Praise from Readers of
The Bridge

"*The Bridge* is a reminder that all things aren't as they seem. That things really do work together for good. That God *is* in control even when we can't see it. Karen's books make you laugh, cry, and leave you wanting more! Her characters are so real you feel like you know them and want to be friends with them. Once I read the first page of *The Bridge,* I couldn't put it down. I read the entire book in one day!"

—Hellen (Annette) H.

"Karen Kingsbury once again uses her beautiful talent to illustrate God's awesome love and grace for us! Each new story speaks to so many hearts across the world. Karen's gift is certainly a loving legacy that I share with others!"

—Cyndi A.

"Gripping from the beginning, *The Bridge* is an amazing story where we learn even in tragedy or loss that God is the God of second chances, and we should learn to treasure the miracles He sends our way."

—Chris V.

"Karen Kingsbury's newest book, *The Bridge,* will tug at the heartstrings of old-time bookstore lovers everywhere! Blend in a little romance with the timeless principle of doing unto others as you would have them do unto you, and you have a classic story built around classic books!"

—Annette W.

"*The Bridge* is a story of friendship, love, forgiveness, and God's amazing grace. Join Charlie, Donna, Molly, and Ryan on an adventure of never-ending friendship in this wonderful story showing that God will never leave us and always protect us."

—Hope P.

"Karen Kingsbury has done it again with *The Bridge*. She is more than an author. She is a vessel that God has used to minister to myself, as well as to her other readers. She is a passionate and inspirational woman of God. I am grateful for her faithfulness and obedience to write when God gives her a story. Thank you, Karen, for your faithfulness. Your stories have touched my life more than you could ever know."

—Tami D.

"Once again, Karen writes strong characters that draw such deep emotions, you feel like you are right there, a part of the story. *The Bridge* is a beautiful love story intertwined with many types of love. You will be truly moved and inspired by this story. Have the tissues ready!"

—Renette S.

"*The Bridge* is an incredibly heart-warming collection of love stories—the story of a young couple in love, the story of an older couple who love each other and their business, and the love of a community coming together for one of its own. I could not put *The Bridge* down because I was captivated by the events and anxious to read 'the rest of the story'! Inspirational! A beautiful story about second chances!"

—Lisa H.

"*The Bridge* will be a bridge to your heart. It is a heart-warming story of second chances that you will not want to put down until you finish. You will fall in love with the Bartons and their wonderful store and ministry, as well as with Molly and Ryan. This is a must-read. God does give second chances and answer our prayers."

—Marnie M.

"The enduring message of *The Bridge* generates hope for second chances. This powerful love story is guaranteed to tug at your heart, remind you of the essence of friendship, and leave you yearning for God's unfailing love."

—Becky S.

"A story of forbidden love, friendship, loyalty, and God's amazing grace. A must-read for everyone."

—Donna K.

"*The Bridge* has appealing characters, and was a true love story not only with people but also with books! Being an avid reader, I understand that there is nothing like the smell and feel of books. In a world that is so rife with technology, it is refreshing to see that the love of a good book and the people that they touch will never be replaced!"

—Kim F.

"I found the story in *The Bridge* to be relatable to my college days when I, too, walked away from a man who loved me. I was rooting all the way for Molly and Ryan to find a forever love. The power of prayer and the community of friends remained the focus of this book's story. A dying man, a bookstore on its deathbed, and a long-ago lost love. Karen did it again as she kept me reading from one chapter to the next."

—Gigi M.

"Karen Kingsbury's *The Bridge* renews your faith by showing the love of a community for a man who is tragically injured. His obedience to God results in a life of service and compassion for his community through a bookstore, and this book will start you on a path of serving God with obedience."

—Jennifer S.

"*The Bridge* by Karen Kingsbury reaffirmed my belief in the God of second chances! I want to sit in the bookstore with Charlie and Donna as they share their story. Thank you, Karen, for letting God speak through your book and touching my heart. You gave me a moment at *The Bridge*!"

—Jessica E.

"*The Bridge* brings to mind the feeling of coming across a neighborhood bookstore and exploring it for the first time—the enchanting charm of stories yet unread and people unknown except for their shared love of reading. *The Bridge* reminds me of the power and potential of miracles."

—Shannon K.

"'Life-Changing Fiction™' is a profound definition of Karen Kingsbury's books. God has placed the words of this book in her heart with her readers in mind. Through the powerful words and Karen's testimony, don't be surprised if you open your heart a little wider to let God write the story of your life."

—Caitlyn C.

"The whole time you are reading *The Bridge*, not only are you right there in the story, but you also want to get in your car and drive to the bookstore and see this place for yourself! Karen Kingsbury has a way when she writes to help you visualize every aspect of this quaint historical bookstore along with the characters. Long after you have finished reading this book, you will find yourself thinking about *The Bridge*. (I still want to get in my car!) Another fantastic book by Karen Kingsbury!"

—Betty W.

"Moving, inspiring, thought-provoking. A story about finding your way back. Once you start reading, you don't want to put the book down. A story that demonstrates real feelings and shows the consequences of decisions that are not made in faith. It is a reminder that miracles can happen with belief and love. There are amazing messages in this story for everyone as long as you are open to them."

—Natasha D.

"*The Bridge* is an excellent example of God's grace that is extended to us time and again despite our own shortcomings. Karen has created a touching and challenging story yet again."

—Nicole S.

the

BRIDGE

the

BRIDGE

Karen Kingsbury

**SIMON &
SCHUSTER**

London · New York · Sydney · Toronto · New Delhi

A CBS COMPANY

First published in Great Britain in 2012 by Simon & Schuster UK Ltd
A CBS COMPANY

1 3 5 7 9 10 8 6 4 2

Simon & Schuster UK Ltd
1st Floor
222 Gray's Inn Road
London
WC1X 8HB

www.simonandschuster.co.uk

Simon & Schuster Australia, Sydney
Simon & Schuster India, New Delhi

A CIP catalogue copy for this book is available
from the British Library.

Hardback ISBN: 978-1-84983-959-4
Trade Paperback ISBN: 978-1-84983-960-0
eBook ISBN: 978-1-84983-962-4

Printed and bound by CPI Group (UK) Ltd, Croydon, CR0 4YY

To Donald, my Prince Charming . . .

Another year behind us, and already Tyler is almost finished with his first year at Liberty University while Kelsey is taking wing—acting in films that glorify God. Isn't our Lord so faithful? Not just with our kids, but in leading our family where He wants us to be. Closing in on a year in Nashville, and it's so very clear that God wanted us here. Thank you for being so steady and strong and good and kind. Hold my hand and walk with me through the coming seasons . . . the graduations and growing up and getting older. All of it's possible with you by my side. I love you always and forever.

To Kyle, my newest son . . .

Kyle, you and Kelsey are married now, and forevermore we will see you as our son, as the young man God planned for our daughter, the one we've prayed for and talked to God about and hoped for. Your heart is beautiful in every way, Kyle. How you cherish simple moments and the way you are kind beyond words. You see the good in people and situations, and you find a way to give God the glory always. I will never forget you coming to me and Donald at different times and telling us that you wanted to support Kelsey and keep her safe . . . and ultimately that you wanted to love her all the days of your life. All of it is summed up in the way you do one simple action: The way you look at our precious Kelsey. It's a picture that will hang forever on the wall of my heart. You look at Kelsey like nothing and no one else in all the world exists but her. In your eyes at that moment is the picture of what love looks like. Kyle, as God takes you from one stage to another—using that beautiful voice of yours to glorify Him and lead others to love Jesus— I pray that you always look at Kelsey the way you do today. We thank God for you, and we look forward to the beautiful seasons ahead. Love you always!

To Kelsey, my precious daughter . . .

What a joy to see you blossom here in Nashville, Kels! How grateful I am that this is a season of love and laughter and friendship like you've never known before. As you said, God is faithful. Live for Him and watch how He will bless you. How great that you are experiencing that firsthand, newly married to Kyle, the man of your dreams. So glad that in this season you're close to home, still the light of our family, the laughter in our hearts. I pray God will bless you and Kyle mightily in the years to come. In the meantime, you'll be in my heart every moment. And wherever you sing and dance and act for Him, we'll be in the front row! I love you, sweetheart.

To Tyler, my lasting song . . .

Some of my favorite moments since you left for college are when we gather around the kitchen computer and talk to you on Skype. I love that in those moments you slip into your funny self, making us laugh until we cry and pretending to be every cut-up character that comes to your mind. But while you can still make us laugh, you are growing into such an amazing godly young man. Your blog, Ty's Take, is being followed by readers who long to know how God is working in your life while you're at college. Your dad and I are so proud of you, Ty. We're proud of your talent and your compassion for people and your place in our family. However your dreams unfold, we'll be cheering loudest as we watch them happen. Hold on to Jesus, son. I love you.

To Sean, my happy sunshine . . .

You are growing up and listening to God's lead, and in the process you are taking your studies and your homework so much more seriously. God will bless you for how you're being faithful in the little things, Sean. He has such great plans ahead for you. Remember, home is where your heart is always safe. Keep working . . . keep pushing . . . keep believing. Go to bed every night knowing you did all you could to prepare yourself for the doors God will open in the days ahead. I pray that as you soar for the Lord, He will allow you to be a very bright light indeed. You're a precious gift, son. Keep smiling and keep seeking God's best.

To Josh, my tenderhearted perfectionist . . .

Soccer was where you started when you first came here from Haiti, and soccer is the game that God seems to be opening up for you. In a number of ways God is showing you that through soccer, you can be a very bright light for Him. But as proud as I am of your athleticism, I'm most proud of your growth this past year. You've grown in heart, maturity, kindness, quiet strength, and the realization that time at home is short. God is going to use you for great things, and I believe He'll put you on a public platform to do it. Stay strong in Him, and listen to His quiet whispers so you'll know which direction to turn. I'm so proud of you, son—I'll forever be cheering on the sidelines. Keep God first in your life. I love you always.

To EJ, my chosen one . . .

EJ, I wish you could know just how much we love you and how deeply we believe in the great plans God has for you. One day not too far from here, you'll be applying to colleges, thinking about the career choices ahead of you, the path God might be leading you down. Wherever that path takes you, keep your eyes on Jesus, and you'll always be as full of possibility as you are today. I expect great things from you, EJ, and I know the Lord does, too. I'm so glad you're a part of our family, always and forever. I love you more than you know. I'm praying you'll have a strong passion to use your gifts for God as you move through your sophomore year. Thanks for your giving heart, EJ. I love you so.

To Austin, my miracle boy . . .

Austin, I love that you care enough to be and do your best. It shows in your straight A's and it shows in the way you treat your classmates. Of course, it absolutely shows when you play any sport. Always remember what I've told you about that determination. Let it push you to be better, but never, ever let it discourage you. You're so good at life, Austin. Keep the passion and keep that beautiful faith of yours. Every single one of your dreams is within reach. Keep your eyes on Him, and we'll keep our eyes on you, our youngest son. There is nothing more sweet than cheering you boys on—and for you, that happened from the time you were born, through your heart surgery until now. I thank God for you, for the miracle of your life. I love you, Austin.

*And to God Almighty, the Author of Life,
who has — for now — blessed me with these.*

CHAPTER ONE

She should have said something.

Even now, seven years later, with Thanksgiving dishes put away and another lonely December rushing up at her, Molly Allen knew the truth. Her year, her life, her Christmas . . . all of it might be different if only she'd said something.

The possibilities plagued her that Black Friday. They walked with her through the front door of her Portland, Oregon, private foundation office, hovered beside her over lunch at P.F. Changs, and distracted her every time she stopped in to see the cats and dogs at her animal rescue shelter.

This was Video Day. Molly's day after Thanksgiving.

Everyone else in the greater Portland area spent the day hunting bargains and stopping in at her shelter to see if the gift they wanted might be in a cage instead of a Walmart. But now, as the day wound down, while shoppers unpacked their bags and counted their savings, Molly would snuggle beneath a blanket by herself and watch the video.

The way she did every year on this day.

She tucked a strand of long blond hair behind her ear and stooped down to the oversize cage on the bottom row. The room echoed with a dozen different barks and whimpers and cries for attention. A chorus of unrest and slight concern from the animals rescued this month to her shelter, one arm of the Allen Foundation's efforts.

"Okay, Buster." She unlatched the cage and welcomed a curly-haired gray terra-poo into her arms. "It's your lucky day. Yes, it is." She snapped a leash to Buster's collar. The dog was a two-year-old, stuck at the shelter for three weeks. Longer than usual, considering this was Christmastime, and the cute dogs usually went first. She scratched the dog just above his ear. "Let's get you to your family."

For good measure, she made a general announcement to the others. "It's still seven days till December, gang. Your turn will come!"

Buster wagged his tail furiously as Molly led him to the lobby. She liked Buster's new family. Of course, she liked most families. Anyone willing to rescue a pet was a friend of hers, no question. But this family with their twin seven-year-old boys seemed special. Their eyes lit up as Molly rounded the corner with Buster.

"Daddy, that's him! Our Buster dog!" One of the boys ran up and dropped to his knees, hugging Buster around his neck.

The other boy was quieter and hung back by their parents. His grin brightened the room all the same. The family had already signed the necessary paperwork, so this was the last step. Both parents shook her hand as they left. "What you're doing here, it's making a difference." The dad's eyes were warm. "I have a feeling you could be doing many more things with your time." He nodded at her. "Merry Christmas."

"Thank you." Molly hesitated. "Happy holidays."

The family turned their attention to Buster and the excitement of getting him out the door in the pouring rain and into their van parked just outside. As the family drove off, Molly checked the time. Six minutes till closing. She walked to the door and flipped the sign. The cages were clean, and the animals all exercised by ten volunteer high school kids who had worked until an hour ago. She would check the water bowls and head home.

He called the video project "The Bridge."

Somewhere in the opening credits, he wrote this descriptor: *How a small-town boy from Carthage, Mississippi, and a highbrow girl from Pacific Heights, California, found common ground on a daily commute down Franklin Road outside Music City to The Bridge—the best little bookstore in the world.*

Too wordy, too many locations, Molly had told him. The two of them would laugh about how he ever could've gotten an A on the assignment with such a horrific descriptor.

Molly set her drenched things down just inside the door of her walk-up apartment, turned on the lights, and took off her dripping raincoat. She lived well below her means, in a new two-bedroom unit on the famous NW Twenty-third Street. Trees along Twenty-third sparkled with twinkling lights even in July, and

the street boasted local coffee shops, cafés, and boutiques with only-in-Portland art and fashion. The
pace and people took the edge off.

Her father would have hated it.

Dinner simmered in the Crock-Pot, vegetable potato
soup with fresh-diced leeks and garlic and parsley.
The soup he taught her to make. Her Black Friday
soup. A whiny meow came from the laundry room,
and her cat Sam strolled up, rubbing against her
ankles. He was a funny cat. More dog than feline. "Hi,
Sam."

He flopped down on the kitchen floor and put his
head between his paws.

"Exhausted, are you?" She bent down and scratched
beneath his chin. "Good boy, Sam. Don't overdo it."

She ladled out a small bowlful of soup, grabbed her
blanket and the remote control and settled into one
half of her leather loveseat. The top button on the
remote dimmed the lights, and the next would start
the movie, which had been in the player since early
that morning.

Molly caught her hair in her hands and pulled it to
one side.

His name was Ryan Kelly.

Now he was married to the sweet Southern belle he'd dated back in high school, no doubt teaching music at Carthage High in Nowhere, Mississippi. But for two years while they attended Belmont University, Ryan had been hers. She'd dreamed of never going home again and playing violin for the philharmonic, and he'd talked about touring with a country band, making music on his guitar for a living. In the end, he had Kristen, his Southern girl back home, and Molly had her dad's empire to run in San Francisco.

But for those four sweet semesters at the Franklin bookstore, nothing came between them.

The ending was the hardest, the final touch, the turning away, her trembling hands. Every gut-wrenching heartbeat remained etched in her soul forever. Their good-bye had happened so fast, she still wasn't sure she understood why. How they could've parted ways so quickly and finally.

Molly hit the play button, and as the music began, the familiar ache built inside her. She didn't often allow herself this trip back to then. But the day after Thanksgiving belonged to him, to the way things once were, and to the unavoidable, inescapable truth.

Like Rhett Butler in *Gone with the Wind,* she should've said something.

He had set the camera up on the dashboard, rigged it with masking tape and a dowel so he could turn it slightly. The viewfinder flipped out, facing them. "Just act natural," he told her. "Keep your eyes on the road." His taped laughter rang through her living room the way it once rang through her mornings and afternoons.

The video started with the camera on him, and his first question always made her smile. "Okay, Miss Molly, tell the people how we met. The unlikely meeting that started the madness."

"The whole story?" He had turned the camera so she came into view, her face less than agreeable as she drove her BMW sedan. "While we're driving?"

He laughed again. "It's thirty minutes to The Bridge. I think you can multitask."

She made a face at him and then laughed as she glanced at the camera. "Fine. What's the question again?"

"Keep your eyes on the road."

Their laughter came together in an up-tempo waltz, while the camera caught the discreet way their bodies seemed drawn to each other. The slight but intentional way their knees and elbows brushed together and the way she looked at him as he filmed her—as if she'd never been happier in all her life. Molly smiled as the video played. The camera had caught their heart connection, the friendship definitely, but it had also caught the connection they hadn't been willing to talk about. The chemistry between them, so strong it took her breath even now.

Their crazy undeniable chemistry.

As the video played on, something remarkable happened, the reason Molly watched the video every year on this day. She no longer felt herself sitting in front of her TV screen watching footage shot seven years ago. Instead she was there again, the sun on her shoulders, adventure in her heart, the summer after her high school graduation. Not in a flashback sort of way. But really there. Heading into an oversize auditorium with three brand-new girlfriends for August orientation at Belmont.

Maybe it was the sense of freedom Molly felt that

day, the fact that she'd convinced her father to let her do the unthinkable—leave the West Coast to attend college in a flyover state like Tennessee. Or the fact that here she wasn't an heiress biding time until she could take over her father's corporation. She was a college kid, same as everyone else. Whatever it was, that day she felt wonderfully alive and hopeful, every predictable aspect of her life as far removed as the Pacific Ocean.

That day the Belmont auditorium was filled with the energy of college freshmen excited and anxious and desperately trying to fit in. Molly and the girls took the first open seats. Her eyes had barely adjusted to the light in the auditorium when one of her friends nudged the other. "Look at him!" She pointed to a guy one section over. He was tall and built, with short dark hair and piercing blue eyes. "He's looking at me!"

"Nice try." The friend laughed. "He's looking at Molly. Same as every other guy."

"Don't be ridiculous. He's just . . ." Molly giggled, but she couldn't finish her thought. Because in those few seconds, the connection between her and the dark-haired freshman was so strong it took her breath. She'd met a number of kids by then—through registration and lunch and field games earlier that afternoon. This felt different, and Molly knew one thing without a doubt, no matter what else happened in her four years at Belmont.

She would never forget this single moment.

They didn't talk, didn't make their way toward each other when orientation finished that evening. Molly almost wondered if her dad had someone following her, someone who would pay the guy to stay out of her way. Because her time here had come with a stipulation from her parents. She could study music, but she couldn't date. If her father found out she was seeing a Belmont boy, he would bring her home on the next flight.

"You'll marry your own kind," he always told her. He'd say it with a smile, but he was serious all the same. And he didn't mean she'd marry just any guy in their circle of friends.

He meant Preston J. Millington III.

Preston had attended boarding school with her. The guy was smart and kind and personable enough. Their parents were best friends, and Preston was on the fast track for an MBA. Her father had already

promised him a position with his shipping corporation.

Molly had no feelings for Preston, but she'd been
raised to believe she didn't have a choice. No say in
the decisions that would shape her life. Not until she
set foot on the Belmont campus did her life feel remotely like it was her own. Still, by the end of the first
week of school, Molly wondered if she'd ever see the
boy from orientation again.

That Friday one of Molly's friends invited her over
for dinner, and she said yes, the way she said yes to
every invite. She loved the freedom of coming and
going whenever she wanted and spending time with
people regardless of their income and influence. Her
friend lived in downtown Franklin, thirty minutes
south of Nashville. As Molly stepped out of her
sedan, she saw a guy climb out of an old Dodge
truck at the house next door. He had a guitar case
slung over his back, and he stopped cold when he
spotted her.

Again their eyes met, and Molly leaned on her
open car door. It was him, she had no doubt. But what
was he doing here? Before she could ask his name or
why he was there, half an hour from campus, or what

classes he was taking, her friend bounded out the front door. "Molly! You're here! Come in and meet everyone. My mom's been cooking all day and—"

Molly pulled herself away from his deep stare and hugged her friend. They were halfway up the walk when she turned back and looked for him, but he must've gone inside. All through dinner, Molly thought about him, thinking up ways to ask her friend's family who he was and whether he lived there or if he was visiting.

When she left that night, his truck was gone.

But on Monday, Molly arrived early to the music building for her instrumental theory class. As she entered the hallway, she was practically overcome by the beautiful sounds of an acoustic guitar and a guy singing a song she'd never heard. His voice melted her, and somehow even before she rounded the corner into the room, she knew. As if she'd known him all her life, she knew.

Seeing him on the other side of the classroom door only confirmed it.

He smiled and kept playing, kept singing, while she leaned against the wall and watched. When the song ended, he lowered his guitar and looked right through her. "I was beginning to think you were a figment of my imagination."

She tried to think of a witty response, but her laughter came first. "You're a music student?"

"I am." He stood and shook her hand with his free one. This close, his eyes looked bluer than they had in the auditorium. "Ryan Kelly. They had me in the wrong class. Just got it all worked out."

"So you're in here?" Her heart soared.

"If I can catch up." He gave her a half grin and raised his brow. "I might have a few questions."

She felt her eyes start to dance. "I might have the answers."

And like that, it started.

Neither of them lived on campus. He couldn't afford the room and board, so he lived in Franklin with an older couple, family friends. She lived in a house her parents owned in Brentwood's McGavock Farms. Her dad had bought it well below market value. He hired a crew to renovate it before school started, with plans to keep it until she left Belmont, when he would sell it for a profit. For now the house was staffed with a housekeeper and groundsman, a married couple who lived upstairs. Molly had a suite on the main floor, adjacent to the music room, where she could practice and study. Dorm living was out of the question.

"Communal living is not suitable," her dad had told her. He tried to soften his expression. "You don't know anything about that lifestyle. This way you'll be safe."

From the beginning, her feelings for Ryan were anything but safe. And since her parents' staff would've reported her for having a boy over, Ryan's idea was perfect from the beginning. "I know of this bookstore. New and used books in an old house in downtown Franklin. It has a reading room upstairs that no one uses. My home away from home." He smiled at her, and the sparkle in his eyes touched the depths of her soul. "It's called The Bridge."

Molly was intrigued, and from that first study session, The Bridge became a private world for Ryan and her, a hiding place for the two of them. Sure, there were other patrons, but Belmont students didn't drive that far, and Molly loved the anonymity.

The store was set up in an old house that once was a hiding place for Union soldiers during the Civil War. The floors were old weathered pine, and the walls and doors had settled so that they didn't quite line up. The place smelled of old books and rich leather, and Molly loved everything about it.

The Bridge was run by a man named Charlie Barton, a friend to the people of Franklin. Charlie kept fresh-brewed coffee on a table near the front register where he hung out, quick with the right suggestion of a book or an insightful conversation. Once in a while his wife, Donna, joined him. The couple would sit with Molly and Ryan near the fireplace and listen. Really listen.

"Tell me about your classes," Charlie would say. Then he'd pull up a chair as if he had all day to hear details about music lectures and science tests and the English lit reports they were working on.

Donna would sometimes pull Molly aside. "That boy's in love with you," she'd say. "When are you both going to admit it?"

Molly would laugh. "We're just friends. Seriously."

"Hmm." Donna would raise her eyebrows. "I guess we'll see."

By the end of the first semester, Molly felt closer to Charlie and Donna than she felt to her own parents.

"I'm never going back," she told Ryan more than

one afternoon while they were at The Bridge. "They can't make me."

He would grin at her, his eyes shining in a way that stayed with her still. "No one can make us do anything."

It took only a few study dates to learn all there was to know about each other. Molly told him things she hadn't told anyone. How her life back home suffocated her and how she had never considered crossing her parents or disobeying them. She told him about Preston and her father's corporation and the plans he had for her.

He was honest, too. "I have a girlfriend back in Carthage." He watched her, looking for a reaction. "We've dated since our sophomore year of high school. Our families attend the same church."

Molly felt the sting of the news, but she didn't let him see. She couldn't date him, anyway. He would be her friend, nothing more. Knowing about his girlfriend back home only made him safer, giving her permission to get as close to him as she wanted.

In the beginning, Ryan talked about his girlfriend fairly often. "Her dad's a farmer," he told Molly one day when they were studying at The Bridge. "He's giving her two acres, so later . . . you know, we can live there."

Molly nodded, thoughtful. She didn't look away, didn't waver in her connection to him. "How will you be a professional guitar player in Carthage, Mississippi?"

His quiet chuckle was colored with discouragement. "I wouldn't be. Everyone thinks I'll come back and teach music at the high school."

"What about you?" Her voice grew softer, the quiet of the store's living room encouraging the conversation. "What do you want?"

"It's a good Plan B, teaching music. I like Carthage."

It hit her then how much they had in common, their lives already planned out. Suddenly she couldn't stand the thought. "No, Ryan!" She took hold of his shoulder and gave it a gentle squeeze. "You can't settle. You have to go for Plan A. Tour the world with the top country bands and play that beautiful guitar of yours."

"Me?" He laughed again, but his eyes showed a hint of adventure that hadn't been there before. "What about you? None of this Preston and San Francisco for you, Molly Allen. You have to play violin for the philharmonic." His laughter faded, and he'd never looked more serious. "No matter what they want for you."

Like that, their dreams were set. They promised to push each other, to never settle for anything but the place where their hearts led. They took turns commuting to Belmont, and they shared a ride every day from the beginning. Ryan would pull his truck up at the corner of McGavock Farms and Murray, where she'd be waiting, out of sight of the staff. He'd take her to school and then to The Bridge when classes were done.

Homework wasn't all they did at The Bridge. They also found books, classics that spoke deeply to them. *Gone with the Wind* and her favorite, Charlotte Brontë's *Jane Eyre*. From the beginning Molly related to the heroine and her determination to do the right thing, even at the cost of love. They read *Jane Eyre* aloud to each other, and once in a while, on the drive to The Bridge, they would quote lines to each other.

"'I'm asking what Jane Eyre would do to secure my happiness,'" Ryan would say in his best English accent, quoting Rochester.

"'I would do anything for you, sir,'" she would

quote Jane in her own Victorian accent, stifling the giggles that always came when they were together. "'Anything that was right.'"

When they weren't quoting Brontë's novel, they sang along with the radio and talked about their classes and dreamed of the future. For two wonderful years they never talked about the one thing that seemed so obvious at the time, the thing that could've made all the difference. They never talked about whether their friendship was a cover for the obvious.

That maybe they were in love with each other.

As the video wound down and Sam curled up on the floor beside her, as her tears slid down her cheeks the way they did every time she watched the film, Molly couldn't help but think the one thing she would always think this time of year.

She should've said something.

CHAPTER TWO

Charlie Barton sank into the worn refinished leather sofa and looked around the empty walls of The Bridge. Even stripped bare, the place was home. But for how much longer? He closed his eyes and tried to still his trembling hands, tried to find a reason to believe again.

Please, God . . . show me the way. I'm out of answers.

He waited, but there was no response, no whispered words of hope or gentle reminders or inspiring Scripture. Nothing. *Are You there, God? Are You really there?* With all of his strength, he fought the ocean of tears rising up inside his soul. He was out of money, and the latest loan hadn't come through. He couldn't buy books to stock his store without at least a line of credit. And no books meant no store.

Another wave of despair washed up against the shore of his soul. All he could see was the way Donna had looked at him when he left home an hour ago—like even *she'd* lost faith in him.

After thirty years in downtown Franklin, Charlie understood the gravity of the situation. Like so many bookstores across the country, his was about to become a casualty. Not because of e-readers—Charlie had enough customers who wanted a real book in their hands. But because of something totally out of his control.

The hundred-year flood.

Charlie opened his eyes and leaned forward, digging his elbows into his knees and placing his hands over his weathered face. The floodwaters had come swift and relentless, nearly twenty inches of rain in two days. He hadn't packed up the books. There hadn't been time. If he'd known how bad it would get, he might've come here anyway, risking his life if that's what it took. By the time he thought about clearing out the store, he would've needed a boat to get to The Bridge.

The water had broken through the windows and knocked over shelves, taking even the books that might've been out of reach of the rising flood. Every book. Every single book was either swept away or left in the corners of the store, mushy piles of pulp. Only the furniture remained, and it was too damaged to save. His insurance policy on the store's contents didn't cover a tenth of what he'd invested in books. No, the flood left nothing. With a clean sweep, it removed all that Charlie Barton had spent his life working for, everything that had mattered to him.

Everything but his faith in God and his lovely Donna.

He looked up and squinted through the fading light out the storefront window. What would Franklin be without a bookstore? Without a place where people could come to learn about history and explorations, fiction and political figures? Where would they go to talk about their ideas and experience the feel of a book in their hands? The weight of the binding and smell of the ink, the feel of the paper between their fingers and the sound of turning pages.

A real book.

Charlie gritted his teeth and worked the muscles in his jaw. This wasn't the end. He closed his eyes again. God wouldn't have brought him this far to see him fail, right? Certainly not. He ran through the options one more time, and his burst of confidence dimmed. He hadn't told Donna about the loan.

The bells on the front door jingled and he looked up. The sign out front said he was reopening on December 8—not ideal but still well before Christmas. The bells on the front door and the worn sofa were the only purchases he'd made so far. He watched as the door opened and Donna walked in. At fifty-six, she was still pretty, still petite, with a girlish face that he loved more with each passing year.

"Charlie." She came to him, her expression weary but patient. "How long are you going to sit here?"

"Until they make me leave." His smile felt heavy, and his eyes blurred, the unshed tears finding a way. "You didn't have to come."

"I did." She helped him to his feet and took him in her arms. "The bank called."

His heart sank. He'd wanted to tell her himself. He drew back and searched her eyes. "What'd they say?"

"The line of credit was denied."

Charlie lowered his gaze to his old brown loafers, the ones he'd worn to The Bridge every day for five years. The business had never been lucrative. He and

Donna had sacrificed to keep the place, but neither of them would've changed a thing. The Bridge gave them a purpose. He was quiet for a long while.

"Donna . . ." His voice cracked. He looked at her, his heart aching with sadness. "It was worth it, right?"

"What?" She had hold of his hands now, her eyes kinder than he deserved.

"The Bridge, the bookstore . . . all the years." He touched her hair, her cheek. "You never had nice things. We never traveled."

She looked at him for a long time and then put her hands on his shoulders. "Our time here, it was never about the money. It was about the people." She pointed out the front window. "There's not a person in Franklin who hasn't been touched by your books and your kindness, Charlie Barton."

He let the words soak in and then pulled her close once more. "I don't deserve you." They stayed that way for half a minute, rocking slightly to the sound of their beating hearts and the passing cars and pedestrians outside. Finally, he took a step back and shrugged. "What should we do?"

For the first time since she walked into the store, her face clouded. "That's just it, Charlie." She crossed her arms and turned her back to him, her eyes on the empty spaces. It took her nearly a minute to face him again. "No matter how many people you've touched, they won't pay the bills. Your customers can't buy books we don't have."

He waited, hoping she had something else, some way out that he'd missed.

Instead she looked down for a long moment. When she lifted her eyes to his, there was a resolution in her face he'd never seen before. "It's time, Charlie. You had a good run. Three decades." She shook her head. "But no more. You need to let it go."

Panic crowded in around him and put its cold fingers against his throat. "I'm a bookseller, Donna." His voice was pinched, his heart pounding. "I don't know what else to do."

She shook her head, glancing about as if the answer might be somewhere on the barren walls. "You know retail." Pain colored her eyes. "Costco or one of the supermarkets. Someone has to be hiring."

Charlie shuddered at the picture. He was almost sixty, his hair whiter than the snow outside. Pushing carts at Costco? Bagging groceries at Kroger? How could that be his swan song when he had planned to work at The Bridge until God took him home? He gave her a weak smile. "I'll figure something out."

"You have to close the store. We can't afford the lease." Her eyebrows raised, she studied him, searching his intentions. "You know that. Right?"

He couldn't have felt more pressure if the roof collapsed and pinned him to the floor. Sweat beaded on his forehead, and he wiped it with the back of his hands. He felt a hundred years old. "I have to do something. I know that."

A long pause followed while she watched him. "I'm going home." She held her hand out. "Come with me?"

"Not yet." He shook his head, and again panic breathed its icy breath down his back. The store *was* his home, his family. Leaving it now without an answer was like putting his mother out in the cold and wishing her the best of luck. He couldn't do it, couldn't promise anything other than the obvious. "I have to think."

A tired sigh sounded in her throat and she put her hand alongside his face. "I love you, Charlie. It's not your fault. Bookstores everywhere are dealing with this." She smiled at him. "I believe in you."

"I know." He gave her a brave smile and a look that said he'd be fine, that she could go and he would find the answers somehow. The truth was, Donna didn't understand completely. This wasn't any other bookstore. It was Franklin's bookstore. A place that defined downtown. If people knew he was in trouble, they'd help, right? They'd come together and do whatever it took to save The Bridge.

Donna kissed him good-bye, pulled up the hood of her winter coat, and headed out into the cold. When he was alone again, Charlie thought about the town coming together. He walked slowly to the window and watched Donna hurry around the corner, out of sight. On both sides of the street, people were walking and laughing and drifting in and out of the small boutiques along the avenue, shopping bags draped on their arms.

Who was he kidding?

People rallying around a bookstore? Things like that only happened in the movies. If The Bridge closed, people wouldn't notice. They would move on and find their books somewhere else, same as any other city in America that lost a bookstore this year. They'd jump on Amazon or get a Kindle for Christmas, and Franklin would go on as if nothing had happened. And that would be that. Charlie Barton and The Bridge, and every memory of anything wonderful that happened here, forever drowned in the flood.

He moved back from the window and shuffled to the checkout counter. The structure was built-in, so it had withstood the rains, and with it, the one item he intended to save. He opened the swollen top drawer and carefully, gingerly, pulled out the scrapbook. Water had risen past the counter and the drawers, but somehow, the scrapbook wasn't destroyed. He ran his hand over the stained canvas cover and the blurred image of The Bridge, the way it had looked in 1972—when Charlie first leased the old house and opened the shop.

The picture on the front of the book was unrecognizable, but between the covers, the photographs remained remarkably unscathed. Charlie opened it and lingered on the first spread. The scrapbook was from a widow named Edna Carlton who had lost her husband in the Vietnam War. In her loneliness and grief, Edna had found her way to The Bridge. "The books, the coffee, the conversation, all of it has been wonderful," she had written across the top of the first page.

"The Bridge has given me a second chance at life. Fill this book with the stories of old souls like me. People who sometimes need a place like this to bridge yesterday and tomorrow. People looking for a second chance. Thank you, Charlie."

Below the inscription, a photo showed Edna Carlton sitting demurely in the upright chair that once stood at the far corner of the store. She held a used copy of *Little Women* in her hands, a story that helped her get through her husband's death. Charlie couldn't read the title of the book. The picture wasn't that clear. Quite simply, he remembered Edna and the book that had spoken so deeply to her.

The way he remembered all of them, generations of regulars who had found a home away from home at The Bridge.

With great reverence, he thumbed through the book, stopping at the photo of the businesswoman Matilda Owens, who had used The Bridge to study for her law degree in the nineties. Last Charlie heard, Matilda had made partner at a law firm off Michigan Avenue in Chicago. Next were a banker and his wife, who had used The Bridge as a romantic hideaway where they often read to each other. Charlie could picture them, whispering beautiful passages from *Wuthering Heights,* together at the end of the old worn sofa that used to sit near The Bridge's fireplace, finding their way back to the feelings that marked the start of their own love story.

Charlie worked his way to the end of the scrapbook and stopped cold, his heart heavier than before. On the last page were two of his favorite people, a couple of college kids who had hung out at The Bridge for most of two years. He ran his thumb along the edge of the photo. Saddest day ever when he heard they separated. He used to tell Donna that the two of them were what love should look like.

Molly Evans and Ryan Kelly.

They had signed their names beneath the photo, but Charlie would've remembered them anyway. Ryan stopped in every once in a while when he was in town. Charlie would ask how he was doing, but they'd lost touch enough over the years that the conversation was never very deep. As far as Charlie knew, Ryan was playing music for a country band. All grown up and famous. Charlie wasn't sure if he ever married. Usually he talked more about Charlie than himself.

Molly hadn't been around since she left town after

her sophomore year. Married some guy on the West Coast, according to Ryan. Such a shame. The two of them should've found a way to stay together. Their differences couldn't have compared to the way the two of them shone so brightly together. Even now Charlie believed that if The Bridge were still standing, still in business, one day Molly would come back. His customers always found a way back.

But not if he closed his doors.

He shut the scrapbook and slipped it carefully back into the drawer. Then he leaned against the wall and breathed in deep. The place smelled dank and moldy. He had plans to paint the walls and bring in new carpet, improvements that would remove the odor. The line of credit was supposed to pay for that, too.

Father, what am I supposed to do? There has to be an answer. My dad said this would happen, and I never believed it, so You can't let me fail. Please, God . . .

He turned and faced the wall, spread his hands against the cool bricks. The Union soldiers had felt warm and safe and dry here, as if things might turn out okay after all. He squeezed his eyes shut, his hands, his arms trembling from the great sorrow crushing in around him. *That's all I want, Lord . . . I'm*

*begging You. Let me rebuild The Bridge so the flood
doesn't win. Give me the second chance Edna talked
about. Please, Lord, show me how.*

A Scripture passage whispered in his mind, one
he'd shared with customers on occasion. It was from
Deuteronomy 20:1: *When you go to war against your
enemies and see horses and chariots and an army
greater than yours, do not be afraid of them, because
the Lord your God, who brought you up out of Egypt,
will be with you.*

God had brought him out of Egypt, for sure, he
and Donna both. Their own personal Egypt. A tragedy no one in Franklin knew anything about.

That horrific time had led them to move here, to
open The Bridge and find solace in books. It was the
only thing Charlie could think of that might bring
meaning to his life after what had happened. Painful
memories tried to work their way to the forefront of
his heart, but he refused them, refused to go back. He
had the photos, the newspaper clippings, tucked in a
small metal box in the drawer beside the scrapbook.
He never opened it, never looked back.

God had rescued them from that, Charlie had been
completely convinced.

Now he wasn't so sure.

Fear and panic stood on either side of him as he turned and faced the front of his store. He had one more shot, one more chance at finding a loan. The banker and his wife—longtime customers—lived in town. The banker ran the branch in Cool Springs. Charlie hadn't wanted to borrow from someone he knew, but he had no choice. He would call in the morning and explain the situation. Then he would know for sure whether God was still with him.

Or if He, too, had left Charlie Barton with the floodwater.

CHAPTER THREE

Donna Barton couldn't stop crying.

All her life she'd counted on Charlie. She relied on him and looked up to him, and from their first date, she'd come to expect his smile and optimism. Even at their lowest point as a couple, Charlie had been rock-solid. Unsinkable. His faith in God strong enough to keep them standing, whatever threatened to topple them. Even death couldn't defeat Charlie Barton.

Until now.

Quiet sobs shook Donna's thin shoulders as she drove south from Franklin to their small ranch house just outside town. She had held it together at the store, but she'd never seen Charlie this way, afraid and without answers. As she left her husband behind, as she stepped into the uncertainty of whatever came next, the sidewalk beneath her feet felt like liquid and her mind raced with uncertainty. Noises around her faded until her senses filled with the sound of her heartbeat. For a moment she wondered if she were having a heart attack or a nervous breakdown. She stopped, grabbed hold of a light post, and prayed. Begged God for the strength to take the next step.

Somehow she'd gotten to her car.

The look in Charlie's eyes, his desperate tone, all of it stayed with her as she gripped the steering wheel. Could she have said anything different, anything that might've encouraged him? Her responses had been honest—The Bridge made a difference in Franklin and to the people who loved it. But that time was past. If they couldn't get a line of credit, then God was closing the bookstore, whether Charlie was ready or not. She had told him how she felt at the core of her existence.

She believed in him. She did.

But her belief in Charlie Barton wouldn't pay the bills or make the lease payment. That would happen only if Charlie picked himself up, headed down to Publix, and found a job. A way to keep them afloat. Maybe that's what scared her the most. She and Charlie didn't see the situation the same way. He wasn't ready to give up, and she loved that about him. Loved that he wasn't a quitter. But at this rate, they were going to lose more than the store. They were going to lose their house. Maybe she'd have to get a job, too. She could do that, right? Either way, Charlie needed to be realistic about the bookstore. She blinked back another rush of tears. Sometimes the only way to fight through a situation was to walk.

Give up one dream and take hold of another.

Donna settled back into her seat and tried to draw a full breath. The trouble had happened so suddenly. Neither of them had seen the flood coming, the flood that God could've prevented. Donna wiped her fingers beneath her eyes and tried to see the road ahead of her.

Snow like this hadn't fallen in November as far back as Donna could remember. Franklin didn't usually have temperatures below freezing until after Christmas, and the cold weather produced mostly flurries. Today two inches were forecast, with another five expected later in the week. By the looks of the snow coming down, the estimates were low. The sun had set hours ago, so Donna was mindful of ice on the road. She turned on the windshield wipers and squinted to see through the thickly falling snow.

Driving took enough of her attention that her tears slowed. The storm drew her back, took her to the place in Charlotte, North Carolina, where she and Charlie had met. Charlie, that handsome, strapping young man with calloused hands and a tender heart. The first person Donna ever trusted.

Her past remained as ugly as it was painful, but while she drove home, she could do nothing to stop it from replaying. Donna was the only child of drug-addicted parents, a bright girl who spent her teenage years visiting one or both of her parents in jail. Routinely, she would come home to find her mom and dad crashed on the floor, Ziploc bags of drugs and dirty needles scattered on the kitchen table.

Sometimes Donna spent the night with a friend down the street. Mostly, she took all her heartache and sorrow out on her studies. Along the way, she developed a fierce determination to succeed, to stay away from drugs and danger and anything that would distract her from her dream. She hid the truth about her home life from everyone and easily carried a perfect 4.0 through high school, and no one was surprised when Donna was named class valedictorian or when she earned a full-ride scholarship to North Carolina State.

Her mom overdosed on heroin three days before her graduation.

A teacher and her husband took Donna in, and she lived with them until she headed off for college. Her dad didn't handle the loss as well. He stayed around for a month or so and then one night went out with his friends and never came home. Police found his car wrapped around a tree the next morning. And like that, Donna was alone in the world.

By the time Donna met Charlie, she was utterly independent. People had let her down and hurt her, so if she could rely on herself, on her academic abilities and her dreams of teaching, then she would survive. Charlie was interesting and different. He was in her freshman English composition class, and from the first day, he found a way to make her laugh. He was the only son of a local cement contractor, a man gruff and quick-tempered who expected Charlie to take over the family trade. Charlie didn't want to spend his life leveling fresh-poured foundations and patios. His decision to study business at NC State was the most rebellious thing he had ever done, and it created a rift with his parents that remained.

Donna remembered what Charlie's father had told him, and the memories made her sick to her stomach. *You'll never succeed in the business world,* his father had told him. *You're a Barton, and Bartons aren't businesspeople. You'll fail and then you'll come crawling back to me and the cement.*

Though his father had sold the cement business fifteen years ago, Charlie was still desperate to hang on to the bookstore. If he walked away from The Bridge now, his father would be right. Donna felt fresh tears fill her eyes. The enormity of that awful prediction must have weighed heavy on Charlie's heart.

"Really, God? You'd let this happen to a man like Charlie?" She whispered the words, her voice broken.

She squinted again, the moments of her past still playing in her mind. No one had ever been able to reach her like Charlie Barton had. When the semester ended, Charlie took her to the beach and walked with her along the shore. "Look out there, Donna." He stopped and stared out at the water, a smile filling his face. "What do you see?"

She laughed, nervous and excited and feeling more alive than ever. "Everything and nothing. I can't see the end of it."

"Exactly." He turned and faced her, touching her cheek with his fingertips. "That's what you deserve, Donna. Everything in all the world. Without end."

"Is that right?" She had felt herself blush, felt the unfamiliarity of caring and wanting and longing for someone. "What if you're the only one who thinks so?"

His smile made her feel dizzy. A sparkle shone in his eyes, and he shrugged. "Then I guess it'll be up to me to make sure you get what you deserve."

Somewhere between his sweet declaration and the walk back to the car, Donna remembered taking note of two things: the feel of the wind and sun on her shoulders and something else. Something was missing from her chest, and she realized by the time they were in his car that it was her heart.

Because from that day on, her heart belonged always and only to Charlie Barton.

Their wedding two years later was a simple affair in front of a justice of the peace, followed by their honeymoon, a weekend trip to a friend's lakeside cabin.

After that, they shared a small apartment, and at night when they had no money, they would sit across from each other at their small kitchen table and dream. One conversation from those days stood out—Donna could see it, hear it as if watching a movie.

"My dad never let me read." Charlie reached across the table and took her hands in his.

"What?" She gave him a doubtful look. "Be serious."

He raised one eyebrow and tilted his head. His sad chuckle told her he wasn't kidding. "I mean, in my early school years, he wanted me to read textbooks. Never for fun." He ran his thumbs along the sides of her hands. "But I loved reading."

Donna smiled. "Me, too."

Charlie told her how, in middle school, he'd head to the school library instead of going outside at recess. "I fought alongside Jim Hawkins in *Treasure Island,* and I felt the splash of water on my face as I sailed on muddy rivers with Tom Sawyer." He laughed. "I was probably the only guy in eighth grade who cried when Beth died in *Little Women.*"

Charlie's fascination with fiction led him to check out books and sneak them home in his schoolbag.

He'd hide whatever he was reading beneath his bed, and long after his dad thought he was asleep, he'd slip under the covers and read by flashlight.

"So I was thinking," he told her early in their marriage, "maybe I'll open a bookstore. New and used books—so everyone has a chance to see the world through the pages of a story."

Donna had been delighted at the idea, impressed with her larger-than-life husband and his grand dreams. His heart had always been bigger than the ocean she'd looked across on that long-ago day. Opening a bookstore had never been about making a fortune or finding the quickest way to success. He simply wanted other people to experience what he had experienced. The feel of ocean water on their feet as they salvaged a shipwreck next to Robinson Crusoe.

Neither of them expected Donna to get pregnant six months into their marriage. They had school to finish and the bookstore to build after that. Even then, Charlie was undaunted.

"God's unexpected blessing," he would say. "He must have mighty plans for this little one."

Donna blinked back the memory. What happened

next was the hardest part, the piece of their past that Donna rarely allowed to surface. Her pregnancy was healthy, nothing out of the ordinary until she went into labor. She had no idea why it had happened or why hers was the one pregnancy in tens of thousands that ended the way it did. There were no warnings, no signs that an emergency was at hand.

One morning a week from her due date, she woke up bleeding.

Charlie rushed her to the hospital, but Donna was already in and out of consciousness. *Losing a lot of blood . . . DIC . . . placenta previa . . . coagulation . . .* Unfamiliar words and terms were thrown around by the doctor and nursing staff as they worked in a panic around her. The last thing she saw before she passed out was Charlie, his wide eyes and pale face as someone asked him to leave the room.

Then there was nothing but darkness.

When Donna woke up, she felt like she'd been run over. Charlie was at her side, tears in his eyes. A hundred questions screamed through her mind, but she didn't need to ask any of them. The pain in her sweet husband's face told her all the sad answers without him saying a word. Eventually, when he could talk, he looked her straight in the eyes and gave her the truth. The baby was dead, a little girl.

That wasn't all. Donna's bleeding had been so bad that the doctor had performed a hysterectomy to save her life. So Donna's chances to ever get pregnant again were dead, too.

In time her body healed, but her heart, her soul, never would have recovered without Charlie. If he questioned God for allowing their loss, he never said so. He clipped their daughter's tiny obituary from the newspaper and placed it with her hospital bracelet and her death certificate in a small metal box. Proof that she had existed. Other than his tears on that first day, he remained solid, convincing her day by day that he loved her unconditionally. Never mind the babies she could never give him. He loved her.

Completely and wholeheartedly.

———

Donna wiped her eyes again and pulled into their driveway. The gravel was slick, covered with a layer of snow. She hoped Charlie was behind her, that he hadn't stayed at the store looking for answers that weren't there. As she parked the car and made her way into the house through the driving snow, she felt the familiar fear again. *Dear God . . . don't let anything happen to him . . . I've never seen him like this . . .*

She made herself a cup of tea and took the seat by the window so she could watch for him. Again the memories returned. It was Charlie's idea that they leave North Carolina and start life over again in Franklin. He had heard from one of his professors that investors were eyeing the small town south of Nashville and that the place was expected to become a retreat for Music City's elite and a destination for tourists.

"The perfect place for our bookstore." Charlie's enthusiasm was contagious, and at the end of the semester, one of his professors connected him with a friend in Nashville who had a room for rent. Charlie was relentless in pursuit of his dream.

They lived in a garage apartment behind the friend's house, and Charlie worked three jobs while attending school so he could save money for the bookstore. Two years after graduation, Donna took a job teaching at Franklin Elementary School, and Charlie leased space for the store.

He called it The Bridge because that was how he felt about books. They connected the past and the present, the present and the future. Books brought people together and gave them a path to worlds they wouldn't otherwise experience.

There was another reason, too.

The bookstore wasn't only Charlie's dream. It was the way to move from the pain of the past to the promise of tomorrow. Forever there would be the tragic and disappointing life before opening the store and the hopeful, fulfilling life after. The store wasn't only called The Bridge.

It *was* the bridge.

From the beginning, Charlie was too generous to make much of a profit. A college kid would come in looking for a classic and end up being a dollar or two short. "Don't worry about it. Someday someone will need a favor from you." Charlie would wink at him and tuck the book in a bag. "Be ready for that moment."

When illness struck the owner of a neighboring pastry business, Charlie gathered up a week's worth of receipts, took the cash to the little shop, and laid it on the counter. "We have to stick together. Community's more important than making a killing."

Donna remembered the woman who owned the pastry shop telling her about Charlie's statement. Donna had laughed out loud. "Sweet Charlie." Her heart swelled at her husband's kindness. "He would give it all away long before there was any danger of making a killing."

That stayed true year after year, decade after decade, while the people of Franklin and tourists who passed through found respite and adventure, hope and direction at The Bridge. Through it all, Charlie never questioned God about the losses of the past, about her parents' drug addiction, or his father's decision to cut him out of the family.

Or about the loss of their little girl.

Even when the flood took every book in the store, Donna didn't see Charlie waver, didn't see him fear for the future. Not until today, when hope of opening again was finally and fully dead. Donna sipped her tea and prayed, begging God on behalf of her husband. Instead of feeling peace and certainty, the more Donna cried out to God, the more she became filled with a sense of dread. If The Bridge closed, then the predictions of Charlie's father would come true. No matter what good Charlie had done at The Bridge, he would be left with the one lie big enough to destroy him.

The lie that somehow Charlie Barton had failed.

CHAPTER FOUR

Music had changed, that was the problem.

Ryan Kelly was a guitar player, and players always had work in Nashville. Now, though, a glut of musicians and too many lesser-known acts had dropped the price for a day's work. Ryan wasn't sure he could still make a living at it.

He silenced his alarm clock, stepped out of bed in his Nashville apartment, and raked his hand through his messy dark hair. How had things changed so fast? A month ago he was touring with a group that used to be the nation's hottest country duo. Now he was unemployed and ready to head back to Carthage, Mississippi.

The past five years were little more than a blur. After graduation from Belmont, he was hired to play with an unknown country act. The pair wound up winning big at the Country Music Awards a year later, and Ryan was set: the lead guitarist for an act that had toured as many as two hundred days a year over the last five years.

But music was a fickle master, and three straight records without a hit were more than the label could take. When the group got dropped over the summer, the lead singer asked Ryan to stay with them through the end of the touring season. Now it was the Saturday after Thanksgiving, and he'd been home a full week without any idea of what was coming next.

He stood and walked to his bedroom window. Crazy snowstorm wouldn't let up. It made him wonder if he was really in Nashville, or maybe some other city, ready to hit the stage. As if all of the past week had been a terrible dream.

He narrowed his eyes against the blinding white outside. *Where do You want me, God? What am I supposed to do next?* He stared at his alarm clock. Seven in the morning. All his life he'd set an alarm—something his father had taught him. "Successful people get up first thing in the morning." His hardworking dad lived out the truth, teaching in the Carthage school system for going on three decades. "Don't get in the habit of sleeping late."

Ryan leaned back against the windowsill. His room was clean, laundry caught up, and every inch of the house dusted and tidied. Getting things in order was the way he always spent the first few days after a tour. This time was different, his alarm only one more reminder of the reality: He had no next tour to prepare for, nothing ahead but the days.

Ryan breathed in deep. How strange that the changes in music hadn't touched him until now.

"It's a new world," his booking agent had told him. The man was a twenty-year veteran in country music. "Players are making a fifth of what they once did. The money's in songwriting and studio work."

"Bands still need guitarists." Ryan hadn't wanted to believe it. He'd assumed for the last six months that when the tour ran out, he'd come home, make a few phone calls, and hook up with a new band.

"It's not that simple." His agent sighed. "The successful acts make their players part of the group. Otherwise it's petty cash for a night's play. Even studio work is different. More competitive than I've seen it. A lot of producers use computerized instruments."

In the dozens of phone calls he'd made over the last week, Ryan had learned of just one job opening.

Studio work for one of the labels, a job coming up the first week of December. His agent said the studio expected more than a hundred players to show up and vie for the job. Ryan breathed in deep and headed toward his bathroom.

There was one other option.

His father had told him about it last night. The music teacher position at Carthage High was opening up at the end of the semester—six months earlier than expected. "It's a good job," his dad told him, "safe, secure."

He thanked his father, but when he hung up, he could only think about the reason he'd gone after his dream of playing guitar professionally in the first place, the reason that, after graduation, he hadn't been able to go back to Kristen and her father's farm and the two acres set aside for them. The reason he had stayed in Nashville nearly a year after graduation, taking odd jobs until he got his shot.

Because even now he could hear her voice encouraging him, pushing him. The voice of Molly Allen. The girl he hadn't been able to forget no matter how hard he tried, no matter how many years.

He showered and dressed in worn dark jeans and

an off-white thermal. Like every day, today offered another chance. He could go to the label and talk to one of the execs, see if he'd missed something—a new band or one of the regulars looking for a replacement. He could be part of a group, right? Throughout his morning routine, while he combed his hair and brushed his teeth, while he made the decision about heading down to the label's office, Ryan thought about her.

About Molly.

Where was she after all these years? Still in San Francisco, married to the guy her parents had chosen for her? Ryan had heard that from someone, and the truth hurt. Not because she'd gone back home or because she'd never fallen for him despite their friendship. But because she'd broken her promise.

The promise to never settle.

Ryan scrambled four eggs and dished them onto a plate. As he did, his eyes fell on the bookcase just off the dining room. The book had been there for the past seven years, but today it might as well have had a neon sign over it. His copy of *Jane Eyre*. He looked at it for a long time before he pushed his plate back, stood, and crossed the room. When he reached the bookcase, he stared at it, unable to fight the way the physical presence of the book took him back.

Molly had bought a copy for each of them one of the last times they were together. "We won't be here to read it off the shelf," Molly had told him. "So we both need a copy."

By then their good-bye loomed, and her voice was tinged with tears. Somehow she had believed that if they each had a copy of *Jane Eyre,* they would keep the connection they'd found at The Bridge. He pulled the book from the shelf and held it carefully, as if it were the most priceless heirloom. His copy was used, one of the earlier editions. Molly had special-ordered it through Charlie once she knew for sure she was leaving.

He opened the worn cover and stared at the inscription. *I would do anything for you, sir. Anything that was right . . . Love, Molly.*

Anything that was right. The line from the novel had stayed with him, haunting him daily at first. How could she have thought that the most right thing was to leave, to find her way back to a life her parents had planned for her? And how could she have married Preston Millington when she had never loved the guy?

Not until two years later had he picked up the book and read through it. He was on the road then, but between shows on the bus, in the quiet of his bunk, he journeyed once more through the story of Jane Eyre. Only then did he see what Molly had written at the back of the book. Another quote from the novel's protagonist, but one that held an insight he didn't quite understand.

Her inscription was this: *All has changed, sir. I must leave you.*

"What changed, Molly?" He whispered the question, as confused today as he was back then. He held the book to his chest and leaned his shoulder against the bookcase. The snow falling out the front window took him back, and gradually, the images around him faded until all he could see was yesterday.

Seven years of yesterdays ago.

————

That day the staff at Molly's house was off—at least that was the plan. Ryan and Molly had reached the end of their second year at Belmont, and finals were a few weeks away. The idea of sharing dinner at the big house in Brentwood was Molly's idea. "I'll make pasta primavera," she told him. Her eyes danced at the thought. "My dad will never find out." She hesitated, and her face lit up. "Actually, come early and we'll work together."

They skipped The Bridge that day. After school they went to the market and bought a cartful of groceries, laughing all the while at how two people could eat so much food. As close as they'd been, Molly had never brought him to her house for fear of her father. Not until they walked through her front door with two bags each did Ryan fully grasp the wealth she came from. The house was a mansion decorated with the sort of furnishings and artwork Ryan had never seen outside magazines and TV shows.

"What's your house in San Francisco look like?" He put his hands in his pockets and cast her a bewildered look.

She grinned and gave a slight roll of her eyes. "You don't want to know."

Ryan had a feeling she was right. "I bet my parents' house would fit in your garage."

"Yeah." She made a face that showed she was uncomfortable with the conversation. "Let's talk about something else."

"Like how come we're starting the primavera sauce with a pile of vegetables." He came over and nudged her with his elbow. "Mine always comes from a jar."

"Yours?" Her eyes sparkled. "Come on, Ryan. Don't tell me you've made pasta primavera before."

"Hmm." He leaned against the kitchen counter and studied her. "Does spaghetti sauce count?"

"No." She washed her hands, her eyes on him the whole time. "True primavera sauce starts with a soffritto of garlic and olive oil."

"Soffritto?" Ryan couldn't say the word without laughing. "You didn't tell me you were a culinary expert."

"I'm not." She dried her hands and pulled two cutting boards from beneath an eight-burner stove. "Just because I can order it off a menu doesn't mean I can make it." She grinned. "You're my guinea pig."

"Oh, is that right?"

"Yes." She laughed and handed him a bag of broccoli. "Start cutting. Let's see what we come up with."

Somewhere between chopping broccoli and sautéing the soffritto, Ryan felt the mood between them change. Molly had turned his head from the first time he saw her, but she was off-limits. Practically engaged to the guy back home. And he had Kristen waiting for him in Carthage. But that night in the kitchen of her enormous Brentwood home, there was only the two of them. Way before they sat down to eat, Ryan felt a sense of inevitability about what was coming. As if they were no longer two college friends aware of their limitations, but characters from some classic love story.

They didn't talk about it, didn't make commentary on the emotions flying between them. They simply lived in the moment. When dinner was over, she turned on music and took him outside. The house backed up to a forest, but the yard sat beneath open skies, and that night the host of stars seemed hung for them alone. She led him to the backside of a gorgeous swimming pool where they sat in a cushioned glider. Usually, at The Bridge, they kept distance between them, enough so they could turn and face each other and read from *Jane Eyre* or compare notes from their various classes.

That night they sat with their bodies touching, and Ryan wondered if she felt it, too. The electricity between them, as if all their lives had led to this. The air was warm, and they wore T-shirts and shorts. As they set the glider in gentle motion, every whisper of her bare arm against his, every touch of their knees, every rapid beat of his anxious heart, made him wonder how long he could wait. Because with everything in him, he wanted to kiss her.

He found a resolve he hadn't known he was capable of and forced himself to look up at the stars. "So beautiful." He was talking about her, but he couldn't let on. Who was he kidding? The feelings between them were impossible, right? She hadn't come to Belmont to fall in love. And even though he and Kristen hadn't talked in over a week, he would have to end things with her before he could think about Molly the way he was thinking about her there in the glider.

A comfortable silence settled around them, and finally, Molly sighed, her eyes still on the sky. "My dad isn't sure about me finishing up here. He wants me to come home."

Fear breathed icy cold down the back of Ryan's neck. "What?" He kept his tone in check. "Why would he do that? You're halfway finished."

Though she laughed, the sound was desperately

sad. "He doesn't care about my music. He wants me to sit at the head of his empire one day." She gave him a weak smile. "I'm the son he never had. That's what he always tells me."

"Molly." He eased away and turned to face her. "You haven't taken a single business class."

"It doesn't matter." She didn't laugh. "He'll have me surrounded by experts. He wants our family to maintain control." She took a slow breath. "He says I'll learn on the job."

"You're only twenty." Ryan couldn't believe the man was serious. "He wouldn't put you in that position now."

"No." She managed a light bit of laughter at the idea. "He wants to groom me, have me finish classes closer to his headquarters, take me to the meetings, and get me familiar with operations. Grooming is like, I don't know, a ten-year process."

It felt like a prison sentence, but Ryan didn't say so. He slid back to his spot beside her and set the glider in motion.

"You think I'm giving up." She sounded hurt, and this time she shifted so she could see him. "That's why you're not saying anything?"

He stopped the glider and met her eyes. "You're the one with a dream, right? Playing in the philharmonic?"

"What can I do about it?" Her tone flashed a rare anger. "My whole life has led to this. I've known what I was supposed to do, where I was supposed to live, since . . . since the first grade."

"He can't make you." Ryan stood and walked to the edge of the patio. For a long time he stayed there, staring into the forest, trying to see clear of the heartache ahead if she left. Suddenly, the reasons seemed clear and he spun around, his own voice louder than before. "It's safe. That's what this is about. You could tell him no, Molly." He was breathing hard, his emotions getting ahead of him. "But going home and doing what he says is safer."

For a few seconds, it looked like she might refute him. Instead, moving slowly, she came to him, and the anger between them kindled a passion they had denied from the beginning. She stood inches from him, her body trembling, and when she spoke, her voice was a whisper. "I hate safe." She came closer still, and tears filled her eyes. "I want to be like Jane Eyre." She sniffed, her voice breaking. "'I am no bird; and no net ensnares me: I am a free human being with an independent will.'" She let her forehead fall against his chest. "Help me, Ryan. Please. Help me be free."

He felt his head spinning, his heart pounding. He took a half step back so he could think clearly, her quote from *Jane Eyre* still playing in his mind. No matter how he fought for control, his voice betrayed the depth of his feelings for her. "How, Molly? How can I help?"

She didn't hesitate and suddenly he could see her again, feel her breath against his skin that summer night. She closed the distance between them once more, and with a determination and anguish that made her breathtakingly beautiful, she took his face in her hands. "Kiss me. Give me a reason to stay."

Here was the moment he had hoped for and dreamed of and wondered about. Though everything about it was wrong, Ryan couldn't stop himself. He caught the back of her head in his hands and slowly, in a losing battle of restraint, he drew her to him and touched his lips to hers. The kiss was more magical than anything in a book. And for the next minute he was convinced for the first time that he wasn't the only one who'd been fighting the attraction. Their kiss grew and built until they were breathless, and then, as if she remembered all the reasons they shouldn't be together, she put her hands on his shoulders and drew back from him. "Ryan . . . we can't."

"Hey . . ." He tried to see into her eyes, but she was staring at the ground, shame covering her face. "Don't be afraid. You said you hate safe, remember?"

"No." When she looked up, the questions in her heart seemed to scream for answers. "You have Kristen. This is . . . it's wrong."

He wanted to remind her that the idea of kissing had been hers, but he was dizzy from the feel of her in his arms, from her lips against his. "I'm sorry." It was the only thing he knew to say. She was right. Until he broke things off with his long-distance high school sweetheart, he had no business kissing Molly Allen. For now, though, if this was what it took to convince her to stay at Belmont, he wasn't really sorry at all. "I'm really sorry, Molly."

"Are you?" She was still breathing fast, as caught up in the wanting and fighting their forbidden attraction as he was. "Are you sorry about this?"

His answer didn't come in words. He took her again in his arms and kissed her the way he had always wanted to kiss her. With all the romance of a character from one of their favorite books. He still wondered what would've happened next, how far things might have gone. But a few minutes later, he caught someone moving in the upstairs window at the back of her house.

"The staff." He gasped the words and moved quickly away from her. "Molly." He nodded toward the window. "You said they were out for the night."

She followed his gaze, and as she did, they watched a light turn off inside the house. Fear flashed like lightning across Molly's face. "Do you think they saw us?"

"I'm not sure." He wanted to say who cared what the staff saw, wanted to draw her close again and pick up where they'd left off. But he respected her too much for that. "Would they tell your dad?"

"Definitely." She glanced around, clearly searching for a way out. "You need to leave." Her eyes pleaded with him to understand. "I can't give my parents another reason to send me home."

For a long moment he hesitated. Did it really matter what her parents thought or what her father threatened? She was old enough to make her own decisions. Ryan felt frustrated to the depths of his being. He could only try to understood a little of Molly's pressures. She'd answered to her father all her life— that much was obvious. But if he knew Molly at all, someday she would find a way to stand on her own. Even if, for now, her determination to please her father overpowered her own dreams.

Ryan blinked, the memory of her kiss lodged in some locked-up corner of his heart. Always when he looked back, he could peg that backyard embrace to the beginning of the end. He put the book back on the shelf, face out. Jane never knew what would happen next. So the only change Molly could've been referring to at the back of his copy had to be the one he couldn't refute.

The change in her heart.

CHAPTER FIVE

That night after their kiss Molly hurried him to the side gate. In the shadows he hugged her, holding on as long as he could. "You said to give you a reason." He touched her cheek, feeling the urgency of the situation. "Give me time, Molly. Don't leave."

A quick nod, and she checked over his shoulder. "We'll talk tomorrow. At The Bridge."

But the next day, before classes, Ryan's cell phone rang. The memory of the phone call still made his stomach hurt. The man was gruff from the beginning. "Is this Ryan Kelly?"

"Yes." It wasn't quite seven in the morning, and Ryan had been rushing around his room gathering homework for class. He stopped and stared at the phone. The caller ID was blocked. "Who's this?"

"Wade Allen. I'm Molly's father." He sounded disgusted. "Look, I know about last night."

Ryan stopped short. "What?" Was this really happening? Molly's father calling him? Why would the man be awake at this hour? "How'd you get my number?"

"That's none of your business." He barely paused. His voice was clipped and pronounced, the talk of an agitated and highly educated man. "Look, I know you have feelings for my daughter. But I'd like to ask you, man to man, to think about Molly and not yourself."

"You don't know her." Sudden venom spewed from Ryan's voice. How dare her father do this, call and try to manipulate him. "She doesn't want to work for you."

"Listen to me, young man. *You* don't know her." His voice maintained a chilling level of calm. "Molly is in love with Preston Millington." A dramatic pause filled the line. "They're engaged to be married."

Slowly, Ryan dropped to the edge of his twin bed. He pressed his elbows into his knees and tried to catch his breath. "She's not engaged. She would've told me."

"They've set a wedding date. Two years from this

summer." He laughed, but the sound came across as condescending. "Molly is very young. This whole Belmont thing was her way of being sure about the engagement."

Hope breathed the slightest air into his lungs. "Have you talked to her lately, sir? She's not sure. I can promise you that."

"She's sure." His answer was quick. "She called Preston yesterday afternoon and told him she was coming home in a few weeks. When she finishes final exams." He sighed as if he could barely be bothered with the conversation. "I'm asking you to stay out of her life. Don't confuse her. She knows what she wants, and she knows where she belongs." This time his quiet laughter mocked Ryan in every way possible. "A guy like you? From Carthage, Mississippi? You could never give her the life she's accustomed to." He chuckled. "You didn't actually *believe* she'd fall for you."

"What if she already has?" Ryan had no trouble standing up to him. "You can't control her."

"I didn't want to have to do this."

"You're not going to do anything. Molly's entitled to live her life, to follow her dreams and—"

"Look." His tone was sharp again, the laughter gone. "Don't believe me. Let her tell you." There was a clicking sound, and what could only have been a recording of Molly's voice. She sounded upset. "Yes, Preston . . . you know how I feel about you. I've known you all my life. I told you I wouldn't stay at Belmont forever." Another clicking sound, and when her father spoke again, satisfaction rang in his tone. "Did you hear that? And yes, I recorded her." He sounded defensive. "She called Preston here at the office. I'm a powerful businessman. I record all my conversations!" He took a breath and seemed to steady himself. "I'm letting you listen to it because I want you to know the truth."

Ryan's head was spinning. He couldn't find the words to speak.

"Look, kid. You heard her. She's in love with Preston, and she's coming home." His words were like so many bullets, steady and well aimed. "If you care about her, you'll cut things off quickly. Let her go. Anything else will only confuse her."

Ryan felt himself drowning, gasping for a way to keep his head above water. There was none. The voice was hers, the message clearly her side of a conversation with the guy waiting for her in San Francisco. Ryan wanted to shout at the man. There had to be an explanation. Molly wasn't in love with Preston. If she were, she would've said so. Shock quickly became fury against her father, rage that rose up and consumed him. He didn't say another word. He ended the call, tossed his phone on his pillow, and punched his fist. Punched it so hard his palm was bruised and swollen by the time he picked her up.

Their routine that day was the same, but their conversation was short and stilted. He had no intention of honoring her father's wishes, so he didn't dream of ending things. But the chemistry that had captured them the night before was gone, and Ryan knew why. With every passing hour, he had to admit the truth. He could be mad at Molly's father, but the voice was hers. Which could mean only one thing: Her father was telling the truth. Molly's true feelings were not for him but for Preston Millington.

When their classes were over that day, they drove to The Bridge, like always. This time when they found their spot upstairs, Ryan faced her. "Hey, listen. I'm sorry. About last night . . . I shouldn't have kissed you."

"What?" Her response was more of a quiet gasp.

"You've got your life back home." He smiled at her as if the words weren't killing him. "I have mine."

She shook her head. "Ryan, that's crazy." She raised her voice and then caught herself. "You told me to give you time. That you would show me why I shouldn't leave."

"I was wrong." He took a step back. With everything in him he forced himself not to think about how she had felt in his arms the night before. "We made a mistake, Molly. We're friends. Let's not let last night change that."

She looked like she might argue with him, but then she must've remembered Preston. A resignation came over her, and when she spoke again, he could see in her eyes walls around her heart that hadn't been there before. "You're right." Her smile looked forced. "I'm sorry, too." She shrugged. "Just one of those things, I guess."

Their study time went late, as usual. But nothing between them was ever the same again. Every time he saw her after that, he could only think of her conversation with Preston and the fact that when the semester ended, she was headed back. He felt like a blind fool. He must've been crazy to think he could win her heart or that she would walk away from her family for him. No matter what he wanted to believe, she was going home.

As the final days of the semester flew by, he and Molly found a way back to their friendship. He never told her about her father's phone call, never asked why she would promise her love to Preston that afternoon and then hours later lead Ryan to believe they were sharing the most wonderful night together. And he never asked her about their kiss, even though the questions plagued him every day. Hadn't they both felt the connection? Felt it to the core of their beings? How could she be so heartless, so conflicted? Every time he asked himself, the answers were the same. Which was why he never brought the matter up to Molly, even when he was tempted to ask. Clearly, she wasn't conflicted at all. She had pulled away from him after that night for one reason.

She was in love with Preston.

The memories lifted and Ryan stepped away from the window, from the snow falling outside. He needed to make calls, needed to check on the studio position. He wasn't ready to give up his dream. Not yet. Not the way Molly had given up when she left Belmont early that summer. Ryan hesitated and touched the copy of *Jane Eyre* as he passed by. He grabbed the keys to his truck and a heavy coat from the closet. Along the way, a thought occurred to him.

Of course he never said anything to Molly about her dad's phone call—not only because of Molly's taped conversation. But because she'd given up on the two of them so easily.

Three weeks later, when she announced she was headed back to San Francisco, there was no surprise, nothing he could say, no real argument or debate. They finished the semester and took their finals, and she bought them matching copies of *Jane Eyre*. Then she was gone. Leaving him with the one thought he couldn't get out of his mind. Her father might've been right about Molly's feelings for Preston. But if Molly truly believed Ryan wasn't good enough, the sad truth was this: He had never known Molly Allen at all.

As on most Saturdays, Molly woke up just after six and climbed into her Nike running sweats, pale pink and tight enough to keep out the cold on chilly November mornings like this. She had a routine that took her down Twenty-third to Everett, up the hill to the right, and through several smaller residential streets back to her apartment. The route was four miles, long enough to stir her heart and clear her head.

At least on most Saturdays.

Today, as she set out, last night's video played in her soul, the unanswered questions hanging from the rafters of long ago. There had never been anyone like Ryan, and Molly fully expected there never would be. How had everything fallen apart? What could have caused him to change so quickly?

There had been so much she wanted to say to him before she returned home. But in the end, the only thing she had done was ask him to kiss her. One kiss. She jogged down her front steps and made the turn onto Twenty-third, the wind biting against her cheeks. The cold didn't matter. All she could feel were his warm hands on her face, the strength of his arms. The way she'd felt safe and loved and whole for those few minutes.

This many years later, that single kiss, those

stolen moments in the backyard of her parents' Brentwood house, were the most romantic of her life. Her whole life. In his embrace, she felt herself falling, changing, finding the strength to stand up to her father. She had meant what she'd said to Ryan Kelly that night. All she needed was a reason—and he was her reason.

She was sure of that back then.

Even after they'd been caught, her only fear was her father, whether he'd find out and buy her a ticket home. Either the staff never saw the two of them kissing in the backyard or they never contacted her dad, because nothing was ever said. She didn't talk to her dad until a few weeks later, and by then she had her answer. She was going back home. Not because of his demands but because Ryan had changed his mind.

She knew something was wrong the moment he picked her up for school the next morning. Molly had planned out the moment. In her dreams, he would jump out and open the door for her—same as always—but when they were inside, he would draw her to him once more, and the kiss that had been cut short the night before would continue. It would continue and it would never end. Not ever.

Instead, Ryan was distant and cool. He opened her door, but he seemed careful not to let their arms brush. On the drive to Belmont, he said very little, talking only about the test he had that day in music theory and how he needed to buckle down and study more for his history class.

By this time Molly began to feel sick. It was almost as if someone had come in the still of the night and kidnapped the Ryan she had known, the best friend of two years who had made her believe he was falling for her. As if he had been replaced with someone who looked like him and dressed like him and smelled like him. Someone who drove his truck and attended his classes.

After that, the Ryan Kelly she knew no longer existed.

All day she worked up the courage to talk to him, to ask him what was wrong and demand that he be honest. But when they reached The Bridge a few hours later, he spoke before she had the chance. In a few rushed sentences, he apologized for the night before, calling it a mistake. He told her she had her life back home and he had his. She remembered wanting to scream at him or cry out or shake him. How many times had she told him she wasn't in love with Preston? Or that her dreams had nothing to do with running her father's corporation?

He was adamant, and in under a minute, the pieces came together. It wasn't her life back home that had caused him to rethink their night together, their kiss.

It was his.

He must have realized that in the end he would go back to Carthage and that he wasn't ready to break up with the girl waiting for him. He was still in love with her. That must have been the conclusion he had reached overnight, and now he could do nothing but apologize.

Molly shuddered, sickened by the thought as much now as she had been then. Could there be anything worse? The guy she'd spent two years with, so regretting kissing her that he had to apologize? In the same minute it had taken Molly to understand the reasons Ryan was sorry, she had known something else. She would never let him see her crumble. She wouldn't beg him or question him or convince him he was wrong. If he wouldn't let go of his past, she would do the only thing she had left.

She would go back home without him.

———

She told Ryan good-bye without tears, before she might've fallen apart. Between that and knowing with all certainty that she'd never see him again, Molly found a strength she hadn't thought herself capable of. It allowed her to go home and face her parents— something she hadn't been sure she could do.

The conversation with her father was short and to the point.

Her dad picked her up at the airport, and before they had her bags in the hired Town Car, he was telling her about meetings for the following day and the method of grooming and why it was important that she spend time watching him work so she'd know what was waiting for her ten years down the road.

Molly let him talk until they reached their gated home in Pacific Heights. When the driver let them out, she faced her father. "Stop."

". . . which is why we have two meetings tomorrow afternoon, the first with . . ." Her father blinked and seemed to register what she'd said. "Stop?"

"Yes." Her heart raced, but there was no turning back. "Here's how it will be. You need to know, because this is the last time I'm going to tell you."

He was quiet for the first time since Molly could remember.

"Okay." She smiled to cover up the fact that she was shaking. "I'm not ever going to be CEO of your corporation. But I have a deal for you."

Her dad looked like he might yell or fly into a dissertation about how she wasn't being rational. But again he remained silent.

"I'll run the charitable branch of your business. We'll help all kinds of people and make a difference in our community. But I will not now nor ever sit at the head of your board."

"You're saying . . . you want Preston to have the job?"

Molly knew what her dad was thinking. If she and Preston married, what difference did it make who was running the company? The business would still be in family hands. She made a hurried decision not to drop that bombshell at the same time. "Okay, yes. That's what I'm saying. I want Preston to run it."

He made a face. "And you'll run the charitable foundation?" He looked baffled, as if she might be certifiably insane to walk away from such an opportunity. "I don't have a charitable foundation."

She smiled at him again. "Exactly." Before her father could say another word, she turned around and grabbed two of her bags. "I'll meet you in the house."

That was that. He tried again later that day and the next and three times a week from then out. Molly held her ground.

Her conversation with Preston Millington was equally brief.

They grabbed coffee on the waterfront the next day, and from the moment he picked her up, she could do nothing but compare him to Ryan. He wasn't funny, and he didn't make her heart beat faster when they were together. He smelled nice, but the whole drive, he asked only a couple of questions about her. Otherwise, he was content to talk about his education, the near completion of his MBA, and his dreams for her father's corporation. He was fit and incredibly handsome, much more mature than his twenty-four years. He wore business pants and a starched white button-down, probably what her father had worn at his age. Most of that day she felt like she was talking to a one-dimensional model, fresh off the pages of *GQ* magazine.

Very quickly, she laid out the situation. "I know we had plans at one point." She took his hands in hers. "That was a long time ago. I've changed, Preston. I don't see you that way."

Preston opened his mouth as if he might refute her, but he hesitated for a long time. "Well." He sounded dazed. "I wasn't expecting that."

"You'll be okay, right?" Molly gave him a weak smile. "I mean, we've barely talked for two years. I sort of thought you'd probably moved on."

"No." It was the most thoughtful Preston had looked the whole time Molly had known him. "A guy could never just . . . move on from you, Molly."

"Thanks." She wanted to tell him he was wrong. Because Ryan was already moving on from her. He would marry his Southern belle and Molly would find her place in his past, a distant memory. This wasn't the time. "We'll be friends?"

Again he waited, but a broken smile tugged at his lips, and he shrugged. "I guess so." He exhaled in a rush. "The truth is, I'm too busy to date."

"Exactly." Molly flipped her blond hair over her shoulder. "That's what I mean. It just isn't right. You know, between us."

She convinced him with little effort, and six months later, Preston and her father helped unveil the Allen Foundation, a charity that initially brought music to orphaned children and eventually expanded to include the shelter for abandoned animals. From the first day of its existence, Molly threw herself into the foundation. The work had a healing effect on her soul. Somehow, when she was teaching a forgotten third-grader how to play the violin, she could keep from spending every waking hour wondering about her dream of the philharmonic and her thoughts about Ryan, the way she still longed for him. The way she hated him for rejecting her.

Every now and then she went to the Christian church down the street. She hoped the key to restoration lay somewhere between the altar and the doors. The pastor talked about hope and redemption and

God, the giver of second chances. Though she liked the peace she felt there, in the end she walked out of the service missing Ryan.

She believed the message. Only God could have given her a second chance with Ryan Kelly.

Three years later, with her father still harping on her to take the reins of the business, a heart attack caught up with him at a gaming table in Las Vegas. A year after they buried him, her mother died after a quick fight with cancer, and Molly couldn't get out of San Francisco fast enough.

Preston took over her father's business, and Molly moved the Allen Foundation to Portland. She began playing violin for a local theater company, and she forced her heart to move on from Nashville and Belmont and every memory of Ryan. It didn't work, of course. Not after she got settled in the Northwest and not after she found new friends and new ways to spend her free time. The memories never died. But once every twelve months, on Black Friday, she gave herself permission to go back, to relive that happiest time when all the world stood still, and to find herself again in that late-spring starry night with Ryan

Black Friday and once in a while on a rainy jog

through Portland the day after. When she couldn't quite return from the trip back to what once seemed so real. When she couldn't convince herself he wasn't waiting for her at The Bridge. When she missed him so much she could hardly breathe.

The way she felt now.

CHAPTER SIX

The hissing was getting louder.

Charlie felt like he had invisible demons on his shoulders, vicious, threatening, murderous demons, and in the last few days, their voices had gotten so loud he could barely concentrate, barely hold a conversation. He parked his '98 Chevy on the curb outside The Bridge, gathered the mail from the front seat, and went inside. Donna was out getting milk and eggs when the carrier came, so he decided to bring it here to open. As if maybe that might help sway the contents to be a little more favorable. The snow from Thanksgiving weekend had melted, but last night another storm had dumped four inches across middle Tennessee. The ground was slippery as he made his way inside.

What's the point, Charlie Barton? He could almost

sense the evil laughter in the empty storefront, the sense of despair so great it nearly consumed him. *You already know what the mail's going to say. More bad news. Just toss it in the trash and drive off a cliff. You're worthless, a failure, just like your dad predicted.*

"No." His response was audible, and it startled him. *That's not true. I won't believe that.* He gave a quick shake of his head, as if by doing so he could rid himself of the voices. Why was it so cold? He rubbed his hands together. Franklin hadn't been this cold as far back as he could remember. More snow was expected in the next few hours.

The Bridge was freezing inside, the utilities long since turned off due to nonpayment. Not that it mattered. It was Tuesday, December 11, and he was no closer to buying books for his store. No closer to finding an answer to the debt weighing him down and pressing in around him.

Which was why he'd come here this afternoon with the mail. He had submitted a loan application to the banker who once spent his free time here at The Bridge with his wife. If anyone could approve a loan, it was this man. "I have a good feeling about this, God . . . I know how You are. How You like to come through at the last minute." He laughed, the sound lost on his chattering teeth. "That's gonna happen here. I can feel it."

Charlie, you're crazy. No one would loan you money. You're not worth anything. You're a bookseller, Charlie. Banks loan money to people with a way to pay it back. Come on.

"Stop!" This time he raised his voice. "Jesus . . . give me peace. Stop the voices. Please!"

And like that, they were quiet.

His hands trembled more than before. He laid the envelopes out on his front counter. Two pieces, all that he'd brought for this moment. The first from his banker friend. The second from the company that leased him the building. Suddenly, the stone counter-top caught his attention.

As if he might find a way back to the days before the store died, Charlie spread his hands lightly over the counter. How many conversations had he shared over this piece of stone? And how many books had passed over the counter on their way to changing a life? Even saving a life? Books could do that. It was the reason Charlie believed in the bookstore.

It had saved his, after all. No other way he would

have survived the loss of their little girl, the loss of the dream of a family. His hope was found in books, and in novels of redemption and hope, purpose and true love. Through them God had given him a purpose. The purpose of putting books in the hands of other people like him.

Hurting people.

He straightened and took a deep breath. Waiting wouldn't change the contents inside the envelopes. Since only the banker's letter could contain the answer he needed, he started with the letter from the leasing company. A week ago he'd called the manager and asked for time. "The flood did me in," he told the man. "Please give me another two months to start making money. Then I'll find a way to pay you back."

The man reluctantly agreed to take the case to his supervisor. Whatever their answer, it was contained in the piece of mail in front of him. He loosened the flap with his thumb and willed his hands to be still. If only it were warmer in here. He eased the letter from the envelope and opened it. His fingers shook so much, the sound of rattling paper filled the empty space.

Dear Mr. Barton,

As per your request to extend grace in the payment of your lease, we have reached a decision. Ultimately, we would have agreed to your request. However, we have been contacted by the building's owner, and he is no longer in a position to wait on your lease payments. He has decided to sell the building, and he would like to offer it to you first.

Charlie's breath came in short bursts, and as his eyes fell on the asking price for the small house, he felt his knees start to buckle. He couldn't pay the gas bill, let alone buy the building. He skipped ahead to the next section, where the manager regretfully informed him that he had until January 1 to either leave the premises and turn in the key or make an offer on the property.

Less than three weeks.

Even with the loan, he wouldn't be able to make things right now. Although maybe he could use the loan to catch up on his back payments and convince the owner not to sell. Not yet, anyway. He felt a gasping bit of hope, and without ceremony, he grabbed the second envelope and tore it open. This one was longer and less formal.

Dear Charlie,

I love your heart for the people of Franklin, and I love your desire to keep The Bridge open. I can remember a hundred times when my wife and I hung out at your store and shared books that stirred our souls.

As a couple, there was a time when we grew busy. Life and kids and carpools and grocery shopping. We almost forgot how to love. But every time we came to The Bridge, we remembered. You and your books reminded us what was important, Charlie. I'll never forget that.

If anyone would want to loan you this money, it's me. In fact, if I had it myself, I'd be down there handing it to you. I feel that strongly. But banks don't make decisions based on emotions. I personally took your packet to our loan department, but no matter how many programs we looked at, they couldn't make the numbers work. I'm sorry, Charlie. We have to decline your application.

Please know that if anything comes up in the future or if your situation changes, we would ...

Charlie stopped reading and the piece of paper fell to the floor. He grabbed the edge of the counter and leaned into it to keep from falling. His chest hurt, but he wasn't having a heart attack. This was a different sort of pain. The sort of pain that came with defeat. It was a feeling as horrific as it was unrecognizable.

He would lose the store for sure, and without the loan, most likely they would lose the house, too. And then what?

Charlie worked his way to the window and clung to the frame. He rested his forehead on the cool glass and tried to grasp the severity of the blows. As he did, he remembered Donna, out buying groceries. But now she was the only one he wanted to talk to, the only voice he wanted to hear.

He pulled his cell phone from his pocket and dialed her number. They'd already lost their old cell phones. This was a pay-as-you-go phone, one they shared, and it dropped calls constantly. Still, Charlie had to try. He waited while the home phone rang, and just when he was about to give up, she answered.

"Charlie? Where are you?" Her voice held a cry of fear. "I come home from the store and you're gone."

"I came to The Bridge." He squeezed his eyes shut and drew a slow breath. "The mail came. I thought . . . I figured I'd look through it down here."

Her hesitation seemed loud and irritated even before she made a sound. "You left most of it here, by the looks of it. I'm holding seven unopened bills. Your life insurance will be the next thing to go. We can't pay it this month, Charlie."

"I know." He hated this, hated having to voice the truth to her. She had believed in him since the day they met. "Donna, we didn't get the loan. The bank . . . they had no choice, I guess. They turned us down."

"Charlie . . . no." She sounded weak and broken. As defeated as he did.

"There's more." His head was starting to hurt. He kept his eyes closed, trying to imagine the disappointment on her face. "The owner of the building is giving us until the end of the year. Then we have to be out or buy it."

"What?" Her voice was shaky, as if already tears were overtaking her. "Can they do that?"

"Yes." He tried to draw a full breath, but this time

he couldn't. The hurt in his heart was too great. He clenched his teeth, forcing the words. "I need to think. There has to be a way, Donna. Help me think of something. Maybe a banker out of town . . . or out of state. Something online where—"

"Charlie! Stop!" Though she was crying, she was angry, too. The way he had heard her get angry only a handful of times in their decades together. "Please." She lowered her voice, but the frustration remained. "It's time to walk away."

"Donna, people need bookstores. God wouldn't want me to give up on everything—"

"Look. He didn't come through this time. That means we have to figure it out on our own." She seemed more in control, less teary. "Just say your good-byes and come home. Let's figure out a way to put our lives back together."

His mind raced, searching for something to say, something to do. The answers were as nonexistent as the books in his store. What *used* to be his store. "Okay." The word pierced his heart, and when he opened his eyes, he wasn't sure he could do it, wasn't sure he could walk away from The Bridge without ever looking back. But his wife needed him. And since he could no longer make a living at his book-store, he could at least do this.

He could come home.

The voices started in again as soon as he hung up. *Charlie, it's official. You're a failure. It was worthless. Everything you've ever done, all the people you talked to, those thousands of days you worked. The countless books you sold. Worthless. You can't even pay your life insurance.*

"No." He shook his head again, desperate for clarity.

Even Donna doesn't believe in you anymore.

"She does." He slammed his fist against the wall, and a rough sliver of wood from the window frame lodged itself in the side of his hand. "God, where are you?"

Really, Charlie? After all you've been through, you still call out to God?

"Yes." His answer sounded weak. What had Donna said? God hadn't come through for them this time, was that it? So what, then, walk away? Give up on the faith they'd clung to from the beginning? He was already halfway insane, here in this frigid empty store, talking to the voices in his head.

He remembered Donna's disappointment, how she'd made a point of telling him about the seven bills and how the life insurance would be the next to go. The bill was due before the end of the—

Suddenly, everything stopped. His breathing and his heartbeat and his reasons for despair. Before he drew his next breath, only one thought consumed him.

The life insurance.

His policy would pay off every bill they had and leave Donna enough to be comfortable the rest of her days. He looked out the window again. The snow was falling hard, the ground covered. A car accident on a day like this would be believable, right?

Of course it would be believable. Get in the car and do it, get it done. You're worth more dead than alive, Charlie. Good that you finally see that.

The voice literally hissed at him, pushing him to grab his keys. God would understand, right? He hadn't provided any way out, any answers they could stand on. He could end it tonight and never have to face Donna again, never have to see his own failure reflected in her eyes.

So get it done. What are you waiting for?

He wanted to shout at the voices, demand that they be silent. But he felt funny using Christ's name to shut them up when he was on his way to kill himself. The voices couldn't hurt him. Life . . . losing The Bridge . . . having their home foreclosed on. These were the things that could hurt him. He slid the phone back in his pocket and grabbed his keys. He knew the back roads, knew the winding routes that would cause anyone to lose control. If he did it just right, he would slip off the road and into a tree, and that would be that.

His final act of love for his precious Donna.

One last time he looked around the empty bookstore. Even now it was hard to look at it without seeing it the way it once was. Floor-to-ceiling shelves full of novels and mysteries and biographies. Customers thumbing through classics and current bestsellers, looking for the sense of adventure that had made him fall in love with books all those years ago.

He blinked back tears, breathing it in. Too many memories to take with him. Slowly, he backed out the door. At the last possible minute, he turned toward his van and shut the door behind him. Not until he was out of Franklin and headed for Leiper's Fork did he realize he'd forgotten the scrapbook. That was okay. It would be Donna's best reminder of all that had mattered to him. The scrapbook and his Bible.

Charlie felt the back tires of his van slip a little as he took the first corner. He couldn't stage just any accident. It had to be swift and deadly. Straight off a cliff and into a tree.

Make it happen, Charlie. Don't mess this up. You're worthless, a failure. Get this right, at least.

"Jesus, quiet them. Please."

As before, the voices fell silent. Chills ran down Charlie's arms, and he realized the reason more clearly than before. The name of Jesus. Evil had to flee at the sound of that name. The Bible said so. Promised it. He blinked hard and focused on the road ahead of him. There had to be a spot somewhere here, he could picture it. And in a few seconds, he knew just the spot. The sharp turn up ahead that he'd driven past many times before. The one that always made him think, *If a person weren't careful, he wouldn't make it past the curve to the other side.*

The snow fell harder, and all around the images blurred to white. White sky and trees and pavement. Even the air was solid white. The only thing he could see clearly in all the white was yesterday. He and Donna with their broken hearts, moving to Franklin and leasing the storefront. They had always liked that their business would operate from an old house.

"Our home away from home," Charlie had told her when they shared coffee and doughnuts in the empty building that first week. "And the customers will be our family."

Tears gathered in Charlie's eyes. Hope and promise, adventure and purpose. The Bridge had given them all of that, and through every stage, Donna had believed in him. She swept the place and helped patch the mortar between the bricks. She was at his side when they picked out vintage oak shelving and as he ordered new and used books. Together they had decided where fiction and history and travel books would go. Over the first few months, they had shopped antique hideaways for the living room furniture where Molly and Ryan hung out upstairs, and for the Victorian chairs that had stood for decades near the rustic brick fireplace and for the high-back tufted sofa by the front window.

When the books arrived, Donna had helped him unpack every box. With great awareness of each title's potential, they savored the process. They checked the books against their master list and found the perfect spot in the store for each. Once in a while they would take a break, sit near the fireplace, and read a few pages aloud to each other.

He would remember one particular day forever. Charlie had purchased a few early edition copies of *Treasure Island,* the book he loved most as a boy. As he lifted it from the box, he ran his fingers over the cover and stared at it. "How many kids like me have read this book and dreamed they were Jim Hawkins?" He looked at Donna, and what he saw, he had never forgotten.

Donna had tears in her eyes. Happy tears. "Have I told you lately how proud I am of you?" She took the book from him and set it carefully on the shelf. Then she put her arms around his neck and looked deep into his eyes. "This is your dream come true, Charlie. But it's more than that. Books are a love affair for you." She smiled. "Nothing could be more beautiful."

He blinked, and the image of his youthful Donna— gazing admiringly into his eyes—disappeared. He reached out after her, but his fingers connected with the cold windshield instead. What was happening? He blinked a few more times and remembered. He was driving through the snow on the winding roads toward Leiper's Fork. Driving so he could plunge off the road into a tree and—

A quick look at his speedometer grabbed his attention and brought him back to the moment. Sixty miles an hour? Into a steep downhill? He must be crazy driving this fast. Suddenly, he could see the road ahead of him more clearly. This part of the drive was lined with so many trees that the sun never hit it. He was no longer riding on snowy asphalt but on ice.

Black ice.

"No!" He shouted the word, gripping the steering wheel with both hands. He applied the brakes gently, tapping them, struggling to maintain control. But the van only flew faster down the hill.

What had he done? Donna would go to her grave brokenhearted if he ended things this way. *Please, God, I don't want to die. I love her too much.* His tears came harder, and he wiped at them with his shoulder. *God, I see the truth now. Donna might be disappointed, but we'll get through this. Don't let me die, please!* His prayer came in silent furious bursts and already he could feel the wheels beneath him sliding. "Help me, God!" Ahead of him was a tree—the tree he had pictured driving into, the trunk wider than any along this stretch of roadway. Only now he wanted to avoid it with every bit of strength he had left.

"No!" His vehicle flew down the hill out of control, heading toward a hairpin turn and the enormous tree. He slammed on his brakes because he had no other choice. No options left. The van responded by fishtailing one way and then the other until the ice whipped it around in a full spin. "God, please!"

Even as he screamed, he felt the wheels leave the hard surface and take flight. The sounds of breaking glass and crunching metal were the last he heard. Was this God's answer? Charlie would die this way, and Donna would finish her life alone? In a rush of thoughts and regrets, this one surfaced—at least he hadn't done it on purpose. The noises grew louder, and Charlie felt himself thrust against the door and the dashboard. His last thought was the saddest of all.

He hadn't told Donna he loved her.

"God!" Charlie held tight to the wheel, but the van was spinning so fast that he couldn't see anything, couldn't tell what was coming. "I'm sorry! Help me! Please . . ."

Then there was nothing but darkness.

CHAPTER SEVEN

The article in the *Tennessean* was small and otherwise insignificant. A one-column headline in reduced italic font:

Owner of The Bridge in Critical Condition
After Accident

Ryan was flipping through the newspaper when he saw it, and immediately, he felt the blood drain from his face. "No . . . not Charlie Barton." He whispered the words out loud as he raced through the ten-line article.

> Longtime owner of The Bridge bookstore,
> Charlie Barton, 59, is in critical condition
> after his van slid off an icy road in Leiper's
> Fork outside Franklin, TN, Tuesday after-

noon. Barton's vehicle struck a tree and the Jaws of Life were used to remove him from the wreckage. Barton was rushed to Vanderbilt Hospital with life-threatening injuries.

Barton and his wife, Donna, moved to Franklin in 1982 and opened The Bridge, a bookstore that has become iconic in the downtown area. The flood of 2010 gutted Barton's store, destroying its contents and sending him into apparent financial struggles. Records show that The Bridge has not reopened and that Barton's business taxes for the current year remain unpaid.

Ryan felt dizzy with the news. How had he missed this, the fact that The Bridge hadn't reopened after the flood? Other businesses had struggled to find their way back, but The Bridge? While Ryan was busy on the road, he assumed life in Franklin had figured out a way to recover. That Charlie Barton was selling books and making conversation and giving people the one thing they could find less often these days.

A bookstore to call their own.

Ryan read the article again and his heart pounded

inside his chest. Poor Charlie. The man existed to run The Bridge. He must have been desperate every day since the flood to reopen. Along the way, of course, he'd suffered financial trouble. Ryan doubted the man owned the building, so lease payments had probably piled up. An insurance policy on the store's contents wouldn't have been much help. Charlie had invested in the store's stock for decades. How could anyone put a price tag on that?

Suddenly Ryan knew what he had to do.

Charlie had spent his life helping the people of Franklin. Now it was their turn to do something for him, rally around him and let him know the difference he'd made. He pushed back from the table, grabbed his cell phone, and called Vanderbilt Hospital. "Charlie Barton's room, please."

There was a pause as the receptionist looked him up. "He's in ICU. I'll ring his nurse."

"Thank you." Ryan walked to his kitchen counter, and tapped his fingers on the granite. He needed to know the situation, how serious it was. And whether Charlie would survive or not.

A nurse came on the line. "Sixth floor, neurosurgery ICU. How can I help you?"

Ryan closed his eyes, trying to find the words. If Charlie was in the neurosurgery section, that meant he'd suffered a brain injury. Why hadn't he stopped in to see the old man since he'd been home? Ryan clenched his fist and blinked his eyes open. "I'm a friend of Charlie Barton's." He worked to keep the emotion from his voice. "Can you tell me how he is? If there's an update on his condition?"

"No, sir. I'm sorry. That information is for immediate family only."

Ryan wanted to tell her that he was one of Charlie's favorite customers, and that made him immediate family. Instead he cleared his throat. "Okay, then is Donna there? His wife?"

"She is." The woman's voice was kind, but clearly, she wasn't about to provide him any information. "Who can I tell her is calling?"

"Ryan Kelly."

She put him on hold, and after thirty seconds Ryan was thinking about hanging up and driving to the hospital, finding his way to Donna on his own. But just then her voice came on the line. "Ryan?"

"Yes." His words came in a rush. "I read about the accident. Donna, I'm so sorry." He didn't want to ask, but he needed to know before another minute went by. "How is he?"

"Not good." Tears clouded her voice. "He's unconscious. Head injuries and . . . internal bleeding."

Ryan felt the air leave his lungs. "Oh, Donna. I'm sorry." He ran his hand along the back of his neck and tried to find his next breath. "Can I come see him?"

"Yes." She sounded small and frail. "Come quickly, Ryan. Please."

"I will." He found his keys, threw on a baseball cap and a leather jacket, and hurried for the door. "I'm on my way."

————

The hospital was only ten minutes from his house, and Ryan was thankful the roads were clear. Along the way, it occurred to him that Donna was probably alone. If he remembered right, the Bartons had no family in Franklin other than the customers. Maybe no family anywhere. What about his injuries? What if he never woke up or the brain trauma was so severe he was never the same again? How would Donna get by without him?

As he parked and jogged toward the hospital's front entrance, he thought about calling Molly. She would want to know what happened, about the flood and Charlie's struggles and the accident. Just as quickly, he let the thought pass. He'd thought about contacting her before, but a Facebook search for Molly Allen or Molly Millington hadn't turned up anything. She must live in San Francisco with her husband, but someone in Molly's position wouldn't be found easily. Not in the past seven years and not now.

He stepped off the elevator at the sixth floor and checked in at the nursing station. "You can go in." The nurse was in her thirties, kind with serious eyes. "He's in room twelve. His wife is expecting you."

"Thank you." Ryan slowed his pace, trying to prepare for what he was about to see. When he reached Charlie's room, he removed his baseball cap and gave a light knock on the door. "Donna?"

"Come in." She sounded broken.

The entrance was blocked by a curtain. Ryan moved it aside and stepped tentatively into the room. Donna was on her feet and met him near the doorway. "Ryan." She was small and frail-looking, thinner than he remembered, and her eyes were swollen from crying.

He took her in his arms, and they hugged for a long time. "I'm sorry." Only then did he look at the figure in the hospital bed. Never would he have recognized the man as Charlie Barton. Charlie, whose smile never faded, the man who was larger than life. The one whose very presence made The Bridge what it was. His head was heavily bandaged, his face swollen beyond recognition. Half a dozen wires came from his arms and chest, and a tube had been inserted at the center of his throat. He was worse off than Ryan had imagined. *Dear God . . . help him.*

Ryan stroked Donna's back. "I came as fast as I could." He stepped back and helped her to the chair near Charlie's bed. He took the one beside her. "How is he? Really?"

Donna hung her head and for a long time said nothing. When she finally looked up, her eyes were flat. As if she'd cried all the tears she had left to cry. "They say it's a miracle he lived through the night." She looked at him, and three decades of love shone in her eyes. Then the shadows returned to her face.

"They don't know how serious his brain injury is. Even if he lives, he might never wake up."

Ryan took a sharp breath and stared at the ceiling. He wanted to run from the room and find fresh air, a place where this new reality didn't exist and he could pretend he'd never opened the newspaper this morning. But Donna needed him. He put his hand on her shoulder. "I didn't know about the flood . . . your struggles with The Bridge." He shook his head, frustrated with himself once more for not checking in on Charlie sooner.

"It's been a while." There was no accusation in her statement. She found the slightest smile. "Charlie talks about you still. He's proud of you, Ryan. You play guitar for a country band, is that right?"

"I did. The band broke up." Ryan didn't want this to be about him. He looked at Charlie's still figure beside them and then back at Donna. "The accident . . . what happened?" He hesitated. "Can you talk about it?"

Donna took a shaky breath and nodded. She folded her hands on her lap and, with her eyes on Charlie, she recalled the flood and the way it destroyed the contents of The Bridge. "The books, the furniture, the shelving. All of it." She lifted her chin, probably finding the strength not to break down. "Charlie was devastated, of course. But he always knew he'd reopen."

"Definitely. Franklin needs Charlie and the store."

"That's what we thought." Donna's eyes grew deeper, her gaze trained on her husband. "The insurance money wasn't enough." She turned to Ryan. "Without money, Charlie couldn't buy books. And without books, there was no store to open." She shrugged her slight shoulders. "No store meant no income." Her smile was beyond sad. "Charlie never had a backup plan."

Ryan hung his head and sighed. When he looked up, Donna's attention was back on Charlie. "Did things get worse lately?"

"Much." She steadied herself. "The house payment is behind, and the bank is talking foreclosure. Charlie used our savings to pay the lease on The Bridge, but that ran out over the summer. We applied for several loans, but with no working store and no income, we didn't qualify."

"And yesterday?"

"Yesterday was the worst." Though her voice didn't crack, tears filled her eyes and fell onto her cheeks. She turned to Ryan. "He had finally agreed it was time to walk away. Time to admit that there would be no more bookstore, no chance at reopening. It was over." She wiped her tears with her fingertips and leaned closer to the hospital bed, giving a quick check of the wires and tubes and monitors. "He left the bookstore for home, but he must've decided to take a drive. The accident happened five miles out of the way on a winding back road." She put her hand over Charlie's. "He must've been so upset."

Again Ryan felt like he'd been kicked. Charlie was the town's eternal optimist, always sure he could help a neighboring store owner or a customer in need. "He didn't hit another car?"

"No. He hit black ice and lost control." She ran her fingers lightly over Charlie's hand. "That's all we know."

For a while they sat in silence. Ryan stood and walked around the bed to the other side. "Can he hear us?"

"Probably not. His brain isn't showing a lot of activity yet."

Ryan picked up on the hope in Donna's choice of words. Proof that a lifetime with Charlie Barton had rubbed off on her. "Charlie." Ryan kept his voice low, bringing his head close to the older man's. "It's Ryan Kelly." He swallowed, fighting his own tears. "Hey, man, we're praying for you. It's almost Christmas, Charlie. You need to get better so we can get that store of yours up and running."

On the other side of the bed, Donna covered her face with one hand and turned away. Ryan heard her tears, anyway.

"Listen, Charlie, we're going to pull together here, okay? You just get better. God's not finished with you yet." He paused, looking for any reaction, any sign, that somewhere inside his battered head, Charlie could understand.

There was none.

Ryan backed up slowly from the bed and returned to Donna's side. Once more he hugged her and then asked her to sit back down. "I have an idea."

Donna dabbed at her tears again. "Sorry . . . I thought I was done crying."

"It's okay." He put his hand on her shoulder. "Does Charlie still have the scrapbook? He used to keep it in the top drawer near the register."

"He does." She sniffed. "Neither of us could believe it survived."

A plan began to take shape, and as it did, Ryan's heart was filled with hope. This was something he could do, something to help repay Charlie for the decades of kindness he'd given to the city of Franklin. "Is the building locked?"

She nodded. "The key's in the potted plant beside the front door. Charlie left it there so the cleanup crew could come and go after the flood. There's nothing inside for anyone to take."

"If it's okay, I'd like to go through the scrapbook and contact Charlie's customers. Let them know what happened." He didn't want to go into detail. No telling whether people would respond, and the last thing he wanted was to get Donna's hopes up.

She agreed to his plan, and before he left, he took Donna's hands in his and prayed for Charlie. For the miracle of healing and for Charlie to know the difference he'd made through his bookstore.

Half an hour later, Ryan was standing in front of The Bridge.

Traffic passed behind him and the occasional bundled-up pedestrian. Ryan barely noticed them. He stared at the sign over the door, the old lettering that might as well have been something from a Charles

Dickens novel. THE BRIDGE—NEW AND USED BOOKS. Ryan stared at it, and for a moment it wasn't the middle of December, and the store on the other side of the door wasn't gutted. It was seven years ago and springtime and Molly was at his side.

He blinked away the images, found the key, and walked in. The sight made him catch his breath. The place was unrecognizable. Even the single piece of furniture—an old leather sofa—wasn't the one that had been here. He closed the door and leaned hard against it. No wonder Charlie had been broken. No wonder he couldn't focus when he left here yesterday.

A quick search, and he found the scrapbook, the treasured collection of notes and thank-you letters and signatures from hundreds of special customers over the years. The cover of the oversize book was water-damaged, but the inside looked intact. Ryan was about to leave when he caught a glimpse of the staircase. The one that led to what had been the upstairs living room, the place where he and Molly had spent two years of afternoons.

He set the book down on the counter and walked gingerly across the wood floor. It creaked more loudly than before, and some areas didn't feel quite solid.

How hard it must've been for Charlie, knowing he couldn't repair the planks, couldn't fix the walls and fill the building with the books he loved. Ryan walked up the stairs, and each one seemed to take him further back into the past. The upstairs looked as bad as the main floor, the furniture gone, the place painfully empty. Just like Donna had said.

Ryan couldn't stay, couldn't stand to breathe in the dank musty air where once life had shone so brightly. He took a final look and returned to the counter for the scrapbook. Then he drove home and sat at his desktop computer. It was time to get busy.

Time to tell Charlie Barton's family what had happened.

———

The opening page of Charlie's scrapbook doubled Ryan's determination. The book was a gift from Edna Carlton, a woman Ryan didn't know. But her words gave him a single-minded purpose. She wrote that The Bridge had given her a second chance at life.

It was exactly what Charlie needed. A second chance.

Ryan made a few phone calls and easily convinced the owner of Sally's Mercantile to set up a donation center for anyone wanting to help Charlie. He worked through the scrapbook like a detective, and by three o'clock that afternoon he had written private Facebook messages to thirty-seven former customers of The Bridge. His message was the same to all:

You don't know me, but we have something in common. At one point we found solace at Charlie Barton's bookstore in downtown Franklin. The Bridge made a difference for me, and I know it made a difference for you because I found your name in Charlie's scrapbook of customers.

People he considered family.

Now Charlie is in trouble. He was in a serious car accident yesterday afternoon and today he's fighting for his life at Vanderbilt Hospital in Nashville. That's not all. The Bridge suffered devastating damage in the flood that hit eighteen months ago. Charlie tried to reopen, but he didn't have the funds or the books and the place remains closed. The accident happened after Charlie had given up all hope of ever opening his doors again.

I'm not sure how you can help. But I'm asking you to join me in praying for a miracle for Charlie Barton. The miracle of a second chance. Beyond that, if you're in the area, there's a donation drop-off set up at Sally's Mercantile. We're looking for books, new, old, used, anything you can give. I'd like Charlie to wake up to more books than he knows what to do with.

Charlie loved all of us. Now it's our turn to love him.

Sincerely, Ryan Kelly

Ryan felt his hope rising. Certainly, this many people could make a difference. But by late that evening he was deeply discouraged. Though he checked every hour, none of the former customers had responded. Then Donna called with an update. Charlie was clinging to life, but he'd made no improvements. *Please, God . . . don't let it end this way for Charlie.* Ryan stayed by his laptop through the night, but by the time he turned in, he had heard from only two customers, both of whom promised to pray. But since they now lived out of the area, they couldn't do much more.

What good could possibly come from such a weak response? The prayers were great, but where would the books come from? Ryan felt drained physically and emotionally. He would try again tomorrow, contact the *Tennessean* about the city getting behind a book drive for The Bridge, and maybe try to find the rest of the customers. He was surprised how many weren't on Facebook, but maybe if he Googled their names, he'd get further. Even then he doubted he'd find the one person he was desperate to find. The person who would care about Charlie Barton's tragedy as much as he did. The girl he had thought about every hour of that sad day.

Molly Allen.

CHAPTER EIGHT

The week before Christmas was insanely busy at the animal rescue shelter. Parents needed gifts for their kids, and by that Friday, four days before Christmas, lots of people were practically desperate. A rescued pet was often the perfect solution. That and the fact that hearts were softer this time of year—more willing to help, more open to visiting the shelter and leaving with a cat or dog.

Molly hadn't seen so many animals leave with homes since she'd opened the foundation. Even better, she had authorized fourteen music scholarships for kids from foster homes. A music scholarship came only after a child had been a part of the Allen Foundation's music development program through high school. The years of work with her foundation were paying off. Lives were being changed.

The work had been arduous, since Molly liked to be in on researching each scholarship application and the extent of the need. Still, as she walked into her apartment late that afternoon, as she shook off her umbrella and flipped on the lights, she felt more satisfied than she had all month. She brewed a pot of coffee and opened a can of food for her cat.

"It's going to be a good Christmas, Sam." She liked to tell the cat things like that. Saying them out loud made them easier to believe.

Sam meowed in her direction and turned his attention to his food bowl.

Molly pulled out her phone and checked her schedule. She had a show tonight with the children's theater, a performance of *The Nutcracker*. Call time was in two hours. She could hardly wait to be surrounded by the music, lost in the story. The play's director had pulled her aside after the first rehearsal. "You have the talent to play first violin." She'd raised her brow. "But you don't have enough time. Or do you?"

"I don't." Molly had appreciated the compliment. She might not have made it to the New York Philharmonic, and she might never play Carnegie Hall, but she had never let her dream die. Tonight she would play second violin.

She smiled. Ryan would have been happy about that, at least.

Her coffee was ready. Molly poured herself a steaming mug, added an inch of organic half and half, and sat down at the kitchen counter. She picked up her phone and thumbed her way to the Twitter app. Time didn't allow her to check in often, but it was one way to stay in touch with people in the music business, as well as contacts and friends she'd made in Portland. Facebook was too time-consuming, but Twitter was doable.

She scrolled down the timeline, smiling at the occasional reference to shopping frenzies at the mall and failed attempts at wrapping gifts. Then something caught her eye. Maybe out of nostalgia for the past, Molly followed @VisitFranklin—a Twitter account that kept her posted on the happenings of the town she once loved. Somewhere in her heart, she probably hoped to see occasional updates on The Bridge or Ryan Kelly, but that never happened and she generally breezed over the town's posts.

This one made her set her coffee down, made her

breathing quicken. The tweet didn't contain much information, but it was enough.

Charlie Barton, owner of The Bridge, still in ICU after car accident. Find out how you can help. At the end of the tweet was a link, and Molly clicked it, her heart skittering into a strange rhythm. Charlie Barton? In ICU? A website opened with a photo of Charlie and another of The Bridge. The headline read FRANKLIN RALLIES IN SUPPORT OF LOCAL BOOKSTORE OWNER. Molly stared at it and then at the pictures.

It wasn't until she started reading the article that she gasped out loud. Once she got past the details of Charlie's accident and the devastating effects of the Nashville flood on his store, she reached the part about the book drive.

> The effort is spearheaded by Ryan Kelly, one of Barton's longtime customers and a resident of Nashville. Kelly is a professional guitarist who spent the last five years touring with one of the nation's top country bands.

Molly read the line two more times. She felt a smile start in her heart and work its way to her face. "You did it, Ryan . . . you chased your dream." She spoke to the article as if he could hear her. He had done what he told her he'd do, and now he was the one leading the charge for Charlie Barton. Sadness came over her again. She would do whatever she could to help Charlie. At the bottom of the article was information on how to reach Ryan, a Facebook link, and the phone number of Sally's Mercantile.

She checked the time. It was two hours later in Nashville, too late to do anything now. As she finished her coffee and dressed for the show, she couldn't stop thinking about what had happened. The flood and Charlie Barton's accident and Ryan's determination to repay the man for his contribution to the people of Franklin. He had probably married his Mississippi girl and moved her to middle Tennessee. By now he might have a family, two or three children.

As she took her seat for second violin and the opening performance of the weekend run, as she felt the music come to life beneath her fingertips, she was comforted by one thought. For all she didn't know about Ryan Kelly, she knew this much. Their time together at The Bridge had to count for something.

Because he had followed his dream.

Tchaikovsky's music spoke to Molly the way it always did. This time it swept her from the small theater into the past, to the days when she first studied the composer at Belmont University. When they reached the second act and the song for Clara and her prince charming, Molly felt like she was playing a soundtrack to every wonderful moment she'd ever shared with Ryan.

The haunting strains of the violin seemed to cry out the question wracking her heart, the one that wouldn't leave her alone. What had happened? How could he have kissed her that way, held her so closely, and looked at her with the certainty that their friendship had turned a corner? How could he have been so convincing in his feelings for her and then apologized the next day?

One song led to the next, and with every stanza, a plan began to form. She needed to get to Franklin, to the hospital room of Charlie Barton. She had two performances tomorrow, but Sunday was open. She could fly to Nashville in the morning and be at Charlie's bedside before nightfall. Her staff could carry on here, and she could fly home Christmas Eve.

There was one problem.

She had no idea what to do if she ran into Ryan. His pity, his apology, had been part of the reason why she'd left Belmont and made her father happy by returning home. She couldn't stay at school knowing Ryan didn't share her feelings. Her heart would've broken again every day. Ryan had chosen the girl back home over her. She had no way around that fact.

So what about now? How would she feel running into him, seeing his wife on his arm, and facing the awkward moments that were bound to follow? As the ballet ended, she thought of a way. It wouldn't protect her heart, but it would protect her from his sympathy. She'd do what other girls had done to look taken, what her receptionist did when she went out with friends just so guys wouldn't hit on her. It might've been an old ploy and a little outdated, but it would get her through the weekend.

She would wear her mother's wedding ring.

He would think she'd gone home and fallen hard for Preston, and he wouldn't question her, wouldn't feel sorry for her. In that way—and only in that way—could she work alongside him and his wife. She could do her part to help Charlie Barton. Maybe she could even find a way to tell him she was sorry, add her apology to his. She could let him know that she never meant for their friendship to cross lines. It was a crazy idea then, and it seemed even crazier now. In light of where life had taken them.

If she apologized like that, then maybe in time her heart would follow. She could come to believe that their spring night together had been a mistake, and she could find a way to live again. Really live. Without the video or the memories or the Black Friday ritual.

She booked the flight that night, and first thing Sunday morning, she moved her small suitcase by the front door and called for her ride. The last thing she took was the one thing she could donate to the community efforts for Charlie Barton, a book she no longer needed.

Her copy of *Jane Eyre*.

That night after she landed in Nashville and checked into her hotel, she took a walk to the church across the street. With every step, she looked for him, watched for Ryan the way she once searched for him in her dreams. Did he live here near the airport or closer to Franklin? Molly wasn't sure, but Ryan wasn't the only thing clouding her mind.

She had called the hospital and talked to Donna Barton. The news on Charlie wasn't good. He remained in a coma, on a ventilator. Every day his chances of waking up grew slimmer. Molly walked through the back doors of the church. The place was empty, and Molly found a spot in one of the back pews. Quietly, reverently, she dropped to her knees.

Her hands shook and her heart raced along in time with her desperate thoughts. She wasn't used to praying or especially good at it. For all she knew, she was going about it all wrong, so she did the only thing she knew to do. Lacing her fingers together, she closed her eyes. *God, if You're really there . . . I think I'll just talk to You like a friend. I don't know what else to do.* Her lips were dry, and she felt a shiver run down her arms. She liked that, thinking of God as a friend. A friend she very much needed right now. She twisted her mother's wedding ring, the one newly on her left hand. *I really need Your help. For Charlie Barton, so that he'll live . . . and so that I'll have the right words if I run into Ryan.*

That was it. She didn't have much else to say. This last part was the most important of all, so she whispered the words out loud. "And if You're really the God of second chances, maybe You could stay with Charlie Barton. Because no one needs a second chance right now more than he does."

When she finished her prayer, she stood and called for another ride. Tomorrow she would visit Sally's Mercantile and see how she could help with the book drive. She still had one more destination before the night was over.

Vanderbilt Hospital.

———

Donna had started a CaringBridge page, a way to keep people updated about Charlie's progress, his physical condition, and the ways they could help. She sat beside Charlie's bed in the dimly lit hospital room and used a loaner laptop to check the page's guestbook for the first time.

What she saw shocked her. She had no idea how Ryan had garnered so much support, but already Charlie's site had over a thousand views and nearly two hundred comments. Donna started at the beginning, and chills ran down her arms and neck.

Donna, you don't know us, but we're praying for you. A few years ago my husband and I came to The Bridge looking for information about adoption. Charlie led us to a couple of books, which we purchased at a discount. Charlie insisted. One of the books told about how to survive the process of adoption. The other told the fictional story of one couple's journey to add a child to their family. Those books changed our lives. We live in Atlanta now and last month we welcomed home twin little girls from China. Our plan was to bring them to The Bridge so they could meet Charlie. Please know that everything your husband has done with that bookstore mattered. It mattered to the people of Franklin and it mattered to us. When he wakes up, let him know. God bless you.

"Charlie, listen to—" She looked up, excited, before she caught herself. She'd done this more than once. Forgotten that he was in a coma, that he couldn't hear her. As quickly as she chose not to share with him, she changed her mind. What if he could hear her?

Wouldn't it be better for him to know the difference he'd made?

With steady hands and a strong voice, she read the woman's entry out loud. "Can you believe that, Charlie?" She slid her chair closer and took hold of his limp hand. "Two little girls have a family because of your books. That's amazing."

Her joy continued as she shared one post after another. Nothing had filled her heart so completely since Charlie's accident. There was a note from a young woman who had talked with Charlie ten years ago about her broken relationship with her mother.

"'Charlie gave me a novel about forgiveness and told me it would make me see things differently. I wanted to read it, but I was broke. I asked if I could stop by the store and read it in stages and Charlie only smiled. He told me I could have the novel for a dollar. I read the book and when I finished the last chapter I hit my knees. I asked God to forgive me and then I called my mom and asked her to do the same.'" Donna hesitated, overcome by the happiness in her heart. She cleared her voice and continued. "'My husband and I live near her now in Oklahoma. I feel like everything about my current situation can somehow be traced back to that single conversation, that kind act. I've never seen a bookseller love books more than Charlie Barton. Please let him know we are praying. Our church is collecting new and used books. After Christmas I'll drive the carload down there myself. It's the least I can do.'"

One after another, for an hour straight, Donna read the entries to Charlie. His breathing pattern didn't change. He didn't stir or show eye movement or flex the muscles in his hand. But Donna believed with all her heart that somehow he could hear her. The posts were like people lined up in the room, each of them giving Charlie a reason to believe.

A reason to wake up and find a way to keep The Bridge.

She was about to read another post when there was a sound at the door. Donna looked up as a tall young woman walked in. Her long blond hair fell in a perfect sheet against her dark coat, and Donna was struck by her beauty, despite her deeply troubled face. Her ice blue eyes and fine features looked familiar.

"Hello." Donna set the laptop on the table and stood to meet the woman, trying to place her.

"Mrs. Barton?"

The young woman's voice helped, because in a rush, Donna had the answer. "Molly Allen!" She went to the young woman and hugged her. "It's been so long."

"It has. Too long." Molly looked past Donna to the hospital bed. "I had to come."

"Thank you." For all the light that the CaringBridge entries had cast across the room, and even with the joy of seeing Molly, the truth remained. "He's very bad off."

"I'm sorry." She walked slowly to the bed and grabbed hold of the side rail. "Charlie, it's me. Molly Allen." She waited, the way all of Charlie's visitors waited. As if this might be the moment when he would open his eyes and smile and they'd all have him back. Charlie remained motionless. Molly turned to Donna. "Is he . . . any better?"

"No. He's alive, but we've had no improvement since the accident."

Molly looked like she might cry.

"Did Ryan get hold of you? Is that why you're here?" Donna and Charlie always believed that the two college students belonged together. Neither ever heard what happened, why Molly had gone back to California.

"No." She smiled, and a shyness filled her eyes. "I haven't talked to Ryan since I left. I heard about Charlie on the Internet. Through Twitter."

"Hmm. So many people talking about him. He would be amazed. How many lives he's touched."

Molly nodded, and for a few minutes she sat and talked with Donna. Told her about the foundation and how she played violin for a local orchestra.

"So you haven't seen Ryan?" Donna asked.

"No." Molly smiled again, patient with the questions. "Has he been up here?"

"Every day. Several times a day, actually." Donna settled back in her chair. "If you come back tomorrow, I'm sure you'll see him."

"I'm sure." Molly looked at her watch. "I need to get to the hotel. I'll head to downtown Franklin tomorrow. See if I can help. Then I'll be back." She stood and hugged Donna.

"Thank you . . . for coming." Donna looked at her husband. "I have to believe that somehow, deep inside Charlie's brain, he knows what is happening. How people are coming together and praying for him." She smiled. "Even flying in from across the country to be here."

"I believe that, too." Molly waved once more, and then she was gone.

Donna wanted to tell Molly that Ryan was single, that he was a wonderful young man, and that maybe it wasn't too late for the two of them. But at the last moment she noticed something she hadn't before, something that put an end to the thought before she could give it a voice.

The wedding ring on Molly's left hand.

CHAPTER NINE

Ryan knew it was her the moment he walked into the Mercantile.

Her long blond hair, same as it had been back at Belmont, the graceful way she had about her, and the sound of her voice. That most of all. He stopped in the doorway and stared, just stared at her. Like he was seeing a vision, not the real Molly Allen. How had she heard about Charlie and why had she come?

When she had left so easily that long-ago summer?

He took a few steps into the building, ignoring the bustle of last-minute shoppers crowding the aisles of the store. He thought about saying nothing, just standing there and taking in the sight of her. But he couldn't keep himself from her, couldn't let this much distance come between them for another minute. "Molly . . ."

She must not have heard him, because she kept talking, and only then did Ryan realize what she was doing. Molly was dropping off several bags of new books, helping the store owner arrange them in big boxes until they were overflowing with books. He watched her for a moment and then came closer. "Molly?"

This time there was no hesitation. She turned, and for the first time in more than two thousand sunsets, her eyes met his. He had wondered if he would know her as fully if they ever had a moment like this. Whether she would've changed somehow and the connection they once shared would only be one more part of the memory. But now he could see that wasn't the case. In her eyes he watched her shock turn to elation, then temper to something more appropriate, given their hasty good-bye and the years between them.

"Ryan." She uttered a quiet laugh, clearly more breathless than amused. "I wondered if I'd see you."

"You look . . . beautiful." He closed the distance between them, and despite the store owner and customers, he took hold of her hands, their eyes connected as if all of time had led to this moment. But as he held her fingers in his, as he savored the softness of her skin, he felt something else.

Her wedding band.

He released her hands and moved back enough to keep things appropriate. She was a married woman now, and he couldn't let the thrill of seeing her consume him. Her father had been wrong in what he'd told Ryan seven years ago. But here, the man would be right. Ryan had no right to confuse her. Not when she was married.

The floor beneath him shifted as he caught her eyes again. How could she have gone to someone else after the bond they shared? The kiss that night? He steadied himself. "How . . . how'd you hear?"

"Twitter." Her smile was sad, but there was something in her eyes he couldn't quite read. Regret, maybe, or wistfulness. The result of remembering. "I had to come."

Ryan had to keep things on a surface level. He wouldn't survive otherwise. "Looks like you bought a few books."

"I did." She walked back to the counter, and he followed. "Every book I could remember seeing on the shelves at The Bridge."

He sorted through the contents. They were brand-new, but they were classics. *Little Women* and *Tom Sawyer* and *The Call of the Wild*. What looked like the entire C. S. Lewis collection. "I'd say this is a great start."

"It's hardly the start." She pointed to the boxes on the floor behind the register. "You did a good job, Ryan. Word's getting out."

"You can say that again." Sally, the storeowner, walked up, tying her apron around her waist. "These boxes weigh a hundred pounds each. Four of them here and another five in the back. When we're through with this drive, Charlie Barton will need two storefronts."

A flicker of sadness made its way through Ryan. Charlie would need them only if he woke up. For now it was easier to believe that his only problem was re-stocking The Bridge. If not for Charlie, then for Donna. In case she might want to run the store. It was something tangible that the town could get behind, since there was nothing any of them could do to help Charlie recover.

That part was in God's hands.

Molly was grateful for the wedding ring. The moment their eyes met, everything she'd ever felt for him came bursting to the surface. Only the feel of the ring on her finger kept her from gushing about how much she'd missed him and how great it was to see him again.

He must have noticed it, because a few seconds after taking hold of her fingers, he stepped away. Which was only right, since he was married, too. At least she assumed he was. He was wearing a ring. But as she helped him load one of the nine boxes into the back of his truck, she realized it wasn't on his left hand. *Strange,* she thought. Either way, she was glad she had worn a ring. Glad he thought she was married. It was probably why things didn't seem awkward between them. He didn't have to be sorry anymore. Not if she was happy in her new life.

Even if the ring represented nothing but a lie.

On the trip out to the parking lot with the second box, she nearly fell when her foot got stuck in a pothole. She cried out but caught herself before she hit the ground. "Wow, that was close."

"Graceful as ever." He grinned at her. "Remember the time when you fell down the stairs at the music building?"

"Yes. Apparently not as well as you remember it." She adjusted the grip on her half of the box, and they continued on to his truck. "Where are we taking them?"

"To the hospital." He set his edge of the box on the open tailgate, easily hopped into the bed, and slid the box to the back with the other one.

"Really?" She brushed a bit of dirt off the lower part of her jeans. "Is there room?"

"For now. The staff said we could keep the books lined up on one side of the room until tomorrow. Christmas Eve. Then we can move them to my storage unit. I have room." His heart hurt again. "We're all praying for a miracle."

"Definitely."

"That Charlie will wake up and see the books"—he jumped back down to her level—"the day before Christmas. And he'll know how much we care. How much The Bridge mattered."

"Hmmm." She walked beside him as they headed back for the next box. "Why not take the books to the store?"

Ryan felt the weight of her question. "The Bartons have until the first of the year before they have to clear out."

"The first?" She stopped and stared at him. "What happens then?"

"You didn't hear?" He dug his hands in his back pockets. The explanation clearly pained him. She could see that. "The owner is selling the building. If he can't buy it, they want him out. There's a for-sale sign in the window."

Molly felt her shoulders slump. "Then what's the point if he won't have a store?"

"We have to start somewhere." Ryan's smile was bittersweet, the same one he'd given her when she left him way back when. "That's what Scarlett O'Hara would say, right?"

For a moment she wasn't standing here a few days before Christmas, pretending to be married. She was back in her car, driving him to The Bridge and laughing about the plot twists in *Gone with the Wind*. She smiled, and for the first time in years, she felt nineteen again. "Yes. That is what she'd say."

They finished loading the boxes and then drove them to Vanderbilt Hospital. Together they got them through the front door, and Ryan found a dolly. Four trips later, they walked up to Donna, winded from the effort.

"This is unbelievable." Donna put her hand to her mouth, her eyes wide. "I can't believe it. Every one of those books was brought in for Charlie?"

"There's more." Ryan chuckled. "Lots more."

"Amazing." Donna looked like she wasn't sure whether she should laugh or cry. Instead she hugged each of them. "Seeing you here together. Everything feels like it's going to be okay."

"It is." Ryan looked at the boxes stacked against the far wall. He moved closer to the hospital bed. "You need to wake up, Charlie. You have books to stock." Ten seconds passed, but Charlie didn't move, didn't give any sign whatsoever that he could hear. Slowly Ryan turned away and looked at Donna. "Any improvements?"

"Actually, yes." Though the corners of her lips lifted a little, her eyes remained worried. "The doctor said he's seen more brain activity. He tried to let Charlie breathe on his own, but that didn't last long. A couple minutes, maybe."

"That's more than before. Ask the doctor to try that

again." Molly looked from Donna to Charlie and back. The hospital scene was painfully familiar. "I remember when my mom was sick, especially at the end. A doctor needs to be encouraged, working with patients like Charlie. Patients need an advocate, Donna. Seriously."

Donna nodded, listening. "I don't want him to get worse."

"Then keep pushing for them to take him off the ventilator. Being on the vent, that's what makes patients sicker."

"I've heard that," Ryan agreed. "Pneumonia can set in. Molly's right. The sooner they get him breathing on his own, the better."

"Okay." Donna looked more determined. "I'll call for the doctor as soon as you leave."

"Perfect." Ryan hesitated. "Before we leave, let's pray."

Again Molly wasn't sure how to feel. But if Ryan was leading, she was content to listen. He held his hands out to her and Donna, and the three of them formed a tight circle. Ryan asked God to breathe healing into Charlie's lungs and give him the strength to fight for life. Molly caught most of the words, but she was distracted. Not by the feel of her hand in Ryan's larger one. But because while he prayed, an idea came to her.

Maybe the best idea she'd ever had.

They weren't quite in the elevator when Molly turned to him, her excitement bursting. "I know how I can help Charlie."

"How?" He looked mildly amused. As if this might be another of her wild plans, like having him over for dinner that night in Brentwood.

"Ryan!" She didn't want him mocking her. "I'm serious." Her tone sounded wounded, but she kept her expression relaxed. So he wouldn't know her real feelings. "Take me to The Bridge."

"Now?" They had planned to go back to Sally's Mercantile for the rest of the books.

"Yes, now." She smiled, and it felt wonderful. Even if everything about this day together was pretend. "Come on. It won't take long."

"Fine." He chuckled but didn't seem to mind. Besides, the drive would give them a chance to catch up. "I guess it's only fitting, huh? You and I driving from this neighborhood down Franklin, to the Bridge."

She hadn't thought about that. "Can you . . . take the detour? Through campus?"

He hesitated. "Are you sure?" His look said he wasn't, that maybe this was more than either of them could take. But then he was the one who had apologized. He'd seen her only as a friend, so what harm could there be in going back? Just this once.

"Very sure."

They reached his truck and climbed inside. The hospital was a mile from Belmont. Ryan drove south on Twenty-first, left on Wedgewood, and right on Belmont Circle, through the heart of the campus. Neither of them said anything as he drove slowly past Fidelity Hall and the music business center, past McWhorter Hall and Massey Performing Arts Center. Every building, every stretch of sidewalk the two of them had walked and talked and laughed along.

At one point he nearly stopped, clearly as caught up in the remembering as she was. "It feels like yesterday."

"I guess I never thought it would end."

"Yeah . . ." He gave her a strange look but then turned his attention back to the campus. "I thought I was the only one who felt that way."

His comment seemed deeper than the words seemed to imply. Molly couldn't begin to sort through the reason or the meaning.

Ryan circled up to Caldwell and east to Twelfth. From there it was easy to get to Franklin Road. They'd done the drive a few hundred times together. She angled herself so she could study him, the man he had become. "I hear you're famous."

"What?" He looked at her once, and then again, before turning his attention back to the road. "Who says that?"

"The article on Twitter. You play guitar for one of the nation's top country acts."

"I did play." His laugh sounded self-deprecating. "Now I'm just an unemployed famous guitar player."

Her laughter joined his. "Not for long."

"It's been a few weeks."

"Sounds like you could use the break." She smiled, proud of him, regardless of the way he'd hurt her so long ago. Never mind her heartache. He had followed his dream, and she was happy for him. "Did your wife go with you on the road?"

Again he gave her the strangest glance, then a slight shake of his head. "No wife." They reached a red light, and he turned to her. "What made you think I was married?" He sounded more baffled than amused. "Twitter say that, too?"

"No." She had to tread lightly here. She didn't want to take the conversation too far back. "I just thought . . . I mean—" She felt her face getting hot. "You were in love with her, Ryan. She waited for you for two years."

"I cared about her." His eyes held hers. "But I wasn't in love with her."

She looked away first, turned her eyes to the road ahead of them. The light turned green and he did the same. "So you never married?"

"No." He thought for a few seconds. "I barely had time to date between show runs."

"Hmmm." Her heart took the blow, and a handful of emotions filled her senses, stopping her from saying anything else. He had never married, and yet he'd never called her? Had he cared that little for her? It was one thing to think he'd apologized for kissing her because he was in love with the girl back home. This was something entirely different: the idea that he would rather be single than pursue her.

"You okay?" He moved like he might reach for her hand, then he stopped himself. "You're quiet."

"Just thinking." She didn't look at him, couldn't take the way her heart would betray her if she did. "All this time . . . I pictured you married. Maybe with two or three kids by now."

"Nope. Twenty-eight and single." He leaned back, squinting against the glare of the snow on the fields surrounding Franklin Road. "And you, Molly? I assume you're happy?"

She thought for a few seconds. If he came out and asked her, she wouldn't lie. His question assumed she was married, so she let the ruse remain. Better than having him pity her. "Yes. I'm in Portland now."

"Oregon?" He seemed as surprised as she had been a few minutes ago. "I thought you were in San Francisco."

"A lot's changed." She hoped he couldn't hear her pounding heart. "My dad died four years ago. Cardiac arrest. My mom passed away a year after that from cancer."

"Molly . . . I didn't know." His expression softened, and this time he put his hand on her shoulder. "I'm sorry."

"I wasn't close to them. You know that."

"Still . . ." He paused, as if he didn't want to rush the moment. "So what happened to your dad's company?"

"Preston runs it." She wouldn't have been surprised if her heart burst from her chest, it was beating so hard. "I run the Allen Foundation. Transferred it to the Northwest." Though she still hadn't lied, she was close.

Ryan nodded, thoughtful. "So it all worked out. Just like your father wanted."

She didn't deny the fact. If he didn't care enough to call after sending her away with his apology, then he didn't deserve the details.

Neither that nor the truth.

———

They pulled up in front of The Bridge and stepped onto the snowy curb. Someone had cleared the sidewalks, apparently, and even on this late Sunday afternoon, shoppers were making their way along the row of quaint stores and boutiques. Molly didn't want to think about the past for another minute. But here, there was no way around it.

She spotted the for-sale sign in the window, pulled out her cell phone, and snapped a picture.

"I know. I did the same thing," Ryan's voice was heavy, a reflection of his heart. "One of these days the sign will be down. I figured I'd get my picture while I could."

"Exactly." She checked the photo as she followed him to the front door. It was perfectly clear, easy to read the phone number on the sign. She waited while he found the key in a plant beside the door, and they walked inside. Tears stung her eyes as she looked around. She leaned back against the cold brick wall. "I don't know what I expected. But this is worse."

"He lost everything." Ryan walked around the front counter and opened the drawer. "His scrapbook. The one with all his favorite customers."

"His family . . . that's what he called us." She stood opposite Ryan and ran her fingers over the book.

"I used this to find some of the people through Facebook." He gave her a wry look. "Not you, obviously. I wasn't sure what name you were using."

"I'm not on Facebook." Again she tiptoed around her reality. "Too busy."

"Just Twitter, huh?" He smiled at her.

"Mm-hm. Less upkeep." She couldn't take looking

into his eyes. With a quick breath, she turned and walked across the front room to the fireplace. Her eyes followed the stairs up to the second floor. "He can't lose this place."

"Which reminds me." Ryan came to her and stopped a few feet away. "What's your idea?"

"Idea?" She felt her face go blank and she gave him a guilty smile. "I guess I forgot."

Again his expression told her he wasn't sure about the way she was acting. "You sure you're okay?"

"Yes." She laughed. "Let's get back to the Mercantile. We need to get a few more books back to the hospital so Charlie sees them when he wakes up."

She loved turning the focus back to the book drive, back to something real and tangible they could do for Charlie Barton. Molly believed he would wake up. That had to be why his brain was showing more function. The hope that lay in the next twenty-four hours made her trip to Nashville worthwhile, and it dulled the ache in her heart for the one thing she didn't want to think about. Not then and not the next morning, when a group of customers gathered at the Mercantile to pray for Charlie.

If Ryan wasn't married, why hadn't he called?

CHAPTER TEN

Donna couldn't take her eyes off the books. Nine boxes delivered by Molly and Ryan yesterday and another three this morning. She had done a rough count and the number nearly dropped her to her knees. The townspeople of Franklin had collected almost as many books as Charlie had intended to buy. Not only that, but some people had donated cash with notes like the one she'd just read: *You gave me my first book for free, something I never forgot. Back then you told me I could pay for it whenever I had the money. Well, Charlie Barton, I have the money now. Lots of it. So here's a thousand dollars. Keep your bookstore open. We need it—all of us.*

Good thing Ryan had room in his storage unit for them. He'd arranged a group of people to move them the day after Christmas.

Altogether, nearly two thousand dollars had been collected and tucked into the boxes of donations. All that, and the books were not just any titles. In many cases, they were the books they once purchased at The Bridge, or copies of their favorite fiction and true-life titles. Many of the books held messages—another of Ryan's ideas. Like the messages in Charlie's Caring-Bridge, the inscriptions in the books were enough to get Donna through the day, enough to keep her believing for a miracle.

If people loved Charlie enough to do this, then maybe God wasn't finished with him. She could only pray she was right. Especially now, late on the morning of Christmas Eve.

Donna moved closer to Charlie's bedside. "Hello, Charlie." She smiled, studying the lines on his face, willing his eyes to open. "Merry Christmas."

He didn't make a sound. But something in his expression seemed to change. She waited, watching. "You breathed on your own for half an hour this morning." With all the love she had for the man in the hospital bed, she stood and kissed his forehead, touching her lips gently to his forehead. "I love you,

Charlie. Please, honey, wake up." She kissed him once more, on the cheek this time. "I need you."

The sound of voices came from the hallway, and Donna turned around. Carolers, maybe. Charlie's nurse had told her that sometimes on Christmas Eve or Christmas Day, church groups would come through the halls singing. As the voices drew near, Donna was sure that's what this was. Carolers. The song was "O Holy Night," and the refrain filled the sixth-floor ICU.

"O holy night . . . the stars are brightly shining . . . this is the night of our dear Savior's birth."

Donna looked at her husband's still form. "Did you hear that, Charlie? This is the night. It's Christmas Eve, Charlie."

Suddenly, his right hand moved. Not much and not for long, but Donna was convinced. He had moved his hand! Could that mean he was coming out of the coma? She rang for his nurse.

"Yes?"

"He's moving. I promise, I saw his hand move!"

"Yes, Mrs. Barton. Someone will be right in."

Donna turned to watch the door, overwhelmed

and shaking from the possibility. The carolers were getting closer, singing about a thrill of hope and the weary world rejoicing. All Donna could think was there couldn't be a better song for the backdrop of what might be happening at this very moment.

The possibility that Charlie was waking up.

Instead of passing by the room, the carolers filed in. First two, and then three more, and then an entire stream of carolers. Tears filled Donna's eyes, and she sat slowly by her husband's hospital bed, unable to take it all in. They hadn't come for the hospital wing; they had come for Charlie. Donna figured it out when the last of the singers entered the room.

Molly and Ryan.

Ryan winked at her and kept up the song, filling the room with a message of a new and glorious morn. When they reached the part about falling on their knees, Donna saw Charlie move again. Both hands this time. She remembered stories in the Bible where victory came when the people sang. There had never been a song more beautiful than this.

Donna looked from face to face, and another realization hit her. This wasn't a church group coming to cheer Charlie up. These were his customers. Her hand flew to her mouth, tears streaming down her face as she recognized the people who had donated books and money. They had found a way here to sing about the greatest miracle of all.

The miracle of baby Jesus in a manger.

Again Donna saw Charlie move, this time his right foot. This night was as divine as the one Charlie's customers were singing about. Because only the touch of God could stir life back into Charlie after all these days. The song came to an end, and Ryan stepped forward. "We spent the morning praying for Charlie. That he would wake up." He put his hand on Charlie's foot. "A few of us figured he might want a Christmas song to wake up to."

Donna dabbed at her tears. "You sounded wonderful." She looked at Charlie again. "He's . . . been moving. For the last few minutes."

———

Charlie heard the noises, heard them blurring and mixing together. Darkness surrounded him, and he wondered if he were dead, if he were in some stage before he would meet the Lord. His head hurt, and he felt stuck. Locked in some strange kind of metal suit that made the slightest movement next to impossible.

Dear God, where am I? How did I get here?

Again the sound of the voices grew and for a moment they frightened Charlie. Then the words began to make sense. This wasn't the hissing of invisible demons. It was singing. Something familiar and wonderful and filled with joy.

The song built and grew and became the song Charlie loved best at Christmastime. "O Holy Night." *Father, am I with You in heaven? Am I dreaming?*

He remembered the van sliding out of control . . . the sounds of breaking glass and wrenching metal and . . . He had been in a terrible accident. That's what had happened. But then why was everyone around him singing? The answer dawned on him gradually. He had to be in heaven. What other reason could there be?

If he were in heaven, then he hadn't had the chance to tell Donna good-bye. He wouldn't see her again— maybe for decades—and despite the joyful singing and the laughter that followed, the thought made Charlie sadder than he'd been in all his life. In all of heaven, he wanted only one thing.

The feel of Donna's arms around him.

Then the strangest thing happened. Charlie felt a tear slide down his cheek, and suddenly nothing made sense. There was no crying in heaven. The Bible taught him that. If he wasn't in heaven, he had to be . . .

He had to be alive!

Donna . . . I'm here.

"Charlie, it's me, honey. It's Donna."

She was standing right beside him. He felt the touch of her fingers against his face.

Like the rising sun, light began to fill his senses. He wasn't sure how long it took—whether an hour or five minutes passed—but with Donna's voice encouraging him, he opened his eyes. Just a crack at first. The light was blinding, and someone must have realized it, because the light dimmed again and he could open his eyes a little more.

Things were blurry, his mind fuzzy. He wasn't dead. That much was clear. A man who looked like a doctor came up beside him and raised the back of his bed. Only a few inches, but the higher position allowed him to see objects, dark blurs, and lighter smeary areas. He blinked again and again.

"Charlie. I'm here."

Donna! Charlie wasn't sure how much time was passing. The process felt slow and fast and amazing all at the same time. More blinking, and as if the fog had lifted, he could see. Not just colors and shapes but people.

He shifted his eyes and winced at the pain it caused him, and there she was. His sweet Donna. He blinked once more, and she came clearer into view. He couldn't talk. The doctor was saying something. He was waking up . . . good signs . . . vitals good. Charlie realized that something was in his throat. Sticking out of his throat. He reached up to grab it but couldn't lift his hand. Not all the way.

"Hold on there, Charlie." The doctor leaned over the bed and stared straight at him. "You're waking up quickly, and that's a good thing. Give me a minute to see how you're breathing."

Charlie forced himself to relax, to look at the faces of the people gathered around him. Why had they all come? How had they known? It hit him exactly who he was looking at. These weren't just any people. They were customers.

His family.

Around the room, Donna watched several of Charlie's friends start to cry. It was one thing to pray for a Christmas miracle, to believe in one. It was something else entirely to see it happen before their eyes. Charlie moved again and again, twitching and shifting beneath the sheets. He was coming back to Donna, but in what condition? Would he know her? Would he remember The Bridge and the people who loved him? Before she could let her fears consume her, she saw something else.

A tear rolling down Charlie's cheek.

That single tear told Donna that the tenderhearted Charlie she had spent a lifetime loving was in there. As the doctor joined them in the room and smiled at the monitors, as the miracle continued to play out, Donna was filled with heavenly peace and one consuming thought.

This was a holy night she would remember as long as she lived.

CHAPTER ELEVEN

Molly had never seen a miracle before.

She never knew until now that they were really something that happened. Like everyone in the room, she watched the scene through a veil of tears, unable to believe that here—on Christmas Eve—Charlie Barton was waking up.

The doctor explained to the group that Charlie needed a quieter room for the waking-up process. "It's happening very fast. That's a good sign." He checked the clock. "I'd like to monitor him for the next several hours. If you could come back . . . maybe after dinner?"

Molly pulled Ryan aside as they headed for the elevator. "I have some business to take care of. I'll meet you for dinner before we head back here."

"Okay." He looked surprised and a little hurt. They

made a plan to meet at a diner on Main Street in downtown Franklin. Molly called for a ride and spent the next few hours in the office of a branch of her bank. She finished what she'd set out to do ten minutes before the bank's early closing.

Others from the group joined them for dinner, so the conversation wasn't focused on the two of them. Molly was grateful. This trip was about Charlie and The Bridge and maybe finding a faith that had never mattered much. A second chance for Charlie and for her. It was most definitely not about recapturing some long-lost connection with Ryan Kelly. Never mind that they were both single. Ryan wasn't interested, no matter what Molly once thought she'd seen in his eyes.

The truth hurt. The sooner she could get home, the better.

———

They gathered in the lobby, and Molly listened with the others while Ryan placed the call to Donna. "We're here. Can we come up?"

Whatever the answer, Ryan's eyes shone with fresh hope. He assured Donna they'd be there in a few minutes. Then he hung up and looked at the fifteen or so who had gathered. Many of them had returned for this visit, and all of them waited in silence for Ryan's report.

"He's awake. Breathing on his own." His voice caught and he stopped for a moment. He pinched the bridge of his nose and gave a shake of his head, trying to find his voice. He coughed a few times and tried again. "Sorry. It's just . . . he knows who he is. The doctor said he has some confusion, but he doesn't appear to have any permanent damage."

Molly's knees felt week. No damage? After suffering a head injury and lying in a coma for nearly two weeks? *Maybe, God, You really did hear our prayers.*

The others started talking among themselves, remarking that a recovery like this was hardly possible. Let alone on Christmas Eve. Ryan raised his hand to get their attention once more. Molly hated herself for thinking it, but he had never looked more handsome. "Listen up." He looked more serious. "Donna will take the lead. Charlie doesn't know about the books or any of it. He has only mentioned The Bridge once—when Donna asked if he knew where he worked."

A ray of light shone in Molly's soul. She could hardly wait to get to the sixth floor.

It took both elevators to get the group to the sixth floor, and this time they walked into the room quietly, respectful of any confusion their arrival might cause. They filled in the empty spaces of the room, and Molly took the spot beside Donna. Ryan looked for her as he entered at the back of the group. She turned away, and he found a place at the foot of Charlie's bed.

Charlie was sitting almost completely up. The tube in his throat was removed, and as he looked at the faces around him, he reached for Donna's hand.

"They came, Charlie." She leaned in close to him. "Because of The Bridge, they came."

A few of their names came across his lips but he was difficult to understand. His voice was raspy, the result of the respirator. Donna nodded at Ryan, and he stepped forward. "Hi, Charlie." His eyes were damp, his smile shining from deep in his soul. "Merry Christmas."

Charlie squinted a little, as if he couldn't believe what he was seeing. "Ryan Kelly."

"Yes." Ryan smiled and pointed to the others around him. "We all stopped by to give you a gift."

Charlie raised his eyebrows, the look in his eyes as sweet as before the flood. "A gift?"

"Yes, Charlie." Donna took hold of his hand. "Look over there."

For what must have been the first time since he woke up, Charlie shifted his attention to the side of the room. Ryan walked to the first box and picked up a book at the top of the pile. "Books. We all pulled together a few boxes of books. So you can still be a bookseller, Charlie."

"Books?" The raspy whisper couldn't hide the shock. He turned slowly to Donna and then back to Ryan. "Every box?"

"Enough books to fill your store." Ryan walked back to the foot of the bed. He gave Charlie's foot a tender squeeze. "It's the least we can do. After all you've done for us."

Molly felt like she was watching a scene from a movie. In bits and spurts, the news seemed to sink in, and Charlie Barton began to cry. Not in a loud or desperate sort of way, the tears of a man whose struggle had taught him something.

He was not alone.

"That's not all." Donna took over. She faced him

and put her hand alongside his face. "People have given money, Charlie. So you can buy whatever books you don't have in those boxes."

His smile lit up the room, and his tears slowed. Just as quickly, his expression fell, and he looked at Donna. He didn't say anything, but Molly could imagine what he was thinking. What good were books without a store? Before anyone could say anything, a nurse worked her way through the crowd. She was holding a large manila envelope over her head. "Donna Barton."

"Yes?" Donna turned and faced the woman.

"This was left at the front desk for you. It's marked urgent."

Molly took a few steps back and leaned against the wall. Though she had a flight to catch in a few hours, she would've missed it to watch the next few minutes.

The others looked on, curious, while Donna opened the envelope and pulled out a few pieces of paper. As she began to read, her face grew pale and she dropped slowly to the chair. She lifted one trembling hand and put it on her husband's shoulders. "I . . . don't believe it."

"What?" Charlie spoke a little louder than before.

His energy seemed to be returning at a rapid rate. "Read it."

Donna looked at the people gathered around her but paid no special attention when she glanced at Molly.

This is good, Molly smiled to herself. No one needed to ever know. No one but Ryan. And she would be gone before he could ask about it. She moved a few steps closer to the door, her eyes on Donna.

"The first piece of paper is from the bank. Confirming that an anonymous source has purchased the building that housed The Bridge."

A chorus of quiet gasps and whispered discouragement rose from the room. Ryan took a step closer. "Charlie still has a week. It's not the first of the year yet."

"Wait." Donna smiled, but the shock in her lined features remained. She held up the second piece of paper. "This explains everything. It's a letter." She looked at Charlie. "From one of your customers." She took a slow breath. "It says: 'Dear Charlie, it came to my attention that you and The Bridge had fallen on hard times. I have to believe you'll be awake to hear this. The truth is, I couldn't stand by and watch your bookstore fail. The years I spent at The Bridge were the best in all my life. So I bought the building, Charlie.'"

Concern held expressions motionless. The room remained utterly quiet but for the sound of Donna's voice as she continued to read. "'Once, a long time ago, I watched you sell a book to a single mother for a penny. From now on and as long as you wish to run The Bridge, that shall be your annual lease. One cent. The truth is, I would do anything for you, sir. Anything that was right.'"

Silent tears fell on the faces of Charlie's friends, but Molly barely noticed. She was looking at Ryan, and of course, he was looking at her. The line from *Jane Eyre* was proof positive of where the gift had come from. She smiled at him for what would be the last time. Then she turned to Charlie and Donna, who was crying and laughing and hugging Charlie. "You don't have to close, Charlie. Once you're better, you can open The Bridge."

There were no tears on Charlie's face, not this time. Instead he was smiling, looking toward the window, his eyes shining with an innocence and awe usually reserved for children and angels. As if he knew better than to look for an explanation among the people in the room.

Not when the only answer was God alone.

Molly stepped into the hall and remembered something. Her copy of *Jane Eyre*. She had to get to the airport if she didn't want to miss her flight. But maybe she had enough time. Besides, some things were more important than being home for Christmas. She headed for the elevator, and as the door closed behind her, she smiled. Her prayers had been heard. Maybe not for her and Ryan. But for Charlie Barton. Which meant God was exactly who the pastor had claimed He was.

The God of second chances.

CHAPTER TWELVE

She wasn't coming back.

Ryan knew because of the look on her face. The sense of finality and good-bye mixed with a raw pain deeper than anything Ryan had seen in her. As soon as she stepped out of the room, he knew. She was gone. He watched her leave, watched her turn away and disappear, and there was nothing he could do, no way to stop her. Not without upsetting Charlie.

He hurried the remainder of the visit as best he could, and ten minutes later, when everyone was saying good-bye, Donna came up to him. "Ryan, how can we ever thank you?"

"One way." He hugged her. "Reopen The Bridge." He glanced at the clock on the wall. Molly had been gone eleven minutes. He didn't want to rush the moment, but he needed to go. Needed to find her before she boarded the plane. If he let her get away now, he might not have another chance.

Ryan looked back at Charlie. He was visiting with the others. "Donna, I need to run. Tell Charlie I'll be back tomorrow."

"I will." The creases in her forehead deepened. "Wait—where's Molly? I didn't see her go."

"She had to catch a plane." He frowned. "I think she was running late."

"Tell her about the lease. I bet she missed it." Joy and hope and life danced in the older woman's eyes. "Molly should know what happened. It's a miracle."

"Yes. I'll be sure to tell her." Ryan took a few steps toward the door. "See you tomorrow."

He rushed to the elevator, and once he was out the door of the hospital, he flew to his truck, his pounding feet keeping time with his heart. *God, please . . . where would she go? Don't let her get away yet. I know she's married, but this might be my last chance to talk to her. Please.*

Only when he was halfway out of the parking lot did he see the piece of paper. There, tucked beneath his windshield wipers, was something that looked like a note. He slammed on his brakes, jumped out of the truck, and grabbed it. The sky was clear, so the paper wasn't wet. He held it up to the parking lot light and read it.

Ryan, it was nice seeing you. Good luck with the next tour. Molly.

What was this? Anger coursed through him. He crushed the piece of paper in his fist, and threw it to the floorboards. That was all? A quick "good luck" and she was gone? So she was married. Did that mean she couldn't give him a proper good-bye when they'd probably never see each other again?

She couldn't leave like this.

He squealed out of the parking lot and headed to the airport, driving like a maniac until the light ahead turned red. "Come on!" The Nashville airport was at least twenty minutes away. He stared at the signal and checked for cross-traffic. No one was coming. For a serious moment he thought about running it. At the same time, a voice of reason shouted to be heard. *What are you doing? Chasing after her? Driving to the airport and then what?* He would have to park and guess at her airline. By the time he got it right, she'd be through security, and it would be too late.

Same as it always was with Molly.

The unexplainable thing was that she wanted him to know. The reference to *Jane Eyre* in the letter left him no doubt who the mysterious donor was. She was waiting for him to look at her as Donna read the last lines of the letter. For what? So he'd know she had a heart? He already knew that. She'd given it to some other guy before Ryan had a chance. The light turned green, but he felt the fight leave him. Forget the airport. He wouldn't find her, anyway. Instead he would go to The Bridge. He had one more book to give, the one on the seat beside him.

His copy of the Brontë novel.

He hadn't planned to give it away, but after seeing Molly's wedding ring, he'd changed his mind. She had long since moved on. What good would it do to keep something that stirred so many emotions in him, so many memories? Seeing her these past few days had confirmed what he'd always denied in himself: In the deepest part of his heart, he had always held out hope. If he kept the book, if he remembered the girl who gave it to him, then maybe someday they'd find each other again. She'd come back and she'd be single and they could figure out what went wrong.

Now that hope was dead, so his copy of the book would be the first in Charlie Barton's new collection.

He settled into his seat and turned his truck south toward Franklin.

———————

Main Street was pitch dark. Besides the half-moon, only the occasional dim light from inside a closed storefront provided any light at all. Ryan didn't care. He parked his truck in front of The Bridge, climbed out, and leaned against his hood. Charlie Barton was awake and had his store back. What more could Ryan ask for? Especially when everything about the last few days with Molly felt like nothing more than a dream.

He was about to get the key and walk inside when he noticed something. The front door was open a few inches. Franklin didn't have a large community of homeless people, but that had to be it. Someone without electricity and a roof over his head had found a way inside. Ryan wanted to be careful.

Moving without a sound, he came to the front door and listened. A shuffling noise echoed through the empty storefront. The movement seemed to come from upstairs. Ryan took a deep breath and crept inside. If someone were sleeping here, that was one thing; especially with the store in this condition. But if vandals were having their way with the place, he'd have to take action.

He was about to move past the front counter when he heard another sound. A voice or maybe a video player. He couldn't make it out, exactly. Adrenaline poured into his veins and put him on edge. What were these noises? Not until he reached the stairs did he realize what he was hearing.

Someone was crying. Sobbing. Soft and muffled and hopeless. His concern doubled. Whatever the situation, it no longer felt dangerous. He moved catlike up the stairs and peered around the corner, and what he saw made him nearly call her name out loud. It was her, of course. Even from the back he recognized her immediately, her blond hair catching the light of the moon from the nearby window. Molly Allen wasn't on a flight back to Portland.

She was here.

Sitting cross-legged on the floor in the exact spot where they had spent so many afternoons, her face in her hands, her heart clearly breaking. She hadn't heard him until now, but something must have caught her attention, because she shifted and sat up straighter, glancing over her shoulder into the dark room.

He didn't want to scare her. So he did what he would've done seven years ago if he'd known he wasn't going to see her again. He didn't need the book. The lines were in his heart. "'I am no bird; and no net ensnares me.'" He hesitated. "What happened to that girl?"

"Ryan!" She allowed a quick gasp and spun around, facing him. "What are you doing here?"

He came closer and sat on the floor opposite her, their knees inches apart. "That was supposed to be my question."

The shock looked to be wearing off, but she seemed discouraged, resigned in some way he couldn't quite understand. "You . . . you're supposed to be at the hospital."

"And you're supposed to be at the airport."

"I missed my flight." She exhaled, finding control again. But something in her tone was more hurt than defeated. "What did that mean? The *Jane Eyre* quote?"

"What happened to her?" He shrugged. "You didn't give me a chance to ask."

Molly dried her eyes with the sleeves of her sweater and looked at him. She couldn't maintain the connection now any more than she could earlier that day. She let her eyes find a spot on the wooden floor. "I play violin for a local symphony." Her tone settled a bit more. She lifted her eyes to his again. "No net ensnares me, Ryan. I'm still that girl."

She played the violin? He forced himself to remember that they weren't sophomores in college, and this wasn't the backyard of her parents' home. He could barely concentrate outside of the way he was drawn to her. "You didn't tell me. About the violin."

Her face didn't apologize. "You didn't ask." She angled her head, allowing him to see a little deeper into her soul. "When we first met, you told me you might have questions. I told you I might have answers, remember that?"

"Yes." He slid back a little, fighting his emotions. "I remember everything."

"This time you didn't ask." She lifted her chin a little. "You don't know anything about me, Ryan Kelly."

She was right. That was the worst part. He sighed, wishing he could explain himself. He hadn't felt right asking questions, not when she had a man waiting back at home. "Okay." He leaned forward, his elbows on his knees. "Your husband . . . does he like music?" His voice was soft, the question merely his attempt at a window to her heart. The one he hadn't looked for earlier. "And does he know about your obsession with *Jane Eyre*?"

Her gaze fell. For a long time she said nothing, only stared at the floor again and moved her fingers nervously along the old wooden planks. Finally, a shaky breath slid across her lips, and two fresh tears fell onto her cheeks. When she looked up, her eyes were the same as they'd been back at the hospital. Filled with a raw pain that made no sense. "Ryan."

It took all his strength to keep from drawing her close and finding a way to comfort her. "Talk to me, Molly."

Before the words would come, the look in her eyes changed. As if, whatever she was about to say, she was already begging him to understand.

"Look, I never stopped caring about you, Molly. I hate seeing you like this." He reminded himself to be careful, not to say too much. "You and your husband . . . is there a problem?"

She pressed her fist to her forehead, and when she lowered it, she said the words he never expected. "I'm not married." She twisted the ring on her left hand. "This is my mother's wedding band."

Ryan heard the words; he just couldn't register them. Couldn't find a place where they made even a little sense. She wasn't married? The ring wasn't hers? He closed his eyes and then blinked them open. He didn't move, couldn't breathe. The assault of emotions on his heart was so varied, he had no idea which one to tackle first.

Shock seemed to take the lead. "Why, Molly?"

Her voice fell to a whisper, tears choking her words. "It was safer."

"But . . ." His own eyes were damp now. "You hate safe. Remember?"

"Except with you."

Ryan remembered her father's phone call. None of it made sense, why Molly would have run to the guy if she hadn't been in love with him. "All this time I thought you married him." He stood and paced to the window. When he turned around, shock took a backseat to anger. "Why did you call him if you weren't in love with him?"

"What?" She sounded mystified.

"The night we kissed, you called *him*, not me." He didn't hide his fury. For seven years he'd wanted to have this conversation with her. He found a level of restraint. "Don't act surprised. Your father told me." He could feel the disgust in his expression. "He even played me the message."

With that, her eyes no longer held an apology or a broken heart or righteous indignation. They held sheer and complete horror. In that single moment he knew with absolute certainty that he'd based the last seven years on nothing more than a lie.

A wicked, ruinous, heartless lie.

CHAPTER THIRTEEN

Molly tried to get up, tried to scream out over the news, but she could do neither. Instead she rose to her knees and leveled her gaze straight at him, at all he knew about the past that she hadn't known until now. When she could catch her breath, she said only the necessary words. "Tell me everything."

Ryan looked like he'd been shot through the heart, as if the life he'd believed in for almost a decade was emptying onto the floor around him. "You didn't call Preston that night?"

"After we kissed?" She heard the pain in her voice. Even from the grave, her father had manipulated her life. "Really, Ryan? Did you actually believe that?"

He came to her and held out his hands. "This is going to hurt us both." He helped her to her feet. "I won't have this conversation without you close to me."

The feel of his fingers against hers weakened her defenses, and she knew he was right. Whatever was coming next, she wanted nothing more than to hear it from the safety of his arms. His fingers eased between hers, and she felt her head spin. She wanted details, answers, but not as much as she wanted him. She closed her eyes and tried to assess the damage her father had wreaked on her life.

It was too great to get her mind around.

He drew a slow breath. "The staff must've told your dad about our kiss."

"Nice."

"However he found out, the next morning he called me."

"How?" She started to pull away, but he wouldn't let her. "He called on your cell?"

"Yes. He told me not to worry about how he got my number."

She groaned and hung her head. How could her dad have done this? "He had a friend on the board at Belmont." She wanted to run, hide her face from Ryan for all her father had put them through. "What did he say?"

"He basically forbade me to have feelings for you."

Ryan's words were slower, kinder. As if he were well aware of the pain they were causing her. "He told me a boy from Carthage, Mississippi, would never be good enough for you."

"What?" The word was more of a cry. "That was never true."

Ryan didn't stop. "He also told me that you were engaged to Preston Millington. He told me you'd set a date and that you had called Preston the night before—after being with me."

Molly felt faint, felt herself losing hearing and vision and consciousness. "No . . . he couldn't have done that." She tried again to take a step back; this time he eased his arms around her waist.

"I'm sorry . . . I know this is hard." He whispered the words against her face. "I'm not letting you go this time."

She pressed her head against his chest and wished with all her being that when she opened her eyes, it would be seven years earlier and they would've had this conversation before she left. "You said . . . something about a message." She eased back enough to see his face.

"Yes. He played me a message." This part was hard

for Ryan; that much was obvious. Clearly, he had based his belief in her father's words entirely on what had happened at the end of the phone call. "It was your voice." He sighed, deeply discouraged. "I'd like to say I've forgotten what you said, but I haven't. I heard you say, 'Yes, Preston . . . you know how I feel about you. I've known you all my life. You always knew I wouldn't stay at Belmont forever.'"

The light-headed feeling was back, and the room began to spin. The words were familiar, and if Ryan said they were her voice, then they must've been. When had she said that? Her senior year, maybe? Or the summer before she left for college? As she forced her brain to go back, the picture came into focus.

Preston had called from her father's office the day before she moved to Nashville. The entire conversation felt like nothing more than a plea on his part, his way of begging her to forget her plans for Belmont. So she had reassured him. After all the years of boarding school, he had to have known how she felt about him. Like he was her friend. Nothing more. That was what she had meant. She explained to Ryan despite the sick feeling trying to consume her.

When she was finished, the next realization almost

leveled her. "My father . . . he was in the room." The ad-
mission was sickening. "He records calls on his business line. So he must've saved my side of the conversation. He probably planned on using it to convince me
how I felt." She raked her hand through her hair, sick to
her stomach. "My dad knew I didn't love Preston. He
tried everything he could to convince me I did."

The story made sense to Ryan. She could see that
much in his face. "Or in case he ever needed to use
the recording to keep a boy from Carthage away from
his only daughter." His obvious disbelief dropped his
voice to a whisper. "I can't believe this."

"Exactly." Molly wouldn't blame him if he hated her
for the way her father had treated him. "I can't believe
he'd lie to you." She looked deep into Ryan's eyes, all
the way through him. "Can I tell you something?"

"Please." He ran his thumbs along her hands, his
eyes locked on hers.

"I never would've called anyone that night." Her
eyes locked on his. "All I could think about was you.
That night . . . it was one of the best in my life."

He stared at her, defeated once again. She watched
a pair of tears slide down his cheeks. "Then why,
Molly? Why'd you leave?"

"Because." She shrugged one shoulder, her lip quivering. "You didn't want me. You apologized the next day. And an apology after a night like that was as good as telling me you never wanted to kiss me again."

"Molly." He released the hold he had on her waist and ran his fingers down the length of her arms. "I missed you every day since then. I thought you were married, but still"—he pulled his copy of *Jane Eyre* from his pocket—"I kept this. Hoping that maybe someday I'd see you again." Another bit of understanding filled his expression. "Everything had changed . . . you wrote that at the back of my book. Because of my apology?"

"I did." She managed a weak smile despite the tears in her eyes. "It's why I wore the ring." Her heart felt like it had been in knots for seven years and only now was it finally beginning to unravel. "I didn't want your pity. Not if you were sorry for kissing me."

He looked like he had a hundred things he might say. Instead he did the one thing she was desperate for him to do. Slowly, with the buildup of far too long, he pulled her to himself and kissed her, a kiss that erased seven years in as many seconds. His lips against hers, the feel of his strong arms around her shoulders. All of it was like some wonderful dream, as if the Ryan in the video had stepped into her world.

All she wanted was to never wake up.

Molly didn't look away, wouldn't dare take her eyes off him, because if she did, he might not be there when she looked back.

"You should know something." His eyes danced.

Molly understood how he could look so happy. With the lies cleared up, there was no distance between them. No lies or doubts or hurt feelings. "What should I know?"

He linked his arms around her waist once more and swayed with her gently, dancing to the sound of creaking boards in their favorite room at The Bridge. "You should know that I've always wanted to kiss you." His grin continued to lighten the mood between them. "Even when I thought you were married."

"Ryan!" She giggled, and then the reality of what he'd said sank in. "You've always wanted to kiss me?"

"Always. From the first day I saw you in the auditorium during orientation."

"Why didn't you say anything?" Her voice fell to a whisper. She put her hand on his cheek, searching his eyes. "We lost so much time."

"Not anymore."

"So what do we do?" Her mind spun with the impossibilities of their lives, the logistics they would need to work out. "My office is in Portland."

"You mean your Portland office is in Portland." He swayed with her again, his eyes sparkling in the soft light from the window. "Your Nashville office will be here. Isn't that what you meant?"

He made it sound so easy, but after a few seconds of wrestling with herself, she realized he was right. With her money, she could open branches in ten cities. "So I move to Nashville?"

"Tomorrow." He kissed her again and one more time. When he drew back, he spoke straight to her soul. "You marry me, and I chase my dream of being a studio musician, and when the babies come . . . you know where we'll take them, right?"

She laughed, not believing this was real, that he was actually saying these things. Marriage? And babies? The joy in her heart was as foreign as it was wonderful. "Where do we take them?"

"To The Bridge, of course."

"Right. Because someone has to teach our little girl that no net will ever ensnare her."

"Mmm." He kissed her again.

She let herself get lost in the feeling. When she took a breath, she whispered near his face. "Is this happening? Are we really doing this?"

"Dreams don't feel this good." His voice was thick with passion. When he kissed her the next time, he seemed to force himself to take a step back. "Don't leave me, Molly. Ever again."

She smiled. "I kept your memory alive. Every year on the same day."

"You did?" They were completely comfortable together. As if no time had passed between them. "When?"

"Black Friday."

"Nice. A reference to your hatred for me, I assume."

"No." She laughed. "Just wound up that way. The one day when I blocked off time after work. That's when I would play the video."

"What video?"

"Come on, Ryan." Her heart hadn't felt this good since that night in her Brentwood backyard. "The one you made for your cinematography class."

"Where I interviewed you in the car?" He chuckled at the way he'd made the project seem like a serious work of art. "You still have that?"

Her laughter faded, and her eyes held his. "I do . . . I play it every year, the day after Thanksgiving. Makes me remember how thankful I was to have you." Her smile felt sad again. "Even for only two years."

"Molly, I had no idea." He looked like he might kiss her again. Then he made a funny face. "What was the name of that video?"

"Remember?" She held onto him, wanting the moment never to end. "You called it 'The Bridge: How a Small-Town Boy from Carthage, Mississippi, and a Highbrow Girl from Pacific Heights, California, Found Common Ground on a Daily Commute Down Franklin Road Outside Music City to The Bridge— the Best Little Bookstore in the World.'"

"Worst title ever."

"I tried to tell you that." She laughed again. "You got an A, anyway."

"Here's a better title." He ran his thumb along her

cheekbone, lost in her eyes. "'Two Years and Forever . . . How a Bookstore Changed Everything.'"

"Hmmm." The longer they stayed like this, the more real it felt. The more she could practically see their life ahead the way Ryan had laid it out a few minutes ago. "I like it."

"You know something? I might want to get married right here in this room. Where it all began." Ryan kissed her one last time and then, against the demands of their desires, led her downstairs. "Let's get you back to your hotel. We both need a good night's sleep." He winked at her. "Tomorrow is Christmas."

In the craziness of the last hour, Molly had almost forgotten. She slipped into Ryan's arms, and as they reached his truck, she thought of something. "A pastor once told me that God was the giver of second chances."

"He is." Ryan's eyes made her wonder how she could've ever doubted his feelings. "I've prayed for this moment since we said good-bye. Provided you weren't married, of course."

She laughed. "As if I would marry Preston Millington. Please."

The wind had picked up, and the chill in the air

was biting cold. He swept her into his arms and held her for another long moment. Then they climbed in his truck and headed north on Franklin Road. As if her father had never lied to Ryan and his apology had never happened and she'd never gotten on a plane and left for good. Along the way, they talked and laughed and dreamed about possibilities that were suddenly real.

And as they drove, as Molly felt the warmth of her hand in his, she did the only thing left to do. Treasure the miracle.

And thank the God of second chances.

ACKNOWLEDGMENTS

No book comes together without a great and talented team of people. For that reason, a special thanks to my friends at Howard Books, who combined efforts with a number of people passionate enough about Life-Changing Fiction™ to make *The Bridge* all it could be. A special thanks to my amazing editor, Becky Nesbitt, and to Jonathan Merkh. Thanks also to the creative staff and the sales force at Howard and Simon & Schuster who worked tirelessly to put this book in your hands.

A special thanks to my amazing agent, Rick Christian, president of Alive Communications. Rick, you've always believed in only the best for me. When we talk about the highest possible goals, you see them as doable, reachable. You are a brilliant manager of my career, an incredible agent, and I thank God for you.

But even with all you do for my ministry of writing, I am doubly grateful for your encouragement and prayers. Every time I finish a book, you send me a letter worth framing, and when something big happens, yours is the first call I receive. Thank you for that. The fact that you and Debbie are praying for me and my family keeps me confident every morning that God will continue to breathe life into the stories in my heart. Thank you for being so much more than a brilliant agent.

Thanks to my husband, who puts up with me on deadlines and doesn't mind driving through Taco Bell after a football game if I've been editing all day. This wild ride wouldn't be possible without you, Donald. Your love keeps me writing; your prayers keep me believing that God has a plan in this ministry of Life-Changing Fiction™. And thanks for the hours you put in helping me. It's a full-time job, and I am grateful for your concern for my reader friends. Of course, thanks to my daughter and sons, who pull together—bringing me iced green tea and understanding my sometimes crazy schedule. I love that you know you're still first, before any deadline.

Thank you to my mom, Anne Kingsbury, and to

my sisters, Tricia and Sue. Mom, you are amazing as my assistant—working day and night sorting through the mail from my readers. I appreciate you more than you'll ever know. Traveling together these past years for Extraordinary Women and Women of Joy events has given us times that we will always treasure. Now we will be at Women of Faith events as well. The journey gets more exciting all the time!

Tricia, you are the best executive assistant I could ever hope to have. I appreciate your loyalty and honesty, the way you include me in every decision and the daily exciting website changes. My site has been a different place since you stepped in, and the hits have grown a hundredfold. Along the way, the readers have so much more to help them in their faith, so much more than a story. Please know that I pray for God's blessings on you always, for your dedication to helping me in this season of writing, and for your wonderful son, Andrew. And aren't we having such a good time? God works all things for good!

Sue, I believe you should have been a counselor! At your home far from mine, you get batches of reader letters every day, and you diligently answer them using God's wisdom and His Word. When readers get a response from "Karen's sister Susan," I hope they know how carefully you've prayed for them and the responses you give them. Thank you for truly loving what you do, Sue. You're gifted with people, and I'm blessed to have you aboard.

And to my friends at Premier (Roy Morgan and team), along with my friends at Women of Faith, Extraordinary Women, and Women of Joy, how wonderful to be a part of what God is doing through you. Thank you for including me in your family on the road.

Thanks to my forever friends and family, the ones who have been there and continue to be there. Your love has been a tangible source of comfort, pulling us through the tough times and making us know how very blessed we are to have you in our lives.

The greatest thanks to God. You put a story in my heart and have a million other hearts in mind—something I could never do. I'm grateful to be a small part of Your plan! The gift is Yours. I pray I might use it for years to come in a way that will bring You honor and glory.

*It's never too late for those
willing to take a chance.*

Check out the next novel coming
from Karen Kingsbury!

the
CHANCE

Available March 2013

Read an excerpt in the following pages.

CHAPTER ONE

Summer 2002

Her mom didn't come home for dinner—third time that week.

That was the first hint Ellie Tucker had that maybe her father was right. Maybe her mother had done something so terrible that this time their family would break in two. And no one and nothing would ever put them back together again.

Ellie was fifteen that hot, humid, Savannah summer, and as the Friday afternoon hours slipped away, as six o'clock came and six-thirty went, she joined her dad in the kitchen and helped him make dinner. Tuna sandwiches with a new jar of warm mayonnaise from the cupboard. He stayed quiet, every minute of her mother's absence weighing heavy in the silence. Their refrigerator didn't have much, but he pulled out a bag of baby carrots and poured them into a bowl. With the food on the table, her dad took his spot at the head and she sat next to him.

The place across from her, the spot where her mother usually sat, remained glaringly empty.

"Let's pray." Her father took her hand. He waited for several beats before starting. "Lord, thank you for our food and our blessings." He hesitated. "You know all things. Reveal the truth, please. In Jesus's name, amen."

The truth? Ellie could barely swallow the dry bites of her sandwich. The truth about what? Her mother? The reason she wasn't home when the doctor's office where she worked closed an hour ago?

They said nothing while they ate, though the quiet screamed across the dinner table. When they were finished, her dad looked at her. His eyes were sad. "Ellie, if you would do the dishes, please." He stood and kissed her on the forehead. "I'll be in my room."

She was finishing up in the kitchen when her mom slipped through the front door. Lately Ellie felt more like the mother, or at least the way a mother was supposed to feel when their kids were teenagers. Ellie looked over her shoulder, and her eyes met her mom's. She was still wearing her black pants and white shirt, the clothes she wore for work.

"Where's your father?" Her eyes were red and swollen, her voice thick.

"In his room." She wanted to ask her mom where she'd been and why she was late. But she didn't know how. She turned back to the sink.

Ellie's mother started in that direction, then she stopped and turned to Ellie again. "I'm sorry." Her shoulders dropped a little more. "For missing dinner." She sounded weary. "I'm sorry."

Before Ellie could say anything, her mom turned and walked down the hall. Ellie checked the clock on the microwave. Seven-thirty. Her friend Nolan had another hour in the gym, another hour shooting baskets. Then Ellie would ride her bike to his house, the way she did most nights. Especially this summer.

Since her parents had been fighting.

She dried her hands, walked to her room, and shut the door behind her. A little music and some time with her journal, and then Nolan would be home. She turned on the radio. Backstreet Boys filled her room, and instantly she dropped the sound a few notches. Her dad said he'd take away her radio if she listened to worldly music. Ellie figured worldly was a matter of opinion. And her opinion was that the Backstreet Boys was as close to heaven as she was going to get for now.

The first shout rattled her bedroom window.

Ellie killed the sound on the radio and jumped to her feet. As much tension as there had been between her parents lately, neither of them did much shouting. At least not this loud. Her heart pounded. Before she reached her bedroom door, another round of shouts ripped through the air, and this time she could understand what her father was saying, the names he was calling her mom.

Quietly, too afraid to breathe, Ellie crept down the hall and across the living room, closer to her parents' bedroom door. Another burst of shouts, and now she was near enough that she could hear something else. Her mother's tears.

"You'll pack your things and leave." Her father had never sounded like this before, like he was firing bullets of hatred with every word. "I will not have you pregnant with his child and . . . and living under my roof." His voice shook the walls. "I will not have it!"

Ellie anchored herself against the wall so she wouldn't drop to the floor. Her mother was pregnant? With someone else's baby? The blood began to leave her face, and her world started to spin. Colors and sounds and reality blurred and she wondered if she would pass out. *Run, Ellie . . . run fast.* She ordered herself to move, but her feet wouldn't follow the command.

Before she could figure out which way was up again, her father stepped into the doorway and glared at her, his chest heaving with each breath. "What are you doing?"

The question hung between them, and from behind her father Ellie caught a glimpse of her mom. Sitting in their bedroom chair, her head in her hands. *Get up,* Ellie wanted to scream at her. *Defend yourself! Do something!* But her mother did nothing. She said nothing.

Ellie's eyes flew to her father again, and she tried to step away, tried to exit the scene as quickly as possible, but she tripped and fell back on her hands. Her wrists hurt but she scrambled further from him, anyway. Like a crab escaping a net.

It took that long for her father's expression to soften. "Ellie. I'm sorry." He took a step toward her. "I didn't mean for . . . you weren't supposed to hear that."

And in that moment Ellie knew two things. First, the horrible thing her dad had shouted was true. And second, her life as she knew it now lay splintered around her on the worn, thin hallway carpet in a million pieces. "I . . . I have to go." The words were barely a whisper.

Her father was saying something about this being more than a girl her age could understand and that she needed to get back to her room and pray. Something like that. But all Ellie could hear was the deafening way her heart slammed around in her chest. She needed air, needed to breathe. In a move that felt desperate, she found her way to her feet and ran for the front door. She needed Nolan, and she needed him now. A minute later she was on her bicycle pedaling through the summer night.

Pedaling as fast as she could.

———

He would still be at the gym, but that was okay. Ellie loved watching Nolan play basketball. Loved it whether the place was packed with kids from Savannah High, or just the two of them and the echo of the ball hitting the shiny wood floor. With every push of her foot against the pedal Ellie tried to put the reality out of her mind. But the truth smothered her like a wet blanket. Her mother had come home late again—the way she'd been coming home late since early spring. And today . . . today she must have told her father what he had suspected all along.

She was having an affair. Not only that, but she was pregnant.

The truth churned in her stomach, suffocating her until finally she had no choice but to ditch her bike in the closest bush and give way to the nausea consuming her. One revolting wave after another, her insides convulsing until the only thing left inside her was the hurt. A hurt that would stay with her forever.

Exhausted and drained, Ellie sat on the curb, her head in her hands, and let the tears come. Until then, the horror and shock had kept her sadness at bay. But with her stomach and heart empty, she cried until she could barely breathe. Her mom didn't love her father, which meant she didn't love Ellie, either. Their family wasn't enough for her. There was no other way to look at this. A sense of shame added itself to the mix of sorrow. Nolan's mom would never have done something like this.

She lifted her face to the darkening sky. Nolan. Ellie wiped her face and breathed in deep. She needed to get to him before it got any later, needed to find him before he left the gym. She forced the pedals to move faster, willed the old bike to make time until finally the gym was in sight. The sound of the ball hitting the floor filled her ears as she leaned her bike against the brick wall at the back of the building, next to his.

Nolan kept the door propped open in case a breeze might come up. Ellie slipped through the entrance and moved quietly to the first row of the bleachers. Nolan caught the ball and stared at her, his eyes dancing, a smile tugging at his lips. "You're early."

She nodded. She didn't trust her voice, not when all she wanted to do was run to him and let him wrap his arms around her. Nolan Cook. Her best friend in the whole world.

"Ellie?" A shadow of concern fell over his handsome face. "You okay?"

As much as she wanted to go to him, she couldn't tell him. Didn't want him to know why she was upset, because then . . . well, then for sure it would be true. There would be no turning from the truth once she told Nolan.

He set the ball down and walked to her. Sweat dripped from his forehead, and his tank top and shorts were drenched. "You've been crying." He stopped a foot from her. "What happened?"

"My parents." She felt her eyes well up, felt her words drown in an ocean of sadness.

"More fighting?"

"Yeah. Bad."

"Ahh, Ellie." His breathing was returning to normal. He wiped his forearm across his face. "I'm sorry."

"Keep playing." Her voice sounded strained from her heartache. She nodded to the basket. "You have another ten minutes."

He watched her for a long couple of seconds. "You sure?"

"We can talk later. I just"—a few tears slid down her cheeks—"needed to be here. With you."

Again he studied her, but eventually he nodded. Slow and not quite sure. "Okay. We can leave whenever you want."

"When you're done. Please, Nolan."

One last look, but then he turned and jogged back to the ball. Once it was in his hands he dribbled to the left and the right, and then took the ball to the hoop. In a move as fluid and graceful as anything Ellie had seen in her seven years of dance lessons, Nolan rose in the air and slammed the ball through the net. He landed lightly on both feet and caught the ball. Dribbled back out, juked a few more imaginary opponents, and repeated the move. Ten straight dunks, and then he jogged to the drinking fountain and drank for half a minute. Next came his three-point shots.

Nolan played basketball with his heart, mind, and soul. The ball was an extension of his hand, and every move, every step was as natural for him as breathing. Watching him, Ellie felt her eyes dry, felt herself marveling at the gift he'd been given, the way she celebrated it every time she had the privilege of seeing him play. Nolan's dream was as simple as it was impossible.

He wanted to play in the NBA. It was something he prayed about and worked toward every day. Every hour of every day. From the A's and B's he struggled to earn in class to the hours he put in here every day and night. If Nolan didn't wind up playing professional basketball, it wouldn't be for lack of trying. Not for lack of believing.

He hit five shots from every spot along the arch of the three-point line, then he gulped down more water and finally tucked the ball under his arm and walked back to her. He used his shirt to wipe the sweat off his face. "Could it be more humid?"

"Yeah." She smiled a little and looked at the open back door. "Not much of a breeze."

"No." He led the way. "Come on. We'll go to my house first. I'll shower, and then we can go to the park."

That's all Ellie wanted, a few hours alone with Nolan at Gordonston Park. The place with their favorite oak tree and enough soft grass for them to lay on their backs and watch shooting stars on more summer nights than she could count. She didn't say anything, not yet. They walked silently out the back door, which Nolan closed and locked. Nolan's dad was the coach, and he had given him a key a year ago. Too much trouble to open the gym every time Nolan wanted to shoot baskets.

They rode their bikes down Pennsylvania Avenue and then took the shortcut down Kinzie Avenue to

Edgewood. Nolan's house was only half a mile from Ellie's, but they might as well have been in separate worlds for how different they were. Nolan's neighborhood had fireflies and front lawns that stretched on forever. Ellie's had chain link fences and stray dogs, with low-slung, single-story houses the size of Nolan's garage.

The sort of house Ellie and her parents lived in.

Ellie sat with Nolan's mother in the kitchen while he showered. Her eyes were dry still, so she didn't have to explain herself. Instead, the conversation was light, with Nolan's mom telling her about the new Bible study she'd joined, and how much she was learning about the Old Testament.

Ellie wanted to care, wanted to feel as connected to God as Nolan and his parents. But if God loved her, why was her life falling apart? Maybe He only loved some people. Good folks like the Cook family. A few minutes later Nolan came down in clean shorts and a T-shirt. He grabbed two chocolate chip cookies from a plate on the kitchen counter and kissed his mother's cheek.

Suddenly Nolan looked different, more grown up. She was with him every day, so she didn't always stop and notice, but here, in his kitchen, she could see it. He wasn't a kid anymore. Neither of them were. They'd been friends since second grade, and they'd walked home together since the first day of middle school. She still felt like a kid, but somewhere along the journey of time they'd both done something they hadn't seen coming.

They'd gotten older. They'd grown up.

Nolan was just over six feet already, tanned from his morning runs, his short blond hair cut close to his head the way it was every summer. He'd been lifting weights for basketball, so maybe that was why he looked different: the way his shoulders and biceps filled out the pale green T-shirt as he grabbed the cookies.

Ellie felt her cheeks grow hot and she looked away. Mrs. Cook smiled at her, and Ellie was grateful the woman hadn't caught her looking at Nolan. "Come by any time, Ellie. The door's always open. You know that."

"Yes, ma'am. Thank you." And with that they were out the door. There was no need to talk about where they were going. It was the same place every time. Beneath the biggest oak tree in the park—maybe the biggest oak tree in the city. The one dripping with Spanish moss, with the gnarled tree roots jutting out of the soft Southern ground high enough to make a place for them to sit. The grassy patch was just a few feet away, beneath a break in the branches overhead.

The place where Ellie and Nolan had come to talk about life since the summer before sixth grade. Their place. Back then they played hide-and-seek among the trees, with the enormous old oak serving as home base. During the school year, when it was warm enough, they'd do their homework out here. And on nights like this, they would do what came easiest for them.

They would simply sit down, open their hearts, and share whatever came pouring out.

"Okay. Tell me." Nolan took the spot closest to the massive tree trunk. He leaned back, studying her. "What happened?"

Ellie had been thinking about this moment since she walked through the door of the high school gym. She had to tell him the truth, because she told him everything. But she didn't have to tell him this very minute, right? He was waiting for an answer. Her throat was dry, so her words took longer to form. "My mom . . . she was late again."

He waited, and after a few seconds he blinked. Twice. "That's it?"

"Yeah." She didn't like postponing the truth, but she couldn't tell him yet. "My dad was really mad."

"Oh. I was worried it was something really bad." He leaned back against the tree. "It'll be okay, Ellie. It will."

"Right." She moved to the spot beside him and pressed her back lightly against the tree trunk. Their shoulders were touching, a reminder of everything good and right in her life.

"One day when we're old and married we'll come back to this very spot and remember tonight."

"How do you know?"

He looked at her. "That we'll remember?"

"No." She grinned. "That I'll marry you."

"That's easy." He faced her fully, shrugged, and folded his arms. "You'll never find anyone who loves you like I do."

It wasn't the first time he'd said this. And always he kept his tone light, so she couldn't accuse him of being too serious or trying to change their friendship to something more. Not yet, anyway. Always she would laugh and shake her head, as if he'd suggested something crazy like the two of them running off and joining the circus.

But this time she didn't laugh or joke or push the subject. She only lifted her eyes to the distant trees and the fireflies still dancing among them. Good thing she hadn't told him about her mother, about how she'd slept with another man and gotten pregnant. Because that would change everything. Nolan would feel sorry for her, and there would be no more teasing about marriage. Not when her parents had made such a mess of theirs.

Ellie exhaled, content. The news could wait.

Because right now she wanted nothing more than to sit here beside Nolan Cook under the big oak tree at the edge of the park on a summer night that was theirs alone and believe . . . believe for one more moment the one thing Ellie wanted more than her next breath.

That they might stay this way forever.

SURROGATE

SURROGATE

SUSAN SPINDLER

virago

VIRAGO

First published in Great Britain in 2021 by Virago Press

1 3 5 7 9 10 8 6 4 2

A CIP catalogue record for this book
is available from the British Library.

Hardback ISBN 978-0-3490-1377-0
Trade paperback ISBN 978-0-3490-1376-3

Typeset in Palatino by M Rules
Printed and bound in Great Britain by
Clays Ltd, Elcograf S.p.A.

Papers used by Virago are from well-managed forests
and other responsible sources.

Virago
An imprint of
Little, Brown Book Group
Carmelite House
50 Victoria Embankment
London EC4Y 0DZ

An Hachette UK Company
www.hachette.co.uk

www.virago.co.uk

For my family

PART ONE

THE OFFER

1

Ruth was hosting a cast and crew screening in Soho for *Hurt,*
the drama series she'd been working on for the past five years.
It was in one of those small, underground viewing theatres in
a mews: out of the rain, down narrow, dingy stairs, then into a
brightly lit bar. Secret, but cosy. Laughter and the promise of gin.
In the Ladies she applied lipstick and blusher, threw on a flame-
red scarf to enliven her dark jacket, then rehearsed her warm,
knowing, mother-of-the-show smile. She loved these events.
Fifty or sixty of the actors, technicians and production team were
expected – not bad for a wet Tuesday in October. They'd come
to celebrate the series, before it ventured out into an uncertain
world of critics and audience ratings. On nights like these budget
crises, overruns and shouting matches were a distant memory,
but the reflex intimacy of the group remained.

She worked the room, hugging, laughing and gossiping, until
it was time to start. Then she stepped onto a small stage, raised
her glass, and waited for the crowd to quieten. She told them
how brilliant they all were: how they'd made something ground-
breaking and timely.

'In a moment we're going to show the first episode. But before
that, here's to *Hurt.* And to all of you. Thank you, I'm *so* proud.'

Loud applause, then everyone swarmed towards the screening room. Ruth picked up fragments of chatter and caught her name.

'Don't you just *love* her? ... makes you feel valued, not like most of them nowadays ...'

'I know ...'

She slowed her pace and listened, amused and flattered.

'... gives directors and writers their heads, *fights* for projects, and shows up when the shit hits the fan ... most execs steer well clear ...'

'... yeah, committed, but she's a good laugh, the stories ...'

'... been around for decades ...'

Then, *sotto voce*, but she caught it.

'Early fifties, I reckon.'

'No, older ... I worked with her on the first series of *Casualty*, back in the day ...'

'... used to be so ravishing, that long hair and those eyes, almost Italian ... lovely bone structure even now. But ...'

'... ravages of time ... comes to us all, though, doesn't it? Unless you take steps to turn back the clock ...'

'Right, and she's not the type, is she ...?'

Ruth lifted her head and hurried on, chiding herself for her vanity. She knew what they saw. She remembered the moment she'd first noticed the shift, four years ago in central London: she and Lauren had stopped to buy coffees from a cart. The baristas, men in their mid-twenties, checked out her nubile, taut-fleshed elder daughter and began to flirt. Ruth joined in the banter, smiling and laughing, but they ignored her – as if she wasn't there. She'd taken her sexual attractiveness for granted for more than three decades, then suddenly it was gone: something in her extinguished. Her dark brown hair was veined with silver and she wore it up now; her skin was losing its elasticity and drooped, like uncooked pastry, over the bones of her face; no monthly surge of hormones came to rescue and rejuvenate her.

4

Her moon had set, for good. Not meno*paused*. Finished. Over. She *minded*; and the minding came as a surprise.

She shook her head in an attempt to dislodge the thoughts and recover her equilibrium, then found a seat in the theatre, halfway back in the middle of a row next to Bella (late forties, lots of cleavage, blonde and still very *visible*). The two of them had worked together at the BBC and six years ago they'd started Morrab Films, a small but respected independent drama company with three successful series to its name.

Bella squeezed Ruth's hand. 'Lovely speech, darling. Well done. Been a bit of a marathon, this one, hasn't it?'

The pre-title sequence unfurled: a little girl, running down a dark corridor, whimpering and stumbling as the music built. An adult hand reaching down into shot, lifting her up and out of vision – unclear whether into safety or peril. Muffled screams, and finally a long silence. They'd spent weeks in the edit suite trying to get the thing to gel, and now it worked, forced you to keep watching. *Hurt* was about abduction and shifting identities, based on a real case that had mesmerised Ruth. It was an important story that needed to be told, but a succession of legal obstacles had delayed production and delivery and she was privately worried that it might have missed its moment. The previous year gritty, challenging dramas like this had done well with audiences; now viewers seemed hungry only for fantasy and escapism. If *Hurt* bombed, the company would be in trouble: they were relying on getting a second series commissioned. But she was probably getting things out of proportion: eighteen months of working evenings and weekends had taken their toll.

She snuggled into the big velour seat and allowed herself to daydream. If only she could get off the treadmill for a while. The job was wonderful – a crazy mix of performance, manipulation, crowd control and troubleshooting – but relentless. What would it be like to stop? To do something just for *herself*?

5

She sighed. If only they weren't so reliant on her income to pay the mortgage; if only she wasn't going to have to work flat out over the next three months to ensure Morrab Films stayed on an even keel . . .

The first time her phone buzzed against her hip she was oblivious. The second time she ignored it, and the third. It was only when she felt the pulse of a text that she pulled her coat over her head and squinted at the screen. It was from Dan.

> Laurie lost the baby this morning
> and has had emergency surgery
> Please come – Room F, Gynae
> Ward, Ladyfield Hospital

Ruth bent forward and clutched her abdomen, engulfed by a cramping anguish. She gathered up her coat and bag, leant into Bella and whispered, 'Lauren's had another miscarriage. Got to go.'

'Of course.' Bella squeezed Ruth's arm. 'Send her my love.'

'Can you do the you-were-all-so-fab at the end? And give my apologies.'

Bella nodded.

By the time she had squeezed and sorried her way along the row, Ruth's phone was vibrating again. 'Adam? . . . I know, Dan messaged me too . . . Yes, heartbreaking. Fourteen and a half weeks, *imagine* . . . No, I'll take the Underground, it'll be quicker. See you there.'

It was raining torrentially and there were long delays, but Ruth was glad to be in the anonymous neon-lit carriage where she didn't have to engage with anyone. As she came out of the station the wind sucked her umbrella inside out, baring its metal carcass, and she was soaked by the time she arrived at the hospital. As the doors of the ward slid open she remembered all the other bleak pilgrimages she and Adam had made to this corner of south London to mourn the deaths of six potential grandchildren. She found a toilet cubicle and leant over a basin to wring the water from her hair, then peered at herself in the mirror: the red scarf was an affront to the moment, she took it off and stuffed it in her bag.

Adam was lurking in the corridor outside the room. He was on edge, he'd never been comfortable in hospitals. 'What kept you? I've been here almost half an hour.'

'Flash floods on the line.' She hugged him, then knocked on the door and pushed it open.

It was a cruel parody of a nativity scene: their daughter and son-in-law locked together on the bed, faces buried in one another. Lauren was wearing a pale blue hospital gown, a smudge of dried blood on her right calf. Dan still had his jacket and tie on. The exposed white skin above his socks made Ruth want to cry.

She said, 'Are we OK to come in?'

They looked up, surprised in their grief, cheeks raw and swollen, then Dan stood and helped Lauren haul herself painstakingly into a sitting position. She shivered and he draped a blanket around her thin shoulders. An intravenous tube snaked from the drip above her head into the back of her right hand; her face was shuttered and shockingly pale. She looked like an abandoned child.

Ruth perched on the edge of the bed and embraced her. 'This is *so* unfair,' she said. 'You don't deserve it. *Any* of it.' She tried to rock her, wanting to make it all go away, but Lauren stiffened in her embrace, then broke free.

'Don't, Mum, please.' She swallowed. 'I'm just not meant—' Her face trembled for an instant then closed down again.

Ruth retreated, feeling the surge of love and frustration that Lauren so often provoked: even now, in extremis, she wouldn't yield and be comforted. She'd been like this from the beginning, self-absorbed and private as a little girl, withdrawn and watchful in her teens; so hard to reach, always. And the distance had grown since she'd got together with Dan.

Adam extended an arm towards Dan's shoulder, wanting to hug him, then thought better of it and clasped his hand instead. He walked to the corner of the room, shook his wet coat and hung it behind the door. Dan moved two chairs next to the bed and they sat down.

Lauren told them about the pains that had ambushed her at home soon after Dan had left for work; the bleeding in the taxi, and thinking if only she could stop it everything would be OK; the fear as she waited alone in a side room, the contractions, blood pooling on the lino between her feet and how she'd known it was all over from the expression on the doctor's face while he was examining her. She'd bled much more this time: it had been a sort of delivery, and she'd seen the foetus. It was the size of her fist and perfect, with a head, arms, legs and eyelids. 'I held it here,' she cupped her hands in front of her face and stared at the memory. 'My baby.'

Adam sat forward and put his head in his hands.

'Oh my love.' Ruth felt guilt at her own easy fertility, and something else – the tug of an old wound. 'That must have been so hard, all by yourself. I wish I could have been with you. *Done* something.'

'If you're thinking you could have stopped it happening you're wrong,' said Lauren flatly. 'No one could. I was just sitting in my studio, working on an illustration. It wasn't my fault, Mum.'

'Of course it wasn't,' said Ruth.

'The mistake we made was to assume we were in the clear,' said Dan, as if their reckless optimism had killed the baby. 'According to the midwives, the chance of a miscarriage after thirteen weeks was tiny and we believed them. Should have known better.'

'And now they've said ... ' but Lauren's voice faltered. 'You tell them,' she whispered to Dan.

'The surgeon who operated to stop the bleeding said that if Laurie ever got pregnant again there's a risk she'd die.'

His words hung in the air, then Ruth murmured, 'Oh, darling.'

Lauren said nothing, her eyes were tightly shut. Ruth imagined the tears, banked up like a swollen river behind the lids.

They made stilted conversation for a while, then Adam offered to brave the elements and get a takeaway supper. Lauren shook her head. 'Thanks, Dad, but we're not hungry. Why don't you two head home?' She looked at Ruth. 'They're keeping me in because I need a transfusion, but Dan's going to stay.'

'Are you sure?' Adam got to his feet and began pulling on his coat, his relief palpable. He walked to the bed and kissed Lauren's forehead, then tried to speak, but no words came, so he picked up his briefcase and retreated.

Ruth leant forward and hugged Lauren. 'I'll be thinking of you, darling, and I'll message you tomorrow, but call me when you feel like it, whatever the time. Try to get some sleep.'

Dan followed them to the end of the long corridor.

Ruth said, 'It must have been so hard for you.'

He nodded, then stared at her, with a look of horror on his face, as if he was reliving something. 'There was so much blood, and they couldn't stop it. I thought she was going to die.'

He looked away and Ruth saw he was struggling to maintain his composure, then he said, 'On Monday mornings the blokes in the office show one another videos of what their kids did at the weekend. Normally I just sit there, staring at my screen, but last week, I took in the scan of our baby. They were really chuffed, bought me drinks after work and talked about how great it is being a dad. And now ... ' He bent forward, winded by grief. 'It's all over. Again.'

All through the years of fertility treatment and miscarriages,

Dan had never let his feelings show. It was one of the reasons they'd never felt close to him. Now Ruth's eyes filled with tears. 'I wish you weren't having to go through this, my love.'

'Sorry, take no notice.' He rolled his shoulders back. 'No point me getting emotional, is there? Last thing Laurie needs after what she's been through.' He let out a long sigh. 'The IVF has kept us going for five years. I don't know how she's going to cope.'

Adam nodded. 'It's going to be hard.'

'Understatement.' Dan gave a brief, mirthless laugh. 'There's a freezer full of our kids in the basement of the clinic: all it needed was for *one* of them to make it through a pregnancy.' He winced. 'But it wasn't going to happen, was it? Because we're unlucky, Laurie and me.'

'You mustn't think like that.' Ruth put her hand on his arm. 'How about finding a surrogate to host one of your embryos? Lauren's always said that would be your fallback.'

'We've talked about it,' said Dan. 'But the fact is we've already burned up thirty thousand pounds, nothing's worked and we've been through hell in the process.' He rubbed his hands over his face as if he was trying to wash away the memory. 'I'm not sure I can take any more . . .'

Adam frowned. 'I don't blame you. Surrogacy isn't cheap and it's a minefield.' Ruth shot him a look and mouthed, *Not now.*

'I'm sorry, Dan,' she said. 'I shouldn't have mentioned it. You're exhausted and now's not the right time. I just don't want you to give up hope.'

'Yeah.' Dan looked at them blearily. 'Anyway, thanks for coming over. I'd best go back inside.'

Ruth and Adam watched as he lifted the blue and white sign off its hook, turned it over, went into the room and shut the door.

DO NOT DISTURB

They drove through the London night, staring straight ahead, saying nothing. It was always the same after these hospital visits: their tacit acceptance that no words would do. Did Adam have the same sense of déjà vu, Ruth wondered. Was he reliving that early-morning car journey to another hospital, in another life? She'd never asked him, for fear of disturbing the equilibrium they'd so painstakingly constructed. It was one of those experiences, shared but never properly discussed, that bubbled under the surface of their marriage; over the years it had worn a small, desolate patch in its fabric.

As they crossed Vauxhall Bridge, the Thames slithering shiny and black beneath them, she said, 'I feel guilty that we produced Lauren and Alex so easily. We took it all so much for granted, didn't we?'

'I never took children for granted.'

'Adam.' She said it as a warning.

'What I meant—'

Ruth interrupted. 'We both know what you *meant*, but let's not go there, shall we? Not tonight, when we're both so upset.'

They drove on, in silent separation, along the Embankment and through the dark streets of West Kensington.

'I'm sorry,' said Adam. 'I shouldn't have said what I did.' They were on home ground now, passing the playground of the girls' old primary school in Hammersmith, then Ravenscourt Park where they'd ridden their first bicycles, played rounders at weekends and partied as teenagers. 'The thing is, I hate seeing Lauren like that and not being able to *do* anything. The waste of it all.'

Ruth touched his arm. 'I know,' she said. He reached out and squeezed her hand.

Goldhawk Road was flooded and a Thames Water emergency team was working under floodlights in a cordoned-off area on the corner of their street. The rain had stopped, but there was a brisk wind now and small grey clouds were hurtling across a sky dyed orange by the light pollution that blanketed the city.

On the doorstep Adam fumbled for his keys and Ruth looked up at the tall, narrow house where they'd lived for over thirty years. She remembered bringing the girls home here, first Lauren, then Alex: the tremulous journey from Queen Charlotte's Hospital; Adam driving the car with the careful gravity of a new father while she perched in the back, never taking her eyes off the baby in the car seat next to her; the joy and excitement as they crossed the threshold. That's what she'd wanted for Lauren: a moment of pure exultation as she set off on the adventure of motherhood, after all those barren years. Instead, her daughter would return to the flat meant for a family with her arms empty and her womb condemned. The memory of Lauren's face, slumped, translucent with grief, on the pillow, pierced Ruth's heart: she yearned to make it all right, but there was nothing she could do.

She laid the table in the kitchen mechanically and put out some bread and cheese, but neither of them had much appetite. Adam left a voicemail message for Alex, who was flying from her home in San Francisco to a conference in Seattle, so she'd know the latest when she landed, then they collapsed together on the sofa and watched the news. Afterwards Ruth yawned, 'I'm ready for bed, but you've probably got a ton of work?'

Adam stretched his arms over his head and grunted. 'I'm afraid so, a stack of new documents turned up this afternoon and we're in court again tomorrow. I need to get going.' He smiled at her. 'You go on up, I'll try not to disturb you.'

'It's OK. I'll sleep in the spare room, that way you can work as long as you like.' She hugged him. 'I do *love* you, Adam.'

'I know, I love you too.' He kissed the top of her head.

They clung to one another, separately and silently completing the same sentence: *in spite of everything.*

As Ruth headed up the stairs, Adam said, 'Sorry, I meant to ask: how was your screening?'

She paused; it was an effort to remember. 'It had only just started when I got Dan's message, but I'm sure it went fine.' She looked at him sadly. 'It feels like a long time ago.'

2

Long afterwards, when Ruth looked back, searching for an untroubled time – before she lost her footing and the family tilted out of control – she settled on the memory of her birthday lunch, ten days before the miscarriage happened. It hung there, like a sunlit patch of coast in calm weather, just before the storm blew in.

She had nothing to do, which was unusual, so she lay in a plantation chair and gazed at the scene around her. It was a glorious day for late September: the sky above a deep, insistent blue, jasmine running sweetly rampant over the fence next to her, and yellow and purple daisies jostling for space in the borders. Light splashed from the terrace, through the glass-fronted kitchen, and into the tiled hall beyond. Adam was standing by the stove. He was frowning in concentration over a recipe book, shirtsleeves pushed up to the elbows, dark blond hair flecked with silver plastered to his temples. She smiled, it was still a pleasure to look at him.

Ruth stretched and inspected herself: long tanned legs emerged from a pale green linen shift; her tummy, sheathed in controlling Lycra, was hard and flat; only the pouches of skin that lolled sideways towards her armpits gave her away. Every so often she pushed them back into her bra, then watched as they sidled disobediently out again: gravity plus loss of collagen. Fifty-four: what could you expect?

The phone on the table beside her grunted out another message: this time from Sheila, her best and oldest friend:

> Happy bday! How DID we get to
> be this ancient?? What you up
> to? love Sx

> > Adam's cooking lunch(!) Am
> > banished to garden with
> > newspapers, G&T and instructions
> > to enjoy self. Strangely stressful . . .

> Simon has never done that in 25
> yrs of marriage. Jealous.

> > Not esp relaxing tbh, but he'll be
> > hurt if I offer to help

> Enjoy. I have present for you, drink
> after work soonest?

> > Yes please! V busy this wk with
> > screenings & publicity, but wk
> > after? Will send dates asap Xxx

The enforced idleness was irksome; she was tempted to run upstairs and fetch some scripts that needed editing, but Adam would be cross. The buzz of the doorbell, echoing through the high-ceilinged house, came as a relief. Minutes later Lauren and Dan made their entrance, striding arm in arm down the brick steps towards her. Lauren was wearing a floating floral-print

15

dress that clung to her slender frame and matched the startling blue of her eyes and she'd tied a scarlet bandanna around her fair curls; Dan towered above her, handsome and solidly built. She gazed at her elder daughter, so lovely today, smiling with a girlish sweetness that belied her thirty years. The sheer physical *otherness* of Lauren always came as a small shock: her skin was milky and sensitive, quick to blush and burn, blue in the cold; she had the poise of a dancer, but hated sport; and her hands and feet were tiny. She'd always been an unknown quantity, made of different clay – more like Adam's mother: maybe that explained the distance between them? She loved Lauren, but there was a dislocation in their relationship, none of the easy propinquity she had with Alex.

'Happy birthday, Mum – no, don't get up.' They bent to kiss her.

'What will you drink?' she said. 'Your dad's being bossy and secretive, but he's bound to have something special in there.'

Dan looked at Lauren. 'Water?' he said, and she nodded. 'I'll tell Adam.' He headed indoors.

Lauren added her present to the pile on the table and pulled up a chair. 'Dad's concentrating so hard on the cooking he can barely speak and there are dirty saucepans and bowls every-where.' Her voice bubbled with laughter. 'Lunch may be a while.'

Ruth made a face. 'I know, I'm dying to go inside and help, but he won't let me.'

'He wants to spoil you, so let him,' said Lauren. She was smiling, but there was a note of irritation in her voice. 'Maybe stop trying to control everyone and everything, just for *one* day?'

'Sorry,' said Ruth. 'I'm trying my best and it's lovely of you to come over. It's been a while.' Then she dipped into practised solicitude. 'How *are* things?'

'Life's good and I'm very happy.'

Ruth was so startled she sat up. Lauren's emotional gauge was normally stuck somewhere between stoical and sad: five years of fertility treatment and six miscarriages, all of them followed by surgery, had taken a heavy toll. 'That's wonderful, I'm *so* glad you're in a good place, darling.' She squeezed Lauren's hand. 'Taking a break from the IVF has made all the difference. I knew it would. You're looking better than you have for ages.'

Lauren blushed. 'Thanks,' she said, turning towards the kitchen. 'Dan's taking his time, isn't he? I bet they've got on to football.'

'Yes, and your dad will be so distracted that everything will burn. Maybe I should go in and check?'

Lauren ignored her. 'Has Alex rung you yet?'

'Way too early.' Ruth glanced at her watch. 'It's five a.m. in San Francisco – she'll be fast asleep.'

'Or falling into bed after a long night, knowing her.' Alex was a force of nature, clever, energetic and optimistic. She lived a frenetic life in California where she had a job as a software developer. The girls had always been close. 'Shame she's not here.'

'I know,' said Ruth. 'I miss her so much.'

Adam emerged from the house carrying a tray, followed by Dan.

'Everything's under control,' he said. 'So, before you ask, there's no need to do *anything*, Ruth.' He set the tray down with a flourish. 'Champagne, elderflower cordial, water and some smoked salmon bits.'

The doorbell sounded. No one reacted. Adam was tearing the foil from the bottle, and Lauren and Dan were watching him.

Ruth said, 'Someone's at the door. That was the bell. Definitely.' She went to stand up.

Adam looked unconvinced. 'Stay there,' he said, 'I'll check.'

He went inside and Ruth wondered aloud whether he was going deaf; Lauren and Dan bit into their blinis.

Seconds later he returned, beaming. 'Turns out you were right.' He gestured behind him. 'Look what I found on the pavement.' He moved to reveal a tall, angular figure framed in the doorway, a big yellow bag on her shoulder. Cropped dark hair, high cheekbones, large brown eyes, eyebrows raised, smile ironic. Alex.

'Darling, what a *surprise*.' Ruth jumped up and ran towards her, arms outstretched. 'How *wonderful* of you to come! How long are you staying? I can't believe it!' She was grinning in amazement and there were tears in her eyes.

'Happy birthday, mother mine.' Alex dropped her bag and wrapped herself around Ruth. 'Flying visit – two days. I'm *very* jet-lagged, but it's so great to see you.' She hugged Lauren and Dan, then took Adam's arm. 'It's all Dad's doing, he choreographed this whole thing.'

Glasses were filled and Adam proposed a toast. 'To Alex, for travelling through the night to get here.' Alex bowed extravagantly and everyone clapped. 'And to Lauren and Dan, who've had the decency *not* to run away to America. And most important of all, to Ruth, with apologies in advance for the quality of the lunch.' Laughter. He turned to the others. 'Your mum's promised me that now her series is finished, she's going to take it easy for a while.'

'Good luck with that, Dad,' said Alex. 'Habit of a lifetime, and all that.' She and Lauren rolled their eyes at one another.

'And it starts *today*,' Adam said firmly. 'Happy birthday, my love.' They smiled at one another and everyone clapped.

Ruth took a breath in order to thank them all, but just as she began Dan cut across her. A flush was spreading up his neck and into his cheeks. 'We've got some news, haven't we?' He put an arm round Lauren's waist and looked down at her. 'Go on, you tell them.'

Lauren leant against him. 'This time we decided not to say anything until we were past the high-risk stage, because we didn't dare hope. We were told it wasn't possible – in fact, the clinic says it's a miracle – but I'm thirteen weeks pregnant.' She was beaming.

Dan kissed the top of her head. 'And here's the proof.' He handed out three grainy black-and-white prints. 'We had the twelve-week scan last week and I got you one each. The resolution's not great, but you can see the face in profile on the right, near the top.'

'Fantastic,' said Alex.

'Wonderful,' echoed Adam. He peered at the image. 'And I swear that's a Furnival forehead.'

Ruth was staring at them in disbelief. 'But you'd stopped trying, hadn't you? So did it just happen? Naturally, I mean?'

They explained that after the last miscarriage Lauren had been diagnosed with Asherman Syndrome: her uterus was so damaged by previous surgery that further IVF would be pointless. The clinic advised them to stop, but they were devastated and eventually the specialist agreed to do one last embryo transfer. He'd termed it a 'closure' cycle: it might help them come to terms with the diagnosis, but there was no chance of it working, so they decided not to tell anyone. When, against all the odds, Lauren became pregnant, she was told to expect another early miscarriage. Every day they braced themselves for disaster, but the baby held on; now the antenatal clinic said the pregnancy seemed secure.

'It's weird,' said Lauren, 'I've been in such a bad place over the last few years but, suddenly, I feel as if I've rejoined the human race.' She gazed at them. 'Thank you for putting up with me, especially all those times I was having meltdowns or behaving like a complete bitch. And for all the support you've given us.'

The Furnivals toasted the ghostly image of the baby, then hugged one another in a scrum of congratulation and relief.

'I'm sorry, Mum,' Lauren whispered into Ruth's shoulder. 'I feel so bad for not telling you, but I didn't want to tempt fate.'

'Darling, I'm so happy, I couldn't care less,' said Ruth, untruthfully; she felt hurt.

Adam was grinning. 'This is *such* good news.' He turned to Lauren. 'I'm going to open another bottle, and this time I shall insist you have a drop, even if you spit it out afterwards.'

Lauren's face, tilted triumphantly up at Dan, was luminous; her left hand protected and advertised her abdomen. Ruth was assailed by physical memories of her own pregnancies – the expansion and convolution of flesh within flesh, and the glorious power of it all. She felt a stab of something: envy, almost.

Alex shoved an imaginary microphone towards her mother's chin and adopted an American accent. 'Isn't this the *cutest* birthday gift ever, *Grandmom*? How are *you* feeling?'

Ruth was caught off guard and they were all looking at her, grinning and waiting. It was wonderful news, but she felt wrong-footed somehow. 'I'm thrilled, Alex. I just said so, didn't I? It's great, and a fantastic surprise. Obviously.'

The baby was due on the third of April, Lauren told them.

'So when I'm back here in December my big sister will be six months pregnant,' said Alex. 'Madonna-and-almost-child: how fantastically *Christmassy* Christmas is going to be this year.' She put an arm around Lauren. 'I am so-ooh pleased for you.'

Adam said, 'And with luck a year from now our first grandchild will be crawling around this garden, celebrating his or her grandmother's birthday. I shall ensure that the lawn's in pristine condition.'

'Please,' a look of panic flickered across Lauren's face, 'can we stop talking like this? If I've learnt one thing over the past five years it's to take nothing for granted. When you do, bad stuff happens.' Dan put his arm around her, protective.

Adam said, 'Let's eat.' He looked at Ruth and smiled. 'If you're ready for your birthday feast?'

She felt a little spasm in her chest: the pleasure–pain of their connectedness.

Lunch was generally agreed to be a triumph: tiny rounds of white crab meat topped with avocado, chicken in a lemon sauce with boiled rice and a green salad, and finally meringues with raspberries and whipped cream. Ruth was astonished; Adam didn't often cook, how had he managed it?

'I rehearsed,' he admitted. 'Someone at work gave me a bit of coaching.'

'Emily, I imagine?' said Ruth, her smile complacent.

Alex stared at her mother. 'Not that blonde trainee you always said was in love with Dad?' She turned to Adam. 'Is she *still* hanging around?'

'Emily Sullivan has been a fully fledged barrister for several years and is a highly valued member of my chambers,' said Adam. 'She's a colleague, nothing more, and she kindly helped me practise this lunch last week.'

'Where did the two of you practise?' asked Alex slyly.

'At her flat.'

'And you're fine with that, Mum?'

'Don't be silly. I've known Emily for years: she comes over here sometimes and we've both been to her place. In any case, she has a long-term boyfriend.'

'Had,' said Adam. 'They split up a month ago, but I doubt she'll be single for long.' He put an arm around Ruth. 'Your mother and I have been married for more than thirty years. Nothing's going to jeopardise that.' He looked at Ruth and she knew he wanted affirmation.

'Absolutely, darling,' she said.

And she had meant it.

3

On the night after the miscarriage happened Adam ended up working into the small hours.. He'd got used to these nocturnal sessions as a young criminal barrister and liked having the house to himself, hearing the grunts of its timbers and the guttural sighs of the central-heating pipes. In the kitchen he poured himself another coffee, then headed down the hall towards his study, past the three collages that Lauren had made at college – portraits of the houses that had shaped her childhood. Ruth's parents' granite-faced terrace in Cornwall on the left; the Hammersmith house in the middle, mauve wisteria clambering up its cream front; and next to it the brick and flint of Adam's family home in Buckinghamshire. All three were painted with documentary meticulousness, then embedded in a mass of torn photos, cards, maps and scraps of fabric.

Lauren had been a dreamy child, with a core of stillness and serenity. She was uninterested in anything academic, but loved music and art. Adam thought she was talented and the teachers agreed, but Ruth worried about her grades and organised intensive after-school tuition in maths, science and French, which Lauren detested. She insisted on going to art college, did well on her foundation course and was one of the stars of her year at St Martin's.

Adam remembered buying the three pictures on the first night of her degree show, where they'd taken the gold medal. Lauren's entire portfolio had sold by the end of the evening and she was in her element, fêted by gallery owners and buyers, her face flushed with surprise and pleasure. He and Ruth had been so proud, had imagined the exhibitions, commissions and acclaim that would follow, but two years later she announced out of the blue that she was marrying Dan, an engineer five years her senior. He clearly adored her, but he was so different from them that her choice felt almost like a rebuke.

They wanted a family straight away and when it didn't happen Lauren was distraught. She stopped making her big pieces and now taught two days a week at a school in Hackney and worked from home as a self-employed graphic artist the rest of the time. They lived frugally and, once they'd used up their single NHS IVF cycle, all their spare money went on private clinic fees. Lauren's life seemed to revolve around medical appointments and it had been distressing to watch the change in her as the years went by: weepy and volatile during treatment; tensely hopeful during the brief pregnancies; desolate when they ended. The memory of her, a few hours ago at the hospital, ravaged by this latest, greatest, loss was almost too much to bear.

In the loo Adam balanced his mug on the shelf where Ruth's golden BAFTA nestled among a clutter of books, vases and pebbles. He urinated, long and hard: a dual relief. The GP said if you could pee against a wall from two feet, there was no need to worry about prostate cancer. Not that he worried. Much. A couple of colleagues had fallen by the wayside over the past year, though, the kind of thing that brought you up short. But Adam had managed three feet at the last attempt, not bad for fifty-seven.

The walls around him were crammed with photos of the girls and pictures they'd made at primary school. The largest one was entitled MY FAMILY by Lauren Furnival Year 3. Adam, Lauren and Alex stood holding hands inside a purple house; outside were trees and flowers, a yellow sun in a bright blue sky and, if you looked very carefully, a tiny brown aeroplane.

'You've only drawn three people,' crowed Alex, when Lauren brought it home. 'You forgot Mummy. Silly.'

'No, I didn't,' said Lauren firmly. 'Mummy's in the aeroplane.'

Adam smiled, remembering Ruth's dismay and her extravagant vows to be around more often, *much* more often. The phrase had stuck. After that, whenever she told them she was going to have to stay late in the cutting room, miss a birthday party or work through a weekend, the girls would chorus: 'Mummy's in the aeroplane, Mummy's in the aeroplane'.

He paused at the foot of the stairs and felt the house wrap itself around him, this thing they'd made together. They'd camped in it for the first few years, like everyone they knew, furnishing and carpeting the place with other people's cast-offs or stuff plundered from skips, while they struggled to pay the bills. Weekends were spent filling holes in the walls, papering and painting. He'd learnt how to plaster, made a front gate, built bookshelves, and still managed to do all the grunt work of a junior barrister, working through the night and travelling to courts all over south-east England for a pittance. What energy they'd had, the two of them.

And they'd been happy, hadn't they, mostly? Of course, there'd been difficult times: extreme sleep deprivation after Alex was born; Ruth's long absences on location, often overseas; one disastrous au pair; the girls' teenage-witch phases – but they'd never lost sight of their goals. Ruth had pulled the garden into shape, made it a place for tea and trampolining and cut-and-come-again lettuce. He'd put up a garden shed and built a treehouse. There were table tennis tournaments on summer evenings. Lauren and Alex bickered over homework at the kitchen table while stews simmered and flapjacks baked. Christmas parties, everyone gathered around the piano, singing carols while he played.

Then, quite suddenly, it was all over, and you couldn't get it back: the chaos and shouting, the throb of life, were replaced by silence. Rooms were cleaned and remained plumped and immaculate all week. Phone chargers, teaspoons and bicycles stayed in their respective places and there was scarcely any laughter. He missed the girls like lost limbs: he adored them and was doted on from afar, but nowadays they saw Alex maybe two or three times a year and Lauren only intermittently.

At first he and Ruth had spent more time together – eating out, going to concerts, talking vaguely of downsizing or taking a gap year. Then, at just the moment when Ruth launched Morrab Films with Bella and lost her BBC salary, the cuts to legal aid began to bite and his earnings plummeted. Money was tight and she started working even longer hours to pick up the slack; Adam felt guilty. He found things of his own to fill the time: serving on a couple of committees, playing more tennis. They still had sex, on an occasional basis, which he knew was perfectly normal, but she was often tired, falling asleep as she read scripts in bed and getting up at the crack of dawn during filming. So ten days ago, when Lauren had announced she was pregnant – and beyond the danger zone this time – he'd felt a surge of hope and excitement. He'd imagined the grandchild who would reanimate the house, opening up a new chapter and giving their lives fresh purpose. Then, this evening, Dan's message came and it was over: the child was gone. Now he felt the empty soreness in his chest again.

Adam's study was his private space. In the hectic family years, when he'd been seriously outnumbered, it was the only room that felt one hundred per cent his: no female interloping or embellishment. He loved Ruth and the girls, they were the centre of his life, no question, but there was something debilitating about living in a gynaecocracy: you needed a sanctuary, a place that allowed you to be alone, separate and different. The brass banker's lamp bathed his desk in the green glow of professional toil. It had belonged to his grandfather, a surgeon and mountaineer, who had been something of a father figure; he'd taught Adam to play football and tennis, and shown him how to identify trees and birds on family holidays in Scotland.

When his father became seriously ill Adam was seven and his sister four: it was leukaemia and the decline was rapid. Ever since then nightclothes worn during the day, and certain smells – talcum powder, Dettol and the spicy chrism oil the priest used for the last rites – took him straight back to his parents' bedroom: entropy and the end of childhood; the sense he was to blame. None of it was talked about; it was buried, like the two golden retrievers in the garden. One day the adults dressed in black and went to a funeral, which was *unsuitable for children*; then they changed into ordinary clothes and carried on as if nothing had happened. A few weeks afterwards Adam found five fledgling blackbirds outside the back door: featherless, their skin pink and translucent, with big blind eyes and scrawny necks. Two were dead but the others were still making small movements. He lined a shoebox with socks and twigs, put it on top of his bedroom chest of drawers and laid them inside, scattering leaves on top to keep them warm. He checked on them every morning and as soon as he got home from school. They moved less, but he dripped milk onto their beaks, desperate to keep them alive. One day when he came home the box was gone. He asked his mother if she'd seen it.

'I threw it away, dear. Everything was dead, and the smell was awful.'

'They weren't dead!' He clasped his arms across his chest like a shield and began rocking backwards and forwards, keening for all that he'd lost. 'Why did you take them?'

She stared at him in alarm. 'Sit still and stop that, Adam. Boys don't cry. Remember what I told you: you're the man of the family now. You mustn't let us down.'

But he cried incessantly over the next few weeks and his mother found she couldn't bear it. It was decided that he should be sent to board at a Catholic prep school run by Franciscan monks, partway through the summer term: *to calm him down.* 'Bear up, young man, you're a Furnival,' said his grandfather as he bade Adam goodbye in the headmaster's study.

Money was tight, but a life insurance policy took care of the mortgage so his mother managed to stay in the house, a former rectory, with uneven oak floors, big fireplaces and several generations of family pictures on the walls. He won a scholarship to a public school and it was made clear that he must excel in order to keep his place, so he did. Uncles turned up at cricket matches, took him fishing and filled him in on the facts of life. His Catholic faith evaporated at fourteen and he sidled towards the mild impersonal Anglicanism of school services. He wasn't devout, but he loved the music and liturgy and still attended church on high days and holidays. In the debating society, though, he revealed his Franciscan roots, arguing passionately – and unfashionably – against fox-hunting, the death penalty, abortion and euthanasia; his skill, conviction and charisma generally carried the day. By the time he got to the sixth form Adam had developed the easy charm and courtly manners that characterised the men of his family, but beneath the surface was a layer of reserve that protected the damaged child he'd been. He borrowed and built a moral code for himself and held fast to it: he needed to know where he stood. His ambition was to be a sportsman and lawyer like his father, and to have a tribe of children – a proper family with a dad who stayed alive.

He'd not done badly, all things considered: here he was, still playing tennis and the occasional cricket match, and he'd stuck it out at the bar. The tribe was smaller than he'd imagined – and he regretted that, now it was too late. There were things he wished he'd done differently, but there was no point in dwelling on the past.

Adam had never talked to anyone about his father's illness until he met Ruth. Unencumbered by middle-class reticence, she wanted to know exactly what had happened and how he'd felt. She was unlike anyone he'd ever met: she'd understood him, had woken something in him: he *had* to marry her. What a gamble it had been, in retrospect. They were strong characters, both of them, and they'd come through some tough times: matters alluded to only in anger; never discussed. But they were still together, which was what mattered. The Furnivals: Ruth and Adam; Adam and Ruth. Indissoluble.

He kept two photographs on his desk. The small black-and-white portrait of a skinny boy with a closed expression, taken in his first year at prep school, was a constant reminder that life could get better (he never attended reunions). The other – showing his parents on their wedding day, its silver frame tarnished brownish-grey, their faces brimming with joy and hope – carried a different message: be ready for the worst to happen.

Ruth reached out and turned her phone face up: 02:57. She'd been woken by a torrential night sweat – when would they ever stop, she wondered as she rolled onto the cool, dry side of the spare bed. She felt a dull sadness but couldn't locate its source, then she remembered: Lauren, slumped in the hospital bed, blank and tearless, pushing her away: *Don't, Mum, please*; Dan's face, gaunt with despair: *I don't think I can take any more*; and their family of motherless embryos, waiting in the freezer. If only she could think of a solution. If only she had a bit of spare cash to help with the surrogacy fees. Ruth had a reputation in the industry as a producer capable of moving mountains: she was used to taking on any problem that reared its head and fixing it, but now she felt frustrated and impotent. And she wasn't going to get back to sleep.

She switched on the light. On the bedside table was her childhood copy of *Little Women*, a pale blue hardback, rescued from her parents' loft in Penzance when she'd cleared the house after they died. It was corrugated by years of Cornish damp, its pages choked with dust, 'Ruth Jago' inscribed on the title page in thick, round joined-up writing, and a large ink blot. She remembered the new fountain pen, a seventh-birthday present, and the scolding from her mother, *You've ruined it, you naughty girl, and you're old enough to know better.* Ruth pressed the book against her face – it still smelled faintly of mould and woodsmoke. She remembered the bliss of lying on the sheepskin rug in the back room, as close as she could get to the fire, and reading for hours on end whenever she could get away with it. *Put it away, you'll ruin your eyes, do something useful.* In her teens she'd raced through the fiction section of Penzance public library; books were a refuge and a promise, they hinted at freedom and a kinder, wittier, more exciting world, where passions flared and sex was transfiguring.

Her mother told a different, bleaker story. Spotting a love bite above the collar of Ruth's school blouse at breakfast one morning she flew into another of her rages: *You wicked, filthy creature. No one will want you now. You're soiled goods, like that Christine Warren.* Christine, a buxom, amiable girl with long fair hair, had disappeared in the fifth form and was now to be seen pushing her pram up the high street in the afternoons: a parallel and terrifying life. No one else at school had a Chapel-going fanatic for a mother, who made them sit through two services on Sundays and kept them under house arrest for the protection of their virtue, so Ruth invented a succession of fictional after-school events and excursions as a cover for her illicit social life. But she was careful never to let a boy go too far: her mother's warnings had frightened her into chastity. At first she hated the subterfuge

29

and feared damnation; she tried to find a righteous justification for every untruth, and usually succeeded. By the time she left school she was an accomplished liar. It was a matter of survival, if something of a strain.

She got out of bed and tucked *Little Women* back in its place on the bookshelf in the corner of the room. This was where she kept her most precious books – the ones she returned to again and again – that offered illumination, wisdom and solace. She scanned the spines, searching for something that would suit her mood, and settled on *Mrs Dalloway*. Her battered university copy, crammed with earnest notes that she'd made during her first term, as her eighteen-year-old self struggled to understand the novel's posh, middle-aged central character, her life in London and her splintered identity. Now she understood better. Inside the front cover her name was written in the spiky, semi-italic script she'd adopted for several years: 'Ruth Jago, Brasenose College'. Another incarnation.

Oxford was beautiful, exciting and scary. It was also exhilaratingly unlike 37 Rosvenna Drive, Penzance. Ruth realised immediately that she wouldn't pass muster as she was. Other students brandished vast social networks from their boarding schools, grand London houses that were convenient for overnight jaunts, crumbling second homes and near-fatal gap-year adventures. Those at the opposite end of the social scale told of deprived childhoods on derelict housing estates, violent fathers, battered mothers and family suicides. Her dull, constrained Chapel-going background was devoid of drama; meanwhile her previously unexceptional Cornish name was suddenly the butt of racist jokes: *Ruth Dago, ha ha ha*. She needed an alias.

Her Cornish accent disappeared within weeks and was replaced by the posh drawl that surrounded her in lectures and tutorials. Tea turned into dinner and dinner became lunch. Apart from brief trips back to Penzance (her accent would return to its roots around Plymouth) she stayed in character and prospered. But she never secured the approval of her mother. *Think you're too good for us now, do you? Well, we'll see, won't we. Pride comes before a fall, my lady, just you remember that.*

She found a job working at the BBC, then married, swapping Jago for Furnival. Adam was clever, funny and kind; his family were cultured and confident. They had the glamorous solidity of *Brideshead* characters. She admired them but she hadn't seen any of them clearly. How could she, being in the process of so thoroughly obscuring herself? Finally, she *fitted in* – that was what mattered.

And here she was, decades later, playing yet another character: post-menopausal-married-working-empty-nester-Ruth, who wasn't, after all, going to have a grandchild, which might have provided a new role of sorts. What on earth was she *for*? Who could she be next? Where might she go? The options were constrained, because she was bound to Adam, wasn't she? Shared history and family held them in a web of gossamer-steel threads and the house was a brick corset; its slate roof kept a lid on everything and would stop them making a break for it, supposing they ever wanted to.

Adam never had these thoughts, she was certain; he was always there, present and consistent – never felt the need to question or reinvent himself. She could feel the pulse of him now as he worked downstairs, filleting his documents and planning the structure and pace of his arguments, footsteps in the hall every hour or so, the blustering murmur of the kettle, then the clink of a china mug on granite. She imagined him, pushing back the sleeves of his jumper, yawning and stretching, before picking up his pen and attacking a fresh pile of papers, scribbling acerbic notes in the margins to highlight weaknesses in witness statements or query points of law. He was in good shape for his age – hadn't run to paunchy fat like some of his colleagues at the bar – and he was still attractive; women flirted with him. The voices from the screening came back to her and began to run on a nagging loop.

Used to be so ravishing ... used to be ... used to be ... used to be ...

She went into the bathroom and stared at herself in the magnifying mirror next to the shaving point. A monstrous portion of her face leapt out at her, ten times its normal size. The early indignities of the menopause had been succeeded by the bearded-lady phase and a new crop of hairs had sprouted on her brow, upper lip and chin since yesterday morning. She began plucking at them with tweezers, a process as deadening and futile as sweeping sand from a beach. Friends went to expensive threading parlours to have their Frida Kahlo brows and moustaches removed. Ruth had tried it, once, but the process was so eye-wateringly painful that she'd decided to stick with the DIY approach. It was a losing battle, though. Despite expensive pots of skin cream, occasional facials and much tweezing, the fabric of her body was starting to betray her.

In these interludes, alone, observing her face and trying to improve it – or rather trying to impersonate a woman of forty – she sometimes felt a kind of blank panic. She was making the exterior fit for purpose, but what was that purpose, and where was Ruth? On whose behalf was she mounting this increasingly draconian surveillance and repair? She felt she'd mislaid part of herself a long time ago and the image in the mirror was a sort of assemblage: the gap between the inside and the outside increasing daily. As she pulled her skin taut to harvest a thick ugly hair, she heard her mother's voice, triumphantly pessimistic: *You'll see, my girl, a woman's life is no bed of roses.* She flipped the mirror over. Much better: in the myopic blur she was almost young again, which was the point of it all, wasn't it?

Back in bed she switched off the light and, as she lapsed into sleep, the voices started up again, this time with added malice:

Looking her age now
No bed of roses, my girl
Old enough to know better
Used to be so ravishing
No one will want you
Comes to us all, comes to us all, comes to us all

4

Mid-afternoon in Brockley and a clear day, the room full of light. Lauren, home for five days now, still hadn't been outside; it was safer up here, away from buggies, toddlers, and mothers with babies slung nonchalantly across their ample chests. Early in the pregnancy her own breasts had been alert and purposeful, nipples hypersensitive to temperature and touch, but now they were shrivelled and dead. Her uterus was still bleeding half-heartedly, as if weeping for the child it had lost. During the days, while Dan was at work, she slept or paced around the flat in her grey velour dressing gown, the hood pulled up, gazing at the family home she'd created so painstakingly: pale unblemished walls, spotless wooden floors, books, pots and beautiful sculptures so neat on their shelves. Safe, but sterile.

They'd moved in on their return from honeymoon. How excited they'd been, the day they collected the keys from the estate agent. They'd lain on the bare floorboards in the front bedroom before the furniture arrived and imagined the next phase of their life together: making love in the king-size bed they'd promised themselves; creating a nursery in the small room under the eaves; being shaken awake on Christmas morning by the two children they would have, each hauling a stocking. What blithe confidence

34

they'd had, and how painful their re-education had been. Eggs were harvested from Lauren three times, then fertilised with Dan's sperm; nine embryos had been transferred into her increasingly tattered uterus. They'd grown accustomed to the draining away of spontaneity and passion as sex became a mechanical means to an end, something to be scheduled to the hour for optimum effectiveness. Dan had learnt how to inject Lauren with hormones and cope with the torrent of emotions unleashed by the treatment.

And in spite of the fact she'd been through this so many times before, it came as a shock now, as she stood staring through the sitting-room window at cars and people in the street below, to discover that the pulse of the world was unaffected by her tragedy.

'Don't let yourself go there.' She spoke out loud, channelling the calm, un-catastrophic voice of her cognitive behavioural therapist, and pulling hard on the red rubber band that encircled her right wrist, until the bruising numbness obliterated everything. Keep the band on day and night, they'd told her, and tighten it every time the bad thoughts come – that way, eventually, your brain will learn to avoid the toxic places. They said it compressed the arteries and released adrenalin. She'd come to think of it as a homely alternative to slitting one's wrists: no collateral damage, no one to feel guilty about.

They'd cherished every embryo and mourned its death, experiences that separated them from the rest of the world and bound them closer: no one else understood their particular sorrows. Sometimes, when Dan was at work, Lauren took the envelope of scan printouts from the back of the drawer in her bedside table. Thirteen small, blackish-grey pictures, some already beginning to curl at the edges, the only relics of the seven children who'd lodged themselves inside her, then left. She would lay them out on the duvet cover and look at them for a long time, in love and remembrance.

35

She and Dan were anomalous, out of step, working from a different script. Few of her friends had kids yet, but most of his had one or two. People started sentences, then left them hanging, more or less elegantly. The sensitive ones took care not to provide constant updates on their children's progress or suggest coffee in venues full of yummy mummies; they didn't send invitations to lunch or tea parties where young families would be a danger. Christmas was the worst time.

The ordinary good fortune of others became increasingly intolerable. When friends announced they were pregnant it came as a body blow, and afterwards Lauren would avoid them because she couldn't control the ugly feelings that threatened to choke her. She was corrosively envious when she met or heard stories about women in their *forties* who'd produced babies with ease, or those who'd pumped out three or four while she was denied even one. The obscene *unfairness* of it all left her pinched and full of hate. Their social circle was increasingly composed of childless friends: it was easier that way.

Her phone buzzed; she put a hand into her pocket and extricated it from among the ball of damp tissues.

> Thinking of you all the time
> Why don't I come over? We
> could have tea or go for walk? I
> know how HARD this must be.
> Much love Rxxx

Lauren put the phone on the windowsill. She'd been wary of her mother for as long as she could remember. Once, in her first year at secondary school, she'd been allowed to stay up late at the end of term and go with her to a screening. Afterwards she'd heard one of her mother's colleagues say, with admiration in his voice, 'How do you manage it, Ruth? Juggling a big job, husband

36

and kids so brilliantly, and making everyone fall under your spell. What an *operator* you are!' So that was the word for what Mum did when her attention fell on you, thought Lauren. She didn't want to be operated on: sliced open and messed around with by her tall, beautiful, brazen mother. If she let her into the flat today, Ruth's empathy would penetrate all the wounds that had opened up again since the miscarriage and overwhelm her. Because this time was worse than all the others: she'd allowed herself to talk to the baby – about the life they'd have together and all the dreams that were finally going to be realised. She'd tempted fate, and fate had smashed the two of them. She replied:

Thanks for offering but I'm fine
everything OK so def no need to
come I'll be in touch x

Through the glass she could see into the crowns of the plane trees, a mix of deep yellow and umber leaves. Pink-grey pigeons squatted on the branches, summer-plumped, basking in a shaft of autumn sunlight. Blissful, people would call this day. Other people.

Lauren placed both palms on her abdomen, fitting them in, between the edges of her pelvis. The flesh gave slightly. Eight days ago it had seemed denser, more determined, and she'd done a lot of standing sideways in front of the bathroom mirror, imagining an infinitesimal thickening of her waist.

'Barren. Childless. Useless.' She yanked on the rubber band, a rider reining in a horse that was far too big for her and out of control.

When it gets unbearable, walk away from those feelings, do something else, any physical activity, the therapist had told her. She unlocked the window catch and pushed up the lower sash: it crashed against the frame. Street air poured in: petrol fumes and the sweet autumn fug of vegetable decay, the rumble of traffic, police sirens, squeals from the school playground two streets away. As she stepped back a pigeon dropped, insouciant, from a tree and landed on the narrow window ledge. Its black eyes surveyed her, then scanned the room for plunder.

Lauren tiptoed to the coffee table, took a biscuit from the open packet, and walked slowly back towards the pigeon. She crumbled it on to the sill. The bird tottered for an instant, contemplating flight, thought better of it and cocked its head to examine the food. It looked sidelong at her for a few seconds, then began to eat.

Her phone rang and the pigeon took flight. Lauren pulled the window shut and checked the screen. Alex's face loomed into view. She was sitting at her kitchen table in San Francisco eating muesli.

'Hi, I've got twenty minutes before I have to leave for work and I wanted to let you know what I've found out so far.' Alex stopped. 'Your face is very pale, how have you been today?'

Lauren sighed. 'Not great. I woke up thinking I was still pregnant, then remembered there was no baby. It was like losing it all over again. Since then I've had a couple of really bad panic attacks. I'm thinking, if I can't have children I'm not sure I can cope with being alive.'

'But you *can* have them.' Alex raised her arms above her head like a visiting angel. 'I'm here to bring you tidings of great joy from California, the world capital of surrogacy. Yesterday I took the day off and called all the clinics on the list you sent me.'

'Thanks,' said Lauren listlessly.

'What's more, I drove to the six that are closest to me and picked up these,' she held up a pile of brochures, 'which have detailed price lists that you can't get online. They all offer surrogacy. Shall I get them couriered to you?'

'Maybe just post them. There's no hurry.'

Alex frowned. 'But two days ago you told me it was mega-urgent because you needed to find a clinic fast.'

'I know, but Dan and I were talking yesterday and he suddenly went, "Would it be so completely terrible if we *didn't* have kids?"' Lauren stared at her sister in dismay. 'Can you believe it?'

'It's a point of view,' said Alex gently. 'Most of my mates reckon the best way to save the planet is by *not* having children, and the ones that want them are planning to adopt – they see it as the highest form of recycling.' She checked herself. 'But you've got your embryos, and I can see it makes sense to use them up. I wouldn't worry about Dan, he's still in shock, but he adores you and he'll do whatever you want in the end.'

'I'm not sure.' Lauren was tearing a tissue into long, thin strips. 'When I got pregnant last time, we agreed that if things didn't work out we'd find a surrogate in the States straight away, because the clinic said that was the best option. But now he's not keen.'

'What's changed his mind?'

'He's sick of our whole life revolving around fertility treatment. And he's worried about money – he thinks we won't be able to raise a big enough loan. Plus, he's come across negative stuff about commercial surrogacy online and thinks we'd be exploiting a poor, disadvantaged American woman, who might not understand what she was signing up for. I hate all that wombs-for-rent stuff too. It's not ideal, but what's the alternative?'

Alex reached for a writing pad where she'd made some notes. 'He's right that it's not cheap: looks like a hundred and fifty thousand dollars minimum, and you'd have to pay additional legal fees on top to export the baby to the UK.'

Lauren looked aghast. 'There's no way we can afford that. It's out of the question.'

'Not necessarily,' said Alex. She took a swig of coffee. 'There is one other possibility.' She tilted her head to one side, and made her teasing face.

'What?' said Lauren.

'How about *I* have the baby for you? I'm not poor, I've got a well-paid job, health insurance, plus an apartment with a spare room where you and Dan could stay. And I wouldn't need paying, so there'd be no pesky ethical issues for him to fret about.' She paused and squinted into the screen. 'You're not crying?'

Lauren balled up the strands of tissue and blotted her face. 'Sorry, but I'm just so ... I mean, I know sisters do this sometimes, I've seen all the stories online, but I never considered asking you, because you've always been so clear that you never want kids.'

'I don't have the faintest maternal urge, but I'd have no problem carrying a baby for you.' Alex smiled. 'Provided you *promised* to take it away afterwards.'

'What if something went wrong ... ?'

'It wouldn't. I'm fit, healthy and I have here,' she patted her tummy, 'a reproductive machine that's lying fallow. Fancy giving it a go?'

Lauren blew her nose. 'Sorry, I'm still processing this ... You're being serious?'

'Cross my heart.'

'Then I'd *love* you to have a baby for us.' Lauren was grinning. 'I'll have to talk to Dan, and you'd need to contact some specialists to find out about the risks so you know what you're signing up for. Could you do that?'

'Sure,' Alex glanced at her watch, 'but not today or tomorrow because we've got an off-site conference. I have to be on my bike in four minutes flat because I'm giving a presentation to the executive board. Talk soon, OK?'

'I love you so much and I wish I could hug you.'

'Me too, sister.'

*

40

Lauren made herself a cup of coffee and savoured the unfamiliar hit: caffeine had been on the banned list through the years of striving for a baby, now it was a tiny compensation for all her failures. She wondered what Dan would say about Alex's offer. Would he want something more formal and contractual, less reliant on the largesse of her family? She walked over to the black-and-white photo, taken a few months after the two of them met: they stood facing one another, his hands on her shoulders, he was smiling down at her, she was gazing up at him, laughing. They'd been so carefree and confident, amazed to have found one another. It felt like another country.

She'd been living in an artists' commune in Wanstead at the time, juggling several low-paid jobs alongside her work in the studio, but she'd managed to make enough collages for a solo show at an East London gallery. One lunchtime soon after it opened, a bunch of men from the engineering company next door came in; one bought a print, then asked her out. He wasn't her type, seemed so much older, with his suit, tie and City-boy haircut, but he was attractive and funny. In the wine bar he confessed he'd never set foot in a gallery before and had bought the picture just so he could talk to her. He asked endless questions and she found herself telling him about herself: how she worried that she'd never make a decent living as an artist and would end up having to go to university to train for a 'proper job' that would bore her rigid, just in order to eat. It was what her mum had predicted would happen – she'd advised her to keep art on the back burner, as a hobby.

'That's bollocks! All the online reviews say you're brilliant, plus you've sold half the stuff already. Your mum needs her head looking at.' He was gazing at Lauren, his dark eyes earnest. 'Unless she's some big art expert?'

'No, she makes TV dramas.'

'Sounds like she wanted you to follow her script, not yours. Not the best parenting trick, if you ask me.'

Lauren laughed, she felt a thrill of subversive pleasure. 'Mum loves us, but she's a bit overwhelming and tends to think she knows best, always. My sister had it easier – she's got a brain the size of a planet and was top of her class at school and uni, but Mum and I had endless fights before she agreed I could go to art college. We're so different. I'm dim and arty, she's driven and ambitious.' She stopped. 'But it's mean, me talking like this, because she's not been so bad, since I left home, and whenever I can't make my rent she always bails me out. What's your mum like?'

Dan grinned. 'Polar opposite, by the sounds of it.' He said she was a normal mum, who didn't care what he did as long as he was happy. She was the glue that held their family together, which was why her breast cancer had hit them all so hard. He was the youngest of three boys and was still at uni when she got the diagnosis. His dad went to pieces for a while, so Dan had taken a year off to look after them both.

'She had surgery and chemo, and last year she got the all-clear, but it was an aggressive tumour, so there's a fair chance it'll come back.' His eyes narrowed. 'You take your parents for granted, then something happens and you realise you've only got them on loan. I had to grow up pretty quick.'

'Poor you,' said Lauren, her eyes pricking.

'I know.' They stared at one another.

Lauren said, 'My dad's father died when he was seven and his mum told him he had to be the man of the family from then on.'

'Jesus, who does that to a little kid?'

'Mum reckons a bit of him shut down, and I think it's affected him a lot. He's quite reserved, and he says he had to make up being a father as he went along, because he never had a proper role model.'

Dan sat up straight. 'That sucks. I can't complain, I've still got two parents.' He rolled his shoulders back. 'Sorry, not sure how we got into all that. Let's change the subject.'

They talked easily now, discovering a shared liking for techno music, Glastonbury and Brazilian food. He was crazy about sport and a lifelong Aston Villa fan. He'd grown up in the Midlands, where his dad worked for British Rail and his mum was a part-time dinner lady. He teased Lauren for being middle class, metropolitan and southern – posh, in fact. She pointed out that she was practically living in a squat. He laughed, she hadn't a clue how most of the country lived and it would be his mission to educate her. No more wine bars: he preferred beer and the kind of food you got in ungentrified pubs.

Quickly they were a couple. Her parents were meticulously friendly, but Lauren sensed their surprise – a hint of disappointment, even – and she loved Dan all the more for it. He made her laugh, and when she was with him she could let her guard down and relax. His devotion never wavered and after they married he encouraged her to reduce her teaching hours and spend more time on her work. All through the fertility treatment, they'd been on the same page, determined to keep going, taking turns to encourage one another, which was why his recent change of heart was so disheartening.

As soon as Dan got home from work Lauren told him about Alex's offer. His response was guarded: he said there were pros and cons and he'd like to spend a few days talking them through. They went backwards and forwards for hours, discussing money and timetables and Alex's suitability, until Lauren became distraught and accused him of trying to block her one remaining chance of becoming a mother. Eventually he capitulated.

That night as she lay in bed Lauren messaged Alex:

Dan sends love & thanks, he
wants to do some sums, but we

definitely want to explore it!!!!!!!!!!
THANK YOU, my amazingly
wonderful sister
Xxxxxxxxxxxxxxxxxxxx

She switched off the light and replayed the scene that she'd devised over the previous six hours: they were in the labour room of an American clinic and Alex had just delivered their baby with a final push and a cry of triumph. She collapsed, grinning, on to her pillows while the midwife handed a bloodstained bundle to Lauren and helped Dan cut the umbilical cord. All three of them gazed at the baby and cried with happiness, then Ruth and Adam arrived to greet their first grandchild. For the first night since the miscarriage, Lauren fell immediately into a deep sleep.

5

The following afternoon Alex called Ruth at work and told her what they were planning.

Ruth was astonished. '*You*, Alex?'

'Why not? If they can choose a clinic quickly and fly out here with their embryos I could be pregnant before the end of the year.'

'It's a wonderful gesture, but pregnancy's a big thing to take on – I couldn't have managed without your dad. You'd be on your own.'

Alex said, 'I've thought about that, but I really want to do it. I've felt so guilty, watching Lauren go through infertility hell, while I live my lovely carefree life over here. It's a way of redressing the balance, I guess. Plus, my friends will be so fascinated they'll be round all the time, massaging my back, feeding me raspberry tea and observing me as if I'm an exotic animal in a zoo.'

'And you're sure it's safe?'

'That's what Lauren's worried about, and I haven't spoken to any specialists yet, but from a quick look online the treatment's pretty straightforward. Lots of women are doing it.'

As Alex outlined the mechanics Ruth typed 'surrogate frozen embryo sister' into her computer. Pages of pictures and articles popped up. 'Wow, I'm looking now … all these stories, and pictures.'

'Exactly.'

Alex seemed to have it all planned: she would work right through the pregnancy and wouldn't have to take much time off because there were several clinics only a short drive away. She knew her bosses would be supportive – several people in the company had had babies via surrogacy. But something was bothering Ruth. She typed: 'criteria for acting as surrogate' and skimmed the results. 'I'm sorry, Alex, but I don't think this is going to work: I'm looking at a checklist on a British surrogacy website and it says you can't host someone else's baby unless you've already had one of your own, which makes sense when you think about it.'

Alex laughed. 'That won't be a problem over here. This is America – the reddist, toothiest incarnation of capitalism – surrogacy is an industry and it's a buyer's market. The customer gets what she wants and there's generally much less regulation, but I'm going to contact some clinics tomorrow, so I'll double check.'

'Then I'll stop worrying. I'm so proud of you for offering, darling. Lauren must be thrilled?'

'It's fair to say that she cheered up a bit, once she'd clocked that I was serious.'

Instead of making all the calls to agents and directors that she'd been planning, Ruth spent the rest of the afternoon reading about women who'd produced babies for their infertile sisters. Their stories were riveting and addictive: one sibling lent her body, and transformed the other's life in the process. Alex was right: it was the perfect solution. How wonderful it would be, watching her girls doing this together, and getting even closer in the process. Alex might even decide to come back to London, once the baby was born, to be close to her niece or nephew, which would be a bonus for all of them. Ruth could help: she would research the latest techniques and find the specialists with the best success rates, as she had during Lauren's IVF. She googled several of the clinics near Alex's flat, trying to figure out which ones prioritised cutting edge medicine over luxurious waiting rooms and grounds. And then, just to be completely sure, she checked their guidelines for potential surrogates. To her dismay, she discovered that she'd been right: they all stipulated that hosts must have at least one uncomplicated pregnancy under their belts *and* be permanent residents of the USA. Alex would be disqualified on both counts.

Ruth put her head in her hands: it would be yet another setback for Lauren, another hope extinguished. Why did everything always go against her? Bit by bit she seemed to be shutting down and Ruth was terrified she'd end up having a breakdown. She wondered whether to call Alex and tell her what she'd discovered, then go to Brockley to be with Lauren when she found out, but decided on balance it was better not to interfere. They'd both be upset and Alex would be better at comforting Lauren, would be more likely to find words that didn't antagonise her.

Ruth stared at her screen: she had to *do* something. There *must* be a way through this. She frowned in concentration: they had to find a woman who'd already completed her family and would be willing to have one more baby for Lauren. She needed to be healthy, responsible and trustworthy. Who did she know? There *must* be someone. She felt an idea detach itself from somewhere deep inside her and float to the surface, so that it was just within grasping distance. She hesitated, then slowly typed: 'grandmother surrogates'.

There were scores of them: women of all ages who had given birth to their children's babies and lived to tell the tale in TV interviews, tabloid exclusives and supermarket bestsellers. Most of them were in the States, but there were stories from the

UK, too. Some were in their sixties and seventies. The formula seemed simple: a few months' hormone treatment turned back the elderly surrogate's biological clock and prepared her uterus for an embryo, which was tucked inside it in a quick procedure that didn't even require an anaesthetic. The tabloids called the carriers Tummy-Mummies or Chickens: the chickens incubated the eggs, laid them and handed them over to the parents when they were newly hatched.

Later that evening, while Adam was out at a work dinner, Ruth curled up on the sofa in the kitchen with her iPad, and immersed herself in the world of surrogacy. She sobbed unwillingly as she watched a succession of American daytime TV interviews in which triumphant women in their fifties and sixties sat alongside their sons and daughters as they dandled their 'miracle' babies. Videos from their pregnancies showed them restored to astonishing full-bloom fertility. Ruth was transfixed by their radiant faces, shining eyes and expressions of amazed potency: what would it be like to do that, she wondered, to travel back, deep into the fertile zone, and generate life again? The grateful parents placed reverent hands on the grandmothers' swollen tummies, mute in the face of such abundant generosity. Talk-show hosts broke down as they watched the monitors: it was a triumph of altruism and science – the ultimate feel-good story.

Ruth blew her nose and flipped into TV researcher mode, scanning blogs, joining conversations in chat rooms and reading the latest surrogacy news. She felt a surge of excitement: a baby would transform Lauren's life, and she could be the one to give it to her. It would be a sacrifice, but one she'd be prepared to make; it felt almost like a vocation. She discovered that there was a big fertility exhibition on the opposite side of London the following Saturday. Specialists from the UK and all over the world would be manning stalls and available for one-to-one chats, leading fertility experts would showcase the latest developments, and seminars would cover every area of treatment. There were several sessions about post-menopausal fertility and surrogacy. She was tempted to go, but when she checked her diary Ruth remembered she'd agreed to spend the day in the South Downs, on a six-hour cliff walk that Adam wanted to do. She'd already postponed it once; there was no way she could call it off again.

The call from Alex was as brutal as another miscarriage. When Lauren was too exhausted to cry any more she phoned Dan.

'Hi.' His voice was low and tentative: the office was open plan and Lauren's calls varied in volume and intensity. 'How's it going?'

'Alex can't be our surrogate because she's never had a baby and isn't a permanent US resident. She's talked to tons of clinics and they all said the same.'

'Oh.'

She waited for him to continue. 'Dan?'

'I'm just heading for the stairwell where I can talk more easily ... OK, that's better. I'm sorry, Laurie, you must be gutted,' he hesitated, 'though maybe it's for the best?'

'Did you just say it was *for the best*? Because if you did—'

He broke in, 'Don't get me wrong, I'm gutted too, all I meant was that, maybe, involving family would have ended up being a bit ... messy?'

'So what are we going to do?'

Dan sighed. 'It's barely a week since we lost the baby and I feel like I've been hit by a truck. I don't have an answer right now.'

'I'm not sure I can go on if we can't have a baby.'

'Laurie, we're on the same page, in principle, but—'

'I'm serious, Dan. I keep thinking about *stealing* one, and I'm scaring myself ...'

Dan spoke slowly. 'OK. Stop. Now. Take some deep breaths

and pull on your rubber band. Come on, we'll do it together. In: one – two – three. Out: one – two – three.'

For several minutes they breathed in synchrony until Dan heard Lauren sigh.

'Better?' he said.

'Yes.'

'We'll get through this, I promise.'

'I know,' said Lauren. 'Sorry to take it out on you.'

Dan said, 'I have to go now, there's a bunch of people waiting for me in a meeting room and I can't keep them hanging around any longer. We'll get through this, Laurie. We've been through a ton of bad stuff and it's made us stronger. Hold on to that thought until I get home.'

After another day of surrogacy research it was clear to Ruth that the fertility exhibition was too good an opportunity to miss: it would enable her to find out once and for all whether she might be able to help Lauren. Adam didn't like the idea of surrogacy and he would think the whole idea was crazy, so it wasn't fair to burden him with it at this stage, when everything was hypothetical. On Friday evening she told a small white lie. 'I'm afraid I need to work tomorrow, darling.' She buttressed the fiction with truthful detail to assuage her guilt, 'As usual the American co-producers want lots of changes made to the version of *Hurt* we've made for the BBC and Bella is overseeing the edits. Anya in LA is now asking for a different opening for every episode and, unless we're careful, we'll go way over budget. I'm so sorry.'

Adam gave her an indulgent look. 'I've been half expecting it: whenever you say you've finished, I always know there'll be more. And in any case, it's probably better if we do that walk in the spring, when the days are longer. That way we won't have to get up at dawn.'

'Thank you, darling.' Ruth hoped her smile seemed rueful, rather than crooked. 'I'm so sorry to abandon you.'

'Don't give it a thought,' he said cheerfully. 'I'll tackle the garden, all the shrubs need pruning, and it'll give me an excuse to watch the Arsenal away game.' He kissed her forehead. 'If you're going to be back late, I'll book a table for Ravi's tomorrow evening. 'It feels like ages since we had a proper conversation.'

On Saturday morning Ruth headed for Docklands. The train was crowded and she joined a throng of people streaming out of the station towards the exhibition hall. Almost everyone was in a couple, most of them holding hands. NO PHOTOGRAPHY BEYOND THIS POINT, said the sign at the entrance. It was an off-the-record, secret world and she felt like a private detective investigating a shadowy potential future. She was taken aback by the crowds: the seminar rooms were packed and there were queues at the stalls where fertility companies from all over the world were selling their services.

A saleswoman in a low-cut crimson dress and stiletto heels ambushed her with a glass of cava and bowl of olives; she represented a big clinic in Barcelona whose banner promised value for money, confidentiality and state-of-the-art science, but when Ruth outlined her situation the woman recoiled.

'All types of surrogacy are banned in Spain as well as in many other European countries.'

'Why?' asked Ruth, surprised.

The woman shrugged. 'We have perhaps a different mentality. We consider surrogacy immoral, an abuse of the female body, something unnatural that has many horrible consequences.' The glossy red lips puckered with disapproval. 'We offer IVF only, so we cannot help someone like you.'

Ruth blushed and walked on. Happily, other stands were more friendly: Cyprus, Russia and the Ukraine were avid for her business; she took a sheaf of brochures then moved on to a stand hosted by one of the leading London clinics. A specialist, wearing a well-cut double-breasted suit that said trust me, I haven't bought off the peg for years, was talking quietly to a woman in her forties. Ruth couldn't hear the conversation, but the emotional dynamic was clear: anxiety and doubt meeting attentive reassurance and the most delicate of pitches. The doctor was in his sixties, steel-grey curls, silver-rimmed glasses.

He turned to Ruth at last. 'Madame, I'm sorry to have kept you, how may I help?' Italian or Greek, with the manner of a very charming head waiter.

'My daughter can't carry a child, but she and her husband have frozen embryos left over from their IVF treatment and I've been wondering, could *I* be her surrogate?'

He was smiling. 'Madame, if I may be so bold, what is your age?'

'Fifty-four, just.'

He managed to convey gallant surprise followed by extravagant disappointment. 'Our upper age limit is fifty-one. It used to be higher, but we reduced it because of the risk to the surrogate and the baby.'

Ruth said, 'But I know that women as old as seventy have done this and survived. What are the risks, given that I'm fit and completely healthy?'

'In a normal pregnancy a woman's blood volume goes up by fifty per cent, but elderly blood vessels are sometimes rigid – I'm talking about *my* blood vessels, too, madame.' He twinkled at her, consoling. 'Now I'm much older than you, certainly, but we all get a little more *inflexible* as time passes, and, if that blood volume cannot increase, the baby's growth will be stunted.'

'So I'd need to go abroad?'

'Madame, did I say that?' He gave her a roguish look. 'At what age did you stop menstruating?'

52

'Fifty-two.'

He stroked his chin. 'That could go in your favour: the average is fifty-one.' He lowered his voice. 'Don't quote me, but some of the smaller London clinics, away from Harley Street, have, shall we say, less *exacting* requirements. Give them a ring, all their details are online.' He released her hand and looked into her eyes, his face suddenly serious and kind. 'It might well be possible. I wish you and your daughter the best of luck.'

'Thank you.' Ruth felt herself beaming at him. *It might well be possible.*

She spent the afternoon attending lectures about pregnancy during and after the menopause, the role of hormones in conditioning the mature uterus, and techniques designed to help embryos created in the lab to implant. She took copious notes and was heartened: everything she'd heard made hosting a foetus at the age of fifty-four seem feasible, mainstream even. Before leaving she slipped into the back of a seminar on surrogacy law, where an earnest solicitor from a firm of fertility specialists was outlining the key legal steps required to reassign parenthood from a surrogate to the person or couple who had commissioned her. The intended parents, as the biological mother and father were called, would apply for a court order that named them as the baby's legal parents. Until that order was approved by a judge, the host and her husband, if she had one, were the legal parents of the baby and both of them had to consent to the handover. Ruth felt a shiver of disquiet: that meant Adam would have to be on board. He'd baulk at the idea, she knew he would, but it was the obvious solution. She'd just have to win him round.

There followed a string of heartbreaking stories about commissioning couples who'd split up halfway through the pregnancy, leaving the surrogate holding the baby; parents who'd entered into commercial arrangements with foreign hosts and hadn't been allowed to keep their children; and hosts who'd given birth to babies and then kidnapped them in order to extort money. The courts, warned the lawyer, were increasingly concerned about the commodification of children, so in order to avoid any difficulties, both parties should take independent legal advice and draw up a watertight arrangement before beginning the process. Ruth made a note then crossed it out: they wouldn't need a contract and Adam could handle any paperwork; that way they'd be able to keep the costs down.

The solicitor looked earnestly at his audience. 'If you're considering surrogacy then I urge you to acquaint yourselves with the relevant laws in the country where you make the arrangement. But the most important thing of all is to choose your host with care and build a solid relationship with her.' He put up his final slide:

INTENDED PARENTS & SURROGATE MUST FORM A
STRONG BOND WITH HIGH LEVELS OF TRUST

Ruth closed her notebook and frowned: her relationship with Lauren wasn't quite there yet. They'd have to work on it. But the most pressing challenge was to find a clinic with 'less exacting requirements'. She sat down with a coffee in a quiet corner of the refreshment zone, took out her iPad and found a list of fertility centres in London. Some were open on Saturdays and she called one of them, describing her situation and trying to sound vigorous, healthy and young.

The response was dispiriting. 'Our age limit here is fifty-one. However, I'm sure we can help your daughter if she'd like to make an appointment ...'

She worked her way down the list, but it was always the same story.

'No. All our patients have to be under forty-six. Older ladies tend to go abroad, where the clinics aren't quite so picky ...'

'I'm sorry, our ethics committee sets the rules. They're based on chances of success and risks to the surrogate and the baby ... No, we can't make exceptions, not under any circumstances.'

Then, after two more cups of coffee she struck gold: the Marinella Clinic. Yes, they did sometimes treat older women if the doctors thought there was a good chance of a successful pregnancy. But fifty-four was their cut-off age: clients needed to give birth before their fifty-fifth birthday.

Ruth did a rapid calculation: that would give them eleven and a half months for treatment and pregnancy – it was just about feasible. 'Then I'd like to see your most senior specialist as soon as possible. Can you arrange that?'

The receptionist said the first step was for the commissioning parents and prospective surrogate to meet with a nurse practitioner for an introductory session.

'When could that be?'

'I've had a cancellation for three thirty on Monday.'

'We'll be there,' said Ruth. If Lauren and Dan weren't interested, she could always cancel.

On the train home she felt buoyant: it had been a good day's work. But she knew she mustn't let herself get too hopeful: her body would probably turn out to be unsuitable, or the risks too great. It was an idea worth exploring, that was all.

Her phone buzzed: a message from Sheila:

Where have you been? I still have your
present! You said you'd send dates 2
weeks ago Everything OK?

Sorry, been ultra-busy Lots
happening! Xxx

Ooh! Can you talk now?

Sheila was the only person on the planet she'd be able to confide in and the impulse to call her right away was strong, but Ruth managed to suffocate it. She looked at her diary, then replied:

No and it's too complicated (truly).
Are you & Simon free for supper
the Saturday after next? Totally
informal. Will tell you then Rx

Intrigued! Yes please Can't wait. xx

6

At eight o'clock that evening Adam and Ruth walked arm in arm to the Indian restaurant that had been their favourite for years. Both were nursing secret excitements that fostered hunger. The dining room looked just as it had the first time they peered inside in the late eighties: red velvet curtains, flock wallpaper, and cotton napkins arranged like flowers in thick greenish tumblers; and the smell was the same: spices, cooking oil and air freshener. It was packed, but Ravi, the proprietor, now in his seventies and plump with prosperity, hailed them like family and showed them to a central table. Service was slow and they'd drunk two large bottles of Kingfisher beer by the time the starters arrived.

'How did your editing go?' asked Adam.

'Oh, you know,' said Ruth. 'Usual stuff.' She could feel herself blushing and wanted more than anything to confess – it was an effort not to, because they confided in one another, most of the time. She wanted to explain her idea: how she might be able to solve Lauren's problem and make everything all right. She wanted him to understand the sacrifice she was willing to make and she yearned for his approval, but it was too soon.

Instead, she turned her attention to him. How was *his* work? Was he happy? Did he feel stretched?

It occurred to Adam that he'd married an *extraordinary* woman: she understood him so well, always knew when something was brewing. Her face was tilted towards him, quizzical and knowing, she was waiting. He smiled at her. 'In a nutshell?' he said.

She nodded.

He paused and took a gulp of beer. 'They're going to start the selection process for another batch of circuit judges sometime over the next two or three months and I'm wondering whether to apply.'

Ruth sat back in her chair in surprise. For as long as she could remember Adam had despised colleagues who swapped the cut and thrust of the bar for the more tedious security of the bench. 'They can't stand the heat of the kitchen,' he would observe, 'but they're happy to spend their days in the dining room criticising the chefs.' He'd sat as a recorder for a while, to broaden his experience, but found he missed the adrenalin that came from being on his feet in the well of the court. 'What's changed your mind, all of a sudden?' she asked.

He said he'd been mulling it over for a while because of the way his income was continuing to fall: he was bringing in less now than he had fifteen years ago. And he wasn't the only one, the cuts to legal aid and reduction in fees meant there was a stampede of criminal barristers towards the bench. His friend Julius Mander was on one of the judicial appointments committees and had told him that a recruitment round was in the offing and he thought it was the right moment for Adam to make the move. They'd known one another since university and Julius, a successful commercial lawyer, was a shrewd analyst of the legal landscape; Adam often used him as a sounding board before taking big decisions. 'He says I'd need to put a lot of time and energy into the application, but he reckons I'm probably experienced and well-regarded enough to get appointed.' Adam grimaced. 'Let's face it, you've shouldered the financial burden for the last few years and it's not fair. This way I'd have a guaranteed salary, plus a decent pension.'

Ruth looked uncertain. 'But don't sacrifice a job you love for one that you know would bore you. We can manage.'

'It's not just about money,' said Adam, 'the whole criminal justice system is crumbling around me.'

Ruth leant forward on her elbows and searched his face. 'But surely it's better to stay and fight to make it better? You've always believed in it so passionately.' It was one of the things she loved and admired in him.

'I did – and I still do, in principle – but the practice is becoming a travesty and I can feel myself getting disillusioned and cynical, like everyone else. It's hard to hang on to your self-respect.' He reached for her hand. 'I know what I always used to say, but I'm beginning to change my mind. What do you reckon?'

'If you're really unhappy, then do it – I'm sure they'll snap you up, but it's your decision in the end.'

'No, it's a *joint* decision,' he said, 'because it would affect us both. If I became a judge you could take it a bit easier and I'd never need to work through the night again.' He kissed her hand, then said tentatively, 'We could do more stuff together? Some serious travelling, or a joint project. It feels like the right time. What do you think?' He looked at her, expectant.

Ruth was moved; she felt that tiny lurch in her heart – as if it had fallen slightly sideways, then regained its balance – that no one but Adam had ever provoked. She wanted to say, *Yes, let's do that, I love you*, but she was shamed, by his meticulous consideration of her, and his tender taking-for-granted of their mutuality. Guilt, about her lies and her secret conversations with specialists, made her lash out: 'Oh, for heaven's sake, we're both free agents. Do whatever *you* want to do.'

Adam's face registered shock and pain for the briefest of moments, then closed.

Ruth put her head in her hands. 'Sorry, sorry, sorry.'

'No need to apologise.' Adam was breaking a poppadum into very small pieces with intense concentration. 'I just wanted to know what you thought of the idea.' He surveyed the debris. 'And now I suppose I do.' He paused as she raised her head and met his gaze. 'Thanks to your unfettered frankness.'

They ate in silence for a while. Then Adam said, 'Alex called while you were out. Did you know she'd offered to have a baby for Lauren?'

Ruth said, 'Yes, they told me.'

'You didn't mention it.' Ruth put a pre-emptive forkful of rice and dal into her mouth. 'Turned out she wasn't suitable and apparently Lauren's pretty cut up about it.'

'Mmm.'

'Blessing in disguise, if you ask me.'

Ruth saw an opportunity. 'I've been wondering whether they should try to find a surrogate over here instead,' she said, tentatively.

Adam put down his knife and fork. 'So you think it's perfectly acceptable?'

She said, 'I know you've got reservations, but if it's what Lauren and Dan want then I think we have to respect their choice.' She paused, then said carefully, 'And support them, in whatever way we can.'

He raised his eyebrows. 'But you appreciate that surrogacy has the potential to be an emotional and ethical nightmare for all concerned?'

Ruth realised he was spoiling for a fight now, because of her brusqueness. 'You've gone straight into cross-examination mode, as usual, which is why we never have proper conversations about these things, the way other people do.' She knew she should leave it at that, but the impulse to justify her idea was too strong. 'You *could*, for example, see surrogacy as a

60

humane and generous act that transforms the lives of child-less couples.'

Adam snorted. 'As opposed to a tawdry transaction in which women sell their bodies to the highest bidder, then manufacture babies to order?'

'In poor countries with a lot of infertility tourism that does happen, I grant you, but I'm talking about altruistic surrogacy, *here*, in London.'

'Then why have so many advanced countries banned the practice outright? It's because they recognise there are moral and biological boundaries that it's dangerous to cross. Sometimes we have to accept the limitations our bodies place on us, rather than meddle with things whose consequences we can't fully understand.'

Ruth lost patience. 'Can't you forget your Catholic brainwash-ing, just for once? We're talking here about our own daughter, who would do anything to have a baby. You don't understand how overwhelming it is, that drive.'

Adam was looking at her with frank dislike. 'But a drive that can be switched off when it suits. Eh, Ruth? By *some* women, at least?'

He'd crossed a line that they'd patrolled, silently, for years. 'How *dare* you?'

She stood up so quickly that her chair tipped backwards. There was a shriek of metal on tiles before it clattered to the floor. The sound silenced the table chatter: everyone was staring. Ruth couldn't get her jacket on because her whole body was trembling with anger. Adam, embarrassed, righted the chair and touched her shoulder, motioning her to sit down and stop making a spec-tacle of herself. 'I didn't—' he began.

She pushed him away. 'Let go,' she said, 'you sicken me. I'm going home. Don't forget to pay the bill, will you?'

*

When she got to the house Ruth went up to the spare room and lay on the bed. She did deep-breathing exercises for several minutes until her heart stopped pounding, then relaxed her abdomen and tilted it into a semblance of pregnancy. This was what her old body had been able to do: conjure babies, swell as they grew inside her, then deliver them squealing and blinking into the light. How she'd loved their gestation, and the sensual thrill of the new creatures sucking and snuggling against her. She realised how much she yearned to feel all that again. She arched her back and stroked her rounded belly. Of course, there were regrettable things in the past – things you wished you could rub out – but this wasn't at all the same. If it happened, surrogacy could be a good deed. Redemptive, even.

One of the advantages of a large family house devoid of children was that two warring adults could lead parallel but separate lives, provided they monitored one another's movements from a distance and took the necessary evasive action, so Ruth and Adam contrived to spend Sunday alone. Each replayed the conversation at the restaurant with amendments, inserting unassailable rejoinders and pleas in mitigation, securing the moral high ground and fortifying their positions. They were lonely. Ruth woke early and lay in bed reading until she heard Adam leave for his weekly tennis match in Ravenscourt Park, then she called Lauren.

'How you doing, darling?'

'Fine.' The voice was toneless.

'Really?'

'Really.'

'You don't sound it. Is Dan there?'

'He's gone to Birmingham, to watch the match.'

'Leaving you alone?' Ruth couldn't keep the edge out of her voice.

'I made him go, Mum. We can't spend all weekend cooped up together – it's like being in a pressure cooker.'

'Can I come over?'

'With Dad?'

'No, he's busy. Just me.'

'The thing is, I'm really behind with work and I was just about to go up to the studio, so it's really not the best time—'

'I'm leaving now,' said Ruth firmly. 'I won't stay long.'

It was several minutes before Lauren came to the door, and Ruth was shocked at the sight of her. She was barefoot, her T-shirt was inside out and her jeans undone: she'd clearly pulled some clothes on when she heard the bell. She'd lost weight and her face had a bony vulnerability, the skin around her eyes was puffy and almost raw. She turned and trudged wordlessly back up the stairs, Ruth following behind. They stopped on the threshold of the sitting room: it was warm and sour-smelling, the blinds were closed and a bluebottle was zigzagging noisily in the half-light; a pile of takeaway food containers, empty beer cans and disposable cups lay on the coffee table.

'Shall I open a couple of windows and get this lot cleared up?' said Ruth.

'Leave it,' said Lauren. 'It's Dan's. He'll do it later.' She flopped onto the sofa and stared vacantly, as if some central mechanism in her had shut down.

Ruth hovered, like a carer sizing up a volatile elderly patient. 'At least let me make you a hot drink, or something to eat, I bet you've had nothing since last night?'

'No, I'm fine.' Lauren spoke slowly and without expression. 'But please stop lurking, it makes me nervous.'

Ruth sat down next to her and decided there was no point tip-toeing around. She said quietly, 'I'm sorry that Alex couldn't be your host. It was such a generous offer and you must be gutted.'

Lauren's head snapped up and her eyes locked on to Ruth's. 'How did you know?'

'She called me. She feels she's let you down and she's worried about you. So am I.' Lauren didn't respond. 'Where have you got to? On ... everything?'

'Nowhere. We can't afford any of the US clinics, even in states that are cheaper than California, so we've run out of options.' Her face was blank with resignation.

'I wish we could help, but money's tight at the moment.'

'I know, Mum, and we don't expect it.'

Ruth said, 'Lots of clinics in Britain offer surrogacy, and it's much cheaper, have you ever thought ... ?'

'It's a non-starter.' Lauren was shaking her head. 'In America there are thousands of potential hosts and we'd have had a legal contract, naming us as parents. Over here there's a shortage, so it could take years to find someone, and even if we did, our child would belong to *her* when it was born, because English law favours the surrogate. She could change her mind and keep the baby.'

'And you don't want to run that risk?'

'I can't face losing another one, so I'd rather call it a day.' Lauren turned away, her voice fraying.

Ruth could feel the beating of her heart. She took a deep breath, and tried to adopt a casual tone. 'I was wondering whether you'd like me to do it ... ' She hesitated. 'Have the baby for you, I mean.'

'Oh, Mum.' Lauren looked at Ruth and her face crumpled.

Ruth took her hand. 'Because I've been doing a bit of research and mothers *do* do it for their daughters. There have been lots of them in the States and quite a few here.'

'It's really kind of you,' said Lauren wanly. 'And I do know about mother-daughter surrogacy, but it's not possible at your age, not in this country. It would be so dangerous, for you and the baby, I couldn't put you through it. It's almost thirty years since you were pregnant and if something went wrong ... '

Ruth realised Lauren had considered her for the role long ago, and rejected her. She felt a stab of hurt and resentment, like an elderly applicant with a good CV who hadn't even made the shortlist: she was the invisible woman, again.

'You're wrong, I'm not too old,' she said sharply. She took another breath. 'I've talked to a specialist, who said it *is* possible.'

'In London?' Lauren was sitting upright now and staring, with her mouth open and her eyes alert.

'Yes.' Ruth tried to keep the excitement out of her voice. 'And I found a clinic that would take me on.'

'Seriously?'

'*In principle*, that is,' she added quickly, anxious not to inflate Lauren's hopes. 'I'd need to pass some screening tests and give birth before my next birthday.'

Lauren gave a derisive laugh and slumped back on the sofa. 'Forget it,' she said. 'The fertility treatment could take *years*.'

'Then we'll make them go faster.'

Lauren looked at Ruth coldly. 'With respect, I'm the one who's been through IVF and I'm telling you, it's not like producing a TV series. You're at the mercy of doctors and embryos and bodies that don't stick to schedules. No amount of persuading or bossing – even by you – could meet that deadline.'

They were going to end up arguing if Ruth wasn't careful. She backtracked. 'I'm sorry, darling, you're the expert and I'm a novice, I get that. I'm sure you're right, but the person I spoke to seemed to think there was enough of a chance to have a quick meeting. And just supposing I *was* able to do it, there'd be no worries about losing the baby. And you'd be able to afford it, wouldn't you, because I'd come free, like Alex would have done.' She sat back and shrugged her shoulders, deliberately non-committal. 'But it's your call. I don't have any agenda, I thought it might be worth investigating, that's all.'

Lauren nodded slowly, like someone in a stupor. It was worth a try, she conceded, but she didn't think Dan would go for it: he'd had reservations about Alex.

'And having his mother-in-law as the host would be the nightmare scenario?' They both laughed and something shifted between them. Ruth said, 'I don't think your father would be particularly thrilled either, but we could talk the men round,' she threaded her arm through Lauren's in maternal solidarity, 'couldn't we?'

'Maybe.' It was the first time Ruth had seen her smile since the miscarriage. 'But I don't think you realise what it would involve. IVF takes over your life and you've already got a huge job and a company to run, how would you manage?'

Ruth said, 'It's broken my heart, watching you over the last few years and feeling powerless to help. I'd do *anything* that had the tiniest chance of giving you a baby, and don't worry, I could organise my work to fit around the treatment schedule. I'm very good at juggling.'

Lauren threw her arms around her mother. 'Thank you,' she whispered, 'for understanding what it's like, and for offering. The chances of it working are minuscule, but I so appreciate the thought.' She buried her head in Ruth's chest and whispered, 'I love you, Mum.'

Ruth flushed with surprise and pleasure. She'd never felt *needed* by Lauren, who – unlike Alex – had always been so resolutely undemonstrative. Suddenly she felt potent and useful: a proper mother, *loved*. She could feel tears pricking her eyes. She stroked Lauren's hair. 'I love you too, and I want to see if we can make this happen.'

She explained that she'd booked a preliminary appointment for all three of them the following afternoon. It was short notice, but to have any chance of meeting the clinic's deadline for giving birth they'd need to move fast. Lauren was dubious: it meant she'd have to talk to Dan that evening, when he got back from football. He'd be tired and possibly tipsy; the timing wasn't great.

'It's now or never,' said Ruth. 'Make him his favourite supper, ask him to give you a detailed account of the match, then put it to him. I'll leave you to it.' As they hugged goodbye Ruth said, 'Good luck, darling, give it your best shot.'

When she got home Ruth put on a tracksuit and trainers then drove to Richmond Park, where she ran a seven-mile circuit to exhaust and escape herself. There was a high wind and deer huddled beneath the trees in sheltered spots. She loved pushing her body and trusting to its energy and strength. For years she'd been using her daily runs to clear her mind and resolve intractable problems; she created mantras to help deal with issues at work or family conflicts and chanted them in her head. Now one came unbidden: 'I – Can – Do – This.'

The words lodged, then repeated themselves every four paces. Suddenly she felt exultant and unstoppable, buoyed by a new energy – *almost young*. She was the only one who could make it happen: she'd get the clinic to move fast with the treatment; then she'd get Adam onside; and – with his love and support – she'd put a baby in Lauren's arms within a year.

As she headed across the park the western sky was limbering up for sunset, golden clouds banked up in a gleaming mass. Ruth ran towards it, thinking of what lay ahead and smiling into the wind.

'I – Can – Do – This. I – Can – Do – This. I – Can – Do – This.'

Afterwards she went to the café at Pembroke Lodge, bought a mug of hot chocolate and sat on the terrace, looking down at the Thames Valley stretched out beneath her, the river a steel ribbon snaking from Windsor to London. She checked her phone messages – there was nothing from Adam – then called Bella, who was still at work.

'How's it going?' Ruth asked her. 'Is Anya happy?'

'It's been a bit of a nightmare,' said Bella.

Ruth heard her muffled yawn and imagined the fug of the edit suite, paper cups half-full of cold coffee, the congealing remains of a takeaway lunch brought in by the runner. 'Want me to come across now and give you a hand?' she asked. 'I could make some proper food and take over for a few hours, while you eat and have a break?'

'No, darling.' Bella was emphatic. 'You enjoy your evening with the lovely Adam. But could you call Anya for me? She's rung several times already, and at this rate I'll be here all night. Maybe you could convince her that the cut I've just sent you both meets every one of her extensive – not to say completely bloody exasperating – requirements? She always takes so much more notice of you.'

'Consider it done.' Ruth was ten years older than Bella, and it gave her more clout with some of the industry heavyweights they had to deal with.

'By the way, how's Lauren?'

Ruth was startled by the question. The focus of Bella's life was her work, her long-term boyfriend and her classic sports car; she was childless by design and had taken polite but limited interest in Lauren's problems over the years. Ruth said, 'I was with her this afternoon. She's very up and down. In fact, I meant to say, I'm planning to work from home tomorrow in case I need to go with her to an appointment.' She was telling the truth, but it felt like a lie. She realised she was shivering. 'Actually Bella I'd better go, I'm in the park and it's suddenly turned cold.'

The sun had weakened and threads of mist were suspended across the darkening landscape beneath her. She ran back to the car, then drove home. The front door was double-locked, which meant Adam was still out. She felt at a loss. Once they'd patched things up and he was in a better frame of mind, she needed to talk to him about surrogacy and get him to see that it was a gift, not some sort of moral perversion. If there was even the tiniest chance of her having Lauren's baby, she'd need him with her: without his support, practical and psychological, she wouldn't be able do it.

Dan didn't get home until half past ten: his train had been delayed by signal failures and he was hungover and ravenous. He'd expected to find Lauren in bed, but instead she'd waited up and the flat was clean, tidy and ablaze with lights. There were flowers on the table and places laid for supper with their wedding-present china. She'd been out shopping and made a shepherd's pie and an apple crumble, using his mum's recipes. He was flabbergasted.

'Best meal I've had for months, no kidding.' He took a third helping of the pudding. 'Looks like you're feeling a bit better?' he added, tentatively.

'More hopeful, maybe.'

'That's good.'

'Mum dropped by.'

She was blushing he noticed. 'And?'

Lauren shifted in her chair. 'Dan, please don't interrupt, or dismiss what I'm about to say out of hand, because I know you'll think this is completely bonkers, and ninety-five per cent of me thinks it is too, but if there's an infinitesimal chance that it *could* work ... At first I dismissed it as a non-starter, one of Mum's crazier ideas, but having thought about it, and spent a bit of time on the internet, I want to find out more and I'd like us to talk about it, so please ... ' She stopped, out of breath.

'I swear on *my* mother's life to listen in silence,' he was smiling at her fondly, 'but I haven't a clue what you're on about, so get a move on.'

As she outlined Ruth's proposal Dan's face fell. The thought of sitting with his wife and mother-in-law in a consulting room to 'discuss the mechanics', as Lauren put it, made him feel sick. It crossed *so* many lines. Quite apart from that, there was *zero* chance of Ruth being suitable: IVF would be a total waste of time and money at her age.

'Dan?' Lauren was looking at him, her expression pleading.

He wanted to say, *Seriously? Trying for a baby is private, between you and me; we're not having her barging in and taking over. No way. End of.* But he knew to tread carefully. 'It's really thoughtful, and generous, of your mum, but I'm not sure it's practical.' He leant across the table and took her hands. 'Laurie,' he said gently, 'even if she *could* do it, which is highly unlikely, what are the odds of someone her age getting pregnant inside two months?'

'Tiny, and I'm not suggesting she will—'

'Then why are we even talking about it?'

'Because she *might*. Remember how the clinic said there was no way our last embryo transfer would work, but it did? *Please* can we try this one last thing?'

His heart contracted with pity. She was so fragile at the moment and, though he was repelled by the idea, Ruth's insane plan seemed to have transformed her: perhaps it was best to go along with it for a while? He'd do anything to make her less unhappy; at least this way she'd have something to focus on.

He squeezed her hands. 'How about this: we go to the clinic tomorrow and listen to what they have to say. Ruth can have some tests, and we'll take it from there.'

Lauren was already beaming.

'But *only* if we both agree that we'll view this as another closure cycle. I don't want either of us to invest any emotion in expecting it to work. And when it's over we'll have a *complete* break from everything for at least six months, ideally a year, so we can take some proper holidays and work out what we want long term. OK?'

She was laughing now. 'Yes, yes, yes! To everything,' she said.

7

At eight on Monday morning Adam, clad in his overcoat, came into the kitchen and found Ruth at the table, bent over her laptop. He was rattled by the sight of her: the long white nightdress, hair chaotic over her shoulders. She never did this, because she knew it reminded him so painfully of his father's illness and death, when routines had disappeared and life came to a standstill. For his sake she'd always shooed Lauren and Alex away when they threatened to drift around in their pyjamas during the day.

'Are you ill?' he said, stepping back involuntarily into the doorway as if to escape contagion.

'I'm never ill,' she said briskly. 'You know that.'

'Then why are you playing truant? What's the matter?'

'I'm working from home because it's more efficient.' Ruth didn't look up. 'In the office I get interrupted all the time.'

He walked to the table and stood behind her chair. She quickly closed whatever she'd been looking at and he caught sight of himself in her screensaver photo: in his late twenties, denim shirt and navy shorts, barefoot on a sandy beach with Lauren – a plump toddler peeping out from beneath a blue sun hat – in his arms. Ruth stood next to them, hugely pregnant with Alex. How stunning she'd been, regal and smiling, like a fertility goddess. In her element.

He lifted her hair and laid it painstakingly in a neat, wide skein down her back. 'Please get dressed, Ruth. It upsets me.'

She stiffened. 'Everything I say and do seems to upset you at the moment.'

'Bit over the top, wasn't it? Storming out of Ravi's like that?'

'I'm not discussing it, Adam.'

He kissed the top of her head, wanting to make peace.

'Stop it.' She ducked away. 'I'm the woman you despise and humiliate, remember? And you'll miss your train unless you leave *now.*'

Adam sighed, picked up his briefcase and walked down the hall. 'I've got a meeting so I'll be late back tonight,' he called.

In the silence that filled the house after the front door slammed shut Ruth gazed at her younger self on the screen: face clear and unlined, hair thick and lustrous, emanating an animal vitality that she'd not been aware of until it was gone. They'd been on an Easter holiday in Dorset, but she'd spent most of the time indoors, reading scripts, or talking to anxious writers from phone boxes. Adam, left alone with Lauren for hours, had resented her absences, but it was the only way she'd been able to keep a foot on the career ladder. Alex had been born shortly after the photo was taken. She'd yearned for more babies, but they didn't happen. She felt thwarted and the ache was always there, beneath the frantic surface of her life. When the girls were six months old she handed them to nannies, and later au pairs, a succession of sweet-natured girls who adored children and pets. She picked ones that were maternal, plump and not too pretty. They were no temptation for Adam, but her daughters fell in love.

Work was a salve, her second family, needier, greedier and less forgiving than the one at home, and she'd hurled herself into it. She'd made herself available around the clock, taking calls at mealtimes, flying out to film sets at weekends to manage crises – she felt torn and guilty, but it was the nature of the job. At Morrab, she'd always made sure she was on hand to brainstorm ideas, steady nerves and solve problems. Now, though, she felt distracted in a way she never had before. For the past four days she'd spent all her time on surrogacy research, and three new drafts of scripts, all requiring her immediate attention, lay unread on the desk in her study. She would make a start on them soon, but not yet – right now her duty of care was to Lauren.

Everything was in sharp focus as she picked up the phone. It was a while before Lauren answered; she sounded half asleep and Ruth's heart sank. 'Have you talked to Dan? I need to know whether or not to cancel the clinic appointment.'

'Oh, sorry, he got back late and we stayed up half the night discussing it.'

'And?'

'He said yes and we're coming, but only to explore the possibilities.'

Ruth stood up and looked out into the garden. All her senses seemed heightened. She would remember this day: the morning sun streaming through the French windows; the dogwood in the border gleaming red, like warm blood; the marmalade cat from next door crouching on the wall as two squirrels walked tightrope along a branch of the apple tree, just a pounce away.

'You still there, Mum?'

'Yes, darling. Very well done for persuading him. The place is in Euston and I'm texting you the details now.'

The Marinella Clinic was a queasy marriage of private medicine and three-star hotel. Jack Vettriano reproductions lined the walls and notices proclaimed a continuous supply of cappuccinos and miniature pastries. But there was a slight shabbiness about the place, Ruth noticed. Magazines that were creased and old; a chair with black stuffing bulging through a tear in its orange cover; and the smell – dust with a hint of mildew – not quite masked by something harshly floral. The bronze chrysanthemums perched on a granite pedestal were past their best and shrivelled petals lay like dead insects on the pink stone. The clinic was off Harley Street: fringe, out of the mainstream, a place that didn't quite meet your eye. Ruth was depressed, then comforted: they were more likely to be flexible and accommodating, weren't they? In the waiting room a plump receptionist with long blue nails stopped typing and removed her headphones. She asked Ruth for her name and credit card, 'Just a routine swipe for our records'. Soulless and tawdry, thought Ruth; she missed the scruffy humanity of the NHS.

Lauren arrived late and flustered. 'Dan's downstairs,' she said. 'He stopped off to buy a newspaper.' She hugged her mother; they were a team now, thought Ruth.

When he appeared, Dan was uncharacteristically subdued and sat apart from Lauren and Ruth, reading the paper. Eventually a nurse draped in a hectic floral tunic over black leggings called Ruth's name and all three of them followed her into a bland meeting room.

'Helen Braithwaite, but *do* call me Helen, we're very informal here,' she said.

Ruth explained that they were on a fact-finding visit, but time was of the essence. Helen took them through the services offered by the clinic and then outlined the treatment schedule for post-menopausal surrogates. Time frames varied, she said. 'The uteruses of women over fifty tend to have already shrunk quite a bit, sometimes they're as small as walnuts and very brittle. It can take a while to restore them to childbearing condition.' Ruth inhaled deeply, trying to breathe plumpness and flexibility into her defunct womb; next to her Dan shifted in his seat.

'We usually put our post-menopausal ladies on the pill for

a month and then let them have a really good breakthrough bleed, so they can flush out all the hard lining that's built up since they last had a period. Then we start them on high-dose HRT to make it nice and thick and vascular again.' She smiled at Ruth.

Dan got to his feet. 'Sorry, I need to make an urgent work call. Won't be long.'

'Bless him,' said Helen after the door had closed. 'It can't be easy, hearing all about your mother-in-law's inner workings, but he'll get used to it, won't he?'

When he returned she ran through the Human Fertilisation and Embryology Authority guidelines for surrogacy, which imposed certain mandatory requirements on clinics. For example, they had to inform commissioning parents and hosts of all the possible dangers they might face.

'There are *risks*, Mrs Furnival.' Helen paused and raised her eyebrows for emphasis. 'You need to understand the risks of contemplating childbirth at your age.'

'Sure,' said Ruth, impatient. 'Just tell me the worst-case scenario and the percentage risk of it actually happening.'

'Ooh,' said Helen with relish, like a greedy diner spoilt for choice. 'Pre-eclampsia. Eclampsia. Stroke. Haemorrhage.' She was counting them off on her fingers. 'Then death, of course. Maternal death. The doctors could tell you the percentages.'

Lauren gripped Ruth's arm. 'Mum, I *told* you, didn't I ...? ' But Ruth shushed her.

Helen catalogued further calamities that might befall the elderly host. Then, in a sudden change of gear, she assured them that Marinella patients seldom encountered such problems because the clinic only accepted women who were low-risk into its treatment programme.

'You see,' Ruth turned to Lauren, 'provided your surrogate is fit and healthy – and I *am* – there's no need to worry.'

Helen went on to explain that all three of them would have to attend what she called Implications Counselling, to explore any issues and address individual concerns, before treatment began.

'By the way, is there a Mr Furnival?'

'I'm married, if that's what you mean,' said Ruth coolly.

'Then both of you would be named on the initial birth certificate as the baby's parents. We'd need your husband's written consent before we could transfer an embryo into your uterus and he'd need to come in for counselling too.'

'So your protocol sees my womb as the property of my husband?' Ruth raised her eyebrows. 'How very quaint.' She hadn't bargained for compulsory counselling. Adam would hate it.

Helen shrugged. 'Our standard operating procedure here at the Marinella is to make sure that spouses or partners know exactly what's involved, so there are no difficulties further down the line. That means all four of you would have to sign our forms.'

She explained that the baby's biological parents weren't allowed to start applying for a parental order for at least six weeks after the birth: the law insisted on a cooling-off period to allow the surrogate time to recover and ensure that she was happy with the arrangement. 'We're required to advise everyone who comes to us that surrogacy arrangements are unenforceable and that you should take legal advice before going ahead.'

Lauren turned to Ruth. 'You see, you didn't believe me when I told you: parents have no security in the UK. It's different when everyone's family, like us, but can you imagine watching your baby growing inside a stranger for nine months and the whole time not being sure whether she'll hand it over once it's born?'

'If I turn out to be suitable that's not something you're going to have to worry about,' said Ruth. 'So let's keep our fingers crossed.'

Helen said the next step would be a meeting with the clinic's medical director, Dr Vassily. He would examine Ruth and decide whether she was a candidate for further tests. She looked at them, her expression solemn. 'But don't be in too much of a hurry, because this is a *huge* decision for all of you. My advice is to talk everything through as a family. If everyone's comfortable, then come back to me.'

They shared a taxi to King's Cross. Dan leant forward and rubbed his palms back and forth over his face. Ruth and Lauren watched nervously.

He looked up at Ruth. 'Thanks very much for setting that up. Laurie and I know that the odds are stacked against this working, because of your age and the short time frame, so we're not getting our hopes up at all, but I guess we should discuss it with Adam as soon as possible?'

'No.' Ruth shook her head. 'It's too early. He's up to his eyes in a big case and I don't want to bother him when we don't even know if it's feasible. If we end up going ahead I'll sort it, don't worry.'

Lauren put a hand on Dan's arm. 'That's fine with us, isn't it?'

He looked puzzled. 'Are you suggesting we keep it *secret* from him?'

'Dan!' Lauren rolled her eyes. 'You know what Dad's like, he'd want a big debate about the pros and cons, which we don't have time for right now.'

He shrugged. 'To be honest, I wouldn't mind having a chat about the pros and cons.' He suspected that Adam would be on his side. 'But I get the feeling I'm being out-voted.' He stared out of the window, resenting them.

'OK,' said Ruth briskly, 'so we need to see the specialist.' She took out her phone and started typing:

Dear Helen,
Great to meet you just now. We'd like to arrange a
consultation with Dr Vassily asap. Can you let me
know how soon the other tests you mentioned could
be arranged?
Best wishes,
Ruth Furnival

The response came almost immediately: the specialist could see them in three days' time; counselling would take one or two days; and it was possible that all the screening appointments could be fitted into the following two weeks – but only if Ruth could make herself available to take cancellation slots at very short notice.

She felt a pulse of anxiety: it would mean being away from the office at a critical time, when she should be concentrating twenty-four/seven on getting projects commissioned. But this was more important. She looked up at Lauren and Dan, 'Thursday at three? OK?'

'Yes!' said Lauren. She turned to Dan, her face flushed with excitement, 'Is that time OK for you?'

He sighed. 'I'll have to move things, but I suppose so.'

On her way home on the train Ruth skimmed through scores of work emails that had piled up in her inbox during the afternoon; there was one from Bella:

Hope appointment went OK?
I've just finished chairing your monthly script meeting
because you weren't here (???). There were questions/
concerns I couldn't deal with – editors are feeling
rudderless atm and they need to crack on. Can we talk
asap? I'm back in cutting room first thing, so tonight best
for me. Will you be in tomorrow? Bx

Ruth kicked herself for forgetting to postpone the meeting. Now Bella was annoyed. If the treatment went ahead she'd need to get her onside, fast.

When she got home, Lauren called Alex on WhatsApp. She was working in the café at the top of her office building, the Golden Gate Bridge visible in the distance, through the wall of glass behind her.

Alex was seldom lost for words but she stared open-mouthed as Lauren described the clinic visit. Finally, she said, 'You have to hand it to Mum, she's *brave*, volunteering to get pregnant and give birth at fifty-four.' Then she looked down and started to type. 'I'm looking at loads of grandmother surrogates here and most of them are in their forties. Wouldn't it be super-risky at her age?'

Apparently not, said Lauren, the menopause could be reversed with drugs and the process sounded much simpler than the one Alex would have had to undergo. 'It's quite straightforward, medically speaking.'

'But staggeringly *un*straightforward in every other way.' Alex leant into the screen. 'You have to admit?'

'How's it any different from you doing it?'

'It's much more complicated.' Alex made a cross with her fingers as if warding off an evil spirit. 'She's *our* mum, and the idea of her podding her own grandchild – aka your child, *her* child, my niece or nephew, *our* sibling – there's something messy about it that *bothers* me.' She puckered her lips in distaste. 'Mum's wonderful, she'd lay down her life for us, we both know that, but she does tend to take over and she always somehow ends up being at the centre of the drama, doesn't she?'

'I know,' said Lauren, 'but over the last few days she's been so lovely and thoughtful, not like that at all.'

'I can't believe what I'm hearing. Remember that time she

79

went through our teenage diaries to check if we'd got STDs or were doing drugs? She read out your breathless account of oral sex in Josh Sheldon's car, then said you were wicked, disgusting and would come to no good. Then she laid into me for my erotic fantasies about Mr Eccles, the Latin teacher.' Alex smiled at the memory. 'I kept quiet, but you went ballistic, screaming about boundary violation and abuse, and threatening to report her to Childline.' She paused. 'You said you hated her.'

Lauren bridled. 'That's because she'd been away filming for *months*, then came swooping back and started helicoptering around, trying to find out who we were and what we'd been up to. All my friends had normal mums who made pancakes with them after school and sat quietly in the background. Ours was either absent or much too present, breathing all over us. I *did* hate it.'

'But this is the woman you want to have your baby?'

'That was years ago, and she's changed. She's willing to put her whole life on hold for me, just like you were.'

'If you say so,' said Alex drily. 'Just make sure you don't wind up falling out, because you'll be spending an awful lot of time together if she gets … *pregnant*.' She stumbled on the word, still unsettled by the whole idea, then a slow grin split her face. 'How's Dan handling this? It must be a complete headfuck: his mother-in-law morphing into his baby-mother.' She pulled her lips into an appalled emoji.

Lauren sighed. 'Stop it, Alex. He was a bit freaked out by all the gynae chat today, but he seems fine with the idea in principle, mainly because he thinks there's no chance it will work. And to be fair, he's probably right.'

'And Dad?'

'We're not telling him yet, but Mum says she'll be able to talk him round if it goes ahead.'

'Hmm.' Alex frowned. 'I wouldn't be so sure. He was

indoctrinated by monks, remember. I reckon IVF makes him queasy and surrogacy might be one step too far.'

Lauren looked surprised. 'He's never said he has a problem with IVF.'

'He wouldn't, would he, not to you.' She shrugged. 'It's only a hunch: once a Catholic and all that, and I may be wrong.' She paused. 'And by the way, Mum did make pancakes with us, quite often, when she was around. You've forgotten.'

That evening Ruth and Adam were reconciled. He arrived home bearing flowers and rang the bell, even though he always had a key. She opened the door and met his quizzical look – one that invited her to acknowledge both their shared history and their recent ridiculousness but was just non-committal enough to morph into a cold stare if she failed to reciprocate. It offered a ceasefire and the possibility of a truce. For a long moment they hung in suspension. Then Ruth smiled, and they fell into one another, shaking with laughter and relief. The lilies were crushed in the hug, but Ruth couldn't bear to throw them away: she crammed them all into a big glass vase and stood it on the hall table as a souvenir of battle.

The post-mortem, such as it was, took place over supper.

'I'm sorry,' said Adam. 'I shouldn't have said what I did in the restaurant.'

'No, you shouldn't.' Ruth looked at him, unsmiling and intent, wanting to underscore the gravity of his offence. Then she said, 'But I'm sorry I snapped at you. I can see why you want to be a judge, and of course I'll support you. When's the deadline for applications?'

'I've no idea. They haven't even announced the vacancies yet. And it's not as if I've made up my mind: there are pros and cons.'

'Then let's discuss it. I also want to have a proper conversation with you about surrogacy at some point.' She smiled at him. 'Now that we've stopped hating one another.'

Adam leant across the table and kissed her gently on the lips. 'OK, but not tonight, if you don't mind – I don't want to risk another walk-out.'

And because she didn't want to spoil their easy amiability, Ruth decided not to push it. This was the pattern of their disagreements: an incendiary row, followed by a period of avoidance and icy politeness, then a moment of mutual recognition that melted the residual bitterness. Apologies would be exchanged and equilibrium restored, but they never confronted the underlying issues, so nothing was ever *resolved*. Ruth suspected that other couples did it differently. Over the years she'd noticed that, whenever Lauren and Dan disagreed, they would talk things through until they got to the root of the problem and figured out where each of them stood, then they'd agree a way forward. She poked fun at them sometimes, said they sounded like union negotiators, but that painstaking and often painful process had cemented their marriage when IVF could have destroyed it. Deep down, she was envious. It was constructive and grown up; she and Adam sometimes seemed like children trapped in a haunted house, afraid to name the ghosts that couldn't be laid.

Ruth returned to the marital bed and the room full of mementos of their life together: a collage of photographs and drawings that Lauren had made for their twenty-fifth wedding anniversary; a plaster figurine labelled 'World's Greatest Mother' that Alex had bought her on a school trip to the New Forest when she was ten; and the two Large-billed Puffins that had watched over them since they married. The Audubon print in its battered gilt frame had hung over Adam's parents' bed and his mother had passed it on as a wedding gift, noting in an accompanying card that puffin pairs stayed together for life. Now it sat in the centre of the wall opposite theirs: one of the birds stood on the very edge of a rock, its mate floated in the water below but one leg was raised; they seemed hyper-aware of one another, yet poised for possible flight. 'Look at them,' said Ruth fondly, 'still together after all these years.'

Adam nodded. 'At school, whenever the bullying started, I'd think of them.'

'I know,' said Ruth, stroking his hair. 'And you'd imagine yourself back home and inside that picture, looking down at what was happening to you.'

'You remember,' he said drowsily.

'I remember everything.'

She'd wondered whether they might make love, a thought rather than a physical impulse, but within seconds Adam was asleep: he wasn't built for guerrilla warfare and their rare but brutal arguments exhausted him for days afterwards. She lay awake next to his gently snoring bulk, and for the first time she felt afraid. She was trapped in a clammy, foul-smelling chamber of her mind. Its walls were red and slimy with blood and mucus, and there was a gigantic metal sign hanging from the ceiling: MATERNAL DEATH in heavy black type. A voice, grave and deep, intoned the nurse's warning on a loop: 'Pre-eclampsia. Eclampsia. Stroke. Haemorrhage.' Yoga breathing didn't help. She tried to empty her head and find stillness, but her thoughts flicked back to the red room, where a woman lay helpless and moaning with pain, no one able to hear her.

PART TWO

ANNUNCIATION

8

Ruth was running her regular morning route that wound its way through the backstreets to Hammersmith Bridge, across to the south bank of the Thames, then along the towpath until she reached the railway bridge. The day was crisp and clear and the path dry; she started fast, then settled into a slow, meditative pace.

In two hours' time they would be back at the clinic to meet the fertility specialist. Was the whole thing a bad idea? she wondered, as she pounded up the metal steps of the footbridge, taking them two at a time to test her muscles. Horribly dangerous, against nature, an act of biological hubris? Or benign and constructive, a risk-free way to create a family for Lauren and Dan? Her gut told her it was the latter: she'd be making herself biologically useful again, doing something she was good at as an act of maternal charity. And, besides, it would be so *interesting*. Fitting the treatment around work would be tricky, but she'd manage, somehow.

She began to mentally rehearse for the meeting with the doctor. It sounded as if the compulsory counselling might be a potential stumbling block: she couldn't afford to have Adam there, disrupting their united front and potentially derailing the whole thing from the outset; she needed to find a way to delay his session. She tried thinking of it in terms of a production: she and Lauren had to move fast in order to meet the transmission deadline, her fifty-fifth birthday; Adam was a key player, but he could join later, once he'd heard the pitch and committed. It was all a matter of timing, and careful persuasion.

She stopped in the middle of the bridge and bent over the parapet to recover her breath. Below her the skeletons of huge willows bent into the water, their branches back-lit yellow by the sun. Beyond them the steel-blue river chafed against the rising tide, and over on the opposite bank a row of pastel-painted Georgian doll's houses fronted up the suburban wedge of Barnes. She took in deep draughts of air, it smelled of the distant sea: urgent and female. The wind was against her as she ran back to the house. But she leant into it, full of purpose and conviction. 'I – Can – Do – This. I – Can – Do – This. I – Can – Do – This.'

The medical director of the Marinella Clinic was a short, thickset man with black hair and a close-cropped beard. He met them in reception.

'Mrs Furnival?' He beamed at Ruth and took her hand, pressing it a fraction too long. 'Nicholas Vassily.' He turned to Lauren and Dan. 'Mr and Mrs Ryan? Such a pleasure to meet you. Let's get to work.'

They followed him into a consulting room that overlooked the Euston Road. Dr Vassily ushered them towards a trio of faux-Regency chairs ranged in front of a vast mahogany desk. He clambered onto a swivel chair on the opposite side that gave him a six-inch height advantage.

'Welcome to the Marinella.' He smiled down at them. 'Helen has briefed me, so I know you're in a hurry. We'll move as fast as we can. We have experience with patients in your situation.'

'Post-menopausal women?' Ruth asked, as she opened the

new red notebook she'd bought for the occasion. 'Who have got pregnant and given birth?'

Dr Vassily's smile widened and he placed his hands, large and covered in thick black hair, on the table and leant towards her. 'Several.' He spun away from them and pointed to a shelf behind his desk that was crowded with gilt-framed photos of mothers brandishing tiny babies. 'Just some of my satisfied customers.' At a quick glance none of them looked as old as Ruth.

He turned back. 'I want to help all of you, but everything depends on how you perform in our tests, Mrs Furnival. Age is not so important. What I'm looking for is a healthy uterus and a woman in outstanding physical condition. We shall see.'

'May I ask a question?' said Lauren.

'As many as you like.'

'When a uterus is menopausal—' She broke off and turned to Ruth. 'Sorry, Mum, but I just want—'

'No problem, let's get everything out on the table,' Ruth laughed, trying to soften the moment, but she could feel the muscles in her neck tightening in anticipation of imminent humiliation.

'How does an older uterus differ from one that's the age of mine?'

'That's an excellent question, and the answer may surprise you.' Dr Vassily pressed his palms together and lowered his voice like a magician before the climax of a trick. 'No difference *whatsoever!*' He flung out his arms. 'The mature uterus does not deteriorate. It merely stops functioning. If we can get your mother's working again, she will be as good a carrier now as she was when she gave birth to you thirty years ago. Amazing, eh?'

Ruth felt as if she'd won first prize in a uterus contest.

'Any more questions?' asked Dr Vassily, glancing at Dan. He shook his head, but Ruth noticed the blush, spreading from his neck to his cheeks. 'Very well, then, I need to know *your* story.'

He looked at Lauren then glanced at the notes. 'You were treated at the Framlingham Clinic?'

'Yes,' she said, 'and we've still got eight embryos there.'

He took their history, ran through all the risks of pregnancy at an advanced age in even greater detail than the nurse had done, then described the process of stimulating the surrogate's uterus and transferring one or two of the thawed frozen embryos into it. He turned to Ruth. 'If implantation were to occur first time round you *could* be pregnant in six weeks.' The magician hands fluttered again as he laughed at their astonishment. 'But first we need to know, do you have the *potential* to be a host?'

He ushered Lauren and Dan out, then gestured towards a screen in the corner of the room and instructed Ruth to prepare herself for a 'full examination'. He asked if she wanted him to fetch a chaperone, but she said no. She wasn't sure how much he'd need to access, so in a spirit of helpfulness she removed all her clothes before putting on the skimpy cotton gown he'd given her, then perched self-consciously on the paper-covered examination couch.

Dr Vassily bustled in and seemed surprised and delighted to see her all over again. He listened to her heart and chest, then told her to lie on her back with her knees bent: 'So I can assess your uterus.' He pulled on a pair of pale blue latex gloves, picked up a heavy metal speculum and anointed it with lubricating gel, then inserted it into her vagina. He stooped and squinted. It was cold and uncomfortable despite the jelly, and Ruth felt suddenly old: were her tissues already too thin and frail to withstand further obstetric onslaughts? He pulled the speculum out of her. It made an explosive sound, somewhere between a kiss and a fart. Ruth closed her eyes and tried to imagine she was somewhere else.

'Now just a quick internal examination.' Dr Vassily put one hand on her belly and left it there, wobbling lightly, like the layer of cream on top of a well-made trifle, then he pushed one of his great blunt fingers inside her and felt his way around the neck of her womb. 'Try to relax,' he murmured rhetorically.

The sensory shock of a man's finger inside her took Ruth by surprise. How long had it been since she and Adam had last had sex? Weeks, maybe months. Her body was becoming numb with disuse, more stone than flesh, as if the nerves were perishing. Now she felt a rekindling that hovered disturbingly close to arousal. Did Adam think much about sex nowadays? she wondered.

Now the blue hand on top of her abdomen was plunging into the pad of fat she'd developed since the menopause, searching for her uterus and trying to establish its boundaries. Let it not be shrivelled to a walnut, she prayed. She opened her eyes and searched Dr Vassily's face for clues. His gaze was focused far away, as if he was listening to an intricate and beautiful piece of music, meanwhile he continued to move around inside her. Eventually he grunted opaquely and withdrew his finger, then ripped off the gloves and threw them into a bin.

'Now I need to scan your uterus,' he said, pulling a trolley with what looked like a laptop on it alongside the examination couch. He switched on the screen and the invasion began again, only this time with a probe.

Ruth shut her eyes until it was over. 'Was everything OK?' she asked.

His expression was non-committal. 'Take a moment or two to get dressed, then we can talk.'

Ruth pulled on her clothes, newly aware of the slackness of her flesh, then sat down opposite him, suddenly nervous.

'Mrs Furnival,' he placed a hand on his heart then bowed, 'on examination everything seemed normal.' He smiled and Ruth exhaled. 'However, the scan shows a small mass in the muscular wall of your uterus that bothers me.' She could feel the blood draining from her face. He said quickly, 'Don't worry, it's benign.

A fibroid, and one in three women of your age has at least one. But if it bulges into the uterine cavity even slightly and distorts the surface it could prevent implantation of an embryo, which would rule you out as a host.'

He couldn't see that level of detail on his machine, so he was going to organise a three-dimensional scan of her endometrial cavity at a specialist centre; and because she was in a hurry, it would make sense if the other tests happened in tandem. Counselling sessions were available the following day and, if the whole family could attend and there were no issues, then the screening appointments could start straight away. Ruth thanked him for moving so quickly.

'You're a brave woman, offering to do this.'

'If an expert like you can renovate my womb so that Lauren can borrow it for a few months, it feels like a no-brainer.'

He smiled. 'You're very kind. And your husband, he feels the same, does he?'

Ruth was so taken aback by the question that she told the truth: 'He doesn't know.' Dr Vassily began to smooth his moustache with thumb and index finger in a repetitive movement that made him seem less confident, nervous even. Ruth recovered fast. 'What I mean is, Adam is *hugely* supportive, in principle, but doesn't know precisely where we've got to in this . . . process.'

'I see.' He was looking at her hard. 'But he'll be able to come here and sign our consent form?'

'I'm not sure,' said Ruth, unclasping the clip in her hair to gather up a strand that had escaped, then re-fastening it. 'His job doesn't really allow for . . . interruptions.'

'Then we have a problem, Mrs Furnival.' The doctor's fingers were on the moustache again. 'Because I need his signature, and without that I cannot treat you. The law in this area is complex – some might say perverse – but it gives him shared legal rights and responsibilities for any child you give birth to. If, God forbid,' he crossed himself extravagantly, 'your daughter and her husband died or refused to take the baby, then you and he would be obliged to shoulder the burden. And unless I have his prior agreement, he could sue me for impregnating you without his knowledge.'

'Dr Vassily, my husband and I take these issues very seriously. He's a lawyer himself.'

He lifted his arms towards the ceiling. 'Even *more* reason to tick all the boxes, because he will know the rules!' Then he grinned conspiratorially and leant towards her, confiding, 'It's all about mitigating risk: we have to watch our step, you know. This industry is a minefield. One false step and the HFEA would withdraw my licence, or I could find myself up before the General Medical Council. Neither would be good for business, so I have to cover my tracks.' An odd expression, thought Ruth, but perversely encouraging: he was a man who ducked and dived.

She nodded. 'I promise I'll bring my husband here as soon as possible, but at the moment he's so busy he barely sleeps.' Ruth gazed at him earnestly. 'Is there any way you can be a *little* bit flexible at this stage – about the timing of his counselling session, for example?'

'Of course. At the Marinella we pride ourselves on being patient-centred. We'll work round your husband's availability, but I do need that signature.' One of his eyes narrowed: she wondered if he was winking.

Ruth stood and gathered her coat and bag, Dr Vassily scrambled from his chair and held open the door.

Lauren and Dan were waiting in the lobby. 'We're on to the next stage,' said Ruth. Her phone bleeped again and she peered at it: another text from Bella.

Have tried you 5x Where ARE you?
Please pick up!

93

She sighed and stuffed it back in her pocket. 'Let's find Helen and fix some appointments with the counsellor?'

Adam had a feeling that secrets were being kept: a physical sensation that warned of calamity to come. He'd learnt to recognise the signs when his father was terminally ill: his mother too busy to engage with him, the evasive eyes of other adults, disruption of the familiar rhythm of the days. In this case, though, he was being irrational, because the catastrophe had already happened. The baby had died, Lauren was grief-stricken and Ruth had dropped everything to comfort her. It all made sense, but Ruth had been preoccupied and evasive for several days – the way she was when one of her projects was threatening to collapse and she needed all her energy to hold it together. She was either out with Lauren or in her study with the door shut, almost as if she was avoiding him. He crept down to his study at one in the morning and called Alex. When she was a teenager they hadn't talked much: she'd been spiky, and critical of everything he stood for – he'd been closer to Lauren, who was sometimes happy to snuggle up on the sofa to watch an old film, play music with him, or go for a stroll along the river – but over the past six years he and Alex had developed an affectionate long-distance rapport and often spoke when he was working late and she was at the office in the afternoon.

'Hey,' she began, briskly American. 'You OK?'

'Sleepless in suburbia,' said Adam.

'Where's Mum?'

'Upstairs. Dead to the world.'

'You poor old thing. Hold on and I'll find a meeting space, so we can talk properly.' A succession of corridors, cornices and carpets tumbled across the screen until she re-materialised, leaning against a brilliant green wall. 'So how's it going back in the homeland?' Alex stared up into the camera so that her big brown eyes looked straight into his. She'd inherited Ruth's brand of shrewdly applied empathy, which drove you to unburden yourself, sometimes more than you wanted or was entirely good for you.

'Not much to report, except I've been toying with the idea of applying to be a judge.'

Alex's eyes widened. 'Wow, that's a surprise! You'd be brilliant: his Honour Judge Furnival.' She bowed extravagantly towards the camera.

Adam shook his head. 'I haven't made a decision yet. It's very competitive and there'll be tons of applicants.'

'Do you have to preside at a mock trial to prove you're judgemental enough to get the gig?'

'Nothing so melodramatic,' laughed Adam. There was a long online process, followed by presentations and an interview – if he got that far. 'In order to apply I'd need to spend hours filling in forms, doing research and finding referees. I'm not sure it's worth all the effort.'

'But you'd look so cool in a shoulder-length wig.' Alex laughed, then she leant into the camera. 'Seriously, Dad, you should give it a go, you've had years of stress and all-nighters and you deserve a break. What does Mum think?'

'We haven't discussed it, at least not in any depth. To tell you the truth I've not seen her much recently. She's been so busy.'

'Working?' The eyes narrowed and waited.

'No. With Lauren, who's still very cut up about, you know . . . '

'The miscarriage?'

'Yes.' Adam sighed and lowered his voice. 'Bit depressed, in fact, according to your mum, who's taken quite a bit of time off work to be with her.'

'*That's* a first.'

'Precisely,' said Adam. 'And it worries me.'

'But you've not talked to Lauren yourself?'

'I want to, but your mother has said to wait for a while. She's keen for Lauren to explore the idea of surrogacy in London, and I suspect she thinks I'd try to put her off.'

'Have you seen Dan?'

'Not since the day they lost the baby.' Adam shifted in his chair. 'I've wondered whether I should get in touch. What do you think?'

'You could suggest a drink after work, just the two of you, offer a bit of male bonding.'

'You don't think he'd find it intrusive?'

'He can always say no, and it never hurts to reach out, does it?'

Adam smiled. 'You sound so American. I've never reached out to anyone in my life.' He made a note on the pad on his desk, then yawned. 'What have you been up to?'

Nothing much, Alex told him. She'd done a big presentation about a new software product she'd developed and it had gone well: the CEO had congratulated her and her boss had talked about a possible promotion. The outdoor markets were awash with pumpkins and apples and the maple leaves were on the turn in Golden Gate Park. It would be Christmas in no time: she needed to get a move on and book her flight home; in fact, she would do it right now. She blew him a kiss and was gone.

Adam felt for Dan. Since the menopause Ruth was less volatile and it was a relief to have the turbulent hormonal years over and done with, but Dan was still in the thick of it, and he'd borne the brunt of Lauren's unhappiness. He never talked about it, or complained, but it couldn't have been easy. Ruth said he'd had to give her daily injections for months on end, and he'd dealt with the mood swings, and shouldered the terrible grief every time she lost a baby. Adam didn't feel close to him: football was their only mutual interest, and at matches they talked about work, and whatever was in the news. He always made sure to ask after Dan's mum; she'd had cancer and recovered, but Adam could sense that he still worried about her.

He picked up his phone. He was unsure of the digital vernacular for communicating with sons-in-law. After several attempts he typed:

> Can I buy you a drink one evening
> this week? All the very best, Adam

As an afterthought he added:

> PS I hope your mother is
> keeping well

He checked his messages. One from Alex:

> Good to talk. Now go back to
> sleep Dad! Xxx

Another, from Guy, his tennis partner:

> Court free this Sat 3 p.m. – worth
> having a warm-up for Sunday?

And one from Emily about their current case:

> Some useful stuff in latest
> prosecution disclosures – have
> sent you highlights.

He switched on his computer. Her email, sent at half past midnight, had ten attachments; he'd open them in the morning. Emily was a godsend: she had a brilliant mind and worked like a Trojan. Occasionally she acted as his junior on the bigger cases and they made a great team. Colleagues envied him, he knew.

Recently they'd fallen into the habit of staying late a couple of nights a week to gossip, talk through the fine detail of the current case and split a decent bottle. Adam looked forward to it: she could deliver pitch-perfect imitations of judges, barristers and clients that left him weak with laughter, and it was clear that she liked and admired him, which was a tonic. He was careful to stay the right side of the line (and tried hard not to imagine what it might be like to step over it). Adam and Ruth: indissoluble – Emily understood that.

9

Ruth's one-to-one counselling session took place immediately after Lauren and Dan's. The room looked identical to the others at the clinic, except for the boxes of tissues: two on the coffee table and four plastic-wrapped multi-packs on the floor in a corner. She wondered whether the absence of tears might count against her and resolved to emote vigorously. Vanessa, the Implications Counsellor (tall, thin, fortyish and dressed entirely in brown), unfolded herself from an orange chair and extended a hand.

'Lovely to meet you, Mrs Furnival.'

'Please call me Ruth. It's so kind of you to fit us in at twenty-four hours' notice.'

'It's a pleasure. Dr Vassily has explained that your husband,' she glanced at her notes, 'Adam, isn't it? Will be coming in later on, but we can get all the other sessions out of the way today. When you and I have finished talking Lauren and Dan will join us for a three-way session and then we'll be done.' Vanessa slotted forms into the clipboard on her lap. 'With any family arrangement like yours a lot of what I have to go through will be a formality, but I need to satisfy myself that you understand the potential challenges and are equipped to deal with them.'

Vanessa began by asking Ruth about the experience of having

Lauren and Alex: how had she felt about the changes in her body, the babies, and the transition to motherhood? How had Adam reacted?

'Both times it was very straightforward – I *loved* being pregnant and Adam was so thrilled to be a father. He doesn't show his emotions much, but he cried when the girls were born. In fact we both cried buckets.' Ruth described their childcare arrangements, how she and Adam had taken it in turns to get up at night, and how he'd always done more than his share: they'd handled it as a team and she couldn't have kept working without his support.

The counsellor nodded and looked down at a typed sheet. 'Any other pregnancies: miscarriages, terminations?'

'No miscarriages and both times I got pregnant very quickly, which must be helpful in terms of hosting one of Lauren's embryos?' Vanessa nodded and made a note. Ruth hesitated, but they'd already requested a copy of her NHS notes, so it would be odd not to mention it. 'And when I was a teenager I had an early termination, but it didn't damage my uterus, otherwise I'd have had problems with the girls.' She bit her lip. 'I've never discussed it with them, though, and I wouldn't want Lauren to—'

'Everything in this room stays confidential, Ruth,' said Vanessa. She paused, head tilted to one side, expression solicitous. 'That must have been a very big thing for you to deal with. Yes?'

Ruth shrugged. 'It was an accident and I was very young, so it was the only option. I've never regretted it or felt guilty.'

'Did your parents know?' Vanessa was in serious danger of overdoing the eye contact.

Ruth gave an involuntary bark of laughter. 'No. My mum was a bit of a religious fanatic and an awful lot of things *weren't* discussed in my family, which is probably the reason I got pregnant in the first place.'

The counsellor's eyes were unwavering. 'And the father?'

'He was aware, but I barely knew him and we split up soon afterwards. I pretty much handled it on my own.'

'A lonely time, then?' Vanessa slid the box of tissues towards Ruth, who resisted the temptation to push them back, hard. 'And later on, when you and Adam met, did you tell him about it?'

'Yes, of course.' Ruth hadn't foreseen this. 'Sorry, Vanessa, can I just clarify. Is there a risk that my having had an abortion *decades* ago is going to disqualify me from being Lauren's surrogate?'

'Not in the *least*.' The counsellor crossed her legs towards Ruth as if for emphasis. 'I'm simply trying to get a full picture of your reproductive history. Previous experiences sometimes leave psychological scars, and scar tissue can break down when it comes under stress.' She smiled reassuringly. 'But what I'm hearing is that you don't think it's an issue for you?' Eventually she moved on, asking Ruth how she would describe her relationship with Lauren.

'Good, on the whole,' said Ruth, aware that untrammelled candour might be counter-productive. 'At least that's what I'd like to think. The teenage years are always a bit turbulent with girls, aren't they, but I'd say we're closer now.' She was thankful to discover from the counsellor that Lauren had said more or less the same.

What if the first implantation didn't succeed? asked Vanessa. How would they all cope if Ruth failed to get pregnant within the critical three-month window?

'I start from the assumption that this whole thing *will* work, because that's how I operate. But if it doesn't pan out, then maybe we could find a clinic abroad that doesn't have an upper age limit.'

'How would you say you've handled episodes of failure in your life so far?'

Ruth relaxed: she was back on safe ground, this was the stuff of platform discussions at conferences and training away-days and she could steer clear of the danger zones.

*

101

Lauren and Dan's session with the counsellor had been gruelling: an hour-long exploration of their fertility history and the
impact it had had on them. While Ruth was having her appointment, they escaped from the clinic and sought refuge in a little
Spanish café on the edge of Fitzrovia. Dan went in first: it was
dark inside and almost empty, no children or pregnant women.
In the aftermath of a miscarriage, the sight of a mitten on the
floor or a breastfeeding mother could undo Lauren. He beckoned
her in. They ordered coffee and two little custard tarts at the
counter, then found a wooden booth at the back.

They sat side by side in silence for a while, then he said, 'How
are you doing?' He was staring at the table.

'Wrung out.' Lauren wrapped her hands around her mug,
craving the warmth.

'I know. I'm shattered.' He leant forward on his elbows, chin
cupped in his hands. 'It feels as if we've been doing this ever
since we got married, doesn't it? Sitting in cafés after counselling appointments, waiting for results, processing bad news.
Sometimes I wonder—' He broke off.

'What?'

Dan hesitated, then said, 'Maybe we're just not meant to have
kids?' He turned to look at her, his face grey and empty. 'And
maybe we should stop all this now. There's no *way* Ruth's going
to be able to host our baby, so what's the point of raking over
everything and upsetting ourselves?'

'No, Dan, those are *my* lines.' She stroked his cheek. 'Whenever
I come out with stuff like that you always tell me not to give up,
don't you?' He looked exhausted and Lauren felt a wave of guilt:
overwhelmed by her own grief, she'd scarcely considered the toll
the baby's death must have taken on him.

He kissed her forehead. 'To be honest, I can't really think
straight any more.'

'Same!' She threaded her fingers between his. 'Everything's

happening *way* too fast. Part of me wants to shout, "Leave me alone, I've just had a miscarriage, I need to cry."' She put her forehead against his. 'But we don't have time, do we? We *have* to keep going, and believe we'll get there, one day.'

Dan saw the desperate energy she was putting into being positive against all the odds, and it made him want to weep; he dreaded the moment when reality hit and her hopes lay in tatters again. 'I suppose so,' was the best he could manage.

After that they sat in silence for a while, riffling through the day's newspapers, until it was time to return to the counselling room for their joint session with Ruth. As they walked up Gower Street in a light drizzle Dan said, 'I meant to say, your dad messaged me yesterday and asked me to go for a pint with him.'

'That's nice of him.'

He grimaced. 'Bit awkward, under the circumstances.'

'He's trying to be supportive, maybe Mum asked him to get in touch.'

'Whatever, I don't feel comfortable seeing him right now, not when we're doing stuff behind his back. Which, incidentally, I hate. What shall I say?'

'That you're tired and can it wait – which is the truth, isn't it?'

Dan said, 'I'll say I'm snowed under at work for the next few weeks and suggest we go to an Arsenal match together when things get easier.'

'Good plan.' Lauren threaded her arm through his. 'He loves it when you go with him – it makes up for the fact that he's saddled with two daughters who've never shown the slightest interest.'

'I like going. He takes an interest in my work and always asks how my mum's doing.'

'Do you ever talk about the IVF?' asked Lauren.

Dan thought for a moment. 'Not really. I don't raise it and neither does he. He always asks how you are, but if ever I say you've been upset or depressed, he changes the subject pretty quickly. It's as if he can't cope with it.' He looked down at Lauren. 'Does that make any sense?'

'Completely. My theory is that he's repressed every powerful feeling he's had since his dad died, which is why he chose to marry someone at the opposite end of the emotional spectrum.' They were outside the clinic and Lauren glanced at her phone. 'She's been in there almost an hour. Let's hope she's worked her magic on the counsellor.'

When Lauren and Dan arrived Vanessa took the three of them through a succession of scenarios. How many embryos would they want to be transferred? The higher the number, the greater the chance that one would implant, but if two or three stayed the course, then Ruth could find herself carrying twins or triplets, which would mean a much greater medical risk.

Ruth looked at Lauren and Dan. 'I'm sorry, but that would be the stuff of nightmares.'

'Agreed,' said Lauren. 'We want to minimise the chances of anything bad happening to Mum, so just one embryo.'

Vanessa turned to Ruth. 'And supposing Lauren and Dan separated, or changed their minds? Or died? The baby would be yours and you'd be responsible – how would you cope?'

Ruth suppressed an incredulous smile. 'Their marriage has been tested to destruction and it's rock solid. But if something terrible happened to them, then of course Adam and I would step in and bring up the child as our own.'

Lauren and Dan were asked what they'd do if Ruth became critically ill during the pregnancy, or the baby died. They agreed that Ruth's welfare would take priority; and they hoped that, if they ended up losing yet another child, they'd find the strength to cope.

'And what if your mother kept the baby?'

Lauren and Dan stared at her in astonishment.

'I'm sorry?' said Ruth, before they could reply. She felt a surge of irritation. 'Are you suggesting I might kidnap my own grandchild?'

Vanessa explained that she was obliged to ask the question because Ruth and Adam would be the baby's legal parents: both of them would have to agree to hand it over before the courts would recognise Lauren and Dan as its mother and father. Sometimes people changed their minds, she told them.

'I *know*,' interjected Lauren. 'That's why we want Mum to be our surrogate, to eliminate that risk.'

'Precisely,' added Ruth drily.

Vanessa moved on: how would they react if a baby Ruth was carrying turned out to have a genetic or developmental abnormality?

'It would be entirely up to these two.' Ruth turned to Lauren and Dan. 'It would be heartbreaking, of course, but I assume that you'd want to terminate and try again? Not ideal, by any means, but I think I could cope, if time was on our side.'

'Kill our baby?' Lauren flinched as if she'd been hit. She looked at Ruth with an expression of horror, then at Dan, for support.

He shook his head. 'No way, Ruth.' His face had a pinched, implacable hardness that reminded Ruth of her mother's. 'If there's even the slightest chance of us going ahead you need to understand that we'd *never* go down that road.' He reached for Lauren's hand.

Ruth could feel her cheeks burning. 'OK, but there's no need to jump down my throat.' She was furious with herself for disrupting the united front they'd managed to present until now. 'As I said, it would be *your* choice and I'd go along with whatever you wanted.' She felt as if she'd been judged, and found wanting.

'Everyone brings their own emotional baggage to these

scenarios,' said Vanessa. 'That's why it's so important to understand and discuss *all* the possible issues before starting treatment.' She was looking at Ruth with an infuriating little smile, as if their disagreement was a vindication of her role. 'Which brings us neatly to the paperwork.' She gave them the clinic's consent forms plus a sheaf of explanatory leaflets. 'If you do decide to go ahead, please sign the forms and return them to us as soon as possible.'

'I'm up for it,' said Ruth, 'and I'll get Adam to come in when he can. How about you two?' She looked at Lauren, who turned to Dan.

Dan took a deep breath. 'Yes,' he said. 'We're on board.'

'Excellent,' said Vanessa. 'One last thing, the Marinella Clinic advises both sides in a surrogacy arrangement to take independent legal advice and draw up a watertight arrangement.'

Ruth nodded politely. 'I'm sure that makes perfect sense under normal circumstances, but as we're family,' she turned to Lauren and Dan with an amused frown, 'I don't think we'll be needing a contract, do you?'

'Of course not,' said Lauren.

'In any case,' added Dan, 'if we ever did need help in that area we could call on Lauren's Dad. He's a barrister.'

Vanessa smiled. 'It's your call,' she said. 'You're clearly a close family with high levels of trust, and I've no doubt you'd make a wonderful host, Ruth. That's what I'll be saying in my report.'

Helen Braithwaite was waiting in the lobby with details of several screening appointments she'd already managed to fix; she said she'd be in touch about the others later. When they got outside Ruth suggested they go for a drink to celebrate, but Lauren and Dan demurred. Like adults restraining an overexcited child, they told her not to get her hopes up.

'One quick gin and tonic?' pleaded Ruth. 'As a reward

for surviving Vanessa's interrogation and all those ghastly scenarios.'

Dan shook his head. 'We used to celebrate, years ago, when we started IVF, but after a while we realised that if you build things up, it's that much worse when the bad news comes.'

Lauren said, 'In any case, Mum, gin's off the menu from now on.'

'I'm sorry?' said Ruth, bridling.

'I didn't drink any alcohol the whole time we were trying to get pregnant, that's what the specialists recommend.'

Really, thought Ruth, what a miracle, then, that she'd drunk her way through two pregnancies yet still managed to produce live, healthy babies. But she said, 'Of course, darling, if this goes ahead you and Dan will be in the driving seat. Completely.'

'I've got a list of other things to avoid and supplements to take in the pre-conception phase; I'll email it to you,' said Lauren. 'You can have all the stuff I didn't finish, because it would be best to start straight away, OK?'

Ruth nodded. She realised she'd have to get used to being bossed around from now on because that was the only way Lauren could maintain any semblance of control as she watched her reproductive role being taken over. She resolved to bite her lip, however annoying it might become.

Ruth couldn't face going into the office afterwards, she was too distracted by the excitement of it all and wanted time to think, so she headed straight home. In her study she read through the two consent forms Vanessa had given her: pages of legalistic text about parental status, risks to physical and mental health, legal implications, financial matters, emotional impact, and the provision of counselling. They needed initialling every so often and signing at the end. She filled out hers, then signed and dated it. Adam's lay waiting, like an unanswered question, and she felt a sudden, awful temptation to forge his signature and post it back to the clinic with her own, another obstacle out of the way. But it was out of the question: if he found out he'd be livid – it might be something else he couldn't forget or forgive. And in any case, it was wrong. She would get him to do it himself, when the moment was right. In the meantime, she needed a hiding place.

She chose her father's big family Bible, the oldest book in her study, a fat brown bundle of mottled pages covered in cracked leather, its spine broken in several places; it smelled sour and dusty. The blank pages at the front and back were criss-crossed with copper-plate writing: a record of all the weddings, births and deaths, from the early nineteenth century up until her parents' marriage. Scores of different hands had borne witness to their lives then passed the volume down, through generations of Jagos.

When she was little the Bible had occupied a whole shelf of the big bookcase in the front room of their house, alongside the encyclopaedias and her dad's motoring magazines, piled up in date order to fill the remaining space. Her mother didn't like having the Bible in the house, said it was filthy and full of dust mites, but when she was out Ruth would heave it off the shelf and sit with it on her lap, poring over the lists, marvelling at their antiquity and portentousness. She'd imagined her ancestors lifting their pens to record the ebb and flow of life as new babies opened their lungs, or coffins were nailed shut; she struggled to pronounce the more unfamiliar names, *Thursa, Ephraim, Keturah*; and was alarmed by the brevity of some of the sepia lives that had preceded hers.

She imagined Lauren or Alex coming across it when they cleared the house after she was dead. Would they keep it, or give it to a charity shop? She'd never shown it to them – or Adam – and she hadn't recorded her own marriage or their births. It had never occurred to her, and now she wondered why. But it was just as well: there was no chance anyone would stumble on the forms. She folded them both, tucked them between the Book of Job and Psalms, then replaced the Bible. The skin on the backs of her hands itched, the way it used to all those years ago. Before she could stop herself, she scratched until they were red and sore: the dust mites. She washed her hands, returned to the study and consulted the To Do list she'd made on the train. Bella was the priority.

Ruth called her. 'I'm sorry I've been so elusive, but before I explain why, I just wanted to check something. I never heard back from you about Anya, so can I assume my multiple transatlantic calls did the trick?'

'Oops, I meant to message you. You're a miracle worker: suddenly she loved all the scenes she'd hated before. Said the new version had "a truly momentous and inevitable quality – almost Tolstoyan". You fed her that line, didn't you?'

'Might have,' said Ruth. 'You know me, in a crisis reach for the hyperbole and gush till they start inhaling.' Bella laughed: she sounded like her old self, and Ruth seized her moment. 'I know I've been out of the office and rather unavailable lately, and I feel very bad about it, but as I've explained Lauren needs help, and I'm afraid I need to take the next couple of weeks off.' She paused. 'I realise the timing's a bit tricky—'

'It's *massively* tricky.' There was dismay in Bella's voice. 'I'm stuck in the cutting room and we're *so* behind on script development. I've been counting on you to galvanise the team so we can get something commissioned.'

'I know that, and I'm sorry,' Ruth cut in, 'but this *has* to be my priority.' She wished she could explain what was going on – after twenty-five years at the sharp end of programme making they were old friends and had always been open with one another – but it wouldn't be right, not when she hadn't told Adam. She searched for words that were not untruthful. 'We're going to see some specialists and get some tests – it's complicated.' She paused. 'I've never asked for anything like this before and I wouldn't now, unless I had to.'

'I get that. It's just that we're *so* exposed, financially.' Before launching the company, they'd secured enough investment to pay the salaries of their team of six for the first four years, while they both lived off their savings. Now that money was gone and they needed to get two series commissioned within weeks if they were to stay solvent. Bella's voice was pleading. 'Do you need to go to *all* the appointments? Couldn't you come in at least some of the time?'

Ruth was torn but she steeled herself not to compromise: she had to keep her diary empty in case there were follow-up tests. 'I will if I can, but it depends on the Lauren situation. This last miscarriage was her seventh, can you *imagine* what that must be like?'

Silence, then Bella said in a different tone, 'I'm sorry, I'm being selfish. We'll manage. I'll have all the scripts emailed to you when we get new drafts and you can read them in your gaps. Come back when you can, and give Lauren my love.'

'*Thank you*, darling.' Ruth felt a wave of relief, only slightly beaded with guilt.

10

'The probe they use in a 3D ultrasound is fatter than the one you had at your first scan – in my fertility chat room everyone calls it the dildo wand – but it's the same routine as before: they cover it with a kind of condom, smear it with lubricating gel, then put it into your vagina.' Lauren's voice was matter-of-fact.

In all her imagining of life as a mother, Ruth had never conjured up this scene, in the waiting room of a London clinic, where she was being coached by her daughter in preparation for an intimate investigation that might pave the way to being pregnant with her first grandchild. Over the previous ten days, as the two of them had sat side by side in a succession of laboratories and examination cubicles north of Oxford Street, a subtle role reversal had begun: Lauren was taking over – instructing, coaching, explaining, insisting. Ruth realised it was inevitable, but she wasn't used to it. For most of her adult life *she'd* been the one in control, directing whatever drama was under way at work or at home; here, though, she was merely a potential reproductive receptacle for her daughter, and her own ideas and opinions counted less and less. She smiled and nodded while Lauren lectured, because she loved her and this was what she'd signed up for, but she was privately dismayed by how ancillary and invisible it made her feel.

She knew that any of the tests might reveal tumours skulking in her deepest recesses, unsuspected diseases, or scarred and furry arteries ripe for heart attacks. So far, she'd been to nine appointments, but today's was in some ways the most critical: if the lump in her uterus was in the wrong place, or turned out to be something more sinister than a fibroid, it would rule her out as potential host. Lauren was a veteran of the procedure. 'It isn't painful at all,' she told her mother, then she hesitated. 'I'm happy to go in with you, but I understand if you don't want me there.'

'No, come,' said Ruth. 'But stay at the head end, won't you? No daughter needs to see her elderly mother's genitals – that way madness lies.' They were briefly hysterical: it was a relief to laugh.

There was a bonus: the sonographer who showed them into the cubicle was a middle-aged woman. Lauren pulled up a chair next to the examination couch and held her mother's hand as the probe was inserted. All three women stared as the grey land-scape of Ruth's pelvis appeared on the screen.

'Apparently there's a small mass in the wall of my uterus. Is it going to be a problem, do you think?' said Ruth, trying to sound conversational.

'Depends what you mean by a problem.' The sonographer was making marks on the screen and calculating measurements between them. 'Why do you ask?'

'I'm trying to get pregnant.'

She paused and looked down at Ruth. 'Oh, I see,' she said, with professional impassivity.

Ruth blushed. She could read the woman's mind: well past her sell-by date, but must have a baby at all costs; more money than sense; *selfish*.

'Not for myself. Not *my* baby.' Ruth's voice was sharp with

112

pre-emption and louder than she'd intended. 'It's for my daughter, because she can't—'

Ruth, turning her head, saw Lauren flinch, eyes bright with tears, and was ashamed of her vanity. She tried again: 'Lauren and her husband have frozen embryos, I'd be the incubator. We want to know if my equipment's still in working order and whether there's anything to stop us going ahead.'

The sonographer stared at them both, recalibrating, then turned back to the screen. Her voice softened. 'The lining of your womb is three millimetres, which is normal if you're post-menopausal, and there's a fibroid measuring three centimetres.'

'And is the cavity smooth enough to allow an embryo to implant?'

'This computer will generate a 3D image from all the pictures I'm taking and your consultant will look at it and make a judgement. I can't comment, I'm afraid.'

Was she trying to prepare them for bad news?

Afterwards they went for a quick lunch in an Italian restaurant south of Oxford Street. As they entered, laden with carrier bags, Ruth was spotted by the boss of a rival independent TV production company. There were kisses, introductions and avowals to do lunch soon *promise*, before they managed to find a table out of earshot.

'The competition?' asked Lauren.

'Charlotte Floode. She's lovely, but she gossips for Britain.' Ruth groaned. 'It'll get back to Bella, who was totally supportive when I asked for this time off, but now sounds more stressed and frantic every time she calls me. She'll think I'm bunking off.'

'Oh Mum, this is all because of me. I'm so sorry.'

'Don't be, it's my fault: I'm cross with myself because I should have handled her better.' Ruth paused. 'The truth is – and I never thought I'd say it – compared with what you and I are doing, that whole world – scripts, egos, audience figures – seems so trivial. Unreal, almost.'

Lauren stared. 'But you love it.'

Ruth thought for a moment. 'Maybe, but doing this,' she spread her arms as if to embrace their joint enterprise, 'and being with you, it feels like the most important thing I've done for *years*.'

As she spoke, she realised it was true. During the long gaps between appointments, they'd whiled away their days in cafés and shops: it was probably the longest time they'd spent alone together since Lauren was a baby. When the girls were growing up Ruth had always been preoccupied with work, or managing the house, and on holidays everyone was together all the time. Now they talked freely and without interruption: Lauren described the wild teenage parties she and Alex had held when Ruth and Adam went away for weekends, and how she'd once drunk herself insensible in Ravenscourt Park as a fifteen-year-old: her friends thought she was dead and she was ambulanced to A&E. 'When I look back I realise what a bitch I was a lot of the time, I'm sorry, Mum.'

Ruth reciprocated with tales of the battles she'd fought with her mother and her own secret life as a teenager. She described Angela Jago's religious terror of sex before marriage and her scare stories about the pill that had put Ruth off taking it for years.

Lauren said, 'In my first year at college I took morning-after pills like Smarties, because no one liked using condoms. I'm not proud of it, but they were free, and easy to take. The downside was you had to find a different pharmacy every time so as not to feel judged by the assistants. I ended up going on the pill, but I hated the way it made me feel, so maybe Granny was right? Looking back, the side effects were like a rehearsal for fertility treatment.'

Ruth nodded. 'I *know*, that horrible bloating, as if your body doesn't quite belong to you any more, and not having proper periods. I only took it for a couple of years and I was so glad to stop.'

'What did you use?'

'Nothing,' said Ruth, 'I didn't have to. Your dad had a vasectomy, years ago.'

Lauren's eyes widened. 'Wow, good for him. Even now you don't get many men volunteering to take responsibility for contraception. It must have been an amazing thing to do, back then. Plus he hates hospitals, so it was brave.'

'I suppose,' said Ruth dubiously. 'To be frank I've never thought of it like that.'

'You should be grateful. I'm not sure Dan would be up for having the snip. Not that he'd ever need it, having chosen a wife with a useless uterus.'

Ruth touched Lauren's arm. 'Stop beating yourself up, darling. You always make it sound as though it's your fault, when it's just horribly bad luck.'

Lauren looked at her bleakly. 'I wanted children so badly. *Much* more than I ever wanted to make it big as an artist. When it didn't happen it was like being mugged, over and over again. It was so different for you, you fancied some kids and, bingo, along they came, no big deal, move on to the next thing.' She paused. 'Don't get me wrong, I'm not blaming you.'

'I sense a "but" coming?' Ruth tilted her head.

Lauren frowned, as if she was trying to disentangle a knot of thoughts. 'It's strange, I've never felt that I'm in competition with you before. You're my mum and we're very different – Alex is much more like you – but sitting there over the past few days, watching you being measured up for the role I've failed at . . . it's really hard not to be overwhelmed by a kind of resentment, it's almost physical.'

'I do know.' Ruth scrunched her face in sympathy and reached out again, but this time Lauren pulled away.

'No offence, Mum, but you *really* don't. You don't know what it's like to be pregnant and so terrified of finding blood in the toilet bowl that you stop peeing and wind up with recurrent bladder infections. Or the feeling when a baby's falling out of you and you can't do anything to stop it. Or crying, year after year, on the due dates of all the children who never arrived.' Her voice rose. 'And the other day, when that counsellor asked what we'd do if the foetus was handicapped, you just went, "terminate and try again".' Now her expression was hostile. 'Don't you realise how precious *any* baby would be to Dan and me, after what we've been through?'

She was clenching her fists, as if trying to batten down an uncontainable fury; her face was like Adam's during the argument at the restaurant, full of righteous indignation. Ruth flinched. 'I'm doing my best here, Lauren. Everyone draws their ethical boundaries in different places, don't they? If I end up carrying your baby, I'll do whatever you want, I've said that repeatedly.' She paused. 'And, just for the record, I may put my foot in it sometimes, but I *do* understand.'

They stared at one another, both of them close to tears. Then Lauren reached out and squeezed her mother's hand. 'I'm sorry,' she said. It was over, but Ruth was left shaken.

On Saturday morning they headed back to Harley Street for the final test, an Exercise ECG to assess the strength of Ruth's heart. The young male doctor, tanned, lean and Australian, covered her chest and back with electrodes then asked her to step on to a treadmill.

'If you feel any pain or discomfort stop right away and grab the handrail – we don't want any accidents. Off you go, but take it gently, Mrs Furnival.'

Ruth broke into a furious sprint. Her hair came adrift from its slide and streamed behind her. After five minutes he told her to stop and the treadmill slowed. As she got off, the doctor tore a printout from the machine and grinned at her. 'A fellow runner, yeah?'

Ruth bent forward to catch her breath, then straightened up. 'I run a bit.'

'Understatement, I reckon.' He asked her to sit down while he removed the electrodes. 'Amazing ECG for someone your age.' He shook her hand and winked at her. 'Respect, Ruth.'

'Yuk,' said Lauren on the doorstep of the clinic. 'What a creep. He was coming on to you, Mum.'

'Nonsense,' said Ruth, trying not to sound gratified.

'Lunch?' asked Lauren.

'I'd love to but I can't. Sheila and Simon are coming to supper so I have to shop and cook.'

'Give my godmother a big hug,' said Lauren. 'Does she know I was pregnant, or about the miscarriage?'

'No, we've not talked in ages.'

'You can tell her if you want.' Lauren sighed. 'Everyone's going to have to know at some point, but right now I can't face all the cards and messages and flowers and sympathy. Again.'

'Let's hope these test results go our way, darling.'

'Please don't say that,' Lauren was staring at the pavement, 'it's tempting fate.' As they walked to the Tube she reached into her pocket. 'I've still got your phone. Dad's rung a few times.'

Ruth looked at the screen:

Tried calling but no response. Are
you with L? Is she OK?

Lauren arrived home in Brockley to find Dan sprawled full length on one of the sofas in the sitting room while a Premiership football match played itself out on a huge plasma screen on the opposite wall. They were trying to economise because Lauren hadn't earned anything since the miscarriage, but Dan had so far resisted cancelling the Sky subscription. She bent to kiss him, and he pulled her down until she lay alongside him.

'How was it?' he said, pushing back her hair. Her face was polished pink by the cold. She burrowed her head into his chest and he had to strain to catch the words.

'I feel as if I don't exist.'

'What?'

'Traipsing round London while my mum gets tested to see if she can have a baby for me – because I'm so *useless*. Sitting there watching, while doctors tell her how strong and healthy she is.'

Dan hugged her hard, trying to squeeze away the sadness. 'Laurie, remember the chances are that Ruth won't be suitable, so stop beating yourself up. You're not useless, you're wonderful and I'll always love you, whatever happens. You know that.' There was a roar from the screen and he glanced over her shoulder to catch the replay of a goal.

Lauren extricated herself and stood up. 'I know. I'm just saying, if she gets pregnant then I'm going to have to deal with major womb envy.' She attempted a smile at her own joke.

Dan looked up at her, frowning. 'But I thought that was what you wanted, for your mum to get pregnant with our baby?'

'Yes, of course I want it, but I feel like my whole *life* is getting rubbed out in the process.' She left the room and he heard her feet, heavy on the stairs, as she went up to her studio.

Dan closed his eyes, exhaled and opened them again. He wasn't sure he could take much more. It had been blindingly obvious to him that getting Ruth involved was a bad idea, and now Lauren was beginning to understand why. Maybe he should have followed his gut and vetoed it, right from the start? That way she wouldn't be upsetting herself now, for no reason. He couldn't wait for the moment when the clinic pulled the plug, then they could take a break from this madness. He picked up the remote to boost the volume and went back to the match.

11

In the kitchen, wrapped in her apron, Ruth was in her element. On the counter next to the chopping board, fruit and vegetables were ranged in harvest festival profusion. She hummed to herself as she whipped egg whites to stiff peaks and anointed a pork fillet in an oily poultice of garlic and herbs. She couldn't wait to see Sheila: there was so much to tell. She melted butter and dark brown sugar in a heavy pan and began frying slices of apple in the treacly froth. Adam was drawn to the kitchen by the smell of caramel.

'You seem happy,' he said. 'What's brought this on?'

'Oh . . . I don't know; everything, I suppose.' Then she checked herself, remembering his text. 'Sorry, my phone was out of battery this morning, so I've only just seen your message. I think Lauren's feeling a bit better.' She beamed, lifting a chunk of apple from the pan, blowing on it and holding it towards him. 'What do you think, more sugar?'

Disarmed, he took it, then filched two more slices from the pan to aid his deliberations. 'Perfect, with just that edge of sharpness.' He put an arm round her shoulders. 'When will they be here?'

Eight, she told him; perhaps he could open a bottle or two of red?

*

Sheila and Simon crawled from Muswell Hill to Hammersmith through dense early-evening traffic, stopping at an off-licence in the Finchley Road to buy a chilled bottle of Prosecco. It lay sweating against Sheila's leg alongside a large butternut squash from the allotment – home-grown produce, something to be quietly proud of. She needed that kind of reinforcement when they visited the Furnivals. Very low key, Ruth had said, but she always lied.

Sheila and Ruth had been watching one another out of the corners of their eyes ever since primary school. Ruth Jago and Sheila Nancarrow, in the first year of the Juniors, at the Red Table – the top group – in their green gymslips and pale-blue checked blouses. Ruth was six months younger than Sheila. She'd been put up a year because she was so clever; that was part of the reason why she never quite fitted in socially. Sheila was pretty, sporty and bright – but not excessively so; she was popular and friends gathered at her house, welcomed by her easy-going parents. Ruth's home was understood to be off-limits, patrolled by a sour, unsmiling mother who treated her brusquely; Sheila was the only friend allowed in because her father was a GP and Angela Jago had an exaggerated respect for doctors. Sheila had kept her name when she married Simon. Why change it? It was who she was after all. Ruth, of course, had been delighted to swap hers for a posh, upper-middle-class English one – another box ticked (Ruth had always had a long list of boxes).

They were best friends and had never lost touch. Some people were like that: they served as calibrators for your life, reminding you where you'd come from, and how far you'd got. You measured your progress against theirs. Ruth was always more noticeable and glamorous, more successful in worldly terms, and Sheila found it fascinating to peek into her showbiz world from the public-sector side of the fence. After training as a social worker she'd done years of casework in north-west London, then moved

120

into academia; now she ran a small university department. Simon had been headmaster of a succession of tough schools. Sheila didn't envy Ruth. She knew herself to be capable and useful and was contented with her life, whereas Ruth was brilliant and full of drive, but restless. *Ungrounded*, somehow.

'OK, so remind me quickly.' Simon paused before they got out of the car. 'What's Alex up to at the moment?'

Sheila rolled her eyes in mock exasperation. 'Same as always. In California, earning pots of money as a software engineer and doing a lot of internet dating by all accounts.'

'And Lauren?'

'I don't know the latest, only that she's been taking a break from the IVF.'

Adam and Ruth were ready for them. They hailed and hugged, drawing them down the hall and past the sitting room, where a fire blazed. As they walked towards the kitchen, Sheila smelled spices. Not shepherd's pie then, she thought, and regretted the Prosecco.

Dinner was a bravura performance, though Sheila always felt that there was a competitive tension about these evenings. Ruth was full of smiles and charm but not quite present in the conversation; it wasn't until she'd produced her magnificent third course – a swirl of meringue and cream decorated with apples and chestnuts – and they'd dutifully consumed rather too much of it for comfort, that she began to relax.

Adam took Simon into the sitting room to watch *Match of the Day*. Alone in the kitchen, the women cleared the table, then Ruth made a pot of mint tea and they curled up at opposite ends of the sofa. 'They can wait for their coffee,' smiled Ruth. 'I've been *dying* to talk to you.'

They basked for a moment in the absence of men. Sheila examined Ruth. Her face was flushed and damp with exertion, she'd taken off her scarf, and her neck, which was seldom exposed these days, had the speckled, haggard look that Sheila recognised from her own bathroom mirror. Ruth's hair, streaked with grey and less abundant now, was falling from its clip, but her eyes were shining. She's excited, thought Sheila, there must be some new triumph or acquisition. 'That was a feast, as usual. It must have taken you all day.'

'A couple of hours, I had a lot of nervous energy to burn off. I've had a lot on my mind.'

Sheila turned the china mug around in her hands and read the big red capitals that encircled it: HOME IS WHERE THE HEART IS. She'd learnt early in her training as a social worker that eye contact and questions discouraged confidences.

'Actually, I'm thinking of having a baby,' Ruth said in a rush.

Sheila's head snapped up. Ruth's face was scarlet, and there was a quiver of uncertainty in her voice.

'A baby?' Sheila felt her face tighten in a frown of alarm. She relaxed it into professional blankness. '"Having" in what sense?'

'Egg, sperm, embryo, labour, birth,' said Ruth, laughing nonchalantly, pushing her hair away from her face. 'You remember, third-year biology with Mrs Pascoe? As I recall she also broadened our horizons by putting a condom on a banana.'

'I don't understand.' Sheila uncurled, put her feet on the floor and sat up straight. 'We're too old. And didn't Adam have a vasectomy?'

Ruth tiptoed over to the kitchen door and closed it quietly, obliterating the murmur of television and the intermittent shouts of the men. She sat down cross-legged, closer to Sheila, her voice low and urgent.

'Lauren's had another miscarriage and she can't have any more IVF.'

'No.' Sheila was aghast. 'I didn't even know she was pregnant. When did this happen? Why didn't you ring me?'

'They didn't tell us until thirteen weeks, and she lost it ten days later.'

'*Poor* Lauren,' said Sheila. 'But then why ...?'

'They've got embryos left over and they need a surrogate to carry one of them. I've offered.'

'*What?*' Sheila put the mug down on the coffee table. 'But you've been through the menopause and come out the other side. We both have. So how ...?'

Ruth ploughed on: 'It turns out that doctors these days can spool back the clock and make you fit for childbearing again, provided your basic machinery is still intact. We've seen a specialist and I've had a sort of fertility MOT. I'll get the results next week.' She paused, enjoying the moment. 'Sorry I've been out of touch, but this stuff has taken over my life.'

'What possessed you?' Sheila's face was appalled. 'I've no problem at all with surrogacy, but for women of our age it's insane.'

Ruth shook her head, complacent. 'The oldest woman to host an embryo was in her seventies. And Lauren needs me to do it.' She grinned at Sheila. 'Actually, I quite fancy diving back into the sea of hormones. I get quite nostalgic for my old body. And it's not as if being post-menopausal has much to commend it, has it?'

Sheila looked at her in astonishment. 'I have no nostalgia *whatsoever* for any of it – PMT, bloating, bleeding, oestrogen headaches. What is there to be nostalgic about? Menstruation was a nightmare, especially towards the end. The day the penny dropped that my periods had stopped for good was one of the happiest of my life. I *prefer* my body now.' Sheila paused. 'Seriously, I think you're completely mad even to consider it.'

'Have you quite finished?' asked Ruth tartly.

Sheila ignored her. 'What about Adam? Isn't he worried about what this could do to your health?'

Ruth put a finger to her lips and lowered her voice. 'He doesn't know. So please, don't mention any of this to Simon.'

'Why haven't you told him?'

'He wouldn't like it.'

'But he's going to have to know.'

'Not now though—'

Sheila was shaking her head. 'No, Ruth, you must tell him. Simon would be devastated if I hid something like this from him.'

Ruth rose, went to the sink and started stacking saucepans and roasting dishes with noisy vigour. 'Adam hasn't always been entirely straight with me about things in the past, so I don't feel obliged to give him a running commentary about what I'm doing,' she said over her shoulder. 'Of course he'll need to know at some point, but if I tell him now he'll try to stop me.'

Sheila got up and went to stand behind Ruth. 'So what's the plan? You get yourself pregnant, then wait till he notices your fat tummy and starts asking questions?'

'Oh, for heaven's sake, you sound like the nurse in the clinic.' Ruth wheeled round and, screwing her face into a simper she asked in a voice of high-pitched concern, '"Is there ... a *Mr* Furnival?"' Then she dropped an octave and for the first time her confidence seemed to falter. 'Actually, they want a meeting with Adam to get his consent and I don't know what to do.'

'Consent?'

'Legally it would be *his* baby as well as mine – can you believe that? As if everything inside me belongs to Adam. They want him to go for counselling and sign their forms, it's ridiculous.' She threw up her hands.

Sheila was appalled, and fascinated. 'Lauren's had a terrible time, and of course you want to help, it's very brave of you, an amazing thing.' She reached out and took Ruth's arms. 'But don't do it on your own. *Please* talk to Adam.'

Ruth pulled away. 'Look, this whole thing will almost certainly never happen, but because there's a *tiny* possibility I'm thinking about it a lot and I wanted to talk it through with you.' She turned away and switched on the kettle. 'Silly of me.'

It took Ruth and Adam forty minutes to stack the dishwasher and restore order to the kitchen with the practised speed and efficiency of a long-married dual-career couple.

'That pork was fantastic,' said Adam. He dropped the empty wine bottles into the recycling bin. 'Great combination, the fennel and herbs. You've not made it before?'

'You say that every time.' Ruth was smiling, indulgent.

'Sorry.' He kissed the back of her head as she reached up to stow serving dishes in the cupboard. 'So beguiled am I by your culinary witchcraft, I quite lose my bearings.'

She turned towards him, dropped her eyes and peered sidelong through fronds of hair. 'By the pricking of my thumbs, something wicked this way comes.'

He laughed. 'I don't know where you get the energy. You spent all morning dealing with Lauren, and you haven't stopped since you got back. You deserve the last of the Sauternes.' He filled a glass and handed it to Ruth. 'I think they enjoyed it, don't you? Simon was on good form, but Sheila seemed a bit preoccupied, she was very quiet after dinner. Is she OK?'

'We had a disagreement about something and I snapped at her, which I shouldn't have done. It's nothing to worry about, I'll apologise tomorrow and everything will be fine.' She looked at her watch. 'It's half past midnight, so four thirty in San Francisco. Let's call Alex, upstairs in my study, come on.'

Adam said, 'I talked to her a couple of nights ago. I'll head up to bed while you catch up, but please don't spend too long chatting. Unlike you, I'm exhausted.'

A stack of unread scripts that Bella had forwarded stood like an arresting party on Ruth's desk; she felt a shudder of foreboding as she pushed them aside to make space for her laptop, then cleared a mound of budgets from her chair, so she could sit down. Alex didn't pick up.

Can't talk – shop too noisy

How are you?

Fine three Halloween parties tomorrow so we're choosing costumes How's things on the fertility front?

Terrified cos am so behind with work, but can't focus till I know if I've passed the tests. It's like staring into the void

Well done for getting this far, Mum, SO proud of you. Bet you'll smash it!!

Fingers crossed.

Feel bad Dad doesn't know – I feel awkward whenever I talk to him

All in good time, darling. Going to bed now Have fun.

Sleep well Mum X

12

The Underground train was severely delayed and dawdled all the way to Euston: Ruth would be late for the results appointment and was perversely relieved because she wanted to put off the moment of truth for as long as possible. She arrived at the consulting room flustered and apologetic. Dr Vassily and Helen Braithwaite were chatting to Lauren; Dan was staring at the floor and tapping his fingers impatiently on his knees. Dr Vassily sat upright in his chair and surveyed them, his face solemn, then he turned to Ruth and folded his hands as if in prayer. He's going to turn me down, she thought as he cleared his throat.

'We were looking for a strong heart, good lungs, excellent fitness, and no serious underlying health issues.' He paused. 'And you fulfilled all those criteria, Mrs Furnival. Your test results are those of a woman ten years younger than the age you claim. Congratulations.' He flourished an arm towards her. 'But let's see about your uterus ... ' He reached for a yellow report slip.

Ruth's heart, so reliably temperate during the screenings, began to beat very fast. 'What did the scan show?'

'The fibroid is less than four centimetres and the surface of the endometrial cavity is clear.' He smiled at Ruth. 'I think we can proceed.'

Lauren leant across the desk. 'Dr Vassily, are you saying ...?'

He covered her slim hand with his big animal paw and patted it. 'Yes, my dear. Your mother is medically fit to act as a gestational carrier for your embryo and to give birth to your child.' He sat back and beamed.

Lauren leant against her mother and murmured, 'Well done.' Ruth felt as if she'd just hit the finishing tape at the end of a gruelling sprint race and she wanted to savour the moment: Lauren's head on her shoulder; the look of shock on Dan's face. Dr Vassily was still talking, but she was only half listening: '... nothing, of course, can be guaranteed', 'manage your expectations', then 'begin the hormones right away'.

She sat up straight. 'What?'

'We're starting you on oestrogen today.'

She was dazed by the speed at which everything was moving: she'd expected a gap before the next phase began, a time to take stock, but Dr Vassily was already running through the schedule.

'If your uterus responds and the lining becomes sufficiently thick then we'll give you additional hormones to prepare it for implantation.'

'What thickness does it need to be?' asked Ruth, keen to fix on her next goal.

'Seven millimetres.' His smile was a challenge. 'Let's see what you can manage.'

Lauren was looking at her diary. 'When's the earliest a transfer might happen?'

'Theoretically in three weeks' time, but four to six weeks is more realistic. It all depends on Mrs Furnival.'

'That leaves only ten months before Ruth's fifty-fifth birthday,' said Dan. 'Which is *very* tight.'

He sounded almost relieved, thought Ruth.

*

The hormones were waiting for Ruth on the desk in Helen Braithwaite's office. 'Do I need *all* of those,' she asked, looking at the boxes of tablets and patches with alarm.

'This is just the start,' said the nurse, 'later on there'll be progesterone pessaries as well. Have you ever been on HRT?'

'I've been very tempted, but was freaked out by the possible side effects.'

Helen gave one of her unnerving laughs. 'Well, you're certainly going to notice some side effects now. When you reach the peak level you'll be taking more than seven times the standard dose, so be prepared for headaches, breast tenderness and leg cramps for starters. Read the drug sheet carefully and contact me if you're worried about anything.'

Seven times. Ruth felt suddenly sick with fear. She imagined her body thickening with the onslaught of this unnatural oestrogen, like a sauce heavy with cornflour. Would tumours sprout in her breasts and ovaries, would clots thicken her blood and jam her arteries?

'Now your risk of conceiving is probably zero,' continued Helen, 'but we tell all our potential hosts, including menopausal ones, to refrain from sex. Just in case.'

'Even though my husband's had a vasectomy?'

'I'm not sure we knew that, did we?' Helen made a note. 'In that case, carry on regardless.' She looked up and grinned with disconcerting familiarity. 'You'll probably notice quite an improvement in that department. Oestrogen increases the blood supply, so it'll get rid of any vaginal dryness and thinning of tissues and perk up your libido. It's great for your skin and hair, too.'

'Good to know there's an upside,' said Ruth coolly.

'Still very busy, is he?' asked the nurse as she put the boxes into a carrier bag.

'Sorry?' Ruth was trying to think back to when she'd last had sex.

'Your husband. With his work?'

'Oh yes, horribly. That very complicated case still hasn't finished. I'll let you know when things ease up a bit.'

Adam was in Vienna for a week at a European legal conference. His colleague Nigel Telman was supposed to be there too, but his current case was overrunning and the Head of Chambers had asked Emily to step in at short notice. It was the first time they'd travelled abroad together and Adam had had to put up with some tiresome teasing. The conference was in one of the city's grandest hotels, its austere stone exterior concealing the red velvet plushness within. His room on the sixth floor overlooking the opera house was dominated by a high, wide rosewood bed enveloped in cream silk and littered with crimson cushions; it seemed to rebuke Adam's single occupancy.

After dinner on the second day he phoned Ruth. 'What are you up to?'

'In bed.'

'Already?' He checked his watch: only twenty past nine in London.

'I'm lying here with the twelfth draft of *Courtesan*, which I need to read and annotate before I go to sleep, because it's still nowhere near good enough, but I can barely keep my eyes open. I've slept for ten hours for the last couple of nights.'

'Sounds as though you're clearing your backlog, which must be a relief?'

'To be honest, I'm terrified of the amount I've got to do. I'm *so* behind. I'd need to work solidly for three weeks to catch up. It's getting serious.' She sighed. 'But hey-ho, it's only telly.'

Was Ruth depressed? he wondered. She'd never had any patience with people who affected to despise television, insisting it was a serious and important medium – inside people's homes, capable of changing their lives. 'You OK?' he asked, anxious.

'I'm utterly exhausted and have a blinding headache.' Her voice was flat. 'But it's nothing to worry about,' she added. 'What have you been up to?'

'Until a moment ago I was trying to get my head around the endless instructions and forms for the circuit judge gig on the Judicial Appointments Commission website.'

'So you're definitely going for it?'

'Still not sure. The opening date for applications is in three weeks' time, so I've been going over the pros and cons with Emily. She thinks I'd miss the cut and thrust of the bar and end up regretting it.'

'Advice that may not be entirely disinterested?' said Ruth drily. 'I suspect she's more worried about how much she'd miss *you* if you disappeared to the bench.'

Adam ignored the jibe. 'I'm sorry I didn't call last night. It was our turn to host dinner and give the speeches.'

'And it went OK?'

'Very well indeed, but we had to stay till the last guests left and they kept us there till three, so we've not had much sleep.'

'How very louche of you both.'

'We've not spent any time together,' he hesitated, 'I mean, *in private*, just in case you're worried.'

'I was teasing, Adam. I've never doubted you for a moment. You're much too *upright* for adultery.' She was laughing. 'What time will you be home on Friday, my love?'

He felt rebuffed and wanted reassurance. 'I'm going to suggest to Emily that we switch our flights to Saturday and grab a few hours of sightseeing. It's her first time in Vienna and we've not been outside the hotel so far.'

A tiny pause. 'Text me your new flight details and I'll pick you up at the airport.'

'No need, I'll get a cab as usual.'

'I'd like to.' Her voice was emphatic. 'I'll see you there, Adam.'

He smiled as he ended the call.

Ruth was on edge as she drove to Heathrow. At the traffic lights before the motorway she peered at herself in the driving mirror – her face had the full-moon look she remembered from when she was on the pill, only more so, and her eyes seemed larger and brighter. It was ten days into the course of oestrogen and she was now taking five tablets a day and had to change the plaster-like patches on her tummy every forty-eight hours; she felt restless and voraciously hungry, and was taking painkillers round the clock to combat the pain in her head.

As she negotiated the ramp that led to the Terminal 3 car park, she identified another side effect: the stirring of sexual appetite. It was as if her pelvis had woken from a coma. She'd not experienced it for at least a couple of years and had completely forgotten the euphoria and edge of recklessness she always felt when aroused. She smiled as she locked the car and pocketed the ticket.

Adam and Emily were waiting in the arrivals hall. In the milli-second before recognition kicked in, Ruth saw a couple ahead of her – the woman petite and slim pivoting on the high heel of her green leather boot as she looked up at a tall man – they were laughing, handsome, enjoying one another. Ruth paused: Adam wouldn't ever . . . *would* he? She went over to them and was greeted effusively. It had been a tedious conference, they said, but they'd managed to glimpse the city, last night and this morning.

'Wonderful place,' said Adam to Ruth. 'It's hardly changed since you and I were there, all those years ago. The smell of coffee in the streets. That sense you're in no-man's-land, on the edge of the Orient. The gypsy violinists in the restaurants.' He looked at Emily. 'I gave you a bit of a tour, didn't I?'

Emily turned to Ruth. 'He's such a great guide, isn't he?'

Ruth shrugged. A small silence erupted.

Emily said, 'Well, I'm going to head for the Tube.' She turned to Adam. 'Thank you for your companionship, see you on Monday – and I promise I'll watch *The Third Man*.' She smiled up at him.

When they got back to Hammersmith Ruth and Adam made love: her idea. She led him upstairs, closed the bedroom curtains and undressed him with languid concentration. He was taken aback by her ardour – and by her evident excitement when she finally allowed him to touch her.

She asked him to come into her, quickly. And when he did she cried out, as she used to years ago, when sex was savage and urgent – not the kindly, intermittent thing they did together now-adays, more shared hobby than passion. Her abandon aroused him; afterwards he fell onto her, gasping with shock and relief.

They lay side by side, laughing softly, her head heavy on his shoulder, her hair like a shawl across his chest.

Adam said, 'I think we've scandalised the puffins.' They gazed at the picture: the birds were eyeing them with their usual wary interest. 'To what do I owe this unexpected pleasure?'

Ruth stretched luxuriously. 'I guess I've been missing you.' Then she said, 'Will you love me always?'

'Of course I will. How could I not?' He lifted his head to look down at her. 'Whatever makes you ask?'

'Hug me,' she told him. 'Tight. No, tighter still.'

Adam frowned, flattered but uneasy.

Later, downstairs in the kitchen, they were startled by fireworks exploding outside, their electric colours splattering and shim-mering across the blackness beyond the French windows. They turned to one another in wordless exclamation: it was the Guy

Fawkes display in the park. For years it had been a fixture in the family diary.

Ruth said on impulse, 'Supper won't be ready for another hour and it's ages since we've been. Shall we go, for old times' sake?'

As they walked arm in arm towards the park they remembered all the other times: bundling the girls into duffel coats and wellingtons; stuffing little hands into mittens; Alex, screaming with delight on Adam's shoulders; Lauren, huddled inside Ruth's winter coat, bewitched by the painted sky but terrified of the noise. When the fireworks were over they'd go straight to the fair and ride on the merry-go-round as the steam organ wheezed its music into the frosty air, feeling as if they ruled the world. Afterwards, in the back garden, there would be bonfire sausages and jacket potatoes, never quite cooked, but comforting all the same, and the girls would hold sparklers at arm's length, their jubilant faces flickering in the firelight. A proper family, part of something.

'Good times, weren't they?' said Adam as the final pyrotechnic flourish faded from the sky.

'You say it as if they're all over,' said Ruth.

Neither of them spoke for a while, then Adam said, 'I suppose I imagined it would all carry on and we'd have grandchildren by now. I never thought for a moment . . . ' He broke off.

Ruth threaded her arm through his. 'It could still happen, you know. You mustn't despair. They're still keen to have a family.' She longed to tell him everything. They'd survived so much and her attempt at this baby should be a joint enterprise, not a solitary, furtive secret. 'Adam,' she began, 'I've been wanting to say. About Lauren and Dan—'

But he cut in: 'Take no notice of my mawkishness. I know we've got to stay positive. I've invited Dan to an Arsenal home game in a couple of weeks' time and I shall be optimistic and encouraging, I promise.' He smiled. 'Fancy a ride on the merry-go-round?'

As they clambered onto their separate horses, Adam looked across at her. 'Sorry, I interrupted you just now, what were you about to say?'

But Ruth's courage failed her. 'Nothing,' she said. 'Nothing that can't wait.'

13

Sheila chose a table diagonally opposite the door of the café so that she would spot Ruth straight away. They'd exchanged apologetic emails after their spat and since then Ruth had messaged her almost every day. She'd now been on the tablets for more than a fortnight and must be dripping with oestrogen: Sheila had suggested lunch because she was desperate to see the results. She ordered a bowl of soup and peered through the windows, but it was pouring with rain and all she could make out were the smudged outlines of people and umbrellas.

Finally Ruth arrived, waving as she hung up her mac. She was wearing a loose, plum-coloured tunic over grey leggings, and seemed to dominate the space as she threaded her way between the tables. 'Sorry I'm late. Work is beyond stressful at the moment and people were queuing up to talk to me as I left the office. It's so lovely to see you.'

As they hugged Sheila said, 'Is it my imagination or have your boobs got bigger?'

Ruth laughed. 'It's as if they've sprung back to life, and they're very tender.' She cupped her hands underneath them and looked down. 'I guess it's not surprising – I'm basically taking super-charged HRT, but it's weird.' She picked up the menu. 'Before we start yakking, I *have* to eat.'

Sheila scanned Ruth's face. Her eyes were shining and her skin, taut over her cheekbones as she grinned, was plumper and less lined, as if the tissues beneath it had been inflated. She tried to inspect her neck, but it was swaddled in a thick grey scarf.

Ruth went to the counter and returned with a plate piled high with chicken risotto. 'I know it's gross, but I'm ravenous twenty-four/seven. It's the hormones.'

'How's it been?'

'Weird. All my menopausal symptoms – hot flushes, insomnia, itchy skin – disappeared within days and for the first time in three or four years I've been sleeping, really deeply, right through the night. It's as if I've fallen into someone else's body – a nicer body – and the doctors say my uterus is plumping up according to plan, so it's all good.'

Sheila said, 'You look different. Younger. How's Adam reacted?'

'At first he was freaked out by the oestrogen patches on my tummy, but I told him they were dressings for a skin rash and he calmed down. Otherwise I don't think he's noticed,' she lowered her voice, 'apart from the sex, that is.'

Sheila waited.

'*Every day* since he got back from Vienna. Sometimes more than once.' She leant closer. 'It's like being thirty again, only without children bursting in every few minutes.'

'And it's all down to the oestrogen?'

'Either that or I'm super-suggestible. The nurse at the clinic said things would improve, but I never expected *this*.' She whispered, 'I mean, I get wet just thinking about it.'

'Goodbye vaginal lubricant?'

'Absolutely. And, this is probably too much information, but I even smell like I used to. Do you know what I mean? That sort of heavy, seaweedy smell you have when you're fertile?'

Sheila giggled. 'This is like those conversations we used to have at my house when we were sixteen, remember?'

'Those Saturday-night sleepovers at yours were the highlight of my week,' said Ruth. 'It was the only time I got to impersonate a normal teenager, although I never felt altogether convincing.'

They remembered meeting up with friends on the beach, drinking cider and smoking cigarettes around a driftwood bonfire, and how they'd stayed up till dawn, talking about boys and dreaming of what they might do when they escaped the confines of Penzance. Ruth would creep home early on Sunday morning, so as to be back in time for Chapel. It was a miracle, she said, that her mother had never discovered what she'd got up to.

'You always were good at covering your tracks,' said Sheila wryly. 'Speaking of which, I take it you still haven't told Adam what's going on?'

'He's unaware, but enjoying the benefits.' Ruth gave a defiant smile. 'And you promised not to nag.'

Sheila splayed her hands. 'You're playing with fire, but I shan't labour the point – no pun intended. What about his consent form?'

'The clinic hasn't mentioned it again, and neither have I.'

Ruth said she was having the fourth and final uterine scan that evening. If the lining was thick enough, there was an outside chance she'd have Lauren's embryo inside her by the end of the week. 'Surreal, or what?' She pushed her empty plate aside and yawned. 'I'm dying for pudding, but I must go back and do some work. What with the appointments and feeling knackered I've been bunking off a lot and it's getting a bit scary.'

Sheila looked concerned. 'But the company's still doing OK?'

'Don't ask,' said Ruth. 'The state of my uterus is my priority right now and I don't have the head space to worry about Morrab Films as well, so I'm trying to put it out of my mind.'

As they stood outside on the streaming pavement Ruth said,

'Oh my God, I'm so obsessed with my treatment and Lauren and everything that I've not even asked about you. You've been chairing your international seminar all morning – how did it go? And Simon? The children? Your mum?' She touched Sheila's cheek and made a penitent face. 'I'm sorry. How *are* you – in a sentence.'

Sheila laughed. 'We're all fine and my news can keep. It's much more interesting hearing your dispatches from the frontline of fertility. Message me when you get the results. And take care, Ruth, won't you?'

Ruth and Lauren waited as Dr Vassily rifled through his pile of test results. Finally, he withdrew a blue A4 sheet from the pile.

'Here we are. Mrs Ruth Furnival. Size and shape of cervix and uterus correspond with pre-menopausal values.' Ruth gave Lauren a thumbs-up. 'Normal morphology. Intact endometrium. Minimum thickness six point five millimetres throughout.'

'Oh no!' Ruth's hands flew to her mouth. 'It's not enough, I'll need another course of oestrogen and we'll lose two weeks.' Tears of frustration pricked her eyes.

Dr Vassily fingered his moustache. 'I said seven millimetres was *desirable*, but time is short. We can work with six and a half.' He clapped his hands. 'Ladies, we're ready to go!'

Ruth's heart began to pound.

'Well done, Mum!' Lauren's face was flushed.

Dr Vassily said he had already spoken to the embryologist and the transfer could take place in five days' time, on Saturday morning, if they were available. Ruth checked her diary and hesitated: there was an all-day meeting for everyone in the company on Friday and, because they were so behind with everything, she and Bella had arranged a follow-up session the next morning; Bella would be furious if she cancelled. On the plus side Adam wouldn't be around, he was going to Manchester to have lunch with his cousins. 'Perfect,' she said.

'It's fine for me and Dan too,' added Lauren.

But Dr Vassily explained that only one person was allowed to accompany the patient, because the transfer suite was a small, sterile, theatre environment. Ruth felt relieved, she couldn't bear the thought of another spectator, but Lauren's face fell.

'Dan and I were together for all our previous transfers and it would mean so much if we could both be there. *Please* can you make an exception, just this once?'

The specialist shook his head. 'Those are the rules, Mrs Ryan, and sadly I can't bend them, even for you.' He folded his hands and bowed in a gesture of apology.

Lauren sighed. 'Then it'll be just me and Mum.' She looked at Ruth and they grinned nervously at one another.

Dr Vassily was running through a checklist. 'Collect the progesterone pessaries from Helen Braithwaite on your way out, and take them daily in addition to the oestrogen from now on. And remember, no cosmetics or perfume in the transfer suite, please.'

He turned to Lauren. 'Mrs Ryan, before we can proceed, you and your husband need to give us signed consent for the use of your embryos.'

'No problem,' said Lauren.

'And Mrs Furnival?' He was looking at Ruth now and every muscle in her body tensed: he was going to demand Adam's consent form. Her palms were wet with sweat.

'Yes?' she managed.

'You're sure you want us to transfer only one embryo? The chances of success are significantly higher with two.'

They'd forgotten. It was going to be all right. She was speechless with relief.

Lauren said, 'We've had that discussion already and nothing's changed, we don't want to run the risk of twins, it would be much too dangerous for Mum and her health takes priority. OK?'

'Understood.' Dr Vassily scribbled in the notes, then he looked up at them. 'I look forward to seeing you both on Saturday.'

Afterwards Ruth dragged a reluctant Lauren to a bar in Camden and ordered mocktails to celebrate.

Ruth clinked her glass against Lauren's. 'Here's to a stunningly successful embryo installation.'

'You'll jinx it,' protested Lauren.

But Ruth was euphoric. 'Nonsense,' she said. 'This transfer's happening much earlier than I expected and the timing's perfect. If it doesn't work we should be able to fit in one more go. And they've not even mentioned your dad's consent form, which is a godsend. It means the pressure's off and I can pick the right moment to tell him once the transfer's over.'

'Dan's going to be gutted when I tell him he can't be there,' said Lauren. 'We always take a moment, before the transfer starts, when we *will* the embryo to implant. It sounds crazy, but I think it really has an effect. And this time it's not going to happen.' She was close to tears.

Ruth took her hand. 'You have to stay positive. There'll be three of us willing it to work this time. And remember, it's the outcome that matters, not who's in the room. Dan will understand that, won't he?'

The day before the embryo transfer Ruth trudged from Covent Garden Tube towards the offices of Morrab Films lugging a small suitcase full of documents and hastily scribbled notes. Four days of high-dose progesterone had taken their toll: she'd been warned to expect premenstrual symptoms, but the reality was horrendous: she felt bloated, uncomfortable and savagely bad tempered. A headache had colonised her skull for two days and nights as she attempted to speed-read her way through bundles of paperwork. The BBC's drama supremo had funded the development of two series and was now waiting for the final scripts and budgets, together with confirmed names for directors and lead actors – details that would often clinch a deal – before she decided whether or not to commission them. The surge of adrenalin, which normally kept Ruth focused and energetic before important meetings, hadn't materialised this time. The embryo transfer was dominating her thoughts and she'd been spending hours in surrogacy chat rooms, where hosts and commissioning parents exchanged experiences, instead of working. She was horribly under-prepared.

The company occupied one floor of a narrow Victorian building off the Strand, up a steep flight of stairs above a computer supplies shop. When she opened the door into the main office the whole team was sitting there, waiting for her.

Ruth forced a smile as she shrugged off her coat, then sat down and took a deep breath. 'Thanks so much for everything you've been doing over the past few weeks, everyone. Brilliant teamwork. I haven't been around as much as usual, but I've been keeping up to speed with everything.' Bella shifted noisily in her chair. 'Everything's looking great.'

'Really?' said Bella, her tone almost scornful. She didn't look well: her face was pale and there were cold sores around her mouth.

'Absolutely,' said Ruth with less conviction.

Bella sighed. 'Four episodes of *Match Girls* still need major rewrites. Scripts for Series Two of *Hurt* have to be finalised and sent to the BBC before episode one transmits,' she glanced down at her notebook, 'and there's a problem with *Courtesan*. If we film in the Czech Republic as planned it'll go way over budget.' She turned to Adrian Webster, their head of production, for confirmation.

Adrian was the kind of manager other companies dreamed of having on their senior teams: canny, unflappable, dextrous with finances and great with people. Normally a professional optimist, his expression was grim. 'The only option is to find another location,' he said. 'Probably rural Serbia, which may not please the talent. And speaking of talent,' he and Bella exchanged another look, 'we're in danger of losing the director. The feature he's attached to has been put back, so there's a clash and I've a feeling we won't win.' He turned to Ruth. 'He called yesterday, wanting to talk to you, and I said you'd do lunch with him tomorrow – I realise it's going to squeeze your time with Bella in the morning, but it's his only free day.'

'Thanks, Adrian.' Ruth forced another smile while imagining the embryo transfer suite where she'd be lying in twenty-four hours' time. 'Let's confirm those details after we're finished here,' she said, avoiding his eye. She looked at the bleak faces of the younger team members. 'Cheer up, my darlings,' she tried to keep the panic out of her voice, 'as Bella says, there are one or two things to tweak, but everything's going in the right direction. We're in good shape.'

Bella stood up. 'Could we have a quick word, Ruth? Now. Just you and me.'

Ruth followed her into their shared office and they sat facing one another on the two pale blue IKEA sofas.

Bella said, 'Why are you coming out with all this rubbish? We're *not* in good shape and everyone in there knows it. It's as if you're living in some sort of parallel universe, disengaged from reality.' Her voice wobbled. 'I can't carry on like this, all by myself.'

Ruth said, 'But I'm back now, and I promise—'

'You *promised* to read all the scripts I sent and give notes to the writers, but I checked first thing this morning. No one's heard anything from you.'

Ruth flushed. 'I've been doing nothing else for the past forty-eight hours and the scripts are in my case, all marked up. The editors can send them out today.'

Bella was chewing her lip. 'We've got hardly any commitments from lead actors and the directors are only lightly pencilled. It's all happening too late, and Adrian and I are the only ones losing sleep at the prospect of Morrab Films going bankrupt.'

'I'm sorry, but it hasn't been easy, with Lauren in such a state.'

Bella's face hardened. 'I heard that she looked in pretty good shape when the two of you were spotted having a girls' lunch in Soho recently.'

Ruth folded her arms. 'Guilty as charged. I bought my daughter a quick lunch after we'd spent the morning at a clinic in Harley Street.' She gazed at Bella with the indignation of a liar telling a technical truth. 'Do you have a problem with that?'

'In that case, I'm sorry,' said Bella stiffly, but her expression suggested she wasn't.

That evening Ruth sat on the closed seat in the downstairs loo at home and performed a swift self-assessment. Was her precarious mental state caused by the hormones ('mood swings' were listed among the side effects of progesterone) or by her Himalayan levels of stress? The day had got progressively worse. When the team meeting had ended Ruth told an incredulous Bella that she couldn't make their follow-up meeting, then she called the *Courtesan* director to cancel the last-ditch lunch that Adrian had arranged. He had one of the tantrums for which he was famous throughout the industry and resigned, saying that Morrab Films was no longer a crucible for the kind of work that he aspired to. The old Ruth would have listened patiently and done whatever it took to talk him round, but this afternoon the dangerous tilt in her mood allowed the words, 'Oh, for heaven's sake, Jamie, why not just *grow up*?' to pop out of her mouth. He'd sworn and put the phone down.

Bella, overhearing Ruth's end of the exchange, went from already-very-cross to furious. Now they were casting around for a replacement and the names in the frame were uninspiring. Ruth had apologised profusely and by the time she left the office they were just about back on speaking terms, but she knew there was some serious repair work to be done.

Meanwhile, Lauren had been bombarding her with nervous texts since dawn: please would Ruth take the drugs at exactly the times stipulated; it was vital to rest, breathe deeply and remember to eat; would it make sense to talk through the procedure one more time? Now the phone was buzzing again and when Ruth pulled it from her bag the message read:

> Love you. Hang on in there. Only 14
> hrs to go! Lxxx

Adam was disgruntled and forlorn. She'd had to keep him at bay for the past few days, lest he dislodge or neutralise the progesterone. In an attempt to mollify him and assuage her own guilt she'd cooked him supper every night, when she should have been upstairs working or wrestling a fresh pessary into place. He was outside in the hall now, shouting for her like an anxious toddler: 'Ruth. Where are you? Ruth. RUTH.' Very quietly she turned the key in the lock.

All the women she knew who'd undergone fertility treatment had been able to rely on supportive husbands or partners, who'd taken over the housework and helped organise the drug schedule while shouldering tears and mood swings. Recently she'd felt waves of resentment towards Adam, for his sheer obliviousness, for *not having lifted a finger* to help her. Entirely unjustified words of reproach had bubbled to her lips and very nearly escaped them: she must be going mad. The email from Helen Braithwaite, which she'd received two hours earlier, had brought her significantly closer to the edge. She reached for her phone and read it again.

145

Dear Ruth,

Just a reminder to bring your consent form with you
tomorrow, together with your husband's. The forms need
to be signed and dated by both of you, please. We need
to have them in place before we can go ahead with
the transfer.

Kind regards,

Helen

Here it was, then: the point of no return. She swallowed,
then typed:

No problem, Helen. You'll have everything tomorrow!

This was the moment to tell Adam. She would take him into
the sitting room and explain, calmly and rationally, how much it
meant to Lauren, how it was an opportunity they *must* take, for
her sake. She'd beg him to sign the form, even if it meant sitting
up all night in order to persuade him. Ruth looked at her face
in the mirror: it was puffy and very pale and there were dark
circles under her eyes. She rolled her shoulders back and took a
deep breath. If she could get him onside now, before the transfer,
everything would be all right. She flushed the loo, for form's sake,
and opened the door.

Adam pounced on her in the hall. 'I've been calling you for
ages, why didn't you answer? What have you been doing?'

This was her cue. 'We need to talk, my darling.'

'About?'

He was looking at her with such distrust, arms folded as if to
resist and rebuff, that she almost lost her nerve. 'It's complicated,'
she began.

'We're talking about Lauren, I assume?' he said testily.

She froze. *He knew.* She must have left clinic paperwork lying

146

around, or forgotten to lock her phone. She could feel sweat beading on her forehead and palms. 'What?' she gasped.

'Alex says you're very involved with Lauren's treatment, whatever that means. I haven't a clue, because you told me to leave her alone. I've not seen her since she lost the baby and whenever I call she's always busy, but she seems to talk to you and Alex all the time. What's going on, Ruth?'

She closed her eyes and exhaled: it was OK, he had no idea. But she couldn't face telling him after all. Not now, when she was so exhausted. And he was so on edge.

She put a hand on his arm. 'Seriously, there's *nothing* bad going on, you're imagining it. I've been trying to help Lauren, that's all. She's getting stronger, and she'd *love* to see you – you just need to give her a little while longer.'

Adam looked unconvinced.

Ruth pushed her hair back off her face and attempted a smile. 'I'm sorry, I know I've neglected you over the past couple of weeks. We need a proper catch-up, about lots of things, but it's getting late and I'm so knackered that I'm not really thinking straight.' She yawned. 'Can we leave it till the weekend, please?'

Adam stared at her hard, then his expression softened. 'OK,' he said. 'But could we eat fairly soon? I've got an early start in the morning, so I don't want to be up too late.'

'There's something I have to do, very quickly.' Ruth sidestepped him and headed up the stairs. 'It won't take me a moment,' she said over her shoulder. 'Then I'll come down and rustle something up. Maybe you could lay the table?'

In her study she took down the Bible and laid it on her desk; a cloud of dust erupted and shimmered lazily in the light of the Anglepoise lamp. The pages fell open in the middle, where she'd hidden the two consent forms. She skimmed through Adam's form, pretending she was a legal secretary preparing a document

147

for a client; in all the places where it needed initialling or signing she put a neat pencil cross:

I understand that my wife is acting as a gestational surrogate X
I understand the nature of the treatment ... X
I have been offered counselling at the Marinella Clinic ... X
I have been given every opportunity to ask questions ... X
I understand that I will be the legal parent of any child born as a result of this treatment ... X
I give my consent

Date X
Signature X

Ruth opened her file of financial documents and found a contract they'd both signed the previous year. Adam normally used a fountain pen and all she had was a biro, but it would have to do. She practised writing his signature and initials, covering an A4 sheet until she was satisfied by the likeness, then she filled in his name, address and date of birth at the top of the form. That was the easy bit done. She braced herself.

The first pencil cross was on the following page. As her pen touched the paper her hand began to tremble so violently that she had to stop. She was a forger and this was fraud: she was about to cross a line. Her mother's voice came, sly and triumphant:

Caught you at it.

Don't think you can hide anything from me, my girl.

Wicked, that's what you are ... and you always were.

Ruth clenched and unclenched her right fist, trying to suppress the tremor. She couldn't turn back now. By committing a minor offence, which might annoy Adam but would do him no harm, she would have the chance to transform their daughter's life and happiness. This was the right course of action, for *everyone*, no question. Below her in the kitchen Adam began to slam plates and cutlery on to the table, signalling his hunger and irritation. She was bone-tired, but she had to concentrate, had to see this through. He would never know – this form was a ludicrous patriarchal relic, an administrative fragment, to be noted on a checklist and stuffed in a drawer – it would alter nothing.

In a few seconds it was done.

She put both forms in a Jiffy bag, then into a long-life Sainsbury's carrier, and stowed the package at the bottom of her briefcase. *Everything was in place.*

As she closed the Bible one of the endpapers fell out and she saw her name. In 1863 Thomas Jago had married Ruth Humphrey, from St Buryan; her namesake had given birth to seven children, two of whom survived infancy; she died in childbed having the last one. Ruth found the gap in the family record and tucked the page in, then put the book back on its shelf. Her hands were dusty and red with scratching. She went to the bathroom and scrubbed at them before going downstairs to make Adam his supper.

14

On the day of the transfer Dan and Lauren arrived at the house half an hour after Adam had left for Liverpool. Ruth was grateful for the lift: she'd been drinking water all morning as instructed and now her bladder was tight as a drum.

As they pulled into the clinic's car park Lauren turned around to look at Ruth and said tentatively, 'Mum, we always give our embryos names. This one's called Caterpillar.'

'Caterpillar?'

'Dan chose it, because it starts off in one place, then moves around and changes into something else.'

Ruth saw that the back of his neck had flushed crimson and her heart turned over. 'I'm so sorry they won't let you watch the transfer, Dan.'

His eyes met hers in the rear-view mirror and he nodded. 'Look after Lauren for me, won't you?' he said. It felt like an oblique criticism of her, as a mother.

Helen Braithwaite was waiting for them in reception, wearing pale blue theatre scrubs that gave her an air of urgent seriousness. They stood in silence as the lift creaked towards the second floor and when they got out the nurse pointed Dan towards the waiting room.

Ruth watched as he and Lauren kissed, then stood facing one another for several minutes, eyes locked and palms pressed together; she guessed she was watching the ritual that had preceded their own embryo transfers. It was so raw and intimate that she had to look away.

'Message me, so I know when to start praying,' said Dan as they separated, then he turned to Ruth and hugged her with a desperate ferocity.

Helen led them into an office and asked for the consent forms; they each handed her a sheaf of papers and watched while she read through them, page by page. Then she started counting, 'First commissioning parent. Second commissioning parent. Surrogate. Surrogate's spouse. Four forms, all signed and dated. Excellent, ladies.' She put the forms into plastic pouches and slotted them into a ring binder marked FURNIVAL/RYAN. Ruth was aware that Lauren was staring at her in astonishment, but she didn't meet her gaze.

'As your daughter knows from experience, we have to check the paperwork and your ID repeatedly before we do the transfer,' said Helen. 'It's a legal requirement, to ensure we don't end up putting the wrong embryo inside you. You're going to be asked who you are and when you were born so many times that you'll end up wanting to scream, but can you start by telling me now, please.'

The nurse held up a plastic band that bore Ruth's name, hospital number and date of birth and, having established that the details were correct, wrapped it round her wrist, then led them to a changing room. There was a hospital gown for Ruth, a plastic apron for Lauren and red clogs for both of them. They clomped across the lino and Helen showed them into the transfer suite, then went to fetch Dr Vassily. The heavy door sucked itself closed behind her with a thud. A treatment couch stood in the middle of the room and screens and equipment were ranged along two walls; the blinds were closed and it was very quiet. Ruth climbed onto the table, lay down and closed her eyes. Suddenly she was afraid. Not of the transfer itself – they said it was no worse than a routine cervical smear – but of something being unleashed in this room, something that couldn't be stilled.

Lauren sat down on a chair next to her mother and nudged her arm. 'So they did chase you for Dad's form in the end?'

'They did.' Ruth opened her eyes and stared at the ceiling.

'I'm so glad he knows. It's been awful, having to keep it secret.' Ruth turned, Lauren was smiling with relief. 'Did you have a hard job persuading him, or did he agree to sign straight away?'

'I *was* going to tell him.' Ruth stopped. 'But then I decided not to.'

'But he signed.' Lauren's face was incredulous. 'I saw his writing on the consent form just now.'

'Keep your voice down. Everything's under control. Just leave it to me.'

'Meaning?'

'This transfer is the priority right now, and I don't need any stress. If it works we'll tell your dad. Straight away.' Now they were both whispering.

Lauren was looking at her in consternation. 'Mum, *please* tell me you didn't forge Dad's signature?'

Before Ruth could reply the double doors sprang open and Dr Vassily entered, clad in a theatre gown, followed by Helen and a youngish man whose impassive face was animated by a livid birthmark on his left cheek.

'Dr Hittal is a fertility scientist, who works in the laboratory next door with his team. We're connected to them by intercom and video link.' He paused and pointed to his left. 'An embryo that was thawed earlier is ready on the other side of that wall.'

Dr Hittal showed Ruth a plastic rectangle the size of a credit card, on which were printed details of the embryo's unique identity code. He asked her to tell him her name and date of birth, then double-checked her wrist-band and his card. He gave her a shy smile and slid from the room.

Dr Vassily moved to the end of the operating table, looked down at Ruth and raised his arms, like a priest at the altar. 'We shall now prepare you to receive the embryo.'

Ruth was asked to confirm her identity once again, then Dr Vassily and Helen sat her up and positioned her hips towards the edge of the operating table. They laid her back and slotted her feet into stirrups that suspended her knees at right angles. She felt open and exposed, like an empty vessel, waiting to be filled.

'Comfortable?' enquired Dr Vassily.

'Apart from an overwhelming desire to pee.'

'That's what I like to hear.' He beamed. 'A full bladder straightens my route into the uterus.' The others laughed; Ruth clenched her teeth.

The intercom crackled and the room fell silent.

'Dr Hittal here. You should be able to see the embryo on the direct feed from my microscope.'

Ruth followed Dr Vassily's gaze up to a large monitor on her right. And there it was: a blackish-grey object, very round with bumps on its surface, filling the screen. It looked like an ancient silver coin – Roman or medieval – its face worn away and tarnished, but full of mystery and power; beautiful, in fact.

Ruth turned to Lauren; she was staring at the screen and smiling. 'Hello, Caterpillar,' she whispered.

'Embryo coming through shortly,' said Dr Hittal.

Dr Vassily inserted a speculum into Ruth's vagina then motioned Helen forward. She folded back the drapes. 'I'm going to do an ultrasound scan, so that Dr Vassily has an image to guide the transfer.' She applied jelly to Ruth's tummy and began to roll the scanner backwards and forwards. Another screen came to life and Ruth saw her uterus, plumped up by the weeks of hormone treatment, lying on its side like a long, ripe grey pear.

Dr Vassily began threading a guide catheter up into Ruth's cervix. She felt the invasion, then saw it materialise: a pale line, floating in the cavity in the centre of the pear. It stopped halfway and hung in suspension.

The intercom spluttered again: 'Embryo at the hatch.'

Helen put down the scanner and switched off the overhead light. Everything was in shadow now and for a moment the room fell silent; Ruth remembered Chapel services on winter evenings, long ago and in another life. The nurse was opening a small door in the wall and a pair of pink-gloved hands were holding out a syringe with a long thin tube attached. She cradled it and walked slowly back to the table, holding it in front of her with infinite care, like sacramental bread at a mass.

She smiled at Ruth. 'Your five-day-old embryo is in here, floating in culture medium.'

'*My* embryo, actually,' said Lauren.

'Of course,' said Helen. 'Sorry.' She handed the syringe to Dr Vassily and began scanning Ruth again.

'Now watch the screen very carefully.' Dr Vassily inserted the tube into the guide catheter and slowly depressed the syringe. 'You should see a small movement. Any moment . . . *now*.'

Ruth held her breath. And then she saw it: a tiny flash of white as the embryo surfed into her uterus on a wave of fluid. A shooting star, there for a fraction of a second, before it buried itself in her depths.

Somewhere behind her Lauren was sobbing.

'Excellent,' said Dr Vassily. 'Exactly where we wanted it.'

Ruth said nothing.

Dr Vassily counted to ten out loud, then very slowly withdrew the catheter. Finally, he removed the speculum.

Helen switched the lights on and she and Dr Vassily

completed the paperwork, closed the scanner, and laughed at something Ruth couldn't catch, as if nothing out of the ordinary had happened.

'You need to stay here, lying flat, for twenty minutes,' Dr Vassily told Ruth. 'With luck, the embryo will begin to implant in three or four days. Until then, take it easy. No swimming, and keep away from toxic substances. Don't do *anything* you're going to regret if this transfer doesn't work. And tell your husband from me that he is to spoil you. This is the time for chocolates and flowers.' He bowed to each of them in turn and disappeared.

Helen Braithwaite gave Ruth and Lauren two printouts each – screenshots of the embryo and the moment of transfer.

'Well done, you've both coped so well.' She looked at Ruth. 'I'm sure you'll want to do a home pregnancy test, but remember they're not a hundred per cent reliable. That's why we'll be doing a definitive one here in a couple of weeks' time. And if it's negative, don't panic, only one in three transfers is successful, first time round. Most of our ladies come back for a second or third go. You're in a good position, with all those embryos in reserve.'

In the car park Dan strode ahead and held open the car door. Lauren, following behind with her arm through Ruth's, said: 'Best if you sit in the back again, Mum. I always did, after my transfers, that way you can keep your legs up.'

Dan started the engine but didn't put it into gear. 'Comfortable there, Ruth?' he asked, moving his head a fraction so that their eyes locked again. A beat, and then she realised: he was waiting for her to fasten her seat belt over the body that now housed his embryo. His property now? She said nothing and buckled herself in.

They slid up the ramp and joined a stream of traffic heading west. It was a damp November day in central London but Ruth felt as if she'd been interfered with and adapted, like a science-fiction character, and now inhabited another zone.

As they drove along the Marylebone Road Lauren said, 'You OK, Mum?'

'Bit zonked.' Ruth was struggling for words. 'It's hard to grasp what just happened—' Then she broke off. 'But you know, darling, don't you? All those times you went through it ... I can't imagine how you kept going.' She unpinned her hair and pulled it around her face and neck, for warmth.

Ahead of her Dan reached over and laid an arm across Lauren's shoulders, placing a dark blue barrier between the front and back of the car. Ruth longed suddenly for Adam: she pictured him, sitting next to her now; her legs on his lap, their hands intertwined, his smile proud and approving: on *her* side.

Lauren said, 'If it was me I'd spend today and tomorrow lying flat, just for safety's sake.' She said it tentatively, but Ruth realised it was an instruction – one that would be complicated to comply with.

She pulled out her phone and texted Adam:

> Hope journey OK and cousins
> good. Am feeling wretched, so
> going to bed. Probably best if you
> sleep in spare room – may be
> infectious and I don't want you to
> catch anything! Xxxxxx

Then she messaged Sheila:

> Transfer was banal and
> momentous. Lap of the
> Gods now ...

156

She took the printouts from her bag and stared at them both again: the inscrutable face of the embryo, then the moment when it entered her and an idea became flesh. She felt a stab of lonely terror.

After they'd taken Ruth home Lauren and Dan headed back to Brockley. The afternoon yawned ahead of them. They drove for a while in silence, then Dan put his hand over Lauren's. 'How was it in the transfer suite?'

'Strange.' She was staring straight ahead. 'You weren't there, and I missed you so much. It was all about Mum really, all those ID checks and preparations. I was just a spectator. Seeing everyone fussing around her and watching her womb on the monitor – I suppose it was the final confirmation that it's all over for me.' She sighed. 'So I felt rather small and sad.' He squeezed her hand. 'But I kept telling myself how lucky I am that she's doing this for us, and hoping that maybe she'll succeed where I've so spectacularly failed.'

'Don't get your hopes up, Laurie. It's never worked before and there's no reason to think it will this time.'

'I sometimes wonder if that's what you're hoping, because you'd be horrified if Mum actually got pregnant.'

He turned to look at her and they swerved briefly into the outside lane; cars hooted and Dan swore. 'Let's be clear,' he said, trying to sound measured, 'if it happened I'd be over the moon, but—'

'But?'

'It would be weird, wouldn't it? Come on, Laurie, it would be *super*-weird.'

She smiled. 'Because it's not something *your* mum would ever contemplate?' Dan laughed in spite of himself. It was true, his mother didn't believe in meddling with nature: she wouldn't like the idea one bit.

Lauren said, 'Is that what you're worried about: how she'd react if our baby was in another granny's tummy?'

'Of course not.' He couldn't tell her his greatest anxiety: how, if Ruth ended up carrying their baby, *she'd* be the one calling the shots, and he'd feel less of a man for having allowed it to happen. He knew it wasn't logical. Instead he said, 'Why are we even *having* this conversation? We agreed at the start that there's basically zero chance of it working. It's a closure cycle, remember?'

'You're right, let's change the subject.' Then Lauren froze. 'Oh my God, Dan, I've just remembered something that happened earlier.'

He glanced at her. 'Go on.'

'The clinic must have chased Mum for Dad's consent form, because she handed it in.'

'So he knows.' Dan let out a sigh. 'Thank God for that.' He frowned. 'What did he say, is he OK with everything?'

'I've no idea, because, here's the thing: the form *was* signed, but Dad can't have done it himself, because Mum admitted to me that she still hasn't told him. I was in the middle of asking her to explain, then the transfer started, and afterwards it went out of my mind.' She put both hands to her mouth and he had to strain to hear her words: 'I'm pretty sure she forged his signature.'

'You're kidding me?' The traffic lights ahead were green, but Dan slowed down and stopped dead at the junction. He looked at Lauren, ashen faced. 'That's illegal.'

'I know.'

The lights flicked to amber, then red. 'If she did get pregnant it could invalidate the whole surrogacy process, and where would that leave us?'

'Reading between the lines, I think Mum wants us to pretend we don't know anything about it – she said everything's under control and she'll handle it.'

158

'Making us accomplices in her fraud?' Dan was shaking his head. 'Thanks, Ruth.'

'No, it's the opposite,' said Lauren, her eyes narrowing. 'If we don't ask, we don't know: that way we're not guilty of anything.'

They stared at one another, considering, then Dan said, 'Your mum has us boxed into a corner. This is why I've been so nervous about her being our surrogate from the beginning.' He rubbed his hands over his face, then looked at Lauren wearily. 'OK, this is what I suggest. We don't talk to *anyone* about your dad's form. *Ever.* He'll be furious if he finds out, and I don't want him to think we had any part in it. So that conversation with your mum, during the transfer, it never happened. Agreed?'

'Agreed.' Lauren pointed ahead. 'The lights have changed, you can go now.'

Dan released the handbrake and put his foot down. In lots of ways, he thought to himself, much the best thing would be for this embryo transfer to fail.

Ruth spent the weekend in bed. The symptoms she'd concocted were designed to guarantee bed-rest and isolation, while allowing her access to food. It was nothing major, she'd assured Adam huskily, when he arrived home from Manchester and peered into the bedroom to check on her, probably one of those forty-eight-hour flu bugs.

He looked at her with narrowed eyes. 'You've not been your normal self for weeks – endless headaches, exhaustion, days in bed, mood swings – and now *this.*' He gestured towards the bed. 'I'm worried about you. I'm going to call the out-of-hours GP, and if necessary I'll drive you to hospital.'

'No, don't do that,' said Ruth, her voice suddenly clear and emphatic. She coughed extravagantly. 'Obviously I'm feeling wretched at the moment, but I know it won't last long.'

'Why, have you already seen a doctor?' His face was etched with anxiety; Ruth couldn't bear it.

She sighed and pulled the duvet up until it obscured everything. It was vital to keep calm, horizontal and stress-free. Which meant she couldn't tell Adam now. In any case, what was the point, given the sixty per cent likelihood that this embryo would fail to implant? She searched for words that skirted outright perjury. 'I haven't seen a doctor about any illness,' she paused, 'for the simple reason that I'm not ill.'

It was an odd formulation, clumsily delivered, and Adam's prosecutor's nose smelled deceit. He addressed the lump under the covers. 'Is there something you're not telling me, Ruth? Something Lauren knows about and not me?'

'What?' Her stomach turned over and she stared into the blackness. She coughed several times, playing for time. 'Why do you say that?' Her voice was high and wavering.

'Because I need to know.'

'You're making me feel worse.'

'You said you were looking after her. I've been wondering if it's the other way round, and you're the one that's ill?'

She exhaled. 'I've told you, I'm not ill – I mean, not in any *serious* way. So you can stop worrying, OK?'

'You promise?'

She peered out and whispered, '*Please*. I've given you an answer, and I'll never be better if I don't get some sleep.'

On Sunday morning a thick fog pressed up against the windows, swaddling the roofs of the houses across the street so they became abstract monochrome triangles that swam in and out of focus. Ruth felt detached from the world. Only her phone punctured the strange silence. Lauren was texting hourly with expressions of love and requests for bulletins. Finally, Ruth's patience snapped:

Please, darling, am trying to be
plausibly ill and need all my energy
for that! Going to switch phone off
now. We both have to be patient.
OK? Much love Xxx

Late in the afternoon she heard Adam's footsteps on the stairs. He came into the bedroom, holding his phone at arm's length.

'Alex. She wants to know if you're up to talking?'

Ruth waved him away and mouthed 'No', but he pushed the phone into her hand.

'Darling,' she rasped, 'how are you?'

'Sorry, Mum, I've spoken to Lauren so I know you're pretending to be ill and can't talk, but I wanted to hear your voice. I've been worried in case you're having a bad reaction to the transfer. If you're OK, just say "yes".'

'Yes.'

'That's a relief. I love you, Mum. You being her host is the only thing that's keeping Lauren sane right now. I am *willing* that embryo to implant.'

'Thank you, that means a lot.'

'I'm sure you realise, but Dad's frantic, he's convinced you're at death's door. Is there some way you can reassure him?'

Adam had retreated to the doorway and was watching her, his face drawn; Ruth felt guilty and cornered. 'I'll try,' she said. 'In fact, I'm already feeling *much* better, but still very sleepy, so I'll hand you back to your dad, who's *right here.*'

Adam took the phone from Ruth and went down the stairs.

'You still there, Alex? How d'you think she sounded?'

'I think she's on the mend. Leave her to rest and I bet she'll be back at work tomorrow.'

'Really?'

'*Really,*' said Alex. 'Stop worrying about Mum and think about yourself for a change. Open a bottle of wine, light the fire and binge watch something on Netflix.'

'Thanks for the pep talk. I'll keep you posted.'

Ruth rose from her sickbed and tried to resume work. It wasn't easy: in the mornings she awoke feeling exhausted, and it was hard to concentrate for any length of time because she was constantly monitoring her body for signs of pregnancy.

On Wednesday the following week Bella phoned her at ten a.m. 'Were you by any chance planning on visiting the office at some point today?'

'Sorry.' Ruth heaved herself out of bed. 'I had another bad night and I'm making a slow start, but I'll be in by lunchtime.'

'You've seen the overnights?'

Ruth felt a constriction in her chest: the opening episode of *Hurt* had aired the previous evening and for the first time in her professional life she'd forgotten to check the viewing figures for a series she'd worked on. 'I've not had a chance yet.'

'Maybe you had a premonition?' said Bella grimly.

Ruth felt sick. 'Tell me.'

'Started at three and a half million and fell off a cliff around thirty minutes in; by the end it had dropped to one point two.' They'd been expecting four million viewers and hoping for more: the numbers were disastrous, and a second series was out of the question.

Two days later Ruth took a call from the BBC Drama Commissioner Hannah Stimpson, who'd championed *Hurt* from the outset. She was gutted that audiences hadn't shared her enthusiasm for the series, but in view of the figures she needed to find a 'less exposed place in the schedule' for the remaining episodes. It was code for burying them in a late-night slot, after most people had gone to bed. She also mentioned that, because of budget cuts, she was deferring a decision on *Match Girls* and

Courtesan until the New Year at the earliest. Ruth kicked herself: if she'd been more on the ball both series could have been in production by now.

Adam was working on a big murder case that had just started. Every day when the court rose he went straight into a meeting with the rest of the team and when he arrived home Ruth was either in her study or already in bed. Suddenly she was too busy to cook and the fridge was empty. Despite all the reassurances she'd given him, there was definitely something up, he knew it. After he got back from Vienna she'd been all over him and for several days they'd had athletic sex – she seemed to be thinking of nothing else. Then, just as he was getting used to it, she pushed him away and started snapping at him all the time; it had been like that on and off for the past couple of weeks. Everything he said or did was wrong; it was as if she'd set him a test and he'd failed it.

Perhaps she was thinking of leaving him? His friend Julius's wife had walked out two years ago, when *she* was in her mid-fifties. There had been no warning. One evening Julius got home after work and found a note on the kitchen table. It said she found him intolerable, had been desperately unhappy for years and didn't want him to contact her ever again. Julius had cried when he told Adam.

Or was she seriously ill and intent on keeping it from him? Her collapse at the weekend had been completely out of character and she'd never seemed so tired and listless. It was as if something pernicious was eating away at her: cancer, or leukaemia? Or maybe the stress of being the breadwinner was driving her towards a nervous breakdown? He wouldn't be able to bear it if anything happened to her. He knew there were problems at Morrab Films – he'd heard her talking on the phone to Bella about laying off at least one member of the team, maybe more;

she'd sounded tearful. But when he asked about it she got defensive and changed the subject. If Ruth was too ill to work or her company went bankrupt, he'd need to have a dependable source of income of his own to fill the gap: it was time to act.

Late one evening, after she'd gone to sleep, Adam sat in his study and finalised his circuit judge application. With laborious care he set out his suitability against the four separate clusters of criteria stipulated in the self-assessment notes, then boiled down his pitch until it met the word count. He read the lengthy guidelines on the importance of good character and confirmed there were no crimes or misdemeanours that would render him unsuitable for office or embarrass the judiciary. As he skimmed the documents one last time and confirmed that, to the best of his knowledge, everything he'd said was true, he felt the same shiver of apprehension that ran through him whenever he walked through the Nothing to Declare channel at an airport: certain that he was innocent, but obscurely anxious that something he was carrying unawares might incriminate him. At three thirty a.m. Adam pressed send, then emailed Ruth to tell her what he'd done. He'd given it his best shot and hoped at the very least that it would be good enough to get him an interview. If he was appointed it would take the pressure off her, and open up a new chapter for the two of them. It was the right thing to do.

15

The funnel was on a shelf in the kitchen, behind Ruth's jam-making equipment: wide, shallow and made of stainless steel, it would fit perfectly into the rim of the jar she'd chosen. It was eight days since the embryo transfer, and Lauren had asked her to do the first pregnancy test. She'd been up since seven, desperate to pee but knowing she mustn't, because she needed to use the first urine of the morning. While she waited on tenterhooks for Adam to leave for his tennis match Ruth had listened to the radio. An early-morning church service to mark the first Sunday in Advent featured a sermon about how untimely, unconventional pregnancies often turned out to be blessings in disguise; was it an omen?

She carried her apparatus upstairs and fetched a pregnancy test from the collection hidden in her underwear drawer. She'd driven south into suburban Surrey where, safe from recognition, she chose five of the most expensive test kits. At the till she withstood the flicker of surprise on the pharmacist's face and rejected her whispered offer of a paper bag. Start as you mean to go on, she told herself as she left the shop with the boxes in her hand, braving the sly stares of the prescription queue. It would have been easier to order online, but she'd imagined Adam taking delivery of a damaged parcel and asking questions she wasn't ready to answer: it wasn't worth the risk.

In the bathroom Ruth pushed all her perfumes and creams to one side and assembled everything next to the basin like a lab technician. Though she already knew the instructions by heart, she read them one last time before ripping off the foil wrapping and removing the testing wand. She put the jar on the floor, inserted the funnel, then squatted above it and peed, managing to stop when it was two-thirds full of urine.

With ceremonial slowness she pulled up her pants and jeans and fastened her belt. She moved to her laboratory, picked up the tester and plunged the white fabric tongue at its end into the jar of urine, then counted to five and lifted it out. The tongue was now bright pink, which felt encouraging, even though she knew it demonstrated only that the kit was working. The actual result would appear in the plastic window on one side of the wand: there was already a blue line running horizontally across the middle; if she was pregnant a second, vertical one would appear, creating a cross. It could take up to three minutes. For the first sixty seconds she gripped the wand fiercely, willing it to change colour, then, feeling ridiculous, balanced it on the edge of the basin.

Time stretched and Ruth's vision began to blur: now even the horizontal line seemed to be growing fainter. She was seized by panic and the beginning of nausea. Then ... was she imagining it, or was that a second line? Faint at first, then growing thicker until it formed a fat, blue, utterly emphatic cross. Ruth started to tremble from head to foot; her legs were shaking so much that she had to rest her forearms on the basin for support. The embryo had chosen to fasten itself to her. It was growing inside her. *She was pregnant.* She lifted her head and saw another face in the mirror, one she didn't fully recognise, pale and raw with shock.

Her phone was ringing: Sheila. Ruth lay down on the bed and breathed in and out twice before answering.

166

'Yes?'

'And?' said Sheila.

'And what?'

'You've done the test. I know you have.'

'Just.' Ruth struggled to find words. 'There was a cross. It was ... positive.'

'I don't believe it.' There was a stunned silence, then Sheila said, 'How do you feel?'

'Very sick, probably the adrenalin.' Ruth hesitated. 'And relieved – that it's all been worth it.' She paused again. 'But it's scary, because there's no going back now, is there?'

'I'm guessing that's a rhetorical question?'

'I've been so focused on the screenings, then the treatment and the transfer. I never really thought beyond that.'

'Well, you've done it, which is amazing – congratulations! This is *so* wonderful for Lauren: I bet she's over the moon. How did she react?'

'You rang before I had a chance—'

'You mean she doesn't—'

'I know. I need to call her *now*. Talk soon, OK?'

She went into the bathroom to clear away the debris. Downstairs she broke the testing wand in half and put it with the packaging and instructions in a refuse bag, which she buried at the bottom of the dustbin where Adam would never find it. The house was very still, as if it was holding its breath. She would make the call soon, but first she wanted to savour this moment, have it just for herself. She went upstairs again, lay on the bed and watched the sunlight as it danced on the ceiling, stained pink, green and blue by the Edwardian leaded lights in the upper half of the sash windows. She placed her hands on her tummy and imagined the embryo, squirming and multiplying inside her, requisitioning her body – giving it purpose and meaning. She arched her back with pleasure, and counted the months on her fingers: it would be due in August, safely before her fifty-fifth birthday. Against the odds she'd managed it. The puffins were looking at her with curiosity, admiration even.

She sat up slowly, dropped her legs over the side of the bed, stood up and stretched. Standing in the bay window, so she'd be able to spot Adam at the end of the street if he came back early, she made a video call.

Lauren answered instantly, her face on the screen blank with despair. She was in the bedroom, still in her pyjamas, and behind her the blinds were drawn. She turned away and shouted, 'Dan, it's Mum. I'm upstairs, come quickly.' She looked back at Ruth, reproachful. 'We've been waiting all morning. I woke at six and couldn't get back to sleep. When you hadn't rung by ten thirty I knew it was negative, but I wish you could have—'

'I'm so sorry, your dad's tennis match got put back and I couldn't do the test until he left the house.'

Dan entered the frame behind Lauren and encircled her with red woollen arms. He stooped to look into the camera, straight at Ruth. 'You've done the test?'

'Just now. Yes.'

A beat while they waited for her to continue.

'It was positive.'

'What?' Lauren put her hands to her mouth. Dan looked as though someone had hit him. Then all Ruth could see was a swirl of red into blackness as they hugged one another. Then Lauren was back again. 'I'm amazed it worked first time. Show me the cross, I want to see proof.' She was smiling.

'The kit's in the bin. It's broken.'

'But you took a photo?'

'No, should I have?' Lauren's face slumped, as if Ruth had stolen something precious from her. 'Sorry, darling, that was thoughtless of me.'

Dan pulled Lauren against his shoulder and out of vision.

168

Ruth saw the pattern of his jumper and heard him whisper, 'Laurie, you're not getting hung up about a *test*?' then, 'Yes, but remember a lot can still go wrong – we know that, don't we?' She heard the sound of kissing, then Lauren, saying, 'I know, I love you so much, our Caterpillar's made it,' and then, 'You're right, it's perfect timing.' She felt like an interloper.

Lauren's face loomed back. 'We've just been saying, there's no reason not to tell Dad now, is there? Dan's going to football with him this afternoon, so why don't we all have supper at yours afterwards and celebrate?'

Ruth's stomach lurched. 'Can we wait till we've been back to the clinic to get the absolute all-clear? Just in case, heaven forbid, it turns out to be a false positive.'

'OK, Mum, that makes sense. And thank you! We love you, don't we, Dan?'

Adam and Dan met in a pub near the stadium an hour before kick-off. They normally went straight to the ground, but Dan had suggested getting a few beers in, so Adam found himself drinking more pints than was comfortable in order to lubricate the conversation. The pub was un-modernised: dark wood, ornate lampshades and lots of bevelled mirror glass, and already festooned with Christmas decorations: furry coils of coloured tinsel, red, bright blue and bilious green, snaked round the carved mahogany pillars and hung from the bar above their heads. They engaged in several minutes of football banter, regretting the recent defeats suffered by their teams and the shortcomings of their managers.

Adam said, 'Football's like a marriage, isn't it? You sign up when you're young and impressionable – for better, for worse, through promotion, relegation, victory or defeat – and you try to hang on in there. How's Lauren, by the way? Any brighter?'

Dan took a long gulp. 'Yep.' He was nodding but frowning,

as if working his way towards an answer. 'She's good, a bit on edge, though.'

'Why's that?' Adam looked concerned.

'Oh . . . ' Dan hesitated and his mouth hung open for a second. Then he waved his hand. 'You know Laurie. She worries.' He put his glass down on the bar and scrubbed his face with the palms of his hands.

Adam felt a wave of compassion for his son-in-law and wondered whether to put an arm around his shoulder. Instead he said, 'I've hated seeing you both go through it all, the hospitals and the worry . . . and, you know, *everything*.'

Dan looked at Adam and his lips puckered into a grim line, as if someone had sewn them together roughly, to keep everything in. He nodded heavily and said, 'It's not been good,' then swallowed the rest of his pint.

Adam handed the empty glass to the barman for a refill. 'I know you're still investigating surrogacy,' he said. 'Ruth mentioned it. But you need to tread carefully.'

Dan had never seen Adam in court, but this must be what it would be like to be cross-examined by him. He wondered how much those piercing eyes could see, and began to blush, a deep, schoolboy red.

Adam saw Dan's reaction and knew he'd overstepped the mark. 'Forgive me,' he said. 'It's much too soon, isn't it? You must still be coming to terms with the miscarriage.' He gripped Dan's arm and shook it in a gesture of mute male solidarity. 'I'm sorry, let's change the subject. How's business?'

Immediately they were on safer ground: Dan talked earnestly for fifteen minutes about schedules, logistics and the challenges of motivating his team; he took out his phone and ran through the results for the previous quarter, which he said were the best they'd ever achieved.

'Thanks for taking an interest,' he said, grinning with a

mixture of pride and apology after Adam had congratulated him. 'I've tried tons of times to explain what I do to my dad, but he doesn't really get it – it's not his world.'

'How's your mother?'

'Good,' said Dan. She'd called earlier in the week to let him know that she'd had her annual check-up and everything was fine.

'Excellent,' said Adam. 'That must have come as a relief?'

'Yeah.' Dan nodded. 'It always happens in the run-up to Christmas, which isn't great, and she knows I worry. But she's been fine for years now.'

'So much more they can do, nowadays.'

Dan heard the sadness in his voice and said hesitantly, 'You mean compared with when your dad had cancer?'

Adam looked startled, as if he hadn't realised he'd spoken out loud. 'I suppose I do,' he said. He cleared his throat. 'It's time we got moving; we're sitting together because the chap next to me, who's also a season-ticket holder, is in the States on a business trip. Bit of luck, eh?'

They were carried in a sea of colour towards the stadium. Adam's red and white scarf proclaimed his loyalty; Dan wore a neutrally brown padded jacket. As they queued side by side at the turnstiles Adam, staring straight ahead, said, 'I must say, Dan, it's a great credit to you, the way you've looked after Lauren over the past few years with all you've been through. Don't think Ruth and I don't appreciate all you've done for her.'

'Thank you,' said Dan. His face was red again.

Adam's kindness made Dan feel so bad that he couldn't concentrate on the match. His father-in-law meant well: he was a decent bloke, and he didn't deserve what was coming to him. He looked sideways at Adam: yessing as his team surged forward, half standing as the striker kicked for goal, subsiding with a groan when the opposition keeper vaulted and saved. He imagined how his face would look when he heard about the pregnancy – from all three of them at some excruciating family gathering, or in private from Ruth. To start with he'd laugh in that handsome open-faced way he had, convinced it was a wind-up; then he'd be shocked. Hurt. Angry.

He might forgive his wife and daughter – might put their actions down to the madness of maternal hormones – but not his son-in-law, who should have known better. Dan would be the chief culprit, the guilty party, the man who'd planted a cuckoo in Adam's nest when he wasn't looking. The man he'd taken to the football, who'd accepted his hospitality and said nothing about the weeks of deception and the secret embryo transfer – who'd betrayed his trust. Even if Ruth miscarried, which was most likely, Adam would end up finding out and would judge him. As the little red Arsenal figures on the pitch below ran rings around their visitors, firing two goals into the net in quick succession, Dan knew what he had to do.

When the half-time whistle sounded, Adam turned to Dan, with a grin that split his face. 'This is turning into one of the most satisfying home games this season. So glad you're here for a good one!' He stood up. 'Time to celebrate!'

Dan got to his feet. 'Actually, there's something I need to say.' He pulled his hands over his face, scouring his cheeks. 'Could we maybe find somewhere a bit quieter?'

Adam looked at him in astonishment. 'OK, but you'll let me buy you a pint first?'

Dan shook his head, 'Thanks, but I'm good.' His face was tense and pale.

They threaded their way between the rows of red plastic seats towards the gangway. Then Adam pointed to his left. 'The best bet is probably the staircase right at the bottom,' he said. 'It'll be less crowded while everyone's in the bars.' He was bracing himself for bad news: either Lauren was seriously ill, or they were about to split up. They elbowed their way down until they found an empty landing on the ground floor, then stood at right angles to one another in the corner, each with his back to the wall. 'Well?' said Adam.

It was like an explosion in slow motion. Dan's voice, thickened by tears that brimmed in his eyes but didn't fall. The stink of beer and industrial disinfectant. *Ruth pregnant*. The baby was *Dan's*, and Lauren's. If it continued she'd be having it in August. The wind blew gusts of air laced with the reek of urine into Adam's face. *Ruth had offered to be their surrogate*. A big sacrifice, incredibly kind, they'd accepted. Adam didn't need to worry about the bill: *Dan was paying for everything*. Six weeks of tests and treatment, physically tough for Ruth. *Six weeks*. Polystyrene burger trays and cellophane wrappers scuttled across Adam's shoes like vermin. *She'd asked them not to tell him*, hadn't wanted to worry him in case it came to nothing. He was jostled by a gaggle of young men, their laughter erupting in his face. Dan hadn't wanted the secrecy, but Ruth insisted. They were planning to tell him this coming week, but he couldn't stand it any more. He hoped Adam would understand. *Understand?*

Another crowd surged between them. Red everywhere. Men embracing, swearing, singing, jeering. Adam, rammed into the corner, up against Dan's jacket, pressed into his wet face, felt his son-in-law trembling. He almost lost his footing. When the crowd had passed Adam stepped back, arms across his chest like overlapping shields, eyes narrowing. He saw it now: Ruth's strangeness, absences, illnesses, avoidance of sex, abandonment of work. His feeling of unease.

Bear up, Furnival, be a *man*. He walked away, fast, out of the stadium. When he got past the turnstiles, he wrenched the scarf from his neck and threw it into an overflowing litter bin; it fell to the ground and he stuffed it back in, then punched it deep inside with all his force.

Dan leant back, pushed the length of his spine against the concrete wall and pulled himself up to his full height. He scrubbed his face with his hands. It was over. He'd done the right thing, given Adam a heads-up, separated himself from the women. That was important. Then he saw Adam's face again: open and wounded as he listened, and then, just before he walked away, sharp and hard with understanding. The second face had scared Dan; he was glad it had gone. He would call Lauren in a minute. Definitely. But first he needed another pint.

PART THREE

SCAR TISSUE

THE CORNISHMAN

BIRTHS

JAGO on 21st Sept. at West Cornwall
Hospital to Angela (née Perran), wife
of Frank, a daughter, Ruth.
Grateful thanks to the doctors
and nurses.

Ruth Jago is her father's daughter, everyone says so.

'He wanted a son, but Angela, she told him, straight out, one's enough, thank you very much, after what I've been through, losing all those others. So he's making the best of little Ruth.'

He takes her fishing for bass in the surf at Godrevy and lets her loiter in his garage at Long Rock while he services the cars and sells the petrol. If he's busy stripping an engine she mans the pumps and takes the money, she's been doing it since she was eight. Her mother's contribution to her upbringing is to disapprove and warn. Ruth's eyes, she often says, are bigger than her tummy – a reference to appetites and ambitions that are *unsuitable* for her age, stage, class and gender. Mum wants her indoors, out of harm's way, but her dad is more indulgent. Apart from Sundays, when they put on their best clothes and go to Chapel, he lets her run wild. Fearless and competitive, Ruth excels at gym and rounders, climbs trees and cliffs with the boys, can stand on her head for ten minutes and swim the length of

Marazion Beach. It's a glorious childhood, but it comes to an end, one Saturday morning, when she's fifteen.

Ruth knows she is dying: three days of stabbing pain in her guts and dark brown stains on the gusset of her white knickers; three days of praying to God and Jesus to make it stop; and now, this morning, liquid seeping out of her and a terrible mess in the bed. It's not diarrhoea, nor the curse – Sheila says that comes in a red gush, as if you're peeing blood. It's something much worse: she is rotting from the inside.

In the bathroom she takes a small oblong mirror from the cabinet, puts it on the toilet floor and squats, forcing herself to look. Shocking flesh, purplish pink, like pork on a butcher's slab, then a dark splodge falls and pools. She looks at her watch and waits: seven large drops come in five minutes, and the intervals between them are getting shorter. She yanks a sheet of hard, shiny toilet paper from the china box on the wall and wipes the mirror clean; there's an insinuating raw smell, like meat that's going off.

Downstairs her mother is washing clothes at the sink, shoulder blades hunched in accusation under her beige jumper.

'Mum.'

'What is it?' She doesn't turn.

'I'm ill.' Ruth's voice falters. She puts the knickers next to the sink, stain uppermost.

Angela Jago wheels round. 'What's the *matter* with you? Take that filthy thing off my clean draining board.' Disgust on her face.

'There's brown stuff coming out of me.'

'Don't be ridiculous.' Her mother is whispering, even though there's no one else in the house.

She is marched upstairs and presented with a bundle of sanitary towels, and a belt with hooks attached. A wave of relief passes through her: she will not die and is finally blessed with the curse, no more teasing in PE lessons for being the only girl who hasn't started. But her mother seems cross, as if Ruth should have known what was happening, shouldn't have bothered her.

Back in the kitchen she's whispering again. 'Wrap up your dirty towels and put them in the boiler straight away, so germs don't spread, but not when your father's in the kitchen, he doesn't want to see that sort of thing. And wash yourself properly, *down there*. Otherwise everyone will know.'

'Know what?' asks Ruth.

Her mother's face shrivels. 'You're a woman now. You need to be more careful about how you sit and act. And don't go getting ideas. It's nothing to brag about, you know, no bed of roses.'

Everything changes. Many more things are *unsuitable*: leaving the buttons of her blouse undone below her collarbone, wearing trousers, being familiar with boys. She's under her mother's jurisdiction now and isn't allowed out, for fear of getting into trouble. Her father abandons her, as if she's turned into someone else, he doesn't come to her rescue any more. She is isolated and lonely, books are her only solace. The house is filled with silence and dissatisfaction. Sometimes when her dad's at work or fishing with his mates and Ruth is lying on her bed reading, she can hear her mother crying on the other side of the wall: low rhythmic sobs. She longs to escape. With the encouragement of her English teacher, and against her parents' wishes, she applies to five universities and receives offers from all of them.

Ruth is in the middle of a Freshers' party in college at the end of her first week, surrounded by hugging and hellos, explosions of laughter and the liquid thud of corks leaving bottles. *Everyone* seems to know one another. The grey polyester dress her mother insisted on buying is sticking to her tights and the silly bow at the neck is itchy. The other girls are wearing tight jeans and little jackets: they don't look like Margaret Thatcher impersonators. She fiddles with her hair and tells herself she belongs here. The room, large and high-ceilinged, reminds her of Chapel back home, but it's older – seventeenth century – according to the Senior Tutor, who's just talked to them about work and play and the journey of self-discovery they're embarking on. She feels self-conscious, counterfeit and very Cornish – it's her first time out of the county apart from school trips and university interviews.

The boy coming towards her is one of the organisers; he's circulating with a big silver tray and handing out glasses of wine. He's wearing a sports jacket and jeans, and he *belongs* here, would have fitted in from the moment he stepped into the medieval quadrangle. Everything about him: square shoulders, upright stance, and the chunky gold ring on his little finger. He's tall, so she has to lift her head to read his name badge:

Adam Furnival
JCR Secretary
History

'Hello there.' He's peering at hers. 'Ruth Jago, English Lit.' A smile crinkling his eyes. 'So I'm truth and you're lies? Doomed to be betrayed by you.' Hair the colour of August wheat, curling to his collar. An open, handsome face somehow at odds with the appraising stare. Grey-green eyes. He's waiting for a response, still smiling. She's outwitted, incompetent, flailing. The admissions interview all over again.

'Are you ... ?' She's stammering. 'You're saying that all literature is lies?'

'Lame joke, sorry. Forget it.' He's laughing at her, not sorry at all. 'Where are you from, *originally*, I mean?' Like everyone else he assumes she's an immigrant, because of her surname.

'Cornwall.'

'Right. Gosh. Quite a way. Where were you at school?'

She pushes back her hair. 'You won't have heard of it.'

'Bet I will, try me.'

'Penzance Girls' Grammar.'

'You're right, I haven't.'

'Perhaps because it's a state school?'

'Ouch.'

He laughs, then she laughs. An unlikely equilibrium has been established.

The first time Adam takes Ruth Jago back to his room in college, she runs her long thin fingers over the black-and-white sign painted at the entrance to his staircase: 'A.M.T. Furnival.' She says initials are a secret code that only people like him can read: his three mean posh and public school; her meagre 'R. Jago' reveals her to be nothing of the sort. This anthropological insight is delivered as a challenge – she's daring him to despise and reject her, but it only adds to her allure.

He's never met anyone like her. Dark, heavy-lidded eyes, sometimes self-consciously averted, then disconcertingly direct when happy or furious. Long, heavy hair that gleams, so dark it's almost black, but shot with chestnut lights, falling across the olive skin of her neck. Emphatically un-Furnival. He is arrested and enmeshed. She's from Cornish tin-mining stock: granite-tough and liminal, that's what draws him to her. He relishes her passion and spontaneity, her capacity for emotional recklessness. She takes him to the edge of himself, a place where he discovers unfamiliar thoughts and feelings. He pursues her relentlessly.

Adam Furnival's persistence is flattering and once Ruth has stopped feeling overawed she discovers that she likes as well as fancies him. He's clever, funny and modest: a good person. He's had lots of girlfriends and been to bed with some of them; she fabricates a brief sexual CV of her own, for balance. Her virginity, so effortfully guarded by her mother, is another anachronism that marks her out from her peers – something to be discarded with all possible speed.

They have sex in his room. At first it's a warmer, more urgent variant of the necking she's done back home on beaches and in cars. Then he reaches over to the bedside table for his wallet.

'Unless you're on the pill?'

'Er ... no.'

'Understood.'

He produces a small square packet, tears it and turns away from her to put it on.

She's apprehensive but determined. It's painful when he finally comes into her: she has to bite the inside of her lip while he moves back and forth so as not to whimper. Afterwards there's the taste of iron in her mouth, but he seems happy. 'It was good for you?' he asks, cupping her face in his hands and gazing into her eyes. She says yes, it was, and smiles ecstatically. How uncomplicated he is, how guileless: she likes that. And what a relief to have it over with.

Adam is dismayed to find blood on his sheets the next morning. Did he hurt her? No, she says, her periods are all over the place, it's nothing to worry about. He doesn't want the college cleaner to see, so she washes them in tepid water until all that remains of her defloration are two pale saffron stains.

Ruth is drinking coffee with her New Friend, the medical student who lives across the staircase. Allegra has transformed her room: it smells of incense and there are small lamps everywhere; the floor is covered with patterned rugs in navy, crimson and gold; her bed is swathed in scarlet Indian material studded with tiny mirrors and piled with satin cushions that she picked up in Delhi. Allegra is from London and has been going to bed with men (she doesn't call them boys) since she was fifteen.

Ruth mentions with proud insouciance that she's sleeping with Adam Furnival.

'*You* didn't waste much time. What are you using?'

'Using?'

Allegra sighs. 'Contraception, idiot.'

'He puts on, um, you know ... sheaths.'

'Condoms!' Allegra's lips purse in disgust. She looks severely at Ruth. 'Much too risky. You need to be on the pill. There's a free walk-in clinic just off the Cowley Road, everyone goes there.'

Ruth frowns. 'I can't take the pill.'

Allegra leans forward, interest piqued. 'For medical reasons?'

'Sort of, it's really bad for you. The hormones are so strong that they cascade backwards and damage your brain and all your other glands.'

'Says who?'

'My mother. Apparently the drug companies know but they keep it secret. Teenagers, especially, should never take them.' Allegra is looking sceptical, so Ruth adds, 'My mum does know, she works part time in a chemist.'

'She's a pharmacist?'

'No, but she serves in that section.'

Allegra laughs so much that she knocks two cushions off the bed. Ruth blushes furiously – for her mother, and herself. When Allegra sits up there are tears in her eyes, 'It's complete rubbish. Millions of women take those pills, your mum's just trying to stop you having sex.'

Ruth cycles to the family planning clinic, which is housed in a Portakabin behind a health centre. She's alarmed when they ask for her name and address: it feels as if she's being entered onto a register of wickedness, but everyone is behaving as if this is a normal thing to do. They take her blood pressure, ask a few questions and give her a small white box: three months' supply.

The following morning, she pops one of the tablets out of its foil package: it is pink, shiny and innocuous-looking. She puts it on her tongue and tastes an artificial sweetness. Then, as an afterthought, she unfolds the accompanying drug sheet; there's a long list of side effects and complications: swollen fingers, feet and ankles; headaches; depression; thrombosis; cancer; embolism; death. Her mother was right! Allegra, she reminds herself, is a first-year medical student: what can she know? She spits out the tablet and throws the box in the bin.

Most nights Ruth sleeps in Adam's room, because it's older and more beautiful than her small first-year one. They eat breakfast together then go their separate ways to lectures and libraries. She's teaching herself to cook from Penguin paperbacks: Spanish omelettes, ratatouille, spaghetti with different sauces. In the evenings they eat, drink rough red wine and make love. He has never been happier: he can't believe his luck.

Towards the end of term Ruth is sitting in the common room with a group of friends, looking out over the quadrangle, the low December sun slanting through the windows, bathing them all in light. One of them nudges her and points towards the doorway. 'Here comes your Adam, lissom and lovely.' His smile, when he catches sight of her, lifts her heart. She is dazzled by her good fortune: this place, these friends, this man.

One night Adam wakes to find himself sitting bolt upright in bed, sweating and trembling. Ruth has switched on the light and is crouching beside him. He's been crying out, she tells him, and staring at her with his eyes wide open, as if in fear of his life. She tried talking and shaking him, but couldn't wake him up. Once his heart stops thudding Adam explains: he has night terrors, they started when he was very young. He can't help it, but he should have warned her, it was thoughtless of him. 'I'm fast asleep the whole time, but I gather it's unnerving for spectators.

My mother says it started just after my father died. As you can imagine, it made me something of a talking point in the dormitory at school.'

Ruth throws her arms around him. 'Poor Adam,' she says. 'Tell me about your father. How old were you when he died?'

And for the first time in his life Adam talks about it, and cries – something he thought had been bred out of him when he was seven. She strokes his hair as they fall asleep, curled into one another. Mother Courage, the Mermaid of Zennor, the tin miner's granddaughter: she'll be my rock, he thinks.

This cannot be happening. Her body is heavy and bloated and she feels on the verge of being sick most of the time. She clings to the memory of the doctor's reassuring smile a month ago, when the first pregnancy test came back negative.

'You've just missed a period, probably because of stress, a lot of girls have disrupted cycles in their first year at university.'

Now a second period has failed to arrive and something is amiss; her breasts are swollen and the nipples tender. Every hour she goes to the loo in the hope of seeing menstrual blood. Nothing comes.

She had a second test three days ago and is waiting for the result. The doctor is searching through a pile of flimsy blue sheets on her desk and can't seem to find what she's looking for. Ruth wants this moment to stretch out for ever, so that the next one can't happen. 'Here it is.' The doctor's face is expressionless. 'The test was positive. We'll do another one today but, given your symptoms, I think we should work on the assumption that it's correct.'

'But what about the first test?'

The doctor shrugs. 'A false negative, it happens sometimes.' She is looking at Ruth steadily. 'How do you feel about being pregnant?'

The word winds itself around her until she can hardly breathe: it will bind her, define her. No, she wants to shout, I'm not pregnant, not me, not possible. She says, 'I'm not in a position to ... I hardly know the ...' She tries to gather herself. 'He used a condom, so I don't know how this happ ... I'm in my second term, I can't ...' Her eyes are filling with angry, childish tears. Nothing has prepared her for this.

The doctor nods calmly. Ruth is reminded that she will have done this before, many times. Other girls (fallen women, scarlet women, whores) have sat in this chair and had this same cliché of a conversation. 'Condoms have a failure rate of eighteen per cent if used without spermicide.' She says it gently, informative rather than censorious. Then, 'There is, of course, another option.'

A hard, determined little voice comes out of Ruth's mouth: it surprises her. 'I want an abortion. Please.'

'There can be a long wait for NHS appointments in Oxford because not all of the gynaecologists perform terminations, but I can refer you to the Pregnancy Advisory Service, which is a charity with an office in London. You can pick up a referral letter tomorrow morning and ring them to make an appointment.' She slides a leaflet across her desk, PAS in large letters at the top.

Ruth risks a look at her face: it is blankly professional. 'Will my college find out?'

'Everything will be kept confidential, Ruth.'

And because the woman has done her the small kindness of using her name, Ruth starts to cry in earnest. She gets to her feet, understanding that the doctor wants her to leave, wants not to be further implicated in the mess she has made.

Ruth is sitting on the stone staircase outside Adam's room when he gets back from morning lectures. She's bent over, head on her knees, rocking backwards and forwards. Her black cloak spills out in a big circle around her. She's never turned up during the daytime before; he's pleased, then alarmed. She says they have to talk: now, inside his room. He unlocks the door and ushers her in. She's about to ditch him, she wants someone more real, more like her – he's been dreading this, because he thinks he may be in love with her. Don't plead, Furnival, get it over and done with.

They stand facing one another, almost adversarial.

He musters all the coldness he can. 'Say it.'

'I'm pregnant, almost nine weeks.' He feels a surge of relief, then something close to panic.

'Why didn't you tell me before?'

'The first test was negative, then I missed another period and the GP did a second one. I got the result two hours ago.' She's very pale and her arms are wrapped tightly round her ribcage. 'I came straight here.'

'I'm so sorry.' His fault, he must shoulder the blame. 'I don't know how this could have happened, I didn't notice a problem with any of the cond—'

'No need to apologise.' She is shaking her head violently, as if trying to dislodge something.

His future is disintegrating, but he reaches for the time-honoured formula. 'I'll marry you. I mean, if that's what you want,' he says it uncertainly, like an actor who hasn't yet mastered his lines.

'Thanks, but there's no need, I'm not going to have it.' Her eyes are wet, but the voice is strong and hard.

'Sure, we can discuss—'

'No, I've decided and,' she lets out a sob, 'I have to do it fast.'

This cannot be happening. 'But you don't have to. We could have the baby, together—'

'It's not a *baby*.' She's shouting and tears are pouring down her face. 'It's a cluster of cells that got there by mistake and if I let them stay there my life will be over.'

'Of course, I just wanted—' But she won't let him finish.

'There's a place that may be able to help me, but if they say yes, I have to pay a fee straight away, and there isn't enough money in my account.' She's waiting, stricken.

He steps back. 'I'll pay, whatever it costs, but I'd like us to talk about it, we need to talk more.' He's never fainted, but this may be what it's like: blackness and the smell of Dettol, with an undertow of chrism oil. A sort of obliteration.

London and its Underground system are unfamiliar and Ruth gets lost twice changing trains. Advertisements next to the escalators seem to know why she's come:

IF YOU'RE HAPPY TO BE PREGNANT
CONGRATULATIONS
IF NOT, PHONE US
24-HOUR HELPLINE
PREGNANCY ADVISORY SERVICE

She is led through small pale offices containing potted plants and filing cabinets by clerks and counsellors, all women. They are faultlessly pleasant but not friendly.

'Are you sure this is what you want?'

'Yes.'

'Are you in a relationship with the father?'

'Yes.'

'Does he know you're thinking of a termination?'

'Yes.'

'Would you like to talk about the alternatives?'

'No.'

'Do you believe your mental health would deteriorate significantly if you kept this baby?'

'I would kill myself.' She is not exaggerating.

The woman explains that in view of Ruth's age and

circumstances it is likely that the doctors will agree to perform a termination, but there's a waiting time of at least a week before she'll be able to have the procedure. Ruth signs the forms and hands over sixty pounds.

Afterwards she gets lost on the way back to Paddington Station and goes round and round on the Circle Line, staring straight ahead, thinking about this big, sad, adult thing that has engulfed her. She tests herself repeatedly as the train swooshes from lighted platforms into black tunnels. It's like pushing her tongue into a giant mouth ulcer:

Could she look after it? No.

Does she want it? No.

Should she keep it? No.

The bursting sensation in her breasts and abdomen is unbearable, as if she's being torn apart from within. Her body has been overtaken by intruder cells, *without her permission*. They are threatening her survival and stopping them is an act of self-preservation. She's never been inside a hospital and is terrified by the prospect, but she'll do anything to staunch the flood of hormones that's turning her into a maternal machine.

She spends most of the week's food money on a large bottle of gin and drinks it while sitting in scalding baths. In the library she finds abortifacient recipes in medical dictionaries, encyclopaedias and anthropology textbooks, then scours Oxford Market for ingredients. She cooks them on the gas ring in her room: they taste of death and make her vomit. She wills her uterus to contract and expel its malign contents. Every few hours she pokes hopeful fingers into her vagina in search of menstrual blood. Nothing comes.

The night before the abortion she goes with Adam to New College Chapel to hear Elgar's Cello Concerto. The familiar music washes over her, plangent and beautiful, but she feels remote from it. The place is very cold and she starts to shiver; he puts his jacket around her shoulders, but it doesn't help. She's on an escalator and it's carrying her far away – from family, from friends, from Adam – into another zone, inhabited by people who do unthinkable things. She can't even talk about it to him, because there are no words, and no alternatives – whatever he may think.

It happens on a Saturday morning, so they won't have to miss lectures. The clinic is in Richmond and she has to be there by seven. Adam has borrowed his mother's car, told her they're going to the seaside for the weekend. He picks Ruth up from the entrance to their college at five thirty; it's still dark as they drive out of Oxford towards the motorway. They don't talk much. The seats smell of leather. She feels sick, but doesn't want to ask him to stop in case it makes them late. The map is confusing and they get lost in the red-grey mesh of suburban streets. The clinic, when they find it, is a low concrete building that could be an office block. Adam comes with her to the door, then they part.

She is shown into a room, where four other women are waiting, all older than her. A voice, carefully neutral, says, 'Ruth Jago?' The summons comes as a shock, proves she's here, implicated. She is led down a corridor and strangers take hold of her. She disappears.

Someone is telling her it's all over. She's OK, back in the light. Relief, a warm tide, washes her body and sings in her blood. She retches, but nothing comes. Eventually they let her go.

Adam has arranged to meet her outside, but he's not there. It is half past two in the afternoon, sunny, birds are singing; the air is warm and smells of daffodils. She waits, weak, floating, dissociated.

A man, middle-aged, florid, asks if she needs a taxi.

'No, someone's picking me up. Thank you.'

'How old are you?'

There's no need to answer, but he has the advantage of her. 'Eighteen.'

'Old enough to know better, then, young lady. Eh?' Moist red lips, leering, laughing.

She turns away and there is Adam at last, in the distance; he takes a long time to reach her. His face is pale, like a frightened child's. They bury their heads in one another. The man is still watching; his laughter follows them, all the way back to the car.

As he drives back to Oxford, there's an empty soreness in Adam's chest. His relief that the pregnancy is over is entwined with a desolating sense of loss: the first of his tribe, gone. Ruth's unilateral decision and refusal to talk about it means he has no idea whether she feels the same. He looks down at her, curled up on the seat next to him, asleep and oblivious – it's as if she's erased him.

Afterwards there's a lot of blood. The sanitary towels they gave her are saturated every time she takes one off, and they drip crimson gouts on to the black-and-white floor of her bathroom. She's told Allegra she's got food poisoning and wants to be left alone.

After six days the blurred, bloated queasiness begins to fade, her breasts return to normal and the bleeding is tailing off. She can breathe again. Like millions of women before her she has stared pregnancy down. She expects to be traumatised and braces herself for an avalanche of guilt and regret, a nervous breakdown, even. But they don't come. Adam visits diligently, bringing flowers and fruit from the market. They can't have sex – she has to wait until after her next period, in case of infection – and they're uneasy with one another; he never stays long. They don't refer to the abortion.

The term ends and she returns to Penzance, feeling immeasurably older. She spends six days a week in the public library catching up on work she's missed and attacking the reading list for the term ahead. Her mother shouts at her for being stand-offish and refusing to go to Chapel, says she's using the place like a hotel. Leave her alone, says her father in a rare intervention, she's working at her books, like a *good* girl. She doesn't tell anyone what happened, not even Sheila, who's home from the LSE where she's studying sociology. Ruth has her old body back, burgeoning and bleeding in its familiar monthly rhythm. It's as if it never happened.

They drift apart. In his last term Adam works day and night until Finals; afterwards he's taken up with farewell parties and graduation. Ruth is invited to the college end-of-term ball by someone else and she accepts. During the summer holidays they exchange affectionate postcards, vowing to keep in touch, but they know they won't.

In her third year Ruth acts in plays and does some directing, she gets noticed by reviewers at the Edinburgh Festival. She has many flirtations but no significant relationships. Adam qualifies as a barrister and becomes a pupil in a sought-after set of chambers, where his father once worked. He has a succession of girlfriends, but one after another they are defeated by an unexpected and impenetrable reserve.

After she graduates Ruth moves to London and finds work as an assistant floor manager in the drama department at the BBC. Another new world and, again, she's an outsider. In the bar at lunchtime and after work some of her fellow trainees hobnob with executive producers and heads of department, who turn out to be their godparents, family friends or school alumni; it's a subterranean network of patronage that provides advice, support and sometimes jobs. One day everyone in her department gets an email: there's an emergency – filming's about to start on a big new series and the main location has just fallen through. Ideas, please!

192

One of the runners calls her uncle and secures the ancestral family home, a Jacobean pile in Gloucestershire; everyone says she'll go far, that one: she's got initiative and contacts – that's what it takes to get on. When a producer with a second home in St Ives discovers Ruth grew up nearby she tells her to drop by, next time she's down, and bring her parents, she'd *love* to meet them. Ruth shudders, imagining the gruesome collision of her old and new lives over drinks or a barbecue. Frank and Angela Jago, tongue-tied and awkward in their Chapel clothes, spurning all offers of alcohol; her colleague's face as she realises where Ruth has sprung from; the office gossip and subtle recalibration that would follow. As a working-class girl with no contacts, she knows already that she's going to have to strive harder and longer than the others to make her mark: she can't afford any cross-contamination.

Felicity Wenham is holding a big formal dinner party in her flat in Stoke Newington. What a coincidence, she exclaims, as she ushers everyone into the dining room: she had no idea Ruth and Adam knew one another when she made the seating plan, almost spooky, isn't it? They must have *so* much catching up to do!

Adam pours wine into her glass and asks how long it's been.

'Heavens,' says Ruth, counting back, 'almost five years since that party in my first week.' She adds uncertainly, 'If you remember it?'

'How could I forget: I was captivated by your beauty.'

'Don't be ridiculous,' she's whispering, worried that others will hear.

'Statement of fact. I'd forgotten how easily you blush, though.'

'*Adam!*' she remonstrates, but she's giggling.

'*Ruth.*' He's looking at her with unfeigned pleasure.

They talk all evening, about life and work and families, ignoring the heated debates going on around them about nuclear weapons and trades union rights; they quite forget to turn politely to their neighbours after the first course, and are much too engrossed to break off at the end of the second. They remember how much they *like* one another.

Afterwards they go back to Adam's flat, because it's nearer than hers. When they start to make love she informs him casually that she's on the pill now – all that stuff her mother told her turned out to be Calvinistic brainwashing.

Two weeks later, and Ruth and Adam have fallen back into their old, intimate complicity. They've been to a performance of *Guys and Dolls* directed by one of her friends at a pub theatre in Waterloo, and now they're walking hand in hand by the Thames, laughing and singing the songs from the show. He hasn't planned to ask her to marry him, but suddenly he knows he must. She's so different from all the others: she *knows* him, and it feels necessary, somehow – a way to make sense of everything. A dense drizzle is hugging the air and their coats are already soaked, but he insists on stopping, there's something he wants to say; his voice is trembling.

She's taken aback, but hears herself saying yes, of course she will, her legs are so unsteady that she leans against the river wall for support. She feels both relieved and deprived of agency: she'll be safe, as a Furnival. It's more of an inevitability than a decision. Is that normal, she wonders. Then brushes the thought away.

They cross Hungerford Bridge and drink a bottle of champagne in the bar of the Savoy Hotel, just the two of them.

THE TIMES

BIRTHS
FURNIVAL On 12th January,
to Ruth (née Jago) and Adam, a
daughter, Lauren Sheila Anne.

This time Ruth loves the metamorphosis of her body, the surge of blood and straining of skin and sinew as a new life makes space for itself inside her. She feels exultant and powerful. She even relishes the shockingly painful process of expulsion. When Lauren is laid on her chest she's enraptured by the baby's silken skin and the profound animal pleasure of breastfeeding. She feels a concomitant tugging as her womb contracts, readying itself for the next occupant. She *must* do this again. Soon. She spends six months suckling and being domestic, then hires a nanny and plunges back into work as a script editor at the BBC; it's a wrench, but she loves her job and they need the money.

Lauren is a quiet, self-contained baby. For Adam she comes as a balm, assuaging the wound of his fatherlessness. He agrees that at some point they'll have another, so Ruth's probably right, it's not worth her going back on the pill for a while. But it's harder than he expected, trying to balance two demanding careers, a house and a baby, not to mention maintain any kind of relationship. They've just about got back on an even keel when she tells him she's pregnant again, and Lauren's barely eight months old: *it's too soon.*

THE TIMES

BIRTHS
FURNIVAL On 26th April, to Ruth
(née Jago) and Adam, a daughter,
Alexandra Clare Rose, sister
to Lauren.

Propped up on pillows in the sunny antenatal ward, cuddling both her daughters, Ruth has never felt happier. She will have at least one more, she decides, ideally two.

*

195

But Alex is unlike her sister: she walks at nine months, rampages around the house and lies noisily awake every night demanding food and attention. They take it in turns to sleep, and operate in a blur of exhaustion. When Ruth stops breastfeeding they agree she must go back on the pill: another baby would break them. Six months later she's offered a junior producer role on a costume drama – it's a chance to prove herself and she jumps at it, spending three months on location in Scotland, then days and nights in cutting rooms. The series wins prizes and establishes her as a new talent; soon she disappears into another high-profile series. She's becoming a role model for younger women in television who aspire to have it all: brilliant career, children, husband.

Adam is left holding the babies more often than he'd like, at weekends and on the nanny's evenings off, and, having no role model, he has to make up being a father as he goes along. Tired and harassed, he ends up cutting corners at work: there's less time for preparation and networking. He's proud of Ruth, but the balance doesn't always seem fair and he worries about the effect it's having on his career. And he misses her.

The girls are five and four now, and Ruth adores them, but she'll be thirty this year and she yearns like an addict for the Class-A thrill of a newborn baby's skin against hers. A boy, perhaps, this time?

When she mentions the idea, Adam is appalled. 'No,' he says flatly.

'Because?'

'Because it's been hard enough with two and Alex has only just started sleeping through the night. Because you're hardly ever here and I've done most of the childcare. I can't face doing it again. Ever.' He pauses and looks at her, sceptical. 'Unless you're planning to give up work?'

She ignores the question. 'I know you've done more than

your share with the girls, but my job's more secure now and next time it'll be *much* easier. I could probably wangle a year's maternity leave.'

'There isn't going to be a next time.'

'You've always known I wanted at least one more. It's always been part of the plan.'

'*Your* plan, not mine.' Adam's face is shuttered now. 'You could have had three by now, but *you* chose not to, didn't you?' He's made veiled regretful references to the abortion over the years, as if it's a scab he has to pick at, but this is the first time he's weaponised it.

Ruth says, 'That was years ago. I was a different person, a teenager, you can't compare the two.'

He shakes his head. 'We're the same people, Ruth – morally continuous.'

She threatens to leave if she can't have another, but he's immovable, so there's no alternative: she stops taking the pill. She feels no guilt because when she gets pregnant, he'll come round, she knows he will, and he'll love the new baby, just like he loves the girls. In fact, he'll be grateful for her subterfuge, because it's the right thing to do.

They are about to drive to Adam's mother's house for a big family party to celebrate her sixtieth birthday. Ruth is downstairs corralling the girls and Adam is filling an overnight bag with clothes. Searching their bedroom for his silver cufflinks, he comes across a box of Ruth's contraceptive pills at the back of a drawer, unused. He checks the prescription date and it's clear she's not been taking them for months: she's lied to him. He pushes the box back into its hiding place, and resumes his packing.

As he drives down the M40, Adam considers his options. He looks at Ruth, sitting beside him, lost in concentration as she

197

marks up scripts and makes a succession of work phone calls, apparently unaware of the girls' bickering and screaming in the back. Her *desperation* for more children, when she barely registers the ones she's got, is a kind of madness: reproductive profligacy. It's the way she was at Oxford when she got rid of their baby: single-minded, no discussion, no sense of being a couple and weighing the pros and cons. He went along with it, of course, when he should have taken a stand. He was guilty, too. This time, though, he must stop her.

The urologist, a pale, desiccated man in his sixties, explores Adam's scrotum with cold, nimble fingers, then probes with shocking inquisitiveness into the area just above it.

'I need to check your vas are present and correct on both sides,' he says absently. 'They're the chaps we need to tie off and cut.' The sensation – a gentle rhythmic pumping – is unnervingly pleasant. Afterwards the surgeon washes his hands with a thoroughness Adam finds faintly insulting. When he's reclaimed his trousers and is seated, the urologist peers at him through rimless glasses. 'Your plumbing's in good order and there's no reason why I can't perform a vasectomy, but you are thirty-three years old. Rather young to be sterilised?'

'My wife and I have two children and I don't want any more.'

The eyes don't blink. 'My average patient is over forty, Mr Furnival. Men who have vasectomies in their early thirties often come to regret it. There's no guarantee that the procedure would be reversible. I would counsel you to wait.'

Adam says he's weighed the risks and benefits: his mind is made up.

The urologist nods. 'Your choice. I have a day surgery list next Thursday and you're a good candidate for local anaesthesia and sedation. How would that suit?'

*

Adam leaves home early. He wears a suit, but his briefcase contains a brand-new jockstrap and his baggiest pair of tracksuit bottoms. At the hospital he is stripped and shaved; the injection into his scrotum is shockingly painful, but the next few hours are a Valium-induced blur. He giggles as a solicitous nurse bandages him, then he falls asleep.

When the drugs wear off he wakes in a small beige day room, horribly alert to the throbbing between his legs. His tracksuit bottoms are stretched at the crotch by something the size of a cauliflower; he reaches forward to touch it but falls back, overcome by nausea. A loud groan escapes him.

'You OK there, Mr Furnival? Pain bothering you?'

He stares at the nurse in frank amazement. 'It's awful,' he gasps. 'Something's gone wrong.'

She laughs with callous abandon and pats his arm. 'It's always sore afterwards, just a bit of bruising.' She looks at her watch. 'In fact, you can go home whenever you like. Is someone coming to pick you up?'

'No,' says Adam.

He lets himself into the house and creeps upstairs, so that the girls, who are in the kitchen with the au pair, won't hear him. Shivering uncontrollably, he puts on two jumpers and a coat, gets into bed and tries to sleep.

Much later he hears Ruth's key in the front door. She's calling his name and searching the ground floor, then climbing the stairs. She pauses in the doorway. 'Are you ill? Why didn't you call me, darling?'

'I had an operation this morning.'

She comes towards the bed, her face etched with concern. 'An *operation?*'

'A vasectomy. I had to. I found your pills. You'd stopped taking them, without telling me. It was the only option.'

She hits him hard across the face, repeatedly. He doesn't resist. It blots out the other pain. When she stops he tries to explain, how they've both exercised their reproductive choices now.

She cries for a long time, then regains her breath and speaks quietly and slowly, as if dictating for the record. 'Before I had the abortion I told you what I wanted and you went along with it. You *drove* me there, for God's sake! Today you've forcibly sterilised me, without even having the courtesy to inform me in advance.'

He stares at her, face swollen, eyes red with weeping. He loves her so much, but it's *his* body too.

She tells no one: the humiliation would be too great. She considers her options: divorce, a punitive affair, self-insemination. But she's living the life she dreamed of as a teenager, liberated from the claustrophobia and constraints of 37 Rosvenna Drive, Penzance, and she can't bear to bring it all tumbling down. And she discovers, bit by bit, that she hasn't stopped loving him.

He's waited for six months, uncertain whether she'll ever return to the marital bed, but now she's back, and they've arrived at a sort of truce: not so much a reconciliation as the end of hostilities. The truth is, they are both attracted and repelled by one another: he needs her boldness and drive, she admires his deep integrity; he deplores her slippery pragmatism and she can't bear his pompous inflexibility. But now they've each played their strongest cards, invoked their opposing powers to the limit, and in the process reached a kind of permanent equilibrium. The game is over now, *for good*. He's relieved.

PART FOUR

RUPTURE

16

Ruth was alerted to Adam's return by the explosive slamming of the front door: the sash windows in her study quivered in their frames. She went out on to the landing; he was below her, at the far end of the hall, staring at the floor.

'I didn't expect you back this early,' she said. 'How was the match?'

He didn't look up. Was he ill?

'Come down here.' His voice was quiet. 'Now.'

She took three steps before checking herself. 'Please don't speak to me like that, Adam. What's the matter?' She felt a shiver of disquiet.

'Come here.' Lethally quiet now. '*Please.*'

Dan had told him.

She had imagined this moment, but as a kind of disembodied rhetorical exchange, never a physical confrontation. Now her heart was flinging itself against her ribcage and she was struggling to breathe. She walked down the stairs very slowly, head held high, determined to be dignified, but her legs were unsteady and she ended up scrabbling for the banister with both hands. When she reached the bottom, Adam stepped back, as if recoiling from something toxic. She forced herself to meet his eyes.

They stood in the middle of the hall, facing up to one another, alongside Lauren's three collages. Adam's shoulders were braced and his neck thrust forward, like the stags she avoided in Richmond Park during the rutting season. There was sweat on his forehead and upper lip, his skin looked pale and waxy and there were red-rims around his eyes: he'd been crying. A spasm in her chest, and the smell of beer, sweetly menacing.

He took a step towards her. 'How could you?' His voice was thick and hoarse.

She flinched.

'How *could* you, Ruth?'

'I was going to tell you if the result was confirmed. I've only done one pregnancy test and it could *easily* be a false positive.' If only she could reach him, it might still be all right. '*Please*, Adam, let's sit down and talk about it.'

It was no good: pain flickered briefly across his face, then she saw him clamp it down. 'You have deceived and humiliated me. Systematically. How *could* you?'

Her voice caught in her throat. 'I did it for Lauren.'

He said nothing, only the rasp of his breathing.

'I'd just be a container for their child,' Ruth pleaded. 'It doesn't affect *us* in any way. This is one hundred per cent theirs.' She looked down and spread her hands between her hips, like a wide belt encompassing the foreign body inside her.

She hadn't meant it as a provocation, but as soon as the words were out of her mouth Adam's face convulsed into a snarl of molten hatred. 'No,' he yelled, somewhere between a groan and a scream.

She felt his saliva on her cheek and the tabloid faces, primitive and deadly, of men who'd tortured and murdered their step-children, rogue products of wombs they'd thought they owned, flashed before her eyes. In a protective reflex she doubled over and clasped her abdomen: anything to save the baby. Her bare toes were inches from his black leather shoes, the muscles in her back tensed, waiting for the blow. But it didn't come: the feet withdrew and Ruth's whole body began to shake. She staggered backwards and collapsed onto the stairs in a blur of nausea and relief, vomit crouching sourly, high in her throat. They surveyed one another, shocked by what had been unleashed.

He said, 'I kept asking you what was the matter. When you were in bed, pretending, no doubt, to be ill, I asked you if you'd seen a doctor, and whether Lauren knew something I didn't. You said, "No, don't worry." You lied, *to my face*. Did what you wanted, and damn the consequences.'

When Ruth could speak she said, 'No, this is what Lauren, *your daughter*, wanted.' His expression didn't change, so she ploughed on, desperate to connect. 'I wanted to tell you the truth. I tried, right at the beginning, the night we apologised to each other after the row at Ravi's, but you changed the subject. And there were lots of other times, but I got interrupted, or was too scared. I'm sorry.'

But he wasn't listening. 'Did what *you* wanted,' he repeated. 'As you always have, right from the start. The abortion, stopping the pill, riding roughshod over me. You're on your own trajectory, aren't you? Separate. Ruthless.'

The unfairness of it stung her. 'Don't throw that in my face again, I'm sick of it.'

Adam stared at her for a long time, then he said, 'How do you think this feels, Ruth? I'll be a laughing stock, the man whose fifty-four-year-old wife has furtively embarked upon a pregnancy and is carrying his son-in-law's baby. A public spectacle. Can you *imagine*?' The silence congealed around them. Eventually he said quietly, 'We both know what's going on here. This is your final reproductive salvo, isn't it, the one that renders me completely obsolete?'

She sighed; it was as if they were reading from a very old script. 'You've got it wrong. Hundreds of women all over the world have done this for their daughters, with the love and support of their husbands. Google it and you'll see.' He gave a dismissive snort. 'I'm putting my body and health at risk, for Lauren. *Normal* people see it as an act of altruism.'

He stiffened. 'Who else knows?'

'The staff at the clinic, obviously.'

He was waiting.

'And Lauren told Alex.'

Adam nodded bleakly. 'The whole family was in on the secret. I was the mug, kept in the dark while you concocted your lies, went to your appointments, and embarked upon this ...' he hesitated, then spat out the word, '*mis*conception.'

Ruth said nothing.

'Anyone else?'

'Only Sheila.'

'"Only Sheila. *Only Sheila,*"' he mimicked her viciously, 'who will have told Simon and everyone we know.'

Ruth said, 'She hasn't, I give you my word.'

'Your *word*?' He raised his eyebrows.

Ruth writhed in the glare of his contempt. 'I hear you, Adam.' She stood up, determined to give it one last try. 'I realise what a terrible shock this has been and how I've hurt you. I know I need to do a huge amount to make amends, but we can get through this together, as a *team*.' She held her arms open. 'We've faced lots of challenges in the past. But we're still here, aren't we?'

He put up his hands, as if to ward her off. 'You've broken us, Ruth. However bad things have been, before now we've always sorted them out in private. This time you've gone public, without even bothering to tell me. There isn't a "we" any more.'

She walked towards him, ready to prostrate herself, but he sidestepped her and pushed opened the door to his study. 'I'll sleep in the spare room,' he said.

*

Ruth sat down on the bottom stair and put her face in her lap, grinding her eye sockets into her knees until everything went black, then she clasped her legs and rocked herself backwards and forwards.

It'll be all right. It'll be all right. It'll be all right.

Been here before. You can cope.

Don't worry, don't worry. Don't worry.

She felt his presence, behind the door a few feet away from her, stone-faced and implacable.

You've broken us. You've broken us. You've broken us.

He'll leave. He'll come round. Gone too far this time.

Good thing. Bad thing. Good thing.

The baby! The moment she remembered, she stilled herself and took a deep breath. She imagined the embryo, like a bead at her centre, holding everything together. She remembered its inscrutable pewter face on the screen during the transfer and the moment when it entered her: it was hers to keep secure and safe, to protect from trauma. Nothing else mattered. She uncurled herself and stood up, then climbed the stairs slowly and carefully. In the bedroom she drew the curtains, got into bed and burrowed under the duvet. She fell asleep almost immediately.

As soon as Dan left to go to football Lauren called Alex to tell her the news.

'It's fantastic,' said Alex. 'I'll be rooting for both of you over the next nine months.'

'Even though you've got reservations about Mum being our host?' said Lauren.

'I'm sorry, I shouldn't have said that.'

'It's OK. I know where you were coming from. When we were little I never felt she was really available and that's why we didn't have a great relationship. I still can't understand how she could bear to leave us so much, but over the past few weeks we've spent so much time together and the surrogacy's become our joint project.'

They talked for ages: what a fluke it was that the first transfer had worked and what a force to be reckoned with their mother was when she put her mind to something. Then Lauren sounded a note of caution: 'I'm thrilled we've got this far, but Dan and I aren't taking anything for granted. Until the clinic's done an ultrasound we can't be sure there's actually a foetus there – sometimes a sac full of fluid gives a positive test result. That's why we're not telling Dad just yet.'

Alex promised to keep everything crossed. 'And later on I might go shopping and buy some wool, so I can start knitting a stylish wardrobe for your sprog. Gender-neutral colours, natch.'

Lauren begged her not to tempt fate. But after they'd said goodbye she lay on a sofa in the sitting room for several hours with her laptop, checking out antenatal clinics in West London that she and Ruth could go to, NCT classes in Brockley, pregnancy blogs by women who'd used surrogates, and clothes suitable for babies born in August.

When she heard Dan's key wrestling with the lock she realised it was already ten o'clock. He'd been gone for eight hours: they must have eaten after the match. She'd just finished clearing her search history when he appeared in the doorway. There was a slack grin on his face. 'Hello, babes.' She frowned, he'd called her that when they first met but she'd managed to train him out of it.

'Dan?' Her voice was sharp.

'Hey, don't be cross with me, babes.' He leant against the wall and began to slide down; she thought he might collapse, but he steadied himself.

She'd never seen him this drunk; he prided himself on keeping up with his mates but staying in control. 'Where have you been?'

He lowered his head and peered up at her from beneath his eyebrows. 'I told your dad.'

Lauren's stomach turned over. 'Told him what?' she asked rhetorically.

He extended his arms as if caressing a vast tummy. 'About your mum.'

She sat up. 'Dan . . . ' She was speaking slowly, as if interviewing a small child who'd been a bystander at an accident and was now a vital witness. 'You told *Dad* that Mum's pregnant?'

He crossed the room and stood over her; she could smell the beer. 'Yes,' his face was defiant, 'I had to.'

She stared up at him. 'What did he say?'

'He said . . . ' Dan's face puckered in concentration. After a long pause he yawned cavernously. 'Nothing. He left at half-time. Didn't say goodbye.'

'And you spent the next six hours getting plastered?'

'I tried calling you. Couldn't get through.' He put his hands over his ears and fell backwards on to the sofa opposite her.

'I was talking to Alex, but only for an hour or so. Why didn't you keep trying?' He didn't reply. 'Dad didn't say *anything*? How did he look? Upset? Angry?'

Dan belched loudly, closed his eyes, then subsided into a snoring sleep.

Lauren went to bed and lay on her back, imagining the scene: her father's fury; her mother's defensive explanations; the ensuing row; and the embryo, caught between the two of them, traumatised and vulnerable.

At midnight she messaged Alex:

> Can you talk? Very bad stuff
> happening here

Seconds later Alex called. 'What's up?'

'You know Dan and Dad went to Arsenal this afternoon?'

'The long-planned male-bonding session? Yes.'

'Dan told him.' Lauren paused because she still couldn't quite believe it. '*Everything.*'

'Oh my God. Why?'

'No idea, and he's so drunk I can't get any sense out of him.'

'Better now than in nine months' time, I guess.'

'It's not funny, Alex. Mum was about to tell him, she was just waiting for confirmation from the clinic.'

'That sucks,' said Alex, 'but at least everything's out in the open now.'

'He'll be furious with Mum and she'll be livid with Dan. It's *so* dangerous.' Lauren said she'd been reading the latest research online: during domestic conflict pregnant women secreted high levels of cortisol, which stopped the placenta developing and caused miscarriage. It could kill foetuses in the early weeks. 'Imagine, Mum's stress levels will be through the roof at the moment. Should I drive over to Hammersmith and bring her back here?'

'I think you may be overreacting,' said Alex gently. 'Whatever's been happening this evening, Mum and Dad are going to be fast asleep by now and your embryo will be safe and snug. You need to switch off all your devices and take a sleeping tablet.'

Lauren's face relaxed fractionally. 'You're probably right, but it's hard not to worry. Everything's suddenly got so complicated.'

Alex pointed her forefinger into the screen and grinned. 'I'm tempted to say I told you so, but I wouldn't dream of it. Sleep well, I love you.'

After they ended the call Alex swiped through the photos on her laptop until she found the one she'd taken in the garden at Ruth's birthday lunch, when they'd all been together, celebrating in the sun. She zoomed in: Lauren on the left, in front of Dan, his arms encircling her, holding an ultrasound image of their baby; great grins on their faces, as if joy and relief had cracked them open after years of tension and grief. Alex next to them: she'd nipped in after setting up the shot and propping the camera in position. Adam to the right, beaming, with his arm slung across Ruth's shoulders. Her mother was in the centre, giving one of her practised smiles that radiated happiness; it would have fooled most people, but Alex saw the tension around her mouth and eyes, and sensed the subdued irritation, as if she was enduring something. She remembered asking a joke question about becoming a grandmother, and how Ruth had almost snapped at her. She hadn't relished the prospect of taking on *that* particular supporting role, yet she'd volunteered with enthusiasm to neglect her work and carry Lauren's baby. Paradoxical and peculiar – Alex couldn't make sense of it. She imagined her mother's uterus and the tiny dot inside it. If it turned out to be a fluid-filled sac, the situation was probably salvageable, but if there was a baby ensconced there then it might be a while before the next group photo was taken.

Alex's impulse was to hop on a plane and try to calm things down, but she'd already taken most of her three-week holiday allowance. Instead, she composed a long, bolstering message to Adam, because he was the injured party and would be feeling wretched, then a brief, wryly sympathetic one to Ruth. Then she decided that approach might be divisive, and in any case maybe Lauren was catastrophising. She deleted both texts and messaged them jointly:

> I'm thinking about you both and
> wondering how you are? Please
> call when you can. Much much love
> dear aged Ps from your distant
> daughter XXXXXXX

If they were already on a war footing, she hoped it might encourage them to behave like grown-ups.

211

17

As he drove home on Monday evening Adam rehearsed a conversation in which Ruth listened in silence while he explained what she'd done to him and how he felt, but when he opened the front door the house was in darkness and he remembered: she had a work dinner and would be back late. He changed into jeans and an anorak and headed down to the Thames, then across Hammersmith Bridge and west along the towpath. He walked at a furious pace, slowing only to sidestep cyclists, joggers and pools of liquid mud. He was trying to manoeuvre himself into a less vengeful place but it was a struggle: this business had ripped open all the old wounds.

The previous night he'd had a vivid and disturbing dream in which he unlocked his car and tried to get in but there was another man already in the driver's seat. He asked him politely to move, but the stranger refused. Adam said, 'Get out now, or I'll call the police.' The man took no notice; instead, he started the car and accelerated fast, laughing uncontrollably as they careered down the road. Adam reached across to seize the wheel and tried to steer but they were swerving all over the place: a crash was coming. When he woke up the sheets were soaked with sweat.

There was the familiar stench of sewage as he approached the National Archives: a sweet, insinuating retch of air that floated above the familiar towpath smell of tidal river and leaf mould. As he climbed the steps to Kew Bridge a passing couple bade him good evening – as if the world hadn't tilted out of control. He'd trusted Ruth, but she'd kept things secret then left him in the lurch. It was what always happened, in the end: his father, his mother, his grandfather's car, scrunching over the gravel as it accelerated away from school. He was rocking now as he walked. Making and breaking foetuses, without a thought for him. The idea of her swelling up into visible pregnancy; having to explain it to friends and strangers; the raised eyebrows and the dry one-liners as the story took wing at work: *Poor old Furnival, must be feeling like a bit of a spare prick, hahahahaha.* He was back in the dormitory, curled in a ball, biting his upper lip, *boys don't cry, Adam,* powerless, pretending not to care, while they imitated his night terrors, screaming and laughing – *Furnifreak! Furnifreak!* – and piled themselves on top of him, until he couldn't breathe. He imagined taking Dan unawares and punching him, dead-centre, between the eyes: how satisfying it would be. But Dan was only the messenger, and this was Lauren's child, his grandchild. He must keep things in perspective. *Don't let us down, will you, Adam?*

Along Strand on the Green a high tide was ebbing from the pavement and he picked his way through twigs and seaweed. Curtains and blinds were still open, and the lighted windows of the terraced houses and pubs were like a series of Victorian lantern slides that revealed well-ordered family lives: cosy, snug, smug, safe; enviable now. He'd have to stay with Ruth and be dignified and supportive until this whole thing was over, but he wouldn't be able to stomach intimate contact. He didn't want to see her burgeoning body, or touch her.

When he got home he spent two hours moving all his things into the bedroom under the eaves. He took only one thing that was jointly owned: the Audubon puffins, passed down by his mother as a sort of guardian of their happiness; thank heavens

213

she hadn't lived to see this mess. Its removal left a pale square on the wall. Upstairs he hung the print on a hook opposite his new bed, then realised it would be too upsetting to look at it every day. He opened the bottom drawer of the chest and put it in, face downwards, then went to his study and began to type:

Ruth,
I have moved up to Alex's old room and will sleep there from now on.
I shall respect your privacy and trust you will reciprocate. Perhaps we can attempt to live parallel but separate lives?
Adam

He pressed send: that way she'd see it before she got home and wouldn't come looking for him.

When Ruth awoke the following morning she stretched her legs sideways in order to locate Adam's body and nestle into his warmth, but his side of the bed was cold and empty. Remembering, she reached for her phone and reread his email for the hundredth time. Moving upstairs was a symbolic gesture; he needed to punish her for a while. All the same, she was surprised how much stuff he'd taken. She imagined him marching back and forth with his arms full of suits and ties and shoes, jaw clamped in resignation.

She didn't feel entirely to blame, though: if he'd been less doctrinaire and rigid she'd have been able to talk to him right from the start. She got out of bed, plumped up the pillows and folded back the duvet in a burst of righteous energy. If Adam was going to abandon her for a while she might as well enjoy a tidy room, unsullied by his mess. As she stood back, checking that everything was shipshape, an oblong shape on the wall caught

214

her eye, it was like a watery shaft of projected light, but strangely still. She stared at it with a giddy sense of foreboding: *someone had stolen the puffins.* They'd been burgled. She scanned the room to find out what else was missing. Unless. Ruth sat down on the bed. Unless something much worse had happened?

As Lauren turned into the side street that led to the clinic she spotted Ruth in the distance. She shouted and ran towards her. Ruth looked back for an instant, then walked on. She was sitting in the ultrasound waiting room when Lauren arrived.

'We've been texting and calling all week to find out how you are.' Lauren stopped to catch her breath. 'Why didn't you answer? I've been frantic, what's happening is *terrible* for the pregnancy, Mum.'

Ruth looked at her. 'I'm sorry, I know that none of this is down to you, darling, but the last few days have been hell. It was my decision not to involve your dad and I take full responsibility for that – I was planning to tell him this evening, if the pregnancy was confirmed, and I'm sure I could have got him on board. But now he's convinced I set out to humiliate him and I've never seen him so angry. I think he may leave me. What was Dan *thinking*?'

Lauren sat down next to her. 'Right from the start Dan felt very bad about keeping things secret from Dad – to be fair, we both did – and when they met up he suddenly felt it was his duty to tell him you were pregnant.'

'His *duty*?' Ruth looked at her, incredulous.

'I know, it's insane, but that's what he said. I was furious with him.' She clutched Ruth's arm. 'I can't tell you how sorry he is, Mum.'

Ruth said, 'I have to tell you, if it turns out I'm not pregnant, then I don't think I can face going through this palaver a second time.'

Lauren opened her mouth to protest, but Helen Braithwaite was coming towards them.

'I've tested your urine and it's still showing positive, so we'll do an ultrasound scan and see what's going on in there, ladies.'

Ruth tried to relax as her uterus became visible on the screen. A small black void would mean that a cyst was masquerading as a foetus. That would be the most convenient outcome: Adam would sympathise and relent, faces would be saved and life would eventually get back to normal. *But it wasn't what she wanted.* Lauren put her hand into her mother's and, in spite of herself, Ruth squeezed it. Their breathing was audible above the low machine hum.

'There,' said Helen, she clicked her mouse and two small crosses appeared. 'Can you see that whitish area in the middle?'

'Yes,' they said in unison.

'That's your baby.'

Ruth's heart jolted on its axis and she felt perilously close to tears; she wished Adam was with her. Lauren closed her eyes and dropped her head onto her mother's chest. Ruth stroked her hair. This was what it had all been for – the weeks of interviews and medical invasions, the tests and tablets, the subterfuge and exhaustion – this was what she'd longed for: something *alive* inside her.

Helen emailed them the scan, then printed off two copies. 'May I have an extra one?' said Ruth. 'For my husband.'

They were ushered straight in to see Dr Vassily, who had already seen the result. He jumped to his feet, his face wearing the irrepressible grin of new fatherhood. 'Mrs Furnival, Mrs Ryan, what a team we are! Eh?' They hugged him.

He announced that Ruth was already almost five weeks pregnant, because the embryo had been five days old on the day of transfer. She needed to keep taking oestrogen and progesterone for seven more weeks to maintain the pregnancy, but by the time she got to the end of the first trimester her placenta should be producing enough hormones to take over. She should register with a hospital antenatal clinic as soon as possible and her expected delivery date was the fourteenth of August – comfortably inside the Marinella's deadline.

He turned to Lauren. 'Please give my best wishes to your husband. I'm sorry not to be able to shake his hand on this happy day. And to Mr Furnival, of course.' He winked at Ruth. 'Send me a photograph of the baby for my wall of fame, won't you, my dears?'

In the lobby Lauren phoned Dan. 'Everything's OK, I'm texting you a photo now, you can't see much . . . Yes, of course, she's right by me . . . I'll ask.'

She held out her phone, her face pleading. 'Dan would like a word.'

Ruth took the phone. 'Congratulations,' she said with cool formality.

Dan's voice was gruff. 'I'm sorry I told Adam. It's no excuse, but I'd drunk an *incredible* amount. I've been trying to get hold of you to apologise for being such a prat and causing so much trouble.'

Ruth felt powerful now, and infinitely magnanimous. 'Dan, darling, I'm tough as old boots and this baby will be OK, I promise. We are where we are and we'll sort it out, somehow, so stop worrying . . . OK, I'll say it: I forgive you! . . . Yes, I will, bye.' She handed the phone back to Lauren. 'He says he'll call you later.'

'Thank you, Mum – I couldn't bear the thought of us being on bad terms with you, or Dad.' She stopped. 'About Dad. Dan and I are scared he might refuse to sign the parental order that recognises us as the baby's parents because of what's happened. Does he know about his consent form, and that you . . . ?' She hesitated; they'd avoided the subject since the day of the embryo transfer.

Ruth said firmly, 'He does not, and if I told him right now I'd be chucking petrol on an inferno, so *please say nothing.*' Her expression softened. 'But you can stop worrying about the parental order. Adam has his faults but pettiness has never been one of them.'

Lauren looked relieved. 'OK, I'll tell Dan to keep quiet.' She smiled at Ruth. 'Can I buy you lunch?'

'I'd like nothing more,' said Ruth, 'but we're making two people at Morrab redundant, which as you can imagine is heartbreaking for everyone, and I'm about to meet the accountant to discuss details. Plus, in order to rebuild Bella's trust, I'm trying to get into the office before her every morning *and* be there when she leaves at night. This morning I'm already playing catch-up, so I'd better run.'

They hugged. 'Love you, Mum,' said Lauren.

'You too, darling.'

'By the way,' added Lauren, 'can we not tell anyone else until we've got through the first three months, because of the risk that something might go wrong?'

'Of course,' said Ruth. 'I shan't breathe a word.' Sheila didn't count, she thought to herself.

Two days later Alex called her mother. She thought that maybe, as the one member of the family who bore no parental responsibility for the child Ruth was carrying, she might be able to broker a rapprochement between her parents. Ruth treated her to yet another lurid account of Adam's angry outburst and his icy withdrawal to the top of the house and begged her to have a go at talking him round.

But it did no good. The first time Alex phoned, Adam referred to the family's 'silent conspiracy' against him and implied that she'd been part of it; she insisted that she'd been a bystander, not a collaborator. Later, when she forwarded him the scan image Lauren had sent her, together with a message of congratulation, he replied:

Very thoughtful, thank you. Your
mother also supplied me with a print.

218

Encouraged, Alex typed:

> SO glad you two are communicating
> again! Please keep it up – it makes
> me very happy and relieved!

But he didn't reply.

Alex had been glad to leave London six years earlier: she liked the space and optimism of California and felt she could breathe more easily there. But now, for the first time, she felt cut off from the family and powerless to help. Video calls were no good. She needed to bundle her parents into the same room, work out how big the gap between them was, and have a go at bridging it. She was afraid that, without external intervention, Adam would be unable to climb down from his hurt, lonely perch, up in the moral heights. She worried, too, about Ruth and Lauren: they seemed deeply enmeshed and devoted to one another, but she wasn't sure how long they'd be able to keep it up. She longed for the Christmas holidays, when there would be a chance to see how the land lay and sort everything out.

The domestic stalemate continued as Adam and Ruth went about their parallel-but-separate lives, so she was astonished when he agreed to go to Sheila and Simon's annual Christmas drinks party. As they sat in stationary traffic on the North Circular, Adam flipped between radio stations while Ruth listened to an audiobook through her headphones. Once inside they went in different directions and mingled, but when the usual crowd of friends and neighbours drained dutifully from the house on the dot of half past eight, Simon insisted that the Furnivals stay behind as they did every year, to have a *proper* conversation. 'It's ages since we saw the two of you together,' said Sheila. 'Not since dinner at yours.' Ruth and Adam agreed, managing to be animated and charming towards their hosts while assiduously ignoring one another. Eventually Sheila led Ruth out of the room, leaving the men together; she'd told Simon to talk to Adam and try to get him to open up.

That proved unnecessary. While Simon poured them a finger of whisky each Adam threw a log on the fire and watched as tongues of flame licked the sides, then he turned and rolled his shoulders back a couple of times as if steeling himself. 'You've no doubt had a seat in the stalls from which to observe the unfolding of our squalid little family melodrama,' he began.

Now it was Simon's turn to stare at the fire. 'On the contrary,' he said, 'Sheila has exercised professional levels of discretion. She told me about the ... er ... pregnancy a couple of days ago, and that was only because she knew you'd both be here tonight.' He paused and cleared his throat. 'I had wondered if something was going on, because she's been on the phone to Ruth more than usual, often late at night.' Adam winced. 'I never imagined *this*, though.'

Both of them badly wanted to change the subject, but there was no escape.

Adam's face was taut with pain and bewilderment. 'It's been a nightmare. She spent weeks having hospital appointments, tests and treatments, and I had absolutely no idea.' He looked at Simon. 'Can you believe it?'

Simon said gently, 'Ruth's always tended to forge ahead and rely on you to be there with back-up when it's needed, hasn't she?'

Adam was hugging his chest, as if to soothe himself. 'But she's *pregnant*. How would you feel if this was Sheila?'

'I've asked myself that.' Simon pursed his lips. 'I'd be shocked and hurt at the deception, no question. But if we had a daughter and she'd asked Sheila to do this for her, then I hope I'd manage to put those feelings aside and do all I could to help.' He proffered the bottle and Adam took it. 'My biggest concern would be the risk to Ruth's life and health. She's terribly thin and looks exhausted. I'd want to be sure she was in the very best hands – where's she having the baby?'

'I've no idea,' said Adam. 'We haven't spoken for weeks. We communicate electronically.'

'You can't go on like this.' Simon put a hand on Adam's shoulder. 'Have you considered counselling? Sheila mentioned Relate—'

Adam gave a small, bitter laugh. 'Can you seriously imagine Ruth and me in marriage guidance? We're too proud, and too self-ironising. We'd end up performing competitively for the counsellor.' He stared into his glass. 'No, we either sort this out by ourselves or call it a day.' He smiled grimly at Simon. 'Kind of you to suggest it, though,' he added.

Simon understood that the matter was closed and cast around for a change of subject. 'Thought any more about becoming a judge?' he asked.

Adam's face relaxed. His application was in the bureaucratic maw of the judicial appointments system, he said, it would be months before he even knew if he'd been shortlisted.

'They'll snap you up.' Simon smiled. 'I'll vouch for your fine judgement and incorruptibility.'

'You jest,' said Adam, 'but they make you list every conviction and caution, including speeding tickets. Fortunately, my slate is clean.' He stretched his arms wide and yawned. 'The word is that it's more competitive than ever this year but, having spent weeks deliberating about whether to apply, I've suddenly realised how much I want it. I'll be disappointed if I don't at least get to the next round.'

Sheila sat Ruth down in the kitchen and plied her with peppermint tea and beady solicitude. The initial euphoria had faded, Ruth said, and now she was feeling groggy every day: morning sickness had been a drag when she was in her twenties, but at fifty-four it was a nightmare; some days she'd been too ill to go into the office at all, which was a disaster, given the state the company was in. She hated letting Bella down and their relationship was now strained to breaking point.

'But she knows you're pregnant?'

Ruth shook her head.

'That's crazy. You must tell her straight away, then she'll understand.'

'The office is closed now. I'm going to tell her in January, when I've had a rest and got myself back onto an even keel.' Ruth said that Adam was clearly determined to maintain hostilities indefinitely and was behaving as if Christmas had been cancelled. She was so tired that the thought of ordering a turkey felt like climbing Everest and no shopping had been done; they didn't even have a tree. Alex was arriving the following day and because Lauren and Dan had been to his parents last year, they would be coming on Christmas Eve and staying for two nights. Ruth groaned. 'It's going to be a nightmare. I wish I could cancel the whole thing, or abscond.' She laid her head on the table.

'You say that every year,' said Sheila wryly.

'I know, but this time I *mean* it.'

'The girls will help, you know they will. And maybe you could buy some of those very complicated board games that force everyone to concentrate, to help pass the time.'

Ruth peered up at her through a mess of hair. 'Thanks, Sheila, I reckon that'll do the trick. Happy Families, with a dark twist. Should have thought of it myself.'

'Just trying to be constructive.'

'On the whole, I think I prefer it when you're the angel of doom.'

18

On Christmas Eve the Furnival family walked to Midnight Mass together, their annual moment of religious observance. It was the sort of clear, frosty night when Adam would normally pause, point towards the sky and say, 'Look at that, the one night of the year when you can see the stars properly in London – no light pollution.' The others would gaze dutifully then grin at one another: it was part of the ritual. But now he was mute and the girls talked valiantly to fill the silence.

While the choir sang 'In the Bleak Midwinter' Dan and Lauren went to the altar hand in hand to take communion; after a moment's hesitation, Adam followed them; Ruth and Alex stayed where they were. Ruth watched as Adam walked back towards the pew: he'd lost weight over the past few weeks and his face was sculpted grave and beautiful by the candlelight. Her heart contracted. When the clock struck midnight and everyone turned to those nearest them to offer peace and love, she forgot herself and leant into him, but he moved sideways, brushing her face with his cheek in an expressionless parody of greeting, then turning away to embrace Lauren and shake hands with Dan. She almost lost her balance, but was rescued by Alex on her other side, who caught her in a fierce hug.

'Happy Christmas, Mum,' she said. 'You've made Lauren *so* happy, thank you for that. I know how difficult it's been, you're a star.'

Ruth found she couldn't sing 'O Come All Ye Faithful' at all. Outside the church Lauren enveloped her in another hug and told her she was wonderful, incredible, a saint. 'Don't,' she protested. 'You'll set me off again. Look, we need to catch up with your dad.'

Adam hadn't stopped to view the Victorian plaster baby Jesus, swaddling-wrapped and newly installed in his crib at the back of the church. He was already halfway down the road, head bowed, hands in pockets, marching away from them.

As she lay tossing and turning in the middle of the night Ruth could hear Adam moving about in the room above; he couldn't sleep either. Should she go upstairs now and beg forgiveness, plead with him to come back, so they could be a proper family again? She put a leg to the floor, then remembered his implacable face in the church and curled up again in the centre of the big, cold bed. Living at close quarters with someone for three decades was like having a companionship tap you could turn on whenever you needed: sometimes it dripped infuriatingly, but when it wasn't there you missed it desperately.

It was the bleakest Christmas morning of her life. She got up soon after dawn to stoke herself with the first pills and pessaries of the day. The house was silent as she crept downstairs in her dressing gown to attend to the turkey. She pushed chestnut and pork stuffing inside the bird, then stitched up its neck and bottom with cotton thread. She soaked a muslin cloth in melted butter, draped it over the breast and tucked in the edges. Then suddenly it was all too much: the thin faintly acid smell of the turkey flesh and the cheesy reek of butter; her stomach reared up into her throat. She got to the sink just in time and retched, over and over, as if her body was trying to purge its entire contents.

She was lying on the sofa when Adam came into the kitchen, fully dressed. He sniffed and frowned. 'You're ill?'

'I've just been very sick.' Ruth pointed towards the sink. 'I haven't had a chance to clear it up yet. Sorry.'

Adam folded his arms. 'Food poisoning or a bug?'

Ruth said, 'I'm eight weeks pregnant and I've got morning sickness.' She sighed. 'So you don't need to worry, there's no danger of you catching it.'

Adam looked astonished, then disgusted. He headed for the door. 'This is the kind of thing I was afraid of,' he said over his shoulder. 'It's ludicrous, Ruth, this whole business. I'll call Lauren. She can deal with it.'

Lauren arrived minutes later, kind and competent. She made Ruth a drink of hot water, ginger and honey. She put the turkey in the oven, rinsed the sink, scoured it with bleach and laid the table for breakfast. Everyone took their places, and *made an effort*. Ruth sipped her tea palely. Once she disappeared to the downstairs loo and the others heard the faint sound of retching. No one said anything.

The long hiatus while the turkey finished cooking was a challenge to their brittle amity, so Alex took charge. 'Present-opening time, everyone, just like always.' She wrapped her arms around Adam and nuzzled his chest. 'Dad, can you fix us all some drinks?'

'*What* a good idea,' said Lauren. As Adam busied himself with bottles and ice, she smiled down at Ruth like an encouraging nurse. 'Come through to the sitting room, Mum. You don't have to do anything except lie there, we'll bring everything to you.'

Alex had bought a tree from a stall in the park and festooned it with all the familiar decorations, collected over decades. Now she was squatting by the pile of gifts underneath. 'I'm going to be present monitor and pass them to everyone.'

Ruth sat with her feet up on the sofa in the bay window; she closed her eyes and concentrated on not thinking too much, or being sick.

They got through it. Alex's presents proved a godsend: she'd given them all fitness watches that told the time, and measured your stride and heartbeat. It was the physical equivalent of a complex board game, thought Ruth, as the others ran up and down the hall and stairs to compare their response rates. The house rang with shouts of triumph and breathless laughter: for the first time it felt unforced.

As they sat down to lunch Adam asked Ruth with what seemed like genuine concern how she was feeling. Better, she replied, acquiescing as Lauren put a potato and a spoonful of vegetables on her plate. She discovered that by eating tiny amounts very slowly she could just about manage to keep them down.

'That was a feast,' said Adam when it was over. 'To the cooks. Well done.'

Ruth clinked her mug against the girls' glasses. 'Sorry to land you with all the work. Thank you, darlings.'

'A pleasure,' beamed Lauren. 'And we should be the ones apologising, having let the Christmas pudding boil dry. We can't wait for normal service to resume next year.' She glanced around the table. 'Can we?'

'Hear, hear,' said Dan.

Adam said nothing.

Alex tapped a knife against a glass and cleared her throat. The others waited, nervous.

'OK, everyone, we've all scored ten out of ten for getting to this point in the day without tripping over the elephant that's taken up residence here over the past few weeks.' She paused and looked them in the eye, one by one. 'Forgive me for sounding like a west-coast shrink,' Alex continued, 'but should we now – maybe? – tiptoe up to the elephant and have a conversation about it?'

'We've forgotten to pull the crackers,' said Ruth. She held hers out. The cream cylinder stamped with golden angels trembled in the centre of the table, but no one took it, and after a few seconds she let it fall.

Adam, his jaw clenched, was swilling wine around his glass and gazing at the crimson swirl with furious concentration.

Alex, who was sitting between her parents, put an arm around each of them and said quietly, 'Guys, you have to sort this out.' She leant her head on Adam's shoulder. 'This is *happening*, Dad, whether you like it or not. You can't *not* engage, not least because Mum is going to need tons of support. Look at the state she's in.'

Adam extricated himself. 'So far your mother has managed everything and everybody without involving me at all,' he said, staring straight ahead. 'I'm sure she'll continue to manage.' They watched as the wine slowed and settled; he put the glass on the table.

'But this isn't only about Mum: we're talking about Lauren and Dan's baby. My niece or nephew. Your grandchild.'

'Alex has a point—' Dan began, but Lauren made a face to silence him.

'She, the onlie begetter,' said Adam. He laughed, mirthlessly.

'You what?' said Alex.

'It's from the dedication to Shakespeare's sonnets.' Ruth lifted her head wearily. 'He means this baby is something I've conjured up on my own.' She looked at Lauren for support. 'Which is a travesty.'

Dan said, 'Just for the record, Adam, this baby is one hundred per cent ours, Lauren's and mine.' His cheeks were reddening. 'All Ruth's doing is ... ' he seemed to be fumbling for the right word, ' ... helping.'

Lauren covered his hand with hers. 'Dad knows that,' she said gently. She turned to Adam, her eyes brimming. 'I'm so sorry about everything that's happened. I want you to love this baby. I don't want it to be something that drives you and Mum apart. *Please*, Dad.'

They were all looking at Adam, who was struggling to compose himself. Finally he said, 'Lauren and Dan, I'm delighted that you are on the way to having a baby and I shall love it, have no fear on that score.' The smile he attempted emerged as a rictus of pain. 'Everything else is a private matter, between your mother and me. We will deal with it as best we can.' After a pause he turned to Alex, 'In the meantime you'll have to forgive me, because I've no wish to embark on a DIY attempt at family therapy.' He dropped both palms on to the table with a small thud like a man bringing a meeting to a close, then stood up and began to stack the dirty plates. 'Dan, shall you and I do the clearing up and make coffee, so the others can relax?'

In the sitting room Ruth lay on the sofa, hair splayed across her shoulders. Lauren sat cross-legged next to her. Alex piled logs on the morning's embers then held a newspaper across the chimney to encourage the fire. 'Fat lot of good *that* did,' she said, half to herself. 'Don't know why I bothered.' She pulled back sharply as flames reared and roared, licking the bottom of the paper.

Ruth said, 'He's immovable.' She sat up.

Lauren looked alarmed. 'But you've always said he'd come round, in the end.'

'Mmmm,' said Ruth. A wave of nausea hit her and suddenly she remembered how patient and gently solicitous Adam had been when she'd had morning sickness with Lauren and Alex, how he'd overcome his horror of illness for the duration, holding her hair away from her face as she threw up, tending her afterwards and making endless cups of peppermint tea. She burst into tears. Alex and Lauren put their arms round her. She was

228

fine, she told them as she dried her eyes and shook herself: she'd been awake most of the night, and what with the sickness and hardly eating, she was bone-tired.

She stood up. 'I need to take myself to bed and sleep for ever. I'll be fine in the morning.'

They walked her to the foot of the stairs and watched as she hauled herself up, then went back to the sitting room. Alex harvested four plump chocolate Santa Clauses from the Christmas tree and stuffed two into her mouth. She handed the others to Lauren. 'Comfort food,' she said indistinctly, 'for tug-of-love children torn between their warring parents.'

Lauren sighed. 'All this hostility won't be doing the baby any good at all.' She ate a chocolate and compressed the foil wrapper into a tiny ball, then rolled it around in her palm. 'I'll never forgive myself if they split up.' She stared into the fire. 'I should have forced Mum to tell Dad. Dan said that's what should happen, right from the start. But then Mum wouldn't have helped us.' She turned to look at Alex. 'And I wanted this baby too much, so it's all my fault.'

19

The first Monday of the New Year and Britain was trudging back to work after its extended festive slump. Adam left the house at seven. Ruth fought her way onto the Tube at Hammersmith Broadway then off again at Victoria, where she vomited copiously into a rubbish bin and all down the front of her (unbuttoned) coat. She hailed a black cab and sat shivering, the driver having opened all the windows. She messaged Bella, saying she was too ill to work; could she come to the house as soon as possible. They needed to talk, in confidence.

Bella arrived an hour later. She hugged Ruth. 'Happy New Year.' Then her face corrugated with concern. 'You've lost weight, and you're terribly pale. What's the matter?'

'It's complicated.'

Ruth led her into the kitchen, and they sat opposite one another at the table, nursing mugs of lemon and ginger tea.

Ruth said, 'I've been very sick over the past few weeks, which is why I've been coming in late and working from home so much. I wanted to explain what's going on, so we can make contingency plans.'

'I'm so sorry.' Bella's face was grave. 'I knew there was

something. The way you've been lately, it's been *so* unlike you.' She touched Ruth's hand.

'Don't worry,' said Ruth, 'it's nothing serious.' She realised how much she'd been looking forward to seeing Bella's reaction. 'I'm nine weeks pregnant and right now I have terrible morning sickness.'

Bella's bright red lips parted in astonishment then her mouth sagged into a loose oval. She scanned Ruth's body and her eyes narrowed. *'Pregnant?'* Ruth nodded. 'Oh my *God.*' Bella put her hand to her mouth. 'How awful.' Having children had always been Bella's nightmare scenario. Why had Ruth ever imagined she'd be impressed, or intrigued? 'It must have been such a shock for you?'

'Not at all.' Ruth tried and failed to suppress a note of triumph. 'No baby was ever more carefully planned. It's Lauren's but she can't carry it – so I'm having it for her.' She described the weeks of tests and treatment, and how the odds had been stacked against her because of her age. She'd assumed it wouldn't work. But it had.

Bella said slowly, 'Is that why you took all that time off before Christmas, and left me those endless messages saying how wretched Lauren was and how you were in bed with headaches and gut problems?'

'Yes, but she *was* in a terrible state and I *did* feel terrible, a lot of the time.'

Bella's expression hardened. 'You abandoned Morrab, with no explanation, while I shouldered your workload, managed the team and worried myself sick about our finances. How *could* you?'

Adam's words, again, and they hit home. Ruth said, 'I wish I'd been around more, and you know I'm gutted that we had to make Zoë and Jack redundant. I'm sorry I couldn't explain at the time. I wanted to.'

231

'You're not sorry, though.' Bella leant back in her chair. 'We've worked together for over twenty years, you've been my closest friend in the business, and I thought I *knew* you, but you've turned into a different person over the past three months.' There were tears in her eyes.

Ruth had to make her understand. 'I was torn between work and family. There was a two-month window in which I *had* to get pregnant. Everything else came second, including work. I was planning to make up for it by going into overdrive in December, but then the morning sickness hit me.'

But Bella didn't seem interested in explanations. 'Why did it have to be *you*, Ruth, clambering back onto the fertility train and playing Lady Bountiful? Surely Lauren could have found someone else? Someone younger, who wasn't the full-time director of a struggling production company?'

Ruth slammed her mug down on the table. 'She was desperate for me to do it and I *wanted* to. Believe it or not, *some* things are more important than television.'

Bella pushed her chair back and stood up. 'I'm going back to the office, because if I stay here any longer, I'll end up saying something I regret.' She looked down at Ruth, contempt in her face. 'I'll see myself out. You conserve your energy for that precious baby.'

Heels clattering down the hall, then the slam of the front door.

Ruth sat at the table for a long time in the accusing silence. As the anger ebbed out of her she started to shiver. Was this baby going to cost her everything, she wondered: Adam, Bella, Morrab, her reputation in the industry? They'd been the bedrock of her life, and now they seemed to be slipping away from her, all of them.

That evening an email arrived:

Ruth,

I have never felt more hurt and betrayed. If you'd made Morrab your priority and discharged your responsibilities we wouldn't be in this mess. I am kicking myself for trusting you.

In a perfect world I'd like to buy you out or sell my stake, but neither of us has a chance of raising any finance while the company is so depleted.

Adrian and I have talked and it's clear we need to slash overheads further. We both feel it would be best if you stepped back from your company director role immediately. In the meantime, if/when you're well enough to take on some script work, exec producing, liaising with key talent etc., then we could pay you on an hourly rate until your maternity leave begins. That would save your salary and might allow us to hang on to the rest of the team for a bit longer.

We could review things in the autumn – assuming Morrab survives that long.

Please let me know if you are agreeable asap.

Regards,

Bella

Ruth read it several times and wept. They'd been through so much together. She remembered how they'd first got to know one another during that long, nail-biting shoot in the Czech Republic, when the lead actor, on a three-day bender, refused to leave his trailer and they took turns trying to coax him out while frantically rejigging the schedule; how they'd stared at one another in amazement and pride as they rose to collect their BAFTA; how they'd sat together on the dusty floor of the Morrab office the day they signed the contract, drinking champagne out of mugs and dreaming of a brilliant future. The years of banter in cutting rooms; working late into the night when everyone else had gone home; the excitement of having ideas and realising them; the mutual understanding, honed over years. And laughter, so much laughter.

She spent a long time crafting her reply:

> Dear Bella,
> I'm sorry for my many absences, my thoughtlessness, and for not telling you what was going on. You're right that I haven't pulled my weight recently and have left you to shoulder a huge burden.
> Having said that, I've *loved* working with you over the past twenty years and for most of that time we've been a fantastic team. I'm gutted at the prospect of losing you as a colleague and friend because of my negligence.
> Your plan makes sense: I'm happy for you to take charge and will do whatever you want, working on any projects you want to give me. Maybe you, Adrian and I could meet to discuss details?
> Much love and heartfelt apologies.
> Ruth

Seated in the vast waiting room of the Burlington Hospital antenatal clinic a week later, surrounded by women at all stages of pregnancy, Ruth was reminded that she was now on the obstetric conveyor belt and couldn't get off. This was the largest NHS maternity unit in West London and she was by far the oldest patient: there were a few in their forties, sleek, confident and well-heeled, but the majority were twenties and early thirties, many with bored, fractious toddlers in tow. Three noticeboards, gaudy with laminated sheets about local food banks, how to report domestic abuse and where to get help with housing issues, hinted at the texture of some of their lives. A nurse was writing on a whiteboard above the reception desk in green marker pen:

CURRENT WAITING TIME:
60 MINUTES MINIMUM

The place was hot and smelled of cooked food. Ruth felt a wave of nausea and knew she was going to be sick. The Ladies was crowded and two heavily pregnant women smiled sympathetically as she emerged from the cubicle, then they clocked how old she was and stared. She decided to skip washing her hands and as she navigated the two sets of doors she heard 'No-oh! *Much* too old', followed by an explosion of laughter.

'You OK, Mum?' Lauren moved her bag so Ruth could sit down.

Ruth dabbed her chin, willing herself to ignore the curious glances of the women around them. 'It's so much worse this time than it was with you and Alex,' she whispered.

After a long wait a midwife took blood and measured Ruth's height and weight. She glanced at the GP's referral letter and said: 'Let me get this clear. You're fifty-four, you've been through the menopause, you're now ten weeks pregnant and the plan is to give the baby to your daughter once it's born?' She tilted her head at Ruth, her gaze impassive.

Ruth said firmly, 'This is Lauren, she and her husband are the biological parents. We'd like to see a consultant, and we don't mind waiting.'

'This is a booking clinic run by midwives. There are no consultants here, I'm afraid.'

Ruth went into overdrive: she tracked down the most senior midwife and pleaded with her. Eventually she agreed – just this once, and in view of the unusual circumstances – to squeeze them into a regular antenatal clinic that was happening around the corner. After two hours, a tall, loose-limbed man in his forties called Ruth's name and led them into a side room. His shirtsleeves were rolled up to the elbow and there were shadows under his eyes. His badge said 'Mr Tom Fenton, Consultant Obstetrician'. He greeted both of them and seemed up to speed with everything; without prompting he told Lauren that she was welcome to attend all antenatal appointments and be present at the birth. Ruth would be monitored a bit more closely than normal because of her age and he would advise a C-section at thirty-eight weeks.

Ruth leant forward. 'If it's OK, I'd much prefer a natural birth. I had no problems with Lauren or her sister, and there are always risks with surgery, aren't there?'

The consultant shook his head. Allowing nature to take its course could be far more dangerous, he warned her. There was a higher rate of stillbirth in IVF babies who went to term, and in older women the cervix often failed to open properly during labour. There were other risks: 'Post-partum haemorrhage is a medical emergency where you can bleed to death very fast. Eclampsia causes seizures and strokes, and is also potentially fatal.'

'I know all about post-partum haemorrhage,' said Ruth. 'What happens if you get eclampsia?'

He reeled off the symptoms: very high blood pressure, swollen hands, feet and face, and a bad headache. Patients often said they'd had a premonition that something bad was about to happen. 'The phrase we were taught at medical school was "a sense of impending doom".'

She suppressed a laugh. 'Forgive me, but that doesn't sound very scientific.'

The consultant looked at her intently. 'Maybe not, but these are serious complications, and while an elective Caesarean before term won't eradicate the chance of them happening, it will reduce it.'

Ruth wasn't convinced. 'Over the past few months I've learnt to treat the scary statistics thrown at me by doctors with a degree of scepticism, because I'm healthy and in pretty good shape for my age.'

But Lauren cut in: 'Please take no notice of my mother, Mr Fenton. We'll have a C-section, please, because those risks sound horrendous and I'd quite like my child to have a grandmother.'

The consultant shot her a look of amusement then turned to Ruth. 'You're my patient, Mrs Furnival, and in the end it's your choice – we can only make recommendations. In any case you don't need to decide now.'

'No, this isn't about me,' said Ruth wearily. 'I'll do whatever Lauren wants, she's the boss.' The hormones, dietary supplements and ban on alcohol were bad enough, but now it felt as though she was losing control of her body. She'd imagined giving birth and delivering the baby to them, as a gift; instead they were going to slice her open at a time of their choosing and take it from her. She shivered.

After the appointment they found a café in the basement of the hospital: a large echoing space demarcated on two sides by rows of potted palms and dominated by a red lacquer grand piano. A woman was playing a Scott Joplin number with jaunty abandon, ignored by the motley collection of people clustered around the tables: doctors and nurses in pale blue overalls snatching a break from the wards; wan in-patients wearing slippers and attached to drip stands; others fully dressed and carrying umbrellas and outdoor coats.

They sat down and Lauren opened the notes the midwife had given them. She took a giant red marker pen from her bag and started writing on the outside of the folder. When she'd finished, she held it out to Ruth for inspection.

At the top, in large letters:

237

Below, much smaller:

GESTATIONAL CARRIER:
RUTH FURNIVAL

'It makes everything clear,' said Lauren. 'Don't you think?'

'I suppose so,' said Ruth, in a lacklustre tone.

Lauren said, 'Do you mind if I keep the notes at home? I'll make sure I bring them to every appointment.' Then she paused. 'No, thinking about it, that doesn't make sense: you'd better hang on to them, in case there's an emergency. But I'll write our contact numbers on the front cover, so they can call us straight away.'

Ruth nodded and managed a smile, but she felt a peculiar hollowing out. The effort of fighting to get to see the consultant and then debating the treatment with him had taken all her energy. The relentless cheeriness of the music made her want to weep. Adam had played it often when the girls were small. He never went near the piano now. In fact she barely saw him. It was wearing her down, his unwavering contempt and the grinding loneliness, but she must stay on an even keel, for Lauren's sake: none of this was her fault. It was hot and there was a nauseating smell of coffee. Drops of sweat coursed down her forehead and cheeks and she sucked hard on her peppermint.

Lauren looked up. 'You OK?' she said.

'Not too bad.'

'This sickness won't last much longer, will it?'

'I hope not. With you and Alex I was sick for the first three months, but I felt fantastic after that.' She broke off. 'Sorry, I must stop going on about my pregnancies.'

Lauren threaded an arm through her mother's. 'No need to

apologise. You're good at this stuff and I'm not – I just have to come to terms with that. And we've got so much closer, haven't we, over the past four months? I almost feel as if it's my pregnancy too.'

'That's because it *is*, darling. I'm just the container, everything inside is yours.' Ruth patted her tummy, then leant her head against Lauren's. 'Keep remembering that.'

They were quiet for a moment, then Lauren said, 'I'm *so* lucky to have you, Mum.'

20

The twelve-week scan was nerve-racking for Lauren and Dan. Less than four months earlier they'd sat in another ultrasound room gazing at their seventh baby at the same point in its development, shortly before they lost it. Lauren held Ruth's hand as two sonographers spent what felt like an eternity probing her mother's abdomen, then measuring and checking the image on the screen. Finally, they announced that everything was as it should be: the size was spot on for dates and all the major organs had formed.

'No abnormalities?' asked Lauren.

'Nope.' The younger woman glanced up at her. 'You're looking at a healthy baby that appears to have reached all its developmental milestones.'

'Appears to?' Lauren's face was etched with anxiety. 'So there *could* still be problems? I'm sorry but we've had—' She broke off.

'We know, pet,' said the older woman. 'We read your referral letter. We can never guarantee that everything will be OK, but right now you've nothing to worry about.' She looked at Lauren and smiled. 'Hand on heart.'

They stared at the little grey baby, snug in its black pouch. It was lying on its back. Ruth saw a forehead, nose and mouth, a fat tummy, a little foot, a thumb, and a tiny heart, beating, beating, beating. Five and a half centimetres. She remembered the first foetus, un-scanned and unchronicled, that had briefly occupied her teenage uterus. When she'd first glimpsed Lauren and Alex on one of these screens thirty years ago she hadn't given it a thought: they were so wanted and that one had been such a threat. Now the memory perturbed her: she brushed the feeling away.

They went back to Hammersmith for lunch. Ruth had passed three milestones over the past week: she'd stopped taking the tablets and pessaries because her placenta was able to keep the pregnancy going without them; the morning sickness was finally over; and, at a long meeting in the office to discuss her future workload, Bella had been cool, but not actively hostile, which gave her hope. Life was returning to normal; she was full of energy and ravenous.

'You've no idea how wonderful it is to eat proper food again – I've had nothing but toast and herb tea for months. I filled the fridge up yesterday so we can feast!' She slathered butter onto a slice of bread then stacked it with mozzarella and tomatoes.

Dan and Lauren were watching her approvingly, like the parents of a recovering anorexic, but as she plunged her knife into a Camembert Lauren gripped her wrist. 'No soft, mould-ripened cheese,' she said. 'It's on the list of foods to avoid, together with anything containing raw milk.'

Ruth sighed. 'I do think this is all a bit bonkers. Do you suppose French women stop eating cheese when they're pregnant?' Then she caught Lauren's expression and said, 'Don't worry, I'll do whatever you want. In fact, now my life's returning to some kind of normality, it would be useful if you could give me a few dos and don'ts for the next six months.' She fetched a pen and A4 pad and sat down again, poised to write.

Lauren snatched them out of her mother's hands. 'It'll be easier if I do it, because it's all in my head, and I can type it up later and email it to you.' She started writing in her small, neat hand and Ruth read over her shoulder.

AVOID:
Raw shellfish/ meat/ fish
Cured meat, salami
Liver
Swordfish
Caffeine
Keep blood sugar low and even
Drink lots of water!
No dental X-rays unless essential
Factor 50 in sun
Gloves for gardening/touching soil
Avoid cats
No pesticides at all

TOXIC HOUSEHOLD CHEMICALS –
I will send list, phthalates are the worst

She paused. 'Do say if there's anything you don't understand.'
Ruth knew she didn't mean to patronise. 'Is that it?' she asked
hopefully.
Lauren shook her head and wrote:

Music: play close to bump but not too loud – I'll
email tracks for you to use
Sing songs whenever possible
Talk to baby – no shouting!
Take regular exercise but nothing too strenuous
Keep chart of foetal movements once they start

The muscles at the base of Ruth's neck were beginning to
tighten: she could feel a migraine coming on.

DELIVERY:
Contact us immediately if labour starts early
We've committed to C-section at 38 weeks, but
earlier if consultant advises
Spinal anaesthesia if possible, otherwise we are
willing to have a general anaesthetic
We will be present in delivery room throughout
Baby given straight to us
Mum will NOT breastfeed

There was something about the pronouns – *we've* committed, *we* are willing, given straight to *us* – that chilled Ruth: it was as if they were trying to both control her and somehow erase her from the birth. Relax, she told herself: she was no one's handmaid and they couldn't requisition her body – it was hers, not theirs.

'We also need to agree on communication,' said Lauren, 'because we can share the news a bit more widely now.'

Dan turned to Ruth. 'We're going to drive up to see my mum and dad this weekend, we think it's best to tell them face to face.'

Ruth imagined his parents' faces when they heard the news and repressed a smile.

'What about Sheila, do you want to tell her or shall I? Best friend or goddaughter?'

'No need, she's known for ages,' said Ruth absent-mindedly.

'How come?' Lauren was frowning.

Ruth could feel her cheeks reddening. 'She called seconds after I'd seen the blue cross on the pregnancy test. You can imagine the state I was in. I just blurted it out, without thinking.'

'You mean you took a call from her, before telling us?'

'Laurie,' Dan put his hand over hers, 'what difference does it make?'

She brushed him away. 'That was totally inappropriate, Mum. It was *our* information.'

Ruth looked at this new Lauren, bossy and ascendant. 'I think you may be overreacting.' She sighed. 'But for the record, I'm sorry.'

Dan jumped in. 'Let's leave it, shall we? As far as extended family and friends are concerned, Ruth, we don't want to tell *anyone* else until we get past at least twenty weeks.' He paused and touched the wooden table. 'Assuming we get that far.'

She nodded obediently. 'Understood.'

'One other thing,' Dan said. 'We'd like to compensate you for the income you've lost because of what you're doing for us. If we'd used a stranger we'd be paying them expenses and it's only fair for you to get something out of it, so please say yes.'

Ruth felt torn: she was back to working virtually full time, but earning a fraction of her former salary, so a bit of extra cash would be invaluable, but it might come with strings attached and she couldn't cope with any more strictures. 'That's very considerate, but I'm not a stranger, and I don't need paying. So that's a no.' She looked at them and smiled. 'After all, this is a gift, isn't it? Not a transaction.'

As they drove home Dan said, 'It's fantastic, what Ruth's doing for us, but as I've said many times, one of the downsides is that we don't have a contract. Telling Sheila she was pregnant before she'd rung us is a perfect example of the problems it can cause. I'd be much happier if she'd accept some expenses, because then we could maybe draw up a rough agreement on paper. As things stand, she holds all the cards.'

Lauren shook her head. 'I overreacted just now – Mum and Sheila have always told one another everything and I can see how it happened. I was hurt, that's all. I don't see how a written agreement would change anything.'

'It's hard to explain, but I feel it would give us a bit of control, rather than everything being so one way. She's the giver and we're the takers. It makes me feel awkward.'

'I don't agree.' Lauren held up her pages of lists. 'These are *our* rules, that we've drawn up. Mum thinks some of them are crazy, but she's promised to stick to them, because *we're* the ones in charge. And I'll make sure she does.'

Dan said, 'So you don't think we should wait a while, then offer her some money again?'

Lauren said, 'No, she'd be offended, bigtime. You heard what she said. It's not a transaction.' She squeezed his arm. 'Relax!'

He laughed. 'You're right. If I'm honest, I never thought we'd get to this point, so I'm just beginning to obsess about the small print – or lack of it.' He turned to look at her and grinned. 'But it's looking good, isn't it?'

Lauren froze. 'Don't say it, please. The whole time I was making that list I kept telling myself that we're talking about the *possibility* of a baby, nothing more. Remember the last time. For all we know Mum could be having a miscarriage right now.'

Two weeks later Adam arrived home earlier than usual to find a large package addressed to Mr and Mrs Adam Furnival leaning against the front door. He took it inside and opened the box. Inside was a card covered in padded yellow satin.

CONGRATULATIONS! it screamed in silver glitter over a picture of two embroidered bootees, one pink, one blue, *We hear the patter of tiny feet!* A badge was pinned in the bottom left-hand corner:

He read the handwritten message:

Dear Adam and Ruth,

Dan and Lauren came over on Saturday and told us their wonderful news. They gave us a framed picture of the baby from the scan. He or she is perfect! They looked so happy.

What a gift you have both given them – a miracle really and isn't it amazing what the scientists can do these days? Dan told us how grateful they are to you.

I must admit we were shocked at first – you read about this sort of thing in the papers but don't expect it in your own family!! Dan explained it's the only way and very safe and everything will be all right. It's a very brave thing you are doing.

We are looking forward to sharing our first precious grandchild with you after all these years of loss and sadness. Take care.

Lots of love,

Patrick and Maria (Ryan)

PS Badge is for Ruth – it might get her a seat on the buses and trains!!!

The sound of a key in the front door startled him, then Ruth was in the hall, laden with shopping. They seldom collided like this.

'Oh.' She dropped the bags. 'Adam, I didn't—'

He thrust the card into her arms. 'This was addressed to both of us, so I opened it, but it's clearly meant for you.' He went into his study.

Ruth read the message twice, then on impulse she followed him.

'Adam.' He was standing by the window looking at her, and

246

for a moment she glimpsed a bruise of emotion on his face before it regained its familiar impassivity. 'That card's a bit over the top, but it's very sweet of them.' She pressed on. 'And they're right, this *is* a big thing.'

'Your point being?'

'It's addressed to both of us, isn't it? They're assuming we're in this together and looking forward to being grandparents.'

'But we're not doing it *together*, are we? Because Ruth, sainted giver of life,' Adam put his hands together and closed his eyes in mock piety, 'performed her miracle by stealth. Unilaterally.'

Ruth walked across the room until she was almost touching him. 'Adam,' she whispered, 'please, please, please can we stop this? I hate it. I regret not telling you more than I'll ever be able to say.'

When Adam opened his eyes, they were pink. 'How could you do this? Destroy everything we've built?' His nose was running. Tears slid down Ruth's face, she put her hands out and placed them on his shoulders. Adam hesitated, then took hold of her and crushed her against him. He was trembling.

'I'm so, so sorry.'

Starved of touch, they clung together, neither knowing what would happen next. Then Adam whispered into her hair, 'What hurt most was the deceit. If we're going to start again, there must be no more secrets, Ruth. Or lies. *You understand?*'

She exhaled and her shoulders relaxed for the first time in months. She nodded her head against his chest, but he held her at arm's length and looked into her eyes, his face pale and deadly serious. 'Say it. You have to say it.'

'No more secrets or lies,' said Ruth. 'I promise.'

She made a Spanish omelette and a green salad. It was the first time they'd eaten together as a couple since the football match. Ruth was buoyant with relief, Adam exhausted. He couldn't just snap back to normal, he warned her. He would stay up at the top of the house for a while; they needed to take things gently. Ruth smiled. He must take as long as he needed, she wasn't going anywhere. Adam confessed how much he'd missed her and how he'd hated their estrangement – especially over Christmas. She was looking lovely, he said. Was she feeling OK now? Much better, said Ruth, she was running regularly again and working as normal. She told him about the row with Bella and how she hoped over time they could patch things up.

When they'd finished eating Ruth took a deep breath. 'There's one thing I should mention – in a spirit of full disclosure.' Adam looked at her enquiringly. 'You said no secrets and I've just remembered that I did do something that might make you cross, but I had to do it for Lauren. I hope you'll understand.' She looked at him in entreaty, but he said nothing.

'So ... the Human Fertilisation and Embryo Authority has reams of tedious rules and guidelines if you want to incubate someone else's baby. It's because, for the first few months of this baby's life, until Lauren and Dan can obtain a parental order, technically speaking you and I are ... ' She hesitated.

'The legal parents of the child you are carrying.' Adam chanted the words as if he'd learnt them by rote. 'By the way, Ruth, that isn't a "technicality", it's a matter of law.' She felt cornered: he knew the surrogacy legislation, of course he did.

'Well, the Marinella Clinic had forms that, in theory, we both needed to sign, giving our consent.'

Adam folded his arms. 'And I'm assuming that using your considerable charms you persuaded them to forget about mine?' He was grinning indulgently. 'Am I right?'

She wanted to run from the room, or have a heart attack. Instead she inspected her hands. '*I* signed the form.'

'Of course you did,' said Adam, as if he was advising a

rather dim client. 'But you're saying there should have been *two* forms – one for you and the second for me, and they helpfully overlooked mine? Don't worry, it's a small complication. I can sort it out before we give our consent to the parental order being made.'

'Actually,' said Ruth in a small voice, 'I signed *both* the forms. On your behalf. As it were.' One of her fingernails was split at the side and hanging half off; she tore it and watched as the exposed nail bed began to seep blood.

Eventually the silence dragged her eyes to his face: grey stone, receding. He spoke in a fastidious whisper. 'You *forged* my signature.'

'It wasn't ideal, but—'

He cut her off, louder now but hideously controlled: 'To be clear, it was immoral, duplicitous and a flagrant breach of my rights. I'm a barrister, for heaven's sake, and I've been shortlisted for interview as a judge. I can't afford *any* blemish on my character. But I'm married to someone who thinks nothing of putting my name to a legal document when it suits her purposes.' He was staring at her through narrowed eyes and shaking his head. 'You've probably blighted my chances. But, yet again, you don't give a *toss*, do you?'

Ruth flinched. 'Adam, I'm sorry, but you needn't worry, I only had to sign once and it was *exactly* like your signature. 'No one will ever know.'

He put his head in his hands. After a long time his voice emerged, mashed with emotion. 'You just don't get it.' He looked at her. 'That's it. I can't stay here any longer, festering in the *mess* you've made.'

He walked out of the kitchen and up the stairs. She could hear him in the loft, looking for a suitcase, then moving from room to room as he collected his things.

*

249

The following morning Sheila arrived at eight, bearing flowers and breakfast. She'd picked up a frantic message from Ruth the previous evening when she got back from the theatre, but there'd been no reply when she called. Ruth took her into the sitting room and gave a blow-by-blow account of the rupture. When she'd finished Sheila said, 'You seem calmer now, more . . . resigned?'

'I'm all over the place.' Ruth unravelled a thick strip from her pain au raisin. 'I was gutted when he actually left. On the other hand, after weeks of being ignored, apart from the odd carefully aimed word of criticism, you start to go numb. I had years of it from Mum, it toughened me up.'

'I remember,' said Sheila, 'but your mother was unhappy and unkind. Adam's a good man who's feeling very hurt.'

Ruth's mouth was full, but she nodded and her eyes filled with tears. 'I know, and for those two hours yesterday when we were back to normal, talking, hugging, laughing, I was *so* happy. Then—' She started scrubbing at her cheeks.

'My love.' Sheila reached towards her.

'No, don't.' Ruth waved her away. 'If I'd told him when he first found out I was pregnant, it wouldn't have been such a big deal, but now,' she managed a sardonic smile, 'I can see that a wife with a sideline in forgery isn't great for his CV. Not that anyone will ever find out. That's the trouble with Adam, he gets hung up on principles and loses perspective. He's so morally . . . ' she was searching for the word, *'inflexible.'*

'You mean moral?' said Sheila.

'No, there's a difference,' Ruth insisted. 'He's always been obsessed with drawing ethical lines and colouring either side in black or white, whereas life's much *greyer* than that.' She exhaled. 'But if he feels such contempt for me, then maybe we're better off calling it a day.'

'You don't mean that,' said Sheila. 'He'll be back, you watch.'

Ruth said she wasn't counting on it. She'd already started putting out feelers for freelance work because she was worried about money, now that she was on her own; the trouble was she was already flat out at Morrab, and there were only so many hours in the day. 'I suppose I could take a lodger. A lissom young man who could assist me with gardening and, who knows, maybe other . . . ' she stretched her arms above her head and gazed at Sheila, 'household tasks. What do you reckon?'

'Simon and I are hoping you and Adam will stay together, otherwise none of us can feel safe in our marriages – you two have always been the gold standard. So, no, I don't think *that* kind of lodger is a good idea at all.'

Ruth laughed. 'Look at your face, Mrs Scandalised of Muswell Hill.' Privately, she suspected that Adam would stay away for a week or so, to make his point, before coming back to her.

Julius Mander had a flat in Middle Temple that he seldom used; he was happy for Adam to borrow it and insisted payment was out of the question. It was on the second floor of an eighteenth-century building that overlooked a quadrangle and most of his neighbours were elderly judges and their wives. The furniture was heavy and dark, but the piano provided consolation. There was dinner in hall if Adam wanted company, but he had little appetite for conversation; he worked, read and attended the occasional concert. Colleagues refrained from asking what had happened and he felt the weight of their discretion. He thought often of Ruth – pregnant with the child who was legally his, but conceived by her in secret – and of her metamorphosis into someone he no longer recognised. He slept badly and worried about her. Lauren checked in with him every few days, but he could tell that most of her emotional energy was directed towards Ruth. Alex called regularly, but was careful not to mention the baby. For years he'd felt on the margins of their sorority; now he was in exile.

251

Lauren and Alex were appalled at the turn of events. Lauren wished she'd made Ruth confess to the forgery at Christmas; she blamed herself. Alex thought Adam was overreacting. They analysed the precarious state of their parents' marriage in daily phone calls.

When three weeks had passed and Adam still hadn't relented, Lauren said, 'I so wish you were still in London, Alex. I've pleaded with him to go back, but he takes no notice of me, he probably thinks I'm on Mum's side. He might have listened to you.'

The following day Alex told her boss she needed to take a long weekend, for family reasons. She'd get everything done by working remotely for a day and a half, so they wouldn't even notice she was gone. She left San Francisco on a foggy Thursday afternoon and reached the house at midday on Friday. The weather was mild and in the front garden the cream buds on the magnolia tree Adam had planted when she was little were starting to open. Alex felt hopeful: this was a chance to show solidarity with Ruth and Lauren and get her father to come to his senses. In the kitchen she found a note from Ruth saying she'd be back at six, propped up against a freshly baked orange and almond cake – Alex's favourite. She ate a quarter of it, then headed up to her old bedroom at the top of the house. She'd worked for several hours on the plane and needed to crash out.

By the time her mother arrived home Alex was up, showered, and had polished off the rest of the cake in a regressive orgy. They hugged for a long time in the hall and when they separated Alex saw that Ruth was crying.

'You're having a really shit time?'

Ruth nodded.

'But looking fantastic on it, I have to say.' Her mother was wearing a cream shirt over dark brown culottes and she looked the way she'd done ten years earlier, when Alex was at university.

'I feel great. And your father said I looked lovely, before ... '
Her voice faltered.

'He's being *ridiculous*,' said Alex. 'We're having dinner tomorrow and I'm going to try to talk some sense into him.'

Ruth made her sit down in the kitchen while she made supper, and they caught up with one another.

Alex's company had offered her a job in management, with a big salary attached, but she was torn. 'I love writing code and if I spent all day bossing other people around I think I'd miss it. I remember you telling us that, whatever we ended up doing, we should stick close to the creative action, because that way we'd always look forward to going in to work.'

'I said that?' Ruth laughed. 'It must have been a long time ago, when I was young and foolish.'

'But it's what you've done, isn't it: stayed with programme-making, instead of turning into one of the suits?'

Ruth paused mid-slice and laid down her knife. 'There are upsides to being a suit: right now my life would be *so* much easier if I had a cushy commissioning job.' They were still firefighting at Morrab. The BBC had finally relinquished *Courtesan* and Bella was trying to find an alternative home for it. Ruth was overseeing a pilot for a possible series, in the hope that they could generate enough turnover to keep the company going. The only thing that spurred her into the office these days, she told Alex, was money: she needed to stack up as many hours as possible in order to pay the bills. She'd lost the creative buzz.

When they'd finished eating Ruth said, 'Thanks so much for coming over, darling, it's such a long way and you must be exhausted, but you've no idea how much it means to be able to talk to you in the flesh.' She smiled ruefully. 'It's terribly lonely in this house all by myself, but I can't tell Lauren, because it would make her even more anxious than she is already.'

'I can imagine.' Alex gave a sly smile. 'How are you coping

with Lauren's maternal anxieties? I understand they've drawn up an extensive rulebook?'

Ruth rolled her eyes. 'Strictly between you and me?' Alex nodded. 'It's driving me up the wall. When I signed up for this gig I didn't realise I'd be spoken to like a rather dim five-year-old and be forced to confirm that I've read, understood and will abide by a ceaseless flow of over-the-top instructions.' She made a face. 'I'm sure it's Dan who writes all the emails – there's a managerial tone that doesn't sound like Lauren at all. Sometimes I feel like *screaming.*'

Alex said, 'I guess they must feel so impotent,' she looked at Ruth shrewdly, 'and maybe they're scared that if they don't assert themselves you'll take over completely? During my brief fantasy of life as their surrogate I worried I'd end up doing that.'

'I don't know what you mean,' said Ruth, defensively. 'I'm doing this to *help* them, and you're painting me as an overbearing monster.'

Alex tilted her head, quizzical. 'Come on, Mum, we're the same, you and me: driven, bossy, and think we know best – probably because we do. I'm not saying you're unkind, because you're not, just a bit overwhelming.'

Mollified, Ruth gave her a grudging smile.

After her mother had gone to bed Alex worked for several hours, then slept until Saturday afternoon. She went for a brisk cycle ride along the Thames towpath with Ruth, then took the Tube to Bloomsbury, where Adam had booked a table in a small Italian restaurant. He was there when she arrived, and Alex felt a pang when he got up to kiss her; he'd lost weight and his face was gaunt and preoccupied. She told him straight away that she'd known nothing whatsoever about Ruth's forgery of his signature. Having said that, she didn't think there was *any* risk of it blighting his application to be a judge. She'd read through the section about good character on the judicial appointments website and it was all about the probity of the applicant, not his wife. Even if the panel discovered what Ruth had done, they weren't going to blame Adam. So it wasn't a big deal.

Adam shook his head. 'It would go against me, no question. They'll have plenty of good candidates. They won't pick someone with a skeleton in his cupboard.'

She changed tack. 'How will they ever find out, Dad? You're not going to tell them and neither are any of us. You'd already forgiven Mum and, manifestly, nothing has changed.'

He took a breadstick, snapped it in two, then gave her what she and Lauren used to call his Old Bailey look. 'This is a matter of *principle*. When your mother signed *my* name on that consent form she crossed a line. She showed a flagrant lack of respect for my feelings.' He paused. 'And my rights.'

'I know, Dad, and if I were you I'd be furious too, but you must be able to understand why she did it? She'd set herself a goal and was determined to do whatever it took to achieve it.'

Adam stared at her for a second or two, then nodded, his expression grim. 'I couldn't have put it better myself. That's precisely what your mother has always done, and she always rides roughshod over me in the process. She's got form. This was the final straw.'

Alex asked him to elaborate, but he refused. She begged him to return home; he said it was impossible. As the dishes came and went they recapitulated their arguments, but the outcome was the same: he wouldn't budge.

As Adam toyed with his tiramisu and tried to change the subject Alex lost patience. 'You know what, Dad, Mum did a very bad thing in a very good cause, and you had every right to feel aggrieved. But right now, you're being pig-headed, insensitive and selfish.'

He flushed and said, 'That's quite enough, Alexandra,' in his Old Bailey voice. Then he summoned a waiter and asked for the bill.

Alex met Lauren for brunch the following morning before heading to Heathrow. She gave an edited version of her conversation with Ruth and a fuller account of the sparring match with Adam.

'Does this mean that you and Dad aren't speaking?'

'No, we agreed to differ and parted amicably. I did my best and I'm sorry I failed.' She stole two rashers of bacon from Lauren's plate. 'I'm a truanting vegan until I return to American soil.'

'Thank you for trying. I'm sure he'll come round in the end.'

Alex was pessimistic. 'It'll take something very big to make him change his mind. He's miserable and lonely but doesn't know how to rescue himself. By the way, he said something odd about Mum. He said, "She's got form" – as if he was talking about one of his clients.'

'Weird,' agreed Lauren. 'But maybe not that surprising. All he does is work. I pop over when I can, but the rest of the time he's either on his own or with the people in his chambers.'

Alex tapped her nose. 'Never forget Emily Sullivan,' she said. 'I always said she was a threat but no one took me seriously. She's played a very long game and now she must be thinking that all her Christmases have come at once. I bet she's already on hand offering every form of succour. Hello, Stepmom!'

'Spare me the jokes,' said Lauren sourly. 'You're about to fly away, but this is my life. I'm frantic about the stress Mum's under and the cortisol that's pouring across the placenta into the baby right now. Plus I have the guilt of knowing that if we hadn't asked her to be our surrogate they'd still be together.'

Alex reached over and put her hands on Lauren's shoulders. 'Two things to remember. One, Mum's not having the greatest time, but she *is* coping. Two, it was *her* idea to have a baby for you. You're not responsible for what's happened.'

As her plane took off and she bade farewell to England, it occurred to Alex that she was more concerned about her sister than her mother: if Lauren wasn't careful she was going to worry herself into a frenzy.

When she went to bed that evening Ruth found a note from Alex on her pillow:

Mother mine,
   You are doing brilliantly and I'm SO proud of you.
   Enjoy this time when you're looking and feeling so good.
   Seize the day!
   I'll come back as soon as I can. In the meantime call or message me whenever you feel like screaming.
   Axxxxx

21

Lorenzo lifted Ruth's hair from her shoulders as if weighing it and looked at her in despair.

'If you insist, we'll do what you want, but highlighting this lot will take the best part of a day, because it's so long and thick, and you won't be happy with the result.' He pursed his lips. 'Regrowth of the grey will be a problem.'

He bunched the skein of hair in a dark halo around her head. 'How about taking it *much* shorter? Look at what that does to your eyes and cheekbones – it changes the whole focus of your face.' He met her eyes and his smile was conspiratorial. 'You won't regret it. And the colour will be fabulous.'

Ruth was appalled, then excited. 'OK,' she said. 'Do whatever you want.'

Eighteen weeks into her pregnancy, she was experiencing that heady sense of well-being and confidence that always came with the second trimester. She felt younger and looked it – apart from the long grey streaks that marbled her hair. They would strike a false note when the slight curve of her abdomen became an unambiguous bump, so for the sake of aesthetic consistency and as a strictly temporary measure, Ruth had consulted her best-coiffed friend, then made an appointment with 'the wonderful Lorenzo' in Kensington on one of her days off.

She felt the chill of steel and air around her neck as he chopped away the first section, and shivered, wanting to say: *Can we please take this slowly, Lorenzo? It's a big thing for me. I'm saying goodbye to my old self.* But within seconds it was gone, and there were great splashes of brown threaded with white all over the black tiles. Her head felt light and untethered, her neck exposed. A shorn child stared back at her as he worked around her head, lifting and shaping the wisps of hair that were left. Lauren had agreed to highlights because the chemicals wouldn't touch Ruth's scalp and therefore couldn't reach the baby's bloodstream, but she'd insisted on phoning Lorenzo in advance to specify particular organic products. It left Ruth feeling like a teenager who hadn't been trusted to do the right thing, and for the first time she felt a mutinous impulse to disobey some of Lauren's rules, just for the sake of it, as a small act of self-assertion. The colourist spent two hours daubing strands of her hair with three different tints and wrapping them in tiny packets of silver foil. Then she had to sit for another hour, like a big shiny armadillo, while the dye took hold.

When it was all over the face that gazed out of the mirror was surrounded by thick, glossy chestnut curls, flecked with gold. Her transformation had been the talk of the salon all morning and now staff crowded round to exclaim and admire as Lorenzo angled a large mirror behind her head to show his sculpture in the round. He smiled at her astonished face. 'It's an amazing look and it's taken years off you.'

Afterwards Ruth walked down Kensington Church Street, eyeing her reflection in the shop windows. She was hungry and felt like celebrating, but couldn't think of anyone who'd be available in central London at no notice. In a café she ate a sandwich and drank a bottle of ginger beer, relieved that Lauren and Dan weren't watching (carbonated drinks had been added to the Preferably Avoid list a week ago).

In the Ladies she spotted white flecks in her eyebrows. She'd never noticed before, but now they contradicted her hair. An Ayurvedic spa in a side street offered to tint them right away, using natural vegetable dyes that wouldn't harm the baby. The proprietor, who described herself as a cosmetologist, said they were offering a discount on laser hair removal if she was interested. Ruth said yes to brow rejuvenation and a facial, but declined depilation: her upper lip and chin were now smooth as a baby's, courtesy of the hormones. As she lay on the couch, it occurred to her that she wouldn't have dreamed of doing any of this if Adam was still around: they'd always agreed that attempts to turn back the clock were an undignified waste of time. But he'd abandoned her, and she might as well enjoy this bizarre new body and make the most of it. It was as if she was putting on a familiar costume and finessing her make-up before walking back onto the stage. She felt restless and alert; hungry for something – but she wasn't sure what.

Now that all the distractions of the first trimester had fallen away, she was working at full tilt, editing scripts and meeting key talent. *Courtesan* had been commissioned by an American channel, easing the financial pressure on the company, and there was a slight thaw in the office: Bella seemed grateful for Ruth's judgement and ideas; and she in turn was scrupulous in deferring to Bella's authority.

Five weeks after Adam's departure Ruth had a work lunch with Sam Turner, a director in his late thirties. She'd discovered him just out of film school and had produced his first drama; he'd subsequently directed two series for her. Now everyone wanted a piece of him and he'd just completed his first feature film: this meeting had been booked four months ago. If she could persuade Sam to direct something his name would guarantee a commission and Morrab's future would be secure. As she walked through the dining room in a long floating top that concealed her pregnancy, aproned waiters nodded greetings and male diners held her gaze, their faces animated: she was *visible* again. She found Sam at a corner table, curled up on a banquette, reading a script: the same olive skin, liquid brown eyes and black curly hair, but his body had lost its boyish angularity and morphed into the complacent bulk of success.

'Sam.' He looked up and it was evident for a deliciously long moment that he couldn't place her. Then she saw the jolt of recognition and surprise.

'Wow.' He got to his feet slowly and put his hands on her shoulders. 'When did Ruth Furnival turn into *this*?' He kissed her, laughing with appreciation as his cheeks brushed hers.

Ruth grinned. 'I've only just cut my hair. I did it on a whim.' Sam was smiling at her the way he did when they first met. It was like lifting her face to the sun. He was one of a posse of eager young directors and writers who'd flirted with her when she was at the BBC. He'd bought her copies of his favourite books and written heartfelt messages in them, invited her to late-night screenings of abstruse art-house films. She'd been flattered by his ardour, while making it clear that she was infinitely happy in her marriage.

'It's stunning.' He was staring into her eyes. 'Who could resist you?'

Ruth grimaced and said without thinking, 'My husband, since you ask.'

'Seriously?'

'Just joking.' She shrugged. 'The ups and downs of family life.'

A waiter was hovering. Sam said, 'I'm drinking gin and tonic, you?'

Ruth said, 'Tap water, please.'

They ordered food, then she asked about his film and he told her at length, proud and excited. The script had been through fifteen drafts and three writers; one of the leads insisted on doing her own stunts and ended up breaking her arm, which cost them three weeks; then the studio tried to neuter the ending, but he fought, and won. 'Sorry,' he said finally, 'I'm boring on as if no one else has ever made a film. How are things with you?'

'Fine.' She speared an olive. 'My secret agenda is to blandish you into directing something for us, but I bet you're booked up years ahead, now that you're famous.' She tilted her head, teasing.

He leant forward and looked at her intently. 'I'd work with you again in a heartbeat, Ruth. I'm taking a couple of months off, starting next week, but after that, apart from doing a bit of publicity for the film, I'm free. What's on your slate?'

"We've got a contemporary-set single in development. With your name attached it'd be a guaranteed commission. Clever, political, very topical – you'd like it.'

'And you'd produce?' Sam asked.

'Not sure.' He was frowning. 'I mean, yes, very possibly.' It was years since she'd produced anything.

'I'd love us to work together again, Ruth, but as a proper team – not with you floating around as exec and swooping in for the occasional visit.'

She told him about the script and the thoughts she'd had about casting. They'd be ready to start shooting in eighteen months' time. 'Sounds great– send it to me.'

They ate hungrily, gossiped and laughed. Ruth felt as if she'd re-entered the world. 'How's Matilda?' she asked as they picked at a green salad. Sam had a long-term girlfriend, whom she'd met a couple of times, a high-flying academic who wrote for the broadsheets.

He smoothed the linen tablecloth. 'We're taking a break, it's been six years and she wanted some time out. She's in Australia right now, on a research fellowship at Sydney University.'

Ruth couldn't resist. 'She waltzed.'

Sam rolled his eyes. 'You're not the first. The waltz and witch gags drive her crazy. She says Roald Dahl has a lot to answer for.'

'You miss her?'

'Less than I expected, to be honest. The whole thing may have run its course. Tilda's great, but I'm not sure I'm ready for the two point four kids gig yet. There's so much I want to do, before domesticity wraps its tentacles around me.'

'Such as?'

'Have long lunches in Mayfair with alluring drama producers.' Sam leant back and surveyed her. 'I still can't get used to that hair.'

Ruth laughed. 'People have been quite thrown. My daughter couldn't find me in a café last week, said she felt as if she didn't have a mum any more.'

They shared a tarte Tatin and agreed it was sublime: the sharpness of the apples blunted by the buttery caramel. Ruth tried to pay the bill, but Sam insisted: he was doing OK financially and this was payback time. What was she doing next, he asked, as they emerged into blazing sunshine.

'Heading to Victoria, then home to read scripts.'

'I'll walk with you,' he said. 'It's such a stunning afternoon.'

They walked along Piccadilly like tourists in a foreign city, stopping to gaze up at the Fortnum's clock as it sounded the hour and the two wooden figures emerged. Sam took her arm, then neutralised the gesture by asking how the girls were doing. 'They're fine. Alex is in California and Lauren lives in Brockley with her husband.'

'And Adam? He must be Lord High Executioner by now.'

Ruth laughed. 'Hardly, but he is applying to be a circuit judge.'

'Not much judgement when it comes to you, by the sounds of it, though.'

Pleasure, then alarm. 'Please forget what I said, it's nothing.' She tried to pull her arm away, but he held it there. They were walking through Green Park, staring ahead.

'Are you lonely, Ruth?' He was speaking so quietly that she could have chosen to ignore him. She tried to say something bright and firm that would bat away the intrusion – maintain a proper professional distance – but her throat had closed up. He would be looking at her, speculating. She said, 'Adam's left me.' Her voice was unsteady.

He stopped and put his arms around her, pressing her to him. She felt the weight of his head on hers. Beyond, there were voices, birdsong and the roar of traffic. She was weak with gratitude because someone had noticed her, touched her, liked her. Sam whispered, 'Those scripts can wait. Come home with me, just for a while. We can talk there.'

His house was in Southwark: narrow, Georgian, with limed floorboards and pictures on every wall. He made two tiny cups of bittersweet chocolate and they sat side by side with them on a sofa in the sitting room. 'Adam's a fool,' said Sam, conversationally.

Ruth shook her head. 'It's not what you're thinking.'

'Which is?' He smiled.

'Husband dumps middle-aged wife for younger woman?'

'OK, so he's ditched you for an older man? A less obvious plot line.'

'I'm having a baby.'

She watched as he processed the information. 'A *baby*?'

'Four and a half months.'

He stared as she pulled her tunic tight across the bump. 'And Adam's not its father?'

Ruth sighed. 'He is, and he isn't: it's complicated.' Sam listened with widening eyes as she told him what had happened.

264

'He's gone because he can't bear to be anywhere near me,' she concluded. 'He thinks I'm a very bad person – not unreasonably, perhaps.'

'No, it's amazing what you're doing.' Sam paused. 'And you look *wonderful*.'

She forgave his fatuousness, because of the look of frank appreciation on his face. 'It's the hormones. The effect's a bit like plastic surgery, but without the cuts and bruises.'

He laughed. 'If this was in a script I'd take it out, because it's unbelievable, but here you are. Looking great with child.'

They stared at one another for a second or two, then he leant sideways and kissed her on the lips. Ruth felt a tug as her uterus came to life, followed by the melting collapse of her pelvic floor.

She put her arms around Sam and kissed him back. When they paused for breath, he got up and pulled the wooden shutters closed over the windows. Then he knelt next to her. 'May I look at you?' he asked.

Ruth smiled. 'As long as no one's going to burst in.'

'I'm the only one living here, but for your complete peace of mind ...' Sam went into the hall and she watched as he drew two bolts across the front door. 'Happy?' He was waiting in the doorway.

Ruth stood up, turned her back towards him and took off her trousers, then pulled her tunic over her head. There was a heavy silence in the room. She undid her bra and her breasts fell against her chest. Sam was behind her, his hands on her breasts, cradling her abdomen, kneading her buttocks, slaking the hunger of her skin.

He turned her round and gazed at her, then said with quaint formality, 'Shall we go upstairs?'

She followed him up several flights of painted stairs, past African masks and stuffed animals into a white room with a four-poster bed. He closed more shutters, then removed his clothes with practised efficiency. She was startled by his penis, so unequivocally erect and intent. She lay on her back on the bed and he kissed her again, then worked his way down her body.

'You have a faint dark line descending from your tummy button.'

'It's called the linea nigra – it appears when you're pregnant, then goes away afterwards.' Ruth was surprised by the sound of her voice, low in her throat and thick with desire.

'Like a very erotic tattoo.' Sam traced it with his finger. 'A road map for the uninitiated.'

His hands moved lower, brushing her clitoris, fingers teasing her.

'Come inside me,' she pleaded.

'No, we can't, not yet.' He stroked her towards orgasm then plunged his thumb inside her until she arched and screamed with pleasure and relief.

'I'm so sorry,' she said when she recovered herself.

'What for?' He was smiling, stroking her face.

'I made such a noise. But it was too wonderful. It's been months since . . . '

'A pleasure, Mrs Furnival.' He ran a finger from her chin to her pubic bone.

His penis was against her hip. She moved to take it in her mouth, but he gently deflected her and she used her hands.

'Why wouldn't you come inside me? I wanted it so badly,' she said.

'Need to get tested first.'

'Tested?'

'For STDs.'

Ruth pulled away, outraged. 'I've been married to the same man for thirty years and I was tested for STDs in October at the IVF clinic. I don't have any diseases.' She sat up on the edge of the bed and began searching for her clothes, then remembered they were downstairs. She felt tainted.

Sam put his arm round her. 'You've misunderstood, I don't have any condoms, which is very unlike me, but in my defence I didn't imagine I'd need one this afternoon. I'm sure you're clean, but I have to get tested and I'll do it tomorrow, I wouldn't want to put you or the bump at any risk of infection.' He placed his hand on her tummy.

Ruth gasped, *the baby*, she'd completely forgotten about it. She felt a spasm of guilt, and then a fluttering – the sensation of an eyelash brushing skin – deep inside her: it was as if the baby *knew*, as if it was speaking to her, compelling her attention. Her eyes filled with tears.

She put her hand on top of Sam's. 'Just then, it moved, for the first time. Quickening, it's called.'

'I didn't feel anything.'

'You wouldn't, it's tiny – the size of a globe artichoke, according to Lauren – so all its movements are minuscule, but the sensation is unmistakable if you've had a baby before, it's as if something's flipping over inside you.'

'Maybe I stirred it into activity.' Sam pulled back the duvet and rested his cheek against Ruth's bump.

He looked up at her. 'What's it called?'

'It doesn't have a name. We'll probably know the sex next week.'

As he kissed her tummy she felt the graze of his stubble. 'Hello there, Flipper. Bit of a shock was it, just then? Lots of squealing and contractions, eh, Flipper?'

He began again. She wanted to stop him, knew that she should leave now and phone Lauren to tell her that she'd felt the baby move, but she couldn't bear to. His hands had rekindled sensations and feelings doused by the familiarity and routine of a long marriage. She was becoming herself again.

267

22

Over the next five days Ruth checked her phone every few minutes for a text from Sam. None came. Eventually she messaged him:

Hi Sam, this is Ruth. Are you OK?

He replied two days later just after midnight:

> flat out will get test asap but may
> take a while cheers sam

'Cheers' struck a false note: was it aggressively casual, calculated to obliterate the intimacy they'd shared? She needed a second opinion and longed to ask Sheila, but was scared of appearing ludicrous. In any case, she was probably reading too much into it: Sam was busy putting his first feature to bed, there would be urgent calls, last-minute changes, people to mollify and persuade. She managed to hold off until the next morning before replying:

No worries! Keep me posted. Hope
things ease up.

She was grateful for her huge workload. Bella had asked her to keep an eye on *Courtesan*, which was now in pre-production, and take three more writers under her wing, so the days were filled with meetings and the evenings with script-reading. On Saturday she went shopping because her clothes were starting to cut into her. She bought elasticated skirts, trousers and tunics the size of bin bags that would see her through the next few months, and bras that would contain her ample bosom.

Lauren and Dan went over to Hammersmith for Sunday lunch. They were thrilled to know that the baby was moving and Lauren begged Ruth to tell her every time she felt something. She spent most of the afternoon sitting next to her mother on the kitchen sofa with her hands on the bump, expectant. But no signal came. It was getting harder to observe from the wings as the physical drama of motherhood ramped up. Lauren knew it was unreasonable, but she envied the increasing physical intimacy between her mother and her child. She asked Ruth to fill out a daily kick chart, recording the time and duration of every movement the baby made, and send it to her by email every evening, together with notes describing the sensations as precisely as possible. When she woke up the following morning she would sit up in bed and pore over the results, looking for patterns, trying desperately to imagine how it must *feel*.

Now that the change in her shape was unmistakable, Ruth began to notice the eyes of neighbours in the street lingering on her torso and she imagined their gossip. Was she depressed and overeating? (There were rumours Adam had left her.) Or ill? (Though she looked better than ever.) *Or . . . ??!!* (No, not possible, surely, not at her age?) Ruth reckoned she had another month before her pregnancy became unambiguous, in the meantime, she resolved to leave them guessing and enjoy her last few weeks of flirting and badinage. Some days she was convinced that Sam would never contact her again, on others she knew he would. The baby inside her was somehow complicit – a fluttering witness to their encounter. *Flipper.* Her heart brimmed; the weather was mild and warm: she could imagine being happy again.

The twenty-week scan came as a welcome distraction. She got to the hospital early and made her way to the ultrasound waiting room impersonating a chaste and sober grand-maternal vessel. Lauren and Dan arrived just as Ruth's name was called; they were anxious. This was called the anomaly scan, designed to screen for serious abnormalities like spina bifida, cleft palate and heart malformations. It was also the moment when they could find out the sex of the baby.

Eva, the sonographer, had scanned Ruth before. As she squeezed gel onto her skin she said, 'How's it been over the past couple of months?'

'Fine,' said Ruth. 'I've been feeling great.'

'Enjoy it while you can. I don't see many women who are still saying that at twenty-eight weeks.' She dug the probe deep and Ruth gasped. 'Sorry, I know it's a bit uncomfortable, but I need to get a good view and because the baby's bigger it's harder to get the angle right.'

The scan took almost half an hour. Every time Eva froze the screen, frowned and measured, the three of them held their breath. Her face betrayed nothing. This time only fragments of the baby were visible, most looked like X-rays of birds: bony, angular and indecipherable. Finally, she pushed back her chair and looked at them. 'OK, I can't see any signs of abnormalities – all the structures and measurements seem normal.'

'Thank God,' said Lauren. 'And can you tell what sex it is?'

'You definitely want to know?'

Lauren and Dan nodded.

Eva smiled. 'I have my suspicions.' She pushed the sensor into Ruth's tummy again.

'What are you looking for?' asked Dan, leaning forward.

'Boys are easier – we look for a small penis or large testicles. With girls if the genitals are visible then they're a bit like a hamburger tipped up on its side.'

'Is that fat thing sticking out of its tummy a penis?' asked Lauren.

'No, that's the umbilical cord, but further down here,' Eva froze the screen and moved the cursor towards a tiny white line, '*that* looks very like one. And I reckon those are testicles.' She grinned at them. 'One for the blue team.'

Ruth pressed her fingers into the corners of her eyes.

'A boy,' said Dan. He and Lauren looked at one another, stunned. They still didn't quite believe this baby was going to happen, thought Ruth.

She walked to the Tube in a daze. A *boy*, twisting and turning inside her. She realised that from the outset she'd assumed it was going to be another girl. After Lauren and Alex were born she'd imagined the son she would surely have next: blithe, handsome and affectionate – playing football, building Lego castles. But he didn't happen and for years she mourned his absence. Even now she felt a stab of envy when she saw Sheila with her sons, basking in their tall bulk, leaning against those men she'd made. Now, finally, she was going to give birth to a boy, but would never be his mother. Was it some kind of punishment?

She felt a tiny tumbling sensation as the baby shifted inside her and she was so moved by the thought of him – sharing her blood supply, hearing her voice, aware of her every move – that she stopped in the middle of the pavement. She wasn't the kind of person who talked to animals, or foetuses, so her voice took her by surprise. 'My boy. How are you doing in there?' She looked around, feeling shaky and foolish, but no one had heard. She switched her phone back on and checked for messages. Bella wanted her to call back asap to discuss a meeting she'd had with Netflix; Sheila was suggesting lunch next week; the plumber needed two hundred pounds in cash. Nothing from Sam.

Lauren went to Adam's flat that evening and told him he was going to have a grandson. He blinked back tears as he looked at the printout from the scan. How was Ruth coping, he asked. Lauren realised it was the first time she'd heard him say her mother's name since he moved out.

'She's past the halfway mark and getting bigger. Everything's fine, but the doctors and midwives have warned us that the next few months will be tough. She's going to need all of us helping and supporting her.'

Adam was staring out of the window towards the bank of daffodils in the garden below.

'As in, *all* of us, Dad.'

Silence.

She slipped her arm through his and said quietly, 'It's been almost two months and you've made your point. Please go home now. Mum's beyond sorry and we all want you back, so we can be a proper family again.'

She saw Adam swallow, then he patted her hand. He would contact her mother, he said, promise.

He phoned Ruth a few days later. She picked up the moment he'd finished dialling, as if she'd been expecting a call. She sounded flustered – the hormones, he supposed.

'What is it, Adam?' Her voice seemed to bristle with hostility.

'I rang for a chat. I'm feeling out of the loop and wanted to know what's happening, how things are, that's all.' He was trying to show concern, but Ruth sensed grievance in his tone.

'Never better, thank you.' She gave a little laugh, dismissive, he thought.

'Well, if you ever need any help or support I hope you know that you can call on me,' he said stiffly. 'At any time.'

Ruth felt patronised, also guilty about Sam, despite the fact that, as she reminded herself, it was Adam who'd abandoned *her*: she owed him nothing. 'That's very kind, but I'm coping extremely well on my own. Lauren and Dan are being wonderful, they help me with anything I can't manage. And Alex came to stay, a few weeks ago.'

'I know, I saw her too,' said Adam. He tried a different tack. 'It will be good to have a boy in the family at last – help balance the numbers, eh?'

Was he goading her deliberately, Ruth wondered. 'To be frank, it's been a painful reminder of how much I wanted one myself for all those years.'

Adam sighed, she was point scoring again. 'Oh, Ruth, *must* you?'

'Thanks for your concern, Adam.' She ended the call.

Alex rang, just as Ruth was getting into bed. Since her visit she'd been checking in with her mother every couple of days, making sure she was on an even keel. Today Alex was eating an early lunch at her desk and wielding chopsticks as she talked.

'I gather Dad extended an olive branch and you batted it away?'

'Is that what he told you?'

'Not me. Lauren knew he was planning to call you and she asked him how it had gone. He said you made it clear you weren't interested in a rapprochement.'

'Were those his words?'

Alex's mouth was full but she nodded vigorously.

'Then we were in different conversations.' Ruth could feel her blood pressure beginning to rise, which wasn't good for the baby. 'Let's change the subject. How was date number four with Karl? I've been on tenterhooks.'

'Hmm, turned out he was a bit of a weird one, Mum.' Alex

273

speared two chunks of tofu. 'We watched a film then he invited me back to his flat. It was in a great neighbourhood, but smelled overpoweringly of the dog that sleeps *in* his bed. Every night. When I declined to stay over he quoted stuff I'd put on my profile about loving animals and called me a hypocrite. So, it's back to the drawing board. How are you?'

Ruth longed to tell Alex about her encounter with Sam and draw on her fount of sexual experience: she'd know how to decode his text and could advise on tactics. Instead she said, 'I'm feeling really great,' and felt herself blushing.

'You look it,' said Alex. 'It's been fascinating watching you over the past few months, because you're like some sort of transgressive time-traveller. You've moved from post-fertile back to full-blown fertility, and after he's born presumably you'll flip back to where you came from. What you've done crosses so many boundaries. What's it like, living outside the box?'

Potent, Ruth told her, and disinhibiting: anything seemed possible. It was like defying gravity – death, even – in the sense that the menopause had taken away her capacity to produce life, but now she'd seized it back.

'I reckon one day every woman will be able to do what you're doing – stay fertile for ever and have babies when it suits. How cool would that be?'

Ruth massaged her bump and smiled. 'Do you think I should offer to have another one for them?'

Alex laughed. 'Just so you get to stay in the fertile zone a bit longer?'

'No, because it would be nice if he had a brother or sister, wouldn't it?'

'And you reckon you could put up with Lauren's rules and regs through another pregnancy?'

'If this one goes OK, she'll know I can deliver and hopefully she'd be more laid back a second time.' Ruth looked at her watch.

'Which reminds me, I haven't filled in the kick chart for the past three days and she's been driving me crazy with endless reminders. I'd better get on and send her something, before she starts nagging me.'

'Speaking of which,' said Alex, 'I'm not sure whether you've clocked it, but if Lauren had kept her baby it would have been due next Thursday. She's very sad and stressed. So maybe cut her some extra slack if she's fussing more than normal?'

'Of course. Thank you for reminding me.' Ruth felt a stab of guilt.

23

Ruth had given up hope of hearing from Sam again. She'd started to re-package their encounter into a wry anecdote: lovely woman stoops to folly, but after a frustrating wait realises she's been dumped *before* the consummation she so devoutly wished for. Then another late-night text arrived:

I'm clean lunch++ tomorrow?

Ruth's heart sang. She knew she should play hard to get, but it might be tomorrow or nothing. Striving for an intrigued-but-non-committal note she replied:

Where were you thinking we
might meet?

He replied by return:

my place 1 o'clock

She prepared for the encounter like a new bride: waxing armpits and legs, smothering her most expensive body lotion on neck, elbows and knees, sandpapering heels and lacquering toenails. Knowing that she was betraying the sisterhood she trimmed her pubic hair – Lauren had once mentioned that in its natural form it was unfashionable nowadays, being somewhat repulsive to men, and Ruth had been voluble in her condemnation. But that Ruth, older, blunter and less biddable, was silent now, drowned out by the thrum of hormones. A floating calf-length dress, bought recently for the purpose, would make her now quite noticeable bump disappear.

Her heart was pounding as she rang the bell.

The entryphone crackled. 'Mrs Furnival?'

Her core contracted at the sound of his voice, but the Mrs was irksome. 'It's Ruth, Sam.'

'Of course.' He was laughing as he pressed the buzzer. 'Come on in.'

She walked past the sitting room, down four steps and into a long narrow kitchen. Sam stood with his back to the sink. He was wearing a pale grey linen shirt and jeans, his feet were bare. He bowed extravagantly, then leant forward and kissed her very gently on the lips.

'Even more stunning, the *ripest* of peaches.' He cupped her breasts, then ran his hands over her bump. 'My God, I had no idea pregnancy could be such a turn-on. I'm going to feed you, then fuck you, Mrs Furnival. *If* you're agreeable?'

He'd been to Borough Market and the kitchen table was piled with Parma ham, French cheeses, walnut bread, and a salad of roasted vegetables slick with olive oil and balsamic vinegar. They sat opposite one another and ate greedily. She heard a distant voice, anxious and proscriptive, *No mould-ripened cheese, no cured meats*, but inside this deliciously transgressive bubble she was a different person: it didn't count. When she'd finished, Sam fetched a dish of fat black figs and turned them inside out so that

277

she could suck the crimson pulp. Her body was trembling with excitement; what remained of her mind was clouded with the suspicion that he'd storyboarded this, like a scene in one of his films. Then he brushed his foot against the inside of her leg and slowly pushed it up, under her dress, until it reached the apex of her thighs. She let her hips fall open and pressed herself against his toe. She stopped thinking.

'Have you had enough?' Sam pressed a napkin against her lips.

'I want you. Please.'

'If you insist.' He took her hand and led her upstairs, then removed her clothes and laid her on the bed. Ruth watched through half-closed eyes as he undressed. His body was strong and taut, no sign yet of the slump and slippage of middle age. His desire for her was unambiguous. He stood looking at her. 'Your nipples have got bigger, and your pregnancy tattoo is darker. It's as if you've been re-branded.' He kissed her breasts, traced her linea nigra with his tongue, then lapped her clitoris.

'Come inside me.'

He knelt back on his haunches, put his hands under her buttocks, then lifted her up and entered her hard and deep. He shocked her rhythmically and repeatedly into orgasm before collapsing on top of her. Then she pushed her pelvis against him and circled his semi-erect penis until she fell into a trance.

When she opened her eyes, he was resting on an elbow and looking down at her intently. 'Good?'

'Blissful. Beyond *everything*.' She smiled at him. 'You?'

He nodded. 'You're like a fertility goddess.' He stroked her bump. 'And little Flipper's inside there still, waiting for its life to begin.'

'His life,' she corrected him. 'It's a boy, they told us at the scan two weeks ago.'

Sam put his ear to her tummy. 'How're you doing in there, mate? Sorry about the banging earlier.' He turned and winked at Ruth, pleased with his dreadful pun. She couldn't think of a response. Sam yawned, flung an arm and a leg across her and fell asleep; Ruth lay on her back and drowsed: she felt calm and certain of herself. She stroked his thick black curls and surveyed the intersection of their bodies: his olive limbs and her pale torso beneath them, glazed by the sunlight that was spilling through the muslin blind. It was as if her fading metal was being reburnished by his young flesh. She stretched and yawned: having proper sex again after such a long absence was like being plugged back into the mains, all her joints and muscles felt luxuriously warmed and loosened. The baby began to flutter inside her and she smiled conspiratorially. 'Yes,' she whispered, 'I *know*.' She began to massage her tummy in slow circular movements to soothe him. 'It's all right, there's no need to worry, but let's miss this one off the kick chart, shall we?' She imagined Lauren and Dan's faces, pleated with incredulous disgust at the thought of a stranger invading the vessel she'd commandeered. But it didn't feel wrong; it felt natural, wholesome even.

Below her a door banged shut and the house trembled. Ruth opened her eyes in alarm, held her breath and listened, but there was only silence and the murmur of traffic: nothing else. It must have been one of the neighbours coming or going, these Georgian terraces were so narrow that every sound ricocheted along the row. She waited a few seconds longer, then took a deep breath and let herself relax again. She had nothing to be ashamed of: this wasn't even adultery – Adam had dissolved their marriage with his departure – it was sex between grown-ups, benign and life enhancing. No assumptions, no grudges, no scar tissue. She turned on to her side and burrowed backwards into the warmth of Sam's body.

Then came the unmistakable clatter of a shoe on a wooden stair. And another. Ruth froze. Slow heavy steps. A case bumping in a different rhythm against the treads; small grunts of exertion.

279

Louder, closer. *He hadn't bolted the door.* The case fell to the ground a few feet away, then the bedroom door creaked open and light drenched the room. Sam stirred. Ruth lay entirely still, her face buried in the pillow, like a child willing herself to be invisible: she wasn't here, this wasn't part of her life. She felt Sam roll away from her and the shift of the mattress as he sat up.

'Tilda?'

'Sam.' A woman's voice, tight and triumphant. A long pause. 'I see we have a house guest. Perhaps you could introduce us.'

'Why are you here . . . ? I had no idea you were back.'

Footsteps on Ruth's side of the bed. 'Then I'll have to make the introductions myself.'

Ruth opened her eyes. A young woman with curly red hair was crouching beside her, her pale face a mask of revulsion. 'Ruth Furnival, isn't it? We met once, at a screening. You were fully clothed then, and a lot thinner.'

'Yes,' said Ruth unnecessarily.

'The famous Sam Turner seduction scene.' The woman pursed her lips and raised her eyebrows. '"I'll feed you then I'll fuck you."'

Ruth's mouth fell open; she turned to look at Sam, but he didn't meet her eye.

'You're not the first and I doubt you'll be the last.' Matilda sighed and stood up. 'But, hey, let's look on the bright side – I won't need to go food shopping for a while.' She looked at Sam. 'A word. *Downstairs.*' They disappeared.

The room was cold and full of ugly silence. Ruth prayed she might die now, quickly. She went into the bathroom and washed her face, then pulled on her clothes. In the sitting room below, Sam and Matilda were shouting. She could hear every word.

'What the hell are you even *doing* here? You didn't say you were coming back.'

'I wanted to surprise you. I stupidly thought you'd be pleased to see me. Instead, I arrive back shattered after a twenty-two-hour flight, and find you in my bed with a pregnant granny.'

'Keep your voice down.'

'She probably has age-related hearing loss. When you said on the phone that she was having a baby for her daughter and you were hoping to work with her at some point, I didn't imagine the job description included geriatric sex. That's how naïve I am. *This. Again.* What's the matter with you, Sam?'

'I thought we were finished.'

'We are now, sweetheart.'

'Look, you're tired and you're overreacting, we've been through this before—'

'Go upstairs NOW and tell her to get dressed and get out. Then change the sheets. Go with her if you want, I couldn't care less. I need to sleep.'

Ruth crept downstairs, opened the door and let herself out.

It was the twenty-four-week check-up and Ruth was crouching over a plastic jug in the ladies' loo at the antenatal clinic, in what the midwives referred to as 'mid-stream', when her phone buzzed. She reached over, dragged her bag across the floor towards her, and peered at the screen: Sam.

The pee stopped and her heart began to hammer. She forced herself to read the message.

> sorry for radio silence tilda wants
> us to give things another go & try
> for baby! feel i owe it to her good
> luck to you & flipper sam x

Hateful lack of capitals. Had Matilda dictated the message while they laughed about her? She wanted to burn the phone, cauterise everything, extinguish herself.

She finished peeing, reached for the basin and hauled herself up, but her knees were stiff and she lost her balance for a second. Her left foot hit the jug and knocked it over; three-quarters of a litre of warm urine splashed onto the tiled floor, engulfing her shoes, trouser bottoms and leather handbag. She threw down paper towels to sop up the mess and rinsed her bag under the cold tap. Her face stared out from the mirror, a stranger surprised at close range: bloated, blotched and slumping into decay. *Pregnant granny.*

Lauren, waiting for her outside, was agitated. 'You're not bleeding?'

Ruth shook her head. 'No, he's fine, don't worry.'

'They called your name ages ago and I said you'd be out soon, so we need to go straight to the desk. Was there a long queue?'

'I managed to chuck urine all over myself and had to clear it up. We'll have to wait until I can produce another sample. I've drunk a lot of water, but it may take a while.' She was becoming slightly tearful, so she turned away from Lauren. 'Sorry, darling, I'm not having a very good day.'

Lauren put her arms around her mother. 'Are you feeling ill?' she asked, protective and anxious.

Ruth pulled away, rubbing furiously at her eyes. 'I'm fine, I'll be OK. But tell me honestly, do I smell of pee?'

She lay low for several weeks, going back and forth to the office every day, but avoiding theatres, cinemas and restaurants because she was convinced she'd be the butt of pregnant granny jokes all over London. Then she heard on the grapevine that Sam and Matilda were officially back together and realised they weren't going to gossip: they had as much to lose as she did if the story got out. Whenever she thought of the debacle a line from *Dubliners*, learnt by heart at school, rang in her ears: 'I saw myself as a creature driven and derided by vanity; and my eyes burned with anguish and anger.' As a sixteen-year-old its meaning had eluded her; now it seemed to nail the particular futility and shame of her attempt to shuffle off her fifty-four years. She'd made a fool of herself and she'd betrayed Lauren's trust, because she hadn't kept the baby in mind and focused on his welfare. She needed to make it up to both of them.

One weekend she went into the back garden for the first time in months, lured out by the sun. It was unusually warm for early May: the purple lilacs were in flower and the air smelled green and urgent. In Adam's absence the garden had run out of control: beds had turned into jungles, weeds sprouted between paving stones on the terrace, and shrubs were rampant. It needed tackling. She opened the door of the shed: the place was garlanded with spiderwebs, but otherwise it looked just as he had left it, tools in their allotted places, his old green jacket behind the door and his wellingtons hanging upside down from the special contraption he'd made. She grabbed some secateurs and a fork and set to work, pruning branches, wrenching up brambles and tearing down ivy, in a surge of angry energy. Thorns clawed at her skin and she watched as blood beaded on her inner wrists, the pain came as a relief, bursting the bubble of frustration and self-loathing she'd been carrying around with her. By late afternoon both of the garden waste bins were full and her hands and arms resembled those of a battered woman in a forensic photo. Exhausted, she took off her muddy jacket, made a pot of tea and lay down on the sofa in the kitchen.

The moment she relaxed the baby began to move inside her and kept it up for a couple of minutes, as if reminding her of his presence. Ruth laughed and rubbed her bump. 'Hello,' she said, 'I know you're there, watching and waiting; nothing escapes you, does it? I'm sorry, my love, because for two or three weeks I went a bit mad, and then I was very sad, and I left you on your own too much, didn't I?' She was massaging her tummy now, as if to warm him. 'That Sam was bad news, and I shouldn't have let him near us. I don't know what came over me, but it's not going to happen again, I promise. I've got you safe and sound, and you're my priority from now on. No one else matters.' She smoothed out the creases in her tunic and picked off the thorns and burrs that had caught in its hem. 'We're not going to tell Lauren what happened, though, because she wouldn't understand, would she? It's *our* secret, just the two of us.'

She surveyed the garden. If Adam could see it he'd be impressed at the work she'd done. She took a photo and toyed with the idea of sending it to him, then remembered her curt response when he'd called, several weeks earlier. It had been a peace overture, she could see that now, but she'd been too blinded by lust and self-absorption to realise; she wished she'd been more gracious. She wanted him back, loping around the house in his socks, playing old songs on the piano, shouting to ask if she wanted a coffee. Hugging her. She longed to invite him to dinner and suggest they have a go at patching things up, but the business with Sam had knocked her confidence.

At seven months Ruth began to flag and work took most of her energy: she collapsed into bed soon after she got home in the evenings. She was growing larger and the youthful bloom of the second trimester had disappeared; when she caught sight of herself she saw a face that was heavy, haggard and bore a faint look of surprise. As Adam had predicted, she'd become a public spectacle and it wasn't pleasant. In the street and on the Tube the eyes of strangers raked her abdomen; the bolder ones asked for spurious directions, then enquired how far gone she was. She sometimes imagined him beside her, tall and unperturbed, throwing an arm around her shoulders and staring down the rubberneckers; visibly proud and staunch, telling her she was a heroine, and that it wouldn't be long now.

She lived a solitary life. Lauren came to all the antenatal appointments and she and Dan dropped in every weekend, but otherwise most of her free time was spent reading, or singing and talking to the baby. When Sheila called one Sunday morning, and asked if she could pop over, Ruth laughed and said she might just be able to find a slot in her *very* crowded diary. Sheila didn't laugh and she sounded tense. She said she'd come right away, on her own. Was there a problem with Simon, Ruth wondered. Their relationship had always seemed rock solid, but who knew what went on beneath the surface of a marriage?

When she arrived, Ruth plied her with solicitous questions, but she turned them all back. 'It's *you* I want to hear about.' Sheila stared at Ruth's bump. 'You're like a ship in full sail now.'

Ruth pulled a face. 'I know – and I've still got *weeks* to go.'

'I've messaged you several times, but you've been off-grid lately.'

'Yeah, I was a bit low for a while.'

'Hardly surprising, considering.'

'It was nothing to do with being pregnant,' said Ruth. 'The truth is I had a brief, passionate affair with a man twenty years younger than me and it ended in circumstances of toe-curling indignity.'

'I'm so sorry.' Sheila's face registered shock, awe and curiosity in rapid succession, then she said, 'I hope it was fun while it lasted?'

'I don't want to talk about it,' said Ruth firmly. 'It was a monumental error of judgement and I'm trying to pretend it never happened. But, yes,' she smiled at Sheila, 'while it lasted, it was great.'

'Am I allowed *one* prurient question?'

'Depends.'

'The sex ...'

'Mmm?'

'Was it very different from ... you know ... the usual?'

'Usual as in married-for-thirty-years-to-the-same-man?'

Sheila nodded.

'It was *off the scale* different,' said Ruth.

'In a good way?'

'At the time it felt amazing. But I was like a very lonely teen-ager in a hormone-driven trance – I think I'd have leapt into bed with anyone who showed the slightest interest. When it ended I missed it desperately for a couple of weeks, then it was as if that version of me had gone up in a puff of smoke. So in answer to your question: technically stunning, but emotionally empty. Very *interesting*, though.'

They giggled and suddenly they were back to their Cornish selves, sharing anecdotes and prising details out of one another. Ruth gave Sheila an edited account of her tryst and its denoue-ment, which now seemed hilarious as well as humiliating. Afterwards she wiped tears from her eyes. 'I haven't laughed like that for years. You must come over more often.'

'We could plan one or two evenings out, if that wouldn't tire you out too much.' Sheila paused. 'Which reminds me, there's something I wanted to mention.'

The change in her voice stifled Ruth's laughter. 'Yes?' she said, suddenly alert to every sound in the room – clock, dishwasher, distant aeroplane, the metal bracelets that Sheila was pushing round and round on her wrist.

'I thought you might be upset, but, in view of what you've just said, I was probably mistaken.'

'Upset about what?'

'Simon and I went to see *Guys and Dolls* last night at the Alhambra and our seats were in the front circle, overlooking the stalls. Before the lights went down we spotted Adam just below us. He was sitting next to that woman he works with – we've met her here at parties, long blonde—'

'Emily,' said Ruth. A series of hammer blows in her chest: *she should have known*. It was a struggle to breathe.

'Yes,' said Sheila. 'I was awake most of last night, wondering whether to say anything, but I didn't want you to hear it from someone else, because, they were ... Well, they looked like a couple. Simon thought so too.'

Ruth's face was blank. '*Guys and Dolls*, did you say?'

'Yes.' Sheila looked relieved. 'I'm sorry I mentioned it, because you probably don't give a toss what Adam's up to—'

But now tears were coursing down Ruth's face and she was rocking backwards and forwards. 'No, no, no. I can't bear it.'

Ruth lay awake all night in a state of torture. She imagined Adam in bed with Emily: wanting her, stroking her, inhabiting her. Emily's head heavy in the warm hollow beneath his collar bone as they caught their breath after making love. His arm cradling Emily's shoulders. Her breast cupped in his hand as he looked into her eyes and pulled her towards him. All the physical memories she and Adam had piled up together – year after year, skin against skin, in joy and in sorrow – would be obliterated now by Emily's firmer, younger, more exciting flesh. They had annihilated her.

But what right had she to be surprised and sickened? If Sam, why not Emily? Adam had more cause. *She had thrown him away.* She had no right to complain. All those years – vanished, irrecoverable. He'd played his final card, the one he'd held closest to his chest. She'd taken him for granted, assumed he'd always be there, in the periphery of her vision, reliable, predictable, loyal. She never thought he'd abandon her completely. Without him she would fall over, fall apart. No sounding board, now; no one to blame; no one to console.

You make your bed and lie in it, my girl.

You're on your own now: no one wants you.

287

PART FIVE

DELIVERANCE

24

Ruth asked Lauren to meet her for lunch the following day at a café in Somerset House. When Lauren arrived Ruth was already installed at a table in an alcove; she hugged her mother, then crouched next to her and ran her hands over the bump, feeling for movement.

'I think he's fallen asleep,' said Ruth after several minutes. 'He was bounding around when I was in the office just now.' She shifted awkwardly in her chair. 'Maybe we could take a break? I'm getting cramp in my right leg.'

'Just my luck, he seems to go to ground whenever I'm around.' Lauren sat down. 'But thanks for all the videos of his acrobatics you've been sending, and for singing to him so much. I'm going to nominate you for the world's greatest surrogate award.'

Ruth forced a smile.

'You OK, Mum? You seem a bit tense.'

'There's something I need to tell you.'

Lauren stiffened. 'Is there a problem with the baby? Or you?'

'Nothing like that.' *She mustn't cry.* 'I wanted you to hear it from me, rather than on the rumour mill, because it's obvious people are already talking. I'm going to call Alex when she wakes up.' She paused.

'Mum, you're frightening me. Please just say it.'

Ruth took a breath. 'I guess it's no great surprise, given what's gone on over the past few months.' She pretended she was a newsreader at the end of a long shift, reading a very dull bulletin and anxious to get it over. 'Your father's having an affair. With Emily Sullivan.' Her voice snagged on the final syllable.

Lauren was shaking her head. 'No, that can't be true. What makes you think ...?' Then she remembered Alex's prediction, and how she'd dismissed it.

'Sheila and Simon saw them together, she said they seemed ... intimate.'

Lauren's face crumpled. 'This is my fault.'

'I've no right to be upset, seeing as he moved out four months ago, but for some reason ...' her voice gave way again. 'I can't bear the thought of it.'

'Why would he do this?'

Ruth threw her a sardonic look. 'Come on. He's a good-looking middle-aged man, choosing between his estranged wife and a colleague twenty years younger who adores him. Add in surrogacy and a forged signature and it's a no-brainer. Flattery, excitement, sex—' She caught herself. 'In any case, we're none of us saints.'

'You're a saint, Mum. And this is vile. You *really* don't deserve it – I hope you realise that?'

Ruth was tempted to tell her about Sam, but decided that a pedestal was a more comfortable place than a psychiatrist's couch.

'Apart from anything else, it's such a cliché. Emily's only a few years older than me.' Lauren wrinkled her nose in distaste. 'And he's been so *secretive* about it. I've been to that flat tons of times, but she's never been there and I've not seen any signs.'

'Oh, believe me, your dad can be a dark horse when he chooses.'

'How d'you mean?'

Ruth shook her head; what was the point of raking over the ashes of their marriage.

'Come on, Mum, you can't drop something like that and then not explain. I need to know.'

Self-pity wrestled with maternal discretion, and won. 'I was about your age when I came home from work one day and found Adam in bed. He'd been to hospital and had a vasectomy.' She stopped, reliving the shock of the moment. 'Just like that. No discussion. No warning. I was planning on having at least one more baby, maybe two.'

'No!' gasped Lauren, her eyes filling with tears of sympathy.

Ruth felt vindicated, and guilty. 'It was the worst moment of my life.' She paused and considered. 'Until yesterday.'

Adam's flat was a mess of books, tousled clothes, papers and unwashed mugs. The lovebirds clearly had better things to do than clear up, thought Lauren sourly as she hung up her jacket. She scoured the cloakroom for traces of Emily, but all she found were Adam's coats and scarves; she sniffed them, but there was no perfume, just the familiar smell of her father. They were being *super*-careful.

Adam made coffee and they sat opposite one another on the two brown leather sofas by the fireplace. Lauren seemed tense, her face wore that shuttered look that suggested trouble. 'Everything going OK?' he asked warily. 'Baby and so on?'

'He's fine,' said Lauren stiffly. 'And Mum's fine, under the circumstances. *Just* in case you were interested.'

'Why, what's happened to her?' Adam clasped his chest.

'Dad, don't pretend you *care*.'

'That's a strange thing to say. Of course I care.'

Lauren rolled her eyes, then shifted so that she didn't have to look at him.

'OK, what's this all about?' Adam held up his hands. 'You're behaving as if I've committed some sort of crime.'

Lauren turned slowly and stared at him, as if it was doubly

painful that she had to spell it out. 'I *know* about your affair with Emily. OK? And I'm gutted, because I really hoped you'd support Mum, at least for the next few months – for the sake of my baby, if nothing else. Couldn't you have waited?'

Adam's eyes narrowed. 'What on *earth* are you talking about?'

'You're not about to deny it?'

He leant forward and looked at her intently. 'Lauren, listen carefully. I am *not* having an affair with Emily, or with anyone else for that matter.' His voice was calm and matter-of-fact. 'Is that clear?'

'But Mum said you were, she told us both, yesterday—' Lauren stopped, confused.

'Based on what evidence, may I ask?'

'Simon and Sheila saw you at the theatre on Saturday being . . .' Lauren was blushing, '"intimate" – Mum said that was the word Sheila used.'

Adam sighed, then moved to sit down next to Lauren. 'Your mother always did have a vivid imagination.' He put an arm around her shoulders. 'Emily and I are colleagues and friends. We're both on our own, so sometimes we go to the theatre or cinema together. But we're not in a relationship.'

'And you swear you never will be?' Lauren's eyes were brimming with tears. Adam opened his mouth to reply, then hesitated. They brimmed over.

'Hey, hey, hey, Lauren, stop that.' He hugged her to him. 'Look, I'm not sure of anything any more, how can I be? This is all such a bloody *mess*, isn't it?'

'I can't bear it,' she said, putting her arms around him and burrowing her head into his chest. 'I just want you to be together and happy, the way you were before.'

He said gently, 'Marriage is tough, Lauren. There were things your mum and I didn't talk about enough and, in the end, they broke us. Promise me that you and Dan won't make the same mistake. Don't leave things to fester.'

Lauren let go of him and wiped her face on the sleeve of her jumper. 'Mum said you were a dark horse.'

'She said that?' Adam looked puzzled. 'It's not a description I recognise. I think of myself as pretty straightforward.'

'She told me about the vasectomy, Dad.' Lauren's face was hostile again. 'Sounds like you weren't super-straightforward about that? She said it was a huge betrayal.'

Adam got up, his face flushed with anger and walked towards the door, then he turned, strode back to the sofa and stood looking down at her. 'That's a private matter and she had *no right* to discuss it with you.' Lauren flinched. When he spoke again his voice was under control. 'Believe me, there's a lot more to be said about secrecy and betrayal, but I'm not going to demean myself by sharing it with you. Do you understand?'

She nodded automatically, understanding nothing.

He sat down beside her again. 'I'm sorry. You're caught in the middle, which can't be pleasant. Forgive me.' He put an arm around her, trying to reconnect. 'But just for the record, your mother is mistaken about my so-called affair.' He was looking at her with concern. 'You do believe me?'

Lauren nodded again, but only for form's sake.

Ruth woke in the middle of the night, her heart pounding. The sound of her breath, rapid and rasping, filled the room and a pale shape lingered in the darkness. They'd sliced her open and let it out. Now it was floating above her, a translucent, skeletal thing with a large head and a tadpole spine. Its right eye was turned towards her, lidded shut and staring blindly. Then it moved and she saw its left side: skull stoved in, mashed and bloody limbs. A botched creature, but watching and waiting.

As she rolled onto her side, trying to blot it out, she felt something move in her depths. She shuddered: *it was inside her too.* Then she remembered, and her hands reached down in panic.

But the baby was still there and she heard herself moan with relief and gratitude. 'It's OK,' she told him, massaging her belly, as if he needed reassurance too. 'You'll be fine.'

When the trembling had subsided she switched on the bedside lamp, sat up and shuffled towards the edge of the bed, unsure whether she had the energy to drag herself to the bathroom for a pee, but knowing she must. The faint vestige of the puffin print on the wall caught her attention as she pushed herself up to standing. She pictured the birds in an unknown flat, watching over Adam and Emily as they slept, intertwined and peaceful. Her face in the bathroom mirror was shocked and waxy. She drank two tumblers of water and went back to bed, but sleep wouldn't come.

It happened two nights running. The second time cramp in her left leg yanked her awake. As she clambered out of bed and stood up to get rid of the pain she could feel the presence of the foetus in the corner above the bay window. It seemed to want something from her. Protection? Reparation? Revenge?

When the cramp had subsided, she lay in the darkness, cradling her abdomen. The familiar nocturnal movements of the child inside her were a comfort, a sort of counter-irritant. She tried to focus on them, but her mind took her back relentlessly to the suburban clinic where she'd had the abortion thirty-six years earlier. Pebbledash houses, the mask over her face, flaring light, daffodils. What did it mean? Where did it sit in her life? That secret, inarticulate event? Questions that hadn't occurred to her at eighteen, when everything had seemed so simple and clear-cut.

She wrapped herself into a tight ball around the baby in an attempt to hold herself together and chanted all the justifications like a mantra. Not the right time. Not the right age. Not ready. Wouldn't have been a good mother. But new thoughts assailed her now, as if the membrane separating two long-partitioned zones had suddenly dissolved.

It was troublesome, knowing what she did now about the frailty of embryos and foetuses, how frequently they shrivelled and failed. Her first one had been tenacious, hadn't it, withstanding all the chemical and physical onslaughts that could derail fertilisation and implantation? It had been one of the winners, growing inexorably inside her, *determined* to be born. And the fact that it was made by her and Adam – just like Lauren and Alex – disturbed her now. A male foetus, perhaps, like the one she'd longed for ten years later. Where would he be now, her potential boy? A man of thirty-five. Older than Sheila's sons. Towering over her, broad-shouldered, hugging her with wholehearted male affection – different from the more complex, equivocal love of daughters.

She heaved herself on to the other side and plunged her fingernails into the palms of her hands. She must stop this: it was crazy and unrealistic. She'd been a different person, in a different life. Adam was a boy she barely knew. If they'd married at that time it would have been a disaster. She'd have ended up a bitter, uneducated, incompetent teenage mother. But she wished that they'd talked more about it: this thing that had shackled them together, long before they married, and whose reverberations had finally finished them off. Sometimes she wondered whether they'd ever really *chosen* to be with one another. Because in a way theirs had been a shotgun wedding, hadn't it? An inarticulate quest for meaning masquerading as choice. Not that it mattered any more, now that Adam had so emphatically *un-chosen* her.

She pushed back the duvet and propped herself up on the pillows to ease her aching back. There was a convulsion inside her as the baby adjusted his position. Paradoxical, the effort she was putting into accommodating this one and keeping him alive: same body, same uterus, same uncompromising reversal of the biological clock, but a different *intention* – a reclamation of fertility, rather than its rejection. The truth was, the same woman at different times in the fertile phase of her life could greet her own menstrual blood with joy and relief, or dread its arrival as the harbinger of defeat and childlessness. Freedom and fulfilment meant sometimes thwarting female biology by unnatural means and sometimes enabling it with unnatural interventions.

In a sort of belated vigil Ruth spent much of her spare time over the next few days staring at images of eleven-week-old foetuses on the internet. She found unsettling colour photographs taken by a Swedish photographer in the 1960s, mostly the products of abortions, but perfect-looking creatures with pale orange skins, ghostly in their amniotic sacs, staring, frowning, sometimes sucking their thumbs. She pored over images of embryos, like the one they'd put inside her: clusters of grey cells. She read about the early midwives and wise women who for centuries helped women stop babies as well as bring them to birth. She wrote a loose diary of her reproductive life, studded with fragments of history, science and theology, and tried to make sense of it all, but she couldn't make the pieces fit together. At night she slept fitfully, woke and returned to the internet, like someone revisiting the scene of a fatal accident.

25

Alex and Lauren were holding a video summit on the parlous state of their parents' marriage. Lauren sat cross-legged with her laptop on the floor of the studio, a shaft of late-afternoon sunshine casting jagged shadows over the drawings she'd been working on. Alex was still in bed, sewing a patchwork baby quilt for her nephew.

'Mum's in a bad place,' said Alex. 'Whenever I call her she's wearing the same baggy grey jumper, and because of the way the colour in her hair's growing out she looks like a sad badger. I think all this time she must have been secretly hoping Dad would go back to her, and now she's given up hope.'

'Sheila and Simon have suggested they go for couples counselling,' said Lauren, 'but both of them said no.'

'Probably a good call.' Alex gave a snort of laughter. 'Imagine one of their grade-A rows, performed competitively to an audience of one. Car-crash therapy.'

'Glad you find it funny.'

'Sorry, but sometimes I feel as if I've been given a bit-part in a surrealist pantomime.'

They agreed that the chances of a reconciliation were slim. Alex said that if their father wasn't already sleeping with Emily, by the sounds of it he very soon would be. She wondered now whether he'd had relationships on the side for years: after all, why else did a man of thirty-three have a vasectomy without consulting his wife?

'And I reckon Mum had affairs too,' said Lauren, her lips corrugated in disgust. 'Dad implied that she'd betrayed him, and he told you she had "form", remember? Maybe she was unfaithful and he retaliated? I can imagine that.'

Alex stretched her arms above her head, then exhaled gloomily. 'Suddenly all our cupboards are full of skeletons and secrets, and I haven't a clue who, or what, to believe.'

'I've decided to focus on the baby from now on,' said Lauren. 'And I've given up trying to mediate.'

'Yeah,' said Alex. 'I guess we have to accept that it's over.' She shook her head. 'I took them for granted, so completely. Mum, Dad, the house – I assumed they'd be there, rock solid, whenever I needed.' She drew her knees up to her chest and her face was woebegone. 'Right now I feel kind of homeless and a bit shaky.'

'Same,' said Lauren. 'Ever since Dad talked about the fault lines in their marriage I've been going over all my childhood memories and looking for signs. And once you start doing that, you realise *everything* was fake. They were just pretending to be happy. You're right, it *was* a pantomime. Four third-rate actors reading from a meaningless script in a set made of cardboard.'

'Whoa,' said Alex. 'You're getting carried away. There may have been problems in the background and, yes, there were some rows, but the main reason I'm feeling so bereft now is that they *were* happy. We all were – for *years*. You know that.'

'It's what we wanted to believe.' Lauren's voice was expressionless. 'But now it's fallen apart. Like everything does. In the end.'

Alex frowned. Her sister's face had a heavy, sullen quality that she hadn't clocked until now. 'Are you feeling OK?'

Lauren shrugged. 'I've not been that great lately.' She lifted her left arm towards the camera and Alex saw the red rubber band and the weals on her wrist where she'd been yanking it.

'What's triggered this?'

'My therapist thinks the tablets may have destabilised me.'

'What tablets?'

'Oestrogen.' Lauren explained she was taking them to make her body think it was pregnant. As the birth approached, she would use a breast pump to stimulate milk production. 'In the meantime, I'm getting blinding headaches and my tits feel as if they're on fire and full of static electricity. Right now I'd like to tear them off my chest. Will they ever produce milk? Will I get a live baby at the end of this? Knowing my luck, it'll all be a complete waste of time.'

'No,' said Alex. 'This time it's going to work, and in less than eight weeks you'll be holding your son in your arms and tucking him up in this very splendid quilt I'm making. Cling to that image.'

'Stop patronising me. You don't have a *clue* what I'm going through.' Lauren ended the call without saying goodbye.

The eight-month antenatal check took less time than usual and was uneventful. The consultant remarked that Ruth's blood pressure was up slightly, but it was nothing to worry about, and there were no signs of pre-eclampsia or gestational diabetes. She was doing brilliantly, he said, but in view of her age they would need to see her every two weeks from now on, just to be on the safe side. Lauren didn't say much: she seemed withdrawn. Afterwards they went to the café as usual and Ruth headed for the Ladies; when she emerged an elderly man was sitting at the grand piano and bashing out 'As Time Goes By' on a loop.

Lauren was stirring her cappuccino and poring over the kick chart in Ruth's antenatal notes. She looked up. 'You did say peppermint?'

'Yes,' Ruth sat down. 'Though I'd kill for a triple-shot latte right now. Anything, in fact, to keep me awake.'

'In six weeks' time I'll buy you a lifetime's supply, promise.' Lauren smiled at her. 'You still sleeping badly?'

Ruth said, 'I've tried everything from yoga breathing to counting sheep, but nothing works. If I could take sleeping pills I'd probably be able to break the cycle.' She caught Lauren's look of alarm. 'Don't worry, I know they're forbidden. But I keep nodding off in the office, which isn't a good look when I've got so much to do.'

'Oh Mum, I'm sorry.' Lauren looked stricken. 'What's keeping you awake? Are you worried about the birth?'

Suddenly she had to tell someone, as a way of diluting feelings that threatened to engulf her. 'There was another pregnancy. Before you and Alex. I've been having dreams about it, like a sort of visitation.'

'You lost one too? Why have you never told me?'

'I was only eighteen at the time, so . . . '

Lauren's face registered shock, then sympathy. She put her hand on Ruth's arm. 'Oh Mum, how awful. Did Granny know?'

'I didn't tell anyone, I couldn't.'

'What happened?'

'I went to the Pregnancy Advisory Service and they rescued me.'

Lauren winced. 'It must have been so horrible?'

Ruth folded her arms. 'Quite the reverse. I couldn't let it happen, so an abortion was my only option. I was massively relieved.' Lauren looked away and Ruth felt judged. 'You don't understand, because you've never been there, but I wasn't ready to be anyone's mother, I was just a child.'

She paused until Lauren turned and met her eyes. 'Six years later, I *was* ready, so I had the two of you. I was a different person, and with you and Alex I loved the whole thing. As you know, I

302

was desperate for more.' She gazed at the bump and massaged it gently. 'It's been the same with this one, I wanted him *so* much.' She looked up and frowned. 'What's the matter?'

Lauren face had darkened; she stared at Ruth in silence. Then she said, 'It's the way you talk about it, as if you're filling a shopping trolley. "I won't have that one but these will do". Easy come, easy go.'

'There was nothing easy about it, Lauren, and, just for the record, I've never mentioned the abortion to anyone before. Because, even though one in three women has had one, it's the big female secret. We don't go there because the debate's become so binary. Pro-life or pro-choice – no space in between.' She paused. 'But maybe you think I shouldn't have had a choice?'

'I wouldn't dream of telling other women what to do with their bodies,' said Lauren haughtily. 'But I'd *never* be able to dispose of my own baby.'

Ruth had to dent her prim certainty. 'But you have. Often. All those morning-after pills you took when *you* were a teenager?' She paused for emphasis. '"Like Smarties", I think you said.'

'That's completely different.'

'In moral terms it's exactly the same. It stops an embryo. A life, if you choose to think of it that way. So does the coil.'

'This isn't really about abortion, Mum. It's about *you*. Going on about switching your fertility on and off, whenever you fancy. *Terminate and try again.*'

'And those seven frozen embryos that you've got left over, waiting in the freezer to be thawed and turned into people, what are you proposing to do with *them*?' Ruth raised her eyebrows. 'Try again? Or terminate?'

Lauren looked at her mother with distaste. 'It's not funny. They already are people. And I worry about them, all the time. We both do.'

'I wasn't joking: this whole business is serious and complicated.

Contraception, abortion, infertility – they're central to the physical and ethical experience of being female, but we never join up the dots and talk about them honestly.'

Lauren's face flamed red. '*My* experience is that I've never managed to get an embryo past fourteen weeks. But I have to sit here listening to you, pregnant yet again, with *my* baby, telling me how abortion's a no-brainer and boasting about your amazing, infallible fertility. Are you *trying* to make me feel as bad as you possibly can?'

Startled, Ruth cast around for words that would soothe. 'Of course not, the last thing I want is to hurt you, after all you've been through,' she said. 'You've been so unlucky. All those years of grief and stress—'

Lauren broke in: 'Why don't you say what you really mean? I'm a career disappointment and a reproductive failure.' She paused and narrowed her eyes like a predator going in for the kill. Ruth braced herself. 'But at least I'm not as driven and ruthless as you, and I just hope I'll be a better mother to him,' she pointed an aggressive finger at Ruth's bump, 'than you ever were to me. Because he'll be my priority. I won't spend weeks working away from home. Or dump him with strangers.' She paused, then threw in, 'Or have sex on the side.'

Ruth's patience, stretched taut as a wire, finally snapped. 'It's my drive and determination, which you so despise, that's got us here. *Me*, carrying this baby for *you*, at great personal cost.' Her voice was loud and three nurses at the next table turned to stare. She hissed, 'I'm doing this because I love you and I'm looking after him as well as I possibly can. And this is what I get in return. Well, *thank you.*'

Lauren's hands went to her face and her mouth opened, but she said nothing.

Ruth got to her feet. 'I'll see you at the next appointment.' She walked a few paces, then turned back, arm outstretched. 'May I have *my* antenatal notes?' She paused, then added drily, 'If that's OK with you?'

Lauren handed them over and their eyes met. There was a moment when one of them could have pulled back in appeal or apology, to break the deadlock, but neither did. Ruth knew she'd been at fault for treating Lauren as a confidante and sounding board, not a daughter – her maternal antennae were malfunctioning. But she was stunned by the vehemence of the attack and the sheer dislike that had powered it.

That evening Sheila called to find out how the appointment had gone.

'Fine, no problems.'

'You don't sound fine.'

Ruth said Lauren had accused her of being a bad mother. Sheila asked what had triggered it. 'It came from nowhere. We were talking about contraception and pregnancy and stuff, and suddenly all this poison poured out of her. It was as if she hated me. I was so hurt. She also accused me of having "sex on the side", which probably means she's heard about Sam, and I've been having a meltdown about that too.'

Sheila said she was surprised it hadn't happened before. 'Being on the receiving end of a gift as big as the one you're giving Lauren is a huge challenge, isn't it? She's bound to have a mass of very complicated feelings about you, some of them fairly dark.'

'I know,' said Ruth. 'I keep telling myself that she's full of oestrogen and envy, and that I need to make allowances.'

'Exactly,' said Sheila. 'So try not to take it personally.'

'That's easier said than done, because *I'm* full of oestrogen too. My back aches, and my nipples hurt like hell, plus I'm hardly sleeping and my husband has traded me in for a younger model – all because I offered to be *her* surrogate. Honestly, Sheila,

305

you should have heard her, she was so judgemental.' She checked herself and groaned. 'That's what I used to say about Adam, isn't it?'

'Yes,' said Sheila. Ruth heard her hesitate. 'By the way, have you heard from him?'

'No, and I wouldn't expect to. I think Lauren goes over there quite a bit and Alex calls him, but thankfully they spare me the details. And I'm OK now, I've got used to it.'

'Seriously?'

'No, of course not. I *hate* it. I have this stupid fantasy in which there's a knock at the door and he's standing there and says he prefers me to Emily and begs me to have him back. I hesitate for as long as I can bear, then give in and we live happily ever after.'

'It's not impossible.' But Sheila didn't sound convinced.

'Not a chance. It's all or nothing with Adam: no halfway house. In fact, I've been wondering if he'll try to get his vasectomy reversed and have children with her. It often happens, doesn't it, when men of his age get a second wind.' Ruth sighed. 'Once this baby's born I guess we'll have to sell the house and I'll start a new life on my own. Fun times, eh?'

Sheila said, 'You need a break. I'm driving down to Penzance this weekend to see my mum, why not come? You could relax, do whatever you fancy and forget about everything for a couple of days. Have a think about it.'

Ruth didn't have to: the prospect of escaping the pain and chaos of her own life, and being carried along instead in the slipstream of someone else's, was too tempting and she didn't have any work meetings scheduled. 'If you're happy to make frequent stops, so I can have a pee and stretch my legs, then I'd love to run away to Cornwall with you.'

Ruth lit a candle, then ran a long, hot bath scented with lavender oil and immersed herself. She watched as the baby kicked and elbowed his way around her glistening abdomen, then placed her hands on either side of the bump and sang to him:

Rock-a-bye baby, on the tree top,
When the wind blows, the cradle will rock.
When the bough breaks, the cradle will fall.
Down will come baby, cradle and all.

When she stopped they lay together, still and quiet. Then he somersaulted, as if begging for more. She laughed and began again. After more acrobatics and three more nursery rhymes, she said, 'We're a good team, aren't we, you and me?' She carried on talking to him as she dried herself: 'Everyone's deserted me because I'm an old, fat, pregnant granny. Not to mention a hateful mother. But you've decided to stay.' She pulled her nightdress on over her head and leant against the wall while she eased it over her bump. 'The trouble is it's hard to be a good mother if your own mother was crap at it, but they don't tell you that in the antenatal classes. You learn on the job – and if it was paid work you'd get fired for incompetence. Lots of collateral damage and no gratitude.' She bent to empty the bath and felt him scrabbling inside her. 'Hang on, we'll be the right way up in a minute.' She stood and put her arms around him. 'You don't think I'm ruthless and unavailable, do you?' She waited for a signal, but he was motionless. 'I hope not, because you're all I've got now, my little one.'

26

Sheila picked Ruth up late on Friday morning because she wanted to miss the rush hour traffic. Ruth hadn't left the city for months and the sight of open countryside, stretching out to the horizon, came as a balm. It was a glorious midsummer's day and as they sped along the motorway she felt like a prisoner on day release. Her spirits soared as they crossed the River Tamar, then headed over the sepia wilderness of Bodmin Moor and down into the southernmost tip of Cornwall.

They'd made this journey together often during the years when they both had elderly parents to look after. Sheila's remained lithe and lucid well into their eighties, but Ruth's father died suddenly of a heart attack at seventy-five and within a year her mother was in a care home in Redruth. Sheila remembered the bleak visits she'd made there with Ruth. Alzheimer's turned some people into a better version of themselves – sweeter and more loving – but Angela Jago was afflicted by a bitter and angry variant of the disease. She grew very fat and barely mobile, spending her days wedged into a purple plastic wheelchair just inside the entrance to the day room. After a few months she didn't recognise them any more, but from time to time, when Ruth was talking with valiant brightness about the weather, or the M&S cookies she'd brought with her, Angela would lift her head, squint at her daughter through the chinks in her plump cheeks and shout, '*Will* you be quiet?' And Ruth would stop and press her lips together, in exactly the way Sheila had watched her do as a child, while her mother laid into her and the other residents hunkered down to spectate.

'Talk, talk, talk. You think you're better than us, don't you, little-miss-know-it-all? I can see right through you, always could. Riding for a fall, you are, my girl, wicked.'

'Mum?' Ruth would plead.

'Wicked, wicked, wicked, she's wicked. Get *away* from me, you *naughty* girl.'

When she started lunging at Ruth the carers would materialise. 'Come on, Angela, time to go back to your room for a lie-down. Say goodbye to your daughter and her friend.'

The first time it happened Ruth cried. It was unnerving, she said, hearing the words that had rained down on her as a child; her mother's hostility was so hard-wired, it seemed the last vestige of her identity. They went to a pub and over many gin and tonics Ruth admitted that when the girls were born she hadn't a clue how to mother them: by then she knew the model she'd grown up with was abnormal and damaging, but it was all she had. 'Sometimes I'd hear Mum's voice coming out of my mouth, saying those same dreadful things. Their faces would crumple and I realised they'd end up with the same scars inside them as I had. But I didn't know how to stop myself. I was panic stricken.'

Sheila nodded. 'It must have been lonely?'

Ruth blew her nose, then managed a wobbly laugh. 'In hindsight it was awful, but nobody died, did they?'

Sheila persisted. 'You're still suffering the effects, though, aren't you?' She took Ruth's hands. 'It might help to talk to someone, so you can put it behind you.'

'It *is* behind me. I never think about it any more,' said Ruth, anxious now to close the conversation. 'I've dealt with it by living a life that's as different from my mother's as possible and I reckon I've pretty much succeeded.'

Angela Jago had finally died five years ago and this was the first time Ruth had been back to Cornwall since. 'Look!' she exclaimed as they turned off the main road and caught their first glimpse of St Michael's Mount and the vast blue bay that stretched from the Cudden Point to Long Rock. It happened every time: the shock of recognition as she took in its breathtaking beauty.

'I know,' said Sheila, and they smiled at one another.

They checked into a small hotel surrounded by a jungle of semi-tropical plants near the harbour in Penzance, where Sheila always stayed. Her mother had sold the family home after her dad died and was now in the dementia unit of a nursing home near Helston; Sheila planned to spend Saturday morning there, and said it was pointless Ruth coming. 'Mum won't have a clue who you are and it'll depress you. Stay here and relax in the garden or have a wander round Penzance. We can meet afterwards for a late lunch.'

Ruth explored the town. It was still down-at-heel and resolutely unfashionable, with the occasional hipster café or New Age emporium hidden among pound shops, charity shops and high-street chains. The staring was worse than in London: people stopped, pointed and gawped; a teenage boy took a photo while she was standing at a pedestrian crossing. There were more estate agents than she remembered and she found herself looking to see what was up for sale and whether she knew any of the houses. Prices had gone up but were still a fraction of those in West London. Ruth wondered ... if the house were sold and the mortgage paid off, would her share of what was left be enough to buy something here? Summoning up a brazen briskness that she hoped would fend off impertinent questions, she talked to a few agents, and came away with a bagful of house details, together with assurances that the market was soft and bargains abounded.

By the time she'd browsed the junk shops and booksellers, and bought food for their lunch, Ruth's legs were aching and she found an eco-store at the top of the main street, where she could collapse onto a sofa, sip a turmeric latte and watch the world go by. Young couples were refilling washing-up bottles and shovelling oats into brown paper bags crumpled with re-use; babies wriggled in slings on their chests and toddlers chewed virtuously on strips of sugar-free fruit leather; they hailed one another, exchanged news and scanned the community noticeboard – earnestness offset by laughter. Not a bad life. She took out the stack of estate agents' brochures and was flicking through them, when a voice said, 'Sorry, but this is the only space left, d'you mind if I crash?'

A heavily pregnant young woman with blue hair and crimson dungarees was looking down at her. Ruth moved her bags, and watched as she shrugged off her rucksack and sat down. Despite the difference in their ages they immediately assumed the weary kinship of women close to term. 'I'm Erin, thirty-two weeks and counting, it's a girl.'

'Ruth. Thirty-two and a half. A boy.'

'Synchronicity,' said Erin. 'Where are you having yours?'

'At a hospital in London. You?'

'A water birth in my doula's garden.' Erin pointed at the brochures. 'You're moving down here afterwards?'

Ruth laughed. 'I picked these up just now. I'm on my own and I'll be looking for a house or flat fairly soon. I grew up here and I've been wondering—'

'Come back!' cried Erin. 'This place is *brilliant* for single mums, there's a fantastic support network and lots of play-groups and nurseries. A few of us in my antenatal class are on our own and we're looking for a building where we can set up

311

a Mommune together – I can add you to our WhatsApp group if you want.'

Ruth said she was a host, not a mother-to-be, so she wouldn't be a candidate. When she finished explaining the circumstances of her pregnancy Erin stared at her, round-eyed. 'That's unreal. I've never met a surrogate.'

'Neither had I, until I became one.' Ruth smiled.

'And you're totally chilled about handing him over to your daughter, the moment he's born?' Erin was looking at her, incredulous.

'It's what I signed up for.'

'But you'll feed him for the first few days?'

'No, they'll give me drugs to dry up my milk,' said Ruth, with more equanimity than she felt.

'Ooh, I'd find that so hard.' Erin grimaced and clutched her crimson bump as if the thought pained her. 'The emotional trauma would be bad enough, but you'll be breaking all those chemical bonds between you and him. Our antenatal teacher was telling us about them at the last session.'

Ruth corrected her: 'There's no chemical bond. This baby grew from my daughter and son-in-law's embryo, not mine.'

'Yes, but scientists have discovered that cells from the babies we're carrying swim into our brains and other parts of our bodies and stay there for ever.' Erin was making a stirring motion with her hands. 'We get all muddled up with them, biologically speaking, during pregnancy, so that we'll be inseparable afterwards.'

Ruth said, 'I've not come across that research, I wonder how mainstream it is,' but she felt a tremor of disquiet. She looked at her watch and stood up. 'I must go. Best of luck with everything.'

'You too. And if you end up down here, call me.' Erin scribbled her number on a paper napkin and gave it to Ruth. 'Remember, girl, anything's possible. Jump and the net will appear.'

*

312

Sheila and Ruth sat on a bench in Morrab Gardens picnicking with unhealthy relish on the food of their childhood: Cornish pasties and local tomatoes, followed by saffron buns slathered with clotted cream. Sheila described a difficult half-hour encounter with her mother, who thought she was a new carer and told her politely but firmly to go away; in the end she'd become agitated and it had seemed kinder to leave her in peace. 'I've had meetings with all the people I needed to see and I don't think there's any point in going back tomorrow, so we can do whatever you fancy from now on.'

That afternoon they drove to the Minack, the outdoor amphitheatre carved into the rock in Porthcurno. The two of them had been there on a class outing to *A Midsummer Night's Dream* when they were fifteen: it was the first play Ruth had ever seen, and she was hooked for life; at twenty she'd acted on the stage herself, as Lady Macbeth in a touring university production. Now she sat down next to Sheila on a granite slab near the edge of the cliff. Fat bumblebees burrowed into the clumps of pink thrift that dotted the turf, chased by a retinue of small blue butterflies, and above their heads herring gulls screamed in abandon as they surfed the warm air currents; below them the sea shimmered as if its surface had been sprinkled with crushed sapphires.

Ruth felt she was reclaiming a part of herself that she'd mislaid a long time ago. She turned her face to the sun and sighed. 'Bliss.' She lay on the grass and stretched out her arms and legs. The baby moved further down her abdomen, easing the pressure on her diaphragm, and suddenly it was easier to breathe.

'We were so lucky, having all this as kids,' said Sheila. 'I sometimes feel guilty that our boys grew up in London – it's great, living in a city, but ...'

'I know,' said Ruth. 'I've been wondering whether I should move back to Cornwall and work from home as a script editor. I'd earn less, but the cost of living is lower here and I wouldn't have all the stress of production. Lots of people in TV are doing it. You can get a Georgian house in Penzance for the price of a two-bedroom flat in Hammersmith.'

Sheila laughed. 'Ruth Jago, I don't believe I'm hearing this. You spent your entire adolescence longing to leave and planning your escape route. You wouldn't last a week down here.'

Ruth's phone started to ring, loud and shrill. Without opening her eyes she asked Sheila to fish it out of her bag.

'It's Lauren,' said Sheila.

Ruth took the phone, she'd expected an apology straight after their altercation, but had heard nothing since the clinic appointment. 'Hello,' she said, her voice cool.

'Mum, are you OK? You sound odd.'

'*Fine*, thank you.'

'Only we're inside your house and there are letters on the mat and a newspaper, and you're not here.' She paused. 'You haven't gone *away*, have you?'

'Porthcurno. I'm here for the weekend.' Ruth could hear Dan's voice in the background.

'She's in *Cornwall*. I've no idea why. *Shush, I'll ask.* You might have said, Mum. We've been really worried.'

'Your rules said I needed to inform you if I left the country, not central London.'

'But what if you had an accident, or something happened to the baby, or if you went into labour right now, while we're stuck here, hundreds of miles away. It's not very responsible. When are you coming back?'

'Tomorrow evening. And, trust me, I'm nowhere near going into labour. I haven't had any of the warning signs and there's still more than five weeks before the Caesarean.'

Lauren sighed. 'I just wish you'd *told* me beforehand.'

'In view of your outburst I didn't feel inclined to.'

Lauren's voice changed. 'I'm sorry about all that, Mum. I was in a state and I didn't really mean any of it. I waited till today because I wanted to apologise in person. We brought you flowers. I've put them in a vase on the hall table.'

'Apology accepted,' said Ruth, but her knuckles were white with the effort of keeping her temper. Lauren didn't sound *nearly* sorry enough. 'I have to go, but I'll let you know when I'm home, OK?'

Ruth threw the phone back towards Sheila. 'She talks to me as if I'm a naughty schoolgirl who's out to harm her baby . . . '

'She doesn't mean it, you have to make allowances.'

' . . . when he's my number-one priority. He has to be, because he's totally dependent on me.'

'Lauren's dependent on you, too, and very vulnerable at the moment, I suspect,' observed Sheila. 'Maybe she needs a bit of mothering too?'

'There's only so much of me to go round,' retorted Ruth. 'And she's an adult, whereas he's an unborn child. I have to prioritise.'

On Sunday morning they took a picnic to Marazion Beach. The sand was streaked with large pools of water that mirrored the pale blue sky; Ruth paddled in a vast maternity costume she'd bought for the occasion, then searched for shells and mermaid's purses as she'd done for hours as a child. Afterwards, while Sheila swam, Ruth sat scooping up handfuls of dry sand and letting them trickle slowly through her fingers as she watched a group of young families a few feet away from her. The women lay in a companionable cluster, sunning themselves, chatting and laughing while their children made sandcastles with their fathers or ran towards the waves with fishing nets. One woman was packing up to leave.

'We need to go,' she told her daughter, 'otherwise Jack will be waiting at Harry's and wondering where we've got to, won't he?'

The girl, aged three at a guess, was wearing only her pants.

The mother approached with a T-shirt and skirt. The child snatched them. 'I want to do it *by myself.*' She walked to a patch of sand near Ruth and began to dress slowly and incompetently. She pulled the T-shirt over her head, discovered it was back to front, then shrugged it off and started all over again. She stooped to pick tiny pieces of dried seaweed off her skirt before attempting to put it on. The mother stood watching at a distance, responding when the child spoke, but allowing her to go at her own pace, not intervening.

Ruth remembered how she'd dealt with Lauren and Alex when they were that age: she would have taken over the dressing in a frenzy of impatience and efficiency; the task always more important than the child. A battle of wills would have ensued, then a tantrum, tears, and the burning feeling of anger and guilt in her chest as she yanked a hysterical child away from the beach, curdling the memory of the day. Now the mother had strapped the girl into a buggy and stood watching as she fished small stones out of her pocket then opened her palm to show them: they were smiling at one another.

How differently she would do it now, if she had the chance, thought Ruth. She wondered what it would be like to raise this child inside her *here*, away from the pace and pollution of London. She didn't yet feel ready to step into character as a grandmother, hovering like a greedy seagull over Lauren's life, waiting for juicy titbits, minding the boy she was carrying for a few hours, whenever she was allowed. If only she could have another go at motherhood, a chance to use what she'd learnt: to make up for the mistakes of the past. An opportunity to do it *properly* this time.

The weather broke that evening and they drove home in heavy traffic and lashing rain. The car was a single thread in a loom of red, yellow, white and orange light, refracted through a prism of lorry spray, as the black wipers shuttled back and forth. Sheila leant forward, concentrating so hard to make out the road markings that she couldn't talk.

Ruth was left to her thoughts. She pushed back her seat, closed her eyes and lapsed into a daydream. It was mid-afternoon and she was pushing a buggy through the back streets of Newlyn, having bought fresh fish for their supper, back to the Edwardian harbourside jewel that needed a bit of TLC; he was facing towards her, the way babies did nowadays, and every so often he smiled at her and she laughed. He was perching on her hip, chortling, as she picked plums from the well-established orchard in the walled garden of the Grade 2 Regency house in Penzance. She was baking a crumble in the charming kitchen with its host of original features, while he watched from his highchair; they ate it together, taking all the time in the world. She was watching him on the climbing frame, outside the recently modernised former farmhouse in Perranuthnoe; he was gazing out at the unsurpassed views of Mount's Bay, while she took photos and gently encouraged him to go higher. They were beachcombing together, she was teaching him to read, she was waiting while he did up his shoelaces and finished his story, he was confiding in her, she was listening, she was watching him while he slept in the room she'd painted dark blue with silver stars, he was hugging her and telling her he loved her . . .

Sheila braked hard and Ruth opened her eyes. They were still on the motorway and the traffic in all three lanes was slowing as it skirted a pile-up: eight or ten cars crunched together, blue lights lurching in film-set rain, dark puddles that might be blood, three ambulances with their doors open, fluorescent men carrying stretchers. Cars crawled for the next five minutes, sobered by their proximity to catastrophe and the sudden reminder that death could be seconds away; then the shock abated and everything speeded up again. Soon they were approaching London through a blur of interwar suburbia; it was like driving through the sleeve of an old grey cardigan.

For the first time in her life Ruth didn't want to go home to Hammersmith. They were a unit, the two of them, and they didn't belong in London, they'd be better off in Cornwall, happier. But she knew it couldn't happen. Instead she was being carried back, towards the nightmares, the birth, and the unimaginable rupture that would follow it.

27

Adam couldn't believe the Sunday-afternoon mayhem at the John Lewis baby department in Oxford Street: toddlers everywhere, running, colliding with large objects, falling to the ground and screaming; fathers scooping them up and proffering drinks in foil pouches to silence the racket; expectant mothers leaning heavily on cots as they agonised between brands; couples poring over Moses baskets and sleep cocoons, their faces alight with anticipatory excitement. It took him back. He, Lauren and Dan made an unconventional trio: the only ones without a visibly pregnant woman in tow.

Over lunch he'd offered to buy them whatever baby goods they needed. Dan, protective, said Lauren would probably want to do some research before buying stuff, but it turned out she'd been doing that for months and knew exactly what she wanted. No reason for Adam to pay, though, she said. He'd insisted: 'Your mother's doing all the heavy lifting, this is my contribution. What do newborns expect to find in a well-stocked nursery, these days? I'm thirty years out of date.'

Lauren consulted her phone and reeled off items: the cot was sorted, Dan was organising a car seat, but they still needed a buggy, a crib, a changing table, a bath and a baby monitor.

Adam said why not get all of it, right away? They worked through the list until only the buggy remained. There were ten couples ahead of them in the queue and when their turn came the assistant pointed them towards a collection of contraptions built like quad bikes that morphed into seats, carrycots and shopping trolleys. Lauren said everyone had them nowadays. She was torn between two models: the black and green one was a fabulous design, but maybe a bit too hi-spec, and *so* expensive.

'To hell with the expense,' said Adam. 'You've waited years for this moment, Lauren, get whatever you want.'

Lauren turned to the assistant. 'In case you were wondering, we're expecting a son, but my mum's having him for us, in four weeks' time.'

'Your *mum*?'

Yes, they said: she was acting as their surrogate.

The woman beamed at them. 'What a generous thing to do. So you've left her at home with her feet up while you stock up on everything your young man's going to need? What an amazing lady, I bet you're making a big fuss of her.'

They smiled and nodded, feeling uncomfortable to varying degrees. Everything, said the assistant, would be delivered the following week, just in case the baby decided to put in an early appearance.

In the café over a cup of tea, Lauren explained to Adam that the baby was viable now: even if he was born that afternoon he'd go to Special Care and his prognosis would be excellent. 'That's why I'm finishing off the nursery and starting to buy things.'

'But there's no reason to think he'll be premature,' said Dan firmly. 'The test results are spot on and everything's going to plan, isn't it?' He put an arm around Lauren's shoulder and kissed the top of her head. She snuggled into him and nodded.

Adam decided someone needed to name the ghost at their feast. 'And Ruth? She's doing OK, is she?'

'I've not seen her since the last check-up, but as far as I know she's fine,' said Lauren. Her cheeks coloured and Adam wondered whether they'd fallen out. 'She was well enough to go to Cornwall last weekend.'

'But you're keeping a close eye on her?'

'We're seeing her tomorrow at the clinic.' Lauren sounded defensive. 'And Mum's got a pretty good instinct for self-preservation, hasn't she?'

It was an odd remark, but he let it go: with the birth so imminent Lauren was probably more anxious than she was letting on. He thought of Ruth, alone in the house: what would she be doing, and feeling? Was she scared of what lay ahead? He had no idea, and he realised that their imaginative connection, which had endured for the best part of thirty-five years, was broken for good.

On the way to the hospital appointment the taxi driver eyed Ruth in his mirror.

'Doesn't look like you've got much longer to go before you pop, love?'

'No.' Ruth closed her eyes emphatically.

Her body was feeling the strain now: the bump was very large and low and her bones ached. Varicose veins corrugated the skin behind her knees and down her right calf. Her tummy itched and it was hard to stop herself scratching until it bled. Her breasts were so big that she'd started wearing a nursing bra day and night: it was marginally more comfortable that way. On days like this she wanted it all to be over. The previous week had been her last in the office: the Morrab team had given her a good-luck card and a big box of bath oils and body lotions. Bella hugged her, for the first time since January, and said how much she was looking forward to seeing her back in the autumn.

As she walked down the stairs and out onto the street with her bag of presents and her work notebooks, Ruth remembered embarking on maternity leave before Lauren, then Alex, and the sense both times that a new phase in her life was about to begin, momentous and exciting. This was different: she felt she was falling – away from the life and people she knew – into a void.

'I'm guessing it's not your first, judging by the size of you and your, ahem, mature years, would I be right there?'

'Can't talk, my daughter's texting.' Lauren said they were on their way, but there was a burst water main and traffic was gridlocked: they'd be late. Ruth sighed, Dan was coming too: she would be under dual surveillance. Their relationship had shifted – estrangement was too strong a word, it was more of an infinitesimal distancing. Lauren phoned less frequently and she'd cancelled lunch.

'How are you, Ruth?' asked Dan when they arrived at the clinic. He embraced her gingerly.

Lauren said, 'Have you been waiting ages?' She patted Ruth's arm.

'About half an hour,' said Ruth. 'And I'm not too bad, Dan, thank you for asking.'

Lauren said, 'Have you played him the Mozart album I sent last week yet, Mum?'

Ruth nodded.

'Great. I thought it would be calming for him to hear it every day in the run-up to the C-section, if that's OK with you?'

Ruth felt like a stranger, who'd been hired, impregnated, then subjected to a belated DBS check that had unmasked her as a criminal. But she was probably imagining it – one of the many drawbacks of living alone was that there was no one to tell you if you were getting things out of proportion.

The check-up was uneventful. The midwife said that Ruth's blood pressure was still on the high side and they'd need to keep a close eye on it, but the baby had turned upside down and was getting ready to be born, which was a good sign. Lauren's face flushed with excitement and Dan hugged her to him. Ruth clutched at her bump protectively. She felt the angle of a foot or knee and then the baby started to kick hard; normally she'd have invited Lauren and Dan to put their hands on her skin and enjoy the moment, but for the first time it occurred to her that they didn't deserve it.

Afterwards they bade her an effusive goodbye. 'You're doing such a great job, Ruth,' said Dan, his cheek brushing hers. 'Everything's on track. Fantastic.' Like a middle manager fresh from a team-building course, she thought sourly.

'Thanks so much, Mum. I'll call soon. Look after yourself and – sorry to nag – but don't forget to keep playing him the music, will you?'

As she sat waiting for a taxi in the hospital foyer Ruth felt hot, cross and lonely. Lauren and Dan weren't really thinking about her at all any more, she was just the biodegradable bag in which their precious baby was being carried – convenient but ultimately disposable.

'They don't want me, they're just waiting to grab you and run.'

The elderly couple on the bench opposite stared at her, startled. Ruth realised she'd spoken out loud. 'I'm sorry,' she said to them. 'It's supposed to be the first sign of madness, isn't it? Talking to yourself, I mean.'

They smiled uneasily.

It was as if time had slowed: the baking days and nights of an early July heatwave stretched and slid into one another. Ruth got up late and grazed on cereal, toast and tea. She napped, wrote pages of her diary, went to the loo and watched fragments of

Wimbledon on television. The pattern repeated itself until she went to bed, where she lay, sleepless, in the dark, or went down to the kitchen and pored over the pile of old photo albums that she'd hauled out of a chest of drawers in her study. There were a few small ones that her father had painstakingly filled with the black-and-white photos he'd taken of Ruth as a young child. Here she was in an Aertex shirt and shorts heading for the tape in a sprint race; on a beach displaying a collection of starfish she'd found; halfway up a rope and grinning. Then there was a gap before she emerged in a blaze of colour: gowned for graduation; radiant at her wedding. The Furnival years were documented in a stack of big square albums that charted birthdays, Christmases and holidays; hundreds of pictures, taken to capture happiness and record success, but in many of them Ruth was gazing out, beyond the camera, as if she wasn't really there.

Alex messaged her one night:

> I know you're awake, what
> you doing?

> > Thinking about motherhood and
> > how I cocked it up

> We've been through this! I've
> already said you were great,
> nothing to worry about

> > I wasn't available, wasn't always
> > kind, BE HONEST

> You're the only mum I have so I
> can't compare – I love you and am
> sure you did your best Xxxx

Not always

Stop it! How you feeling?

35 wks pregnant in 35 degrees =
UNBEARABLE

Sheila dropped in the following evening to do some cleaning and cooking. Ruth opened the front door wearing only her underwear and sweating profusely. 'Sorry for the hideous spectacle, but I can't bear clothes against my skin.' She flopped back onto the kitchen sofa.

'Don't mind me.' Sheila surveyed her. 'You look amazing – like one of those monumental Picasso nudes.'

'Beached and beefy, you mean?' Ruth groaned. 'I feel as if I'm wearing the biggest fat suit in the world and I can't find the zip. I don't think I'm *ever* going to get back to normal – whatever normal means from now on.'

She looked down at her breasts. Their hard, spherical cores stood proud and over the past few hours a thin pale liquid had started seeping from her nipples, leaving two primrose stains on her white bra. She'd recognised it at once: colostrum, the early, precious nourishment designed to boost the baby's immune system and make him strong. But it would all be wasted, because Lauren was going to breastfeed him. With hormone-induced milk that wouldn't be as good. There was so much he was going to miss out on. She began to weep. Her body was breaking down. His head pressed on her bladder all the time now and often she didn't get to the loo fast enough. The insides of her ribs were bruised and sore from his kicking, as if he was preparing her for the unimaginable pain to come. If they took him from her she would dissolve into a pool of tears, and milk and urine.

'Ruth?' Sheila was staring at her in consternation.

325

'Take no notice,' she said. 'It's the hormones crying, not me.'

'Are you scared?'

'I'm beginning to face up to what's going to happen at the end.'

'You mean the Caesarean?'

Ruth shook her head. 'The fact that there won't be a baby.'

Sheila was emptying the rubbish bin; she stood up and looked at Ruth in astonishment. 'But there will be.'

'Not *my* baby.'

Sheila frowned. 'But you always knew—'

'Yes. I always knew. I'm just telling you how it *feels*. I've got detachment issues.'

Sheila went to hug her, but Ruth pushed her away.

'I'll get over it. I'll have to, won't I?' She closed her eyes and began to cry again, soundlessly.

When she'd finished tidying up the house Sheila filled a bowl with iced water and sponged Ruth's face, neck and wrists, then combed her hair. She said, 'I've got to go to Leeds tomorrow, for a three-day conference, but I'll come straight over as soon as I'm back. In the meantime, call me whenever you want. It's not good for you, being stuck here on your own, day after day.'

But Ruth was already asleep.

She woke in the night and clambered downstairs to the kitchen, where she ate three shortbread biscuits, then lay on the sofa and began sorting through the Cornwall property details. She made four piles on the coffee table next to her – Penzance, Marazion, villages, countryside – then began triangulating nurseries, play-groups and schools on her laptop and scribbling notes in the margins of every sheet. She logged on to Mumsnet and grazed threads about life as a long-distance commuter in Cornwall, the experiences of recently arrived single mums and the health risks from radon emissions in the west of the county.

Then the baby woke up and moved so violently inside her that

326

she started coughing. 'What was that all about?' she asked him when she'd recovered. 'It's claustrophobic in there, isn't it? You've had enough too, haven't you? I know what you're going through.' *Their cells swim into our brains . . . we get all muddled up, biologically, during pregnancy, so that we'll be inseparable afterwards.* She reached for her laptop and searched for 'foetal tissue in maternal brain'. It was true: his cells would remain part of her until she died, it was called microchimerism and there was a hypothesis that it happened so that mothers could nurture and respond to their babies more effectively. She grabbed her diary and made some notes.

She put the laptop on the table and started singing:

> *Rock-a-bye baby, on the tree top,*
> *When the wind blows, the cradle will rock.*
> *When the bough breaks, the cradle will fall.*
> *Down will come baby, cradle and all.*
> *Rock-a-bye baby, do not you fear*
> *Never mind, baby, mother is near.*

He was still now. She whispered, 'Imagine if it was just the two of us, on our own by the sea. You could run and swim and climb. I'd show you the best places to fish, and where to find crabs and mussels; maybe we'd get a boat. We could have hens and fresh eggs every day, and the air would be clean. You'd be safe, because I'd always know what you needed. I could do it better this time, so much better.'

28

Lauren and Dan called Alex: they'd decided that Ruth needed daily support from now on. She was trying to manage on her own, said Lauren, and got very spikey whenever help was offered, but she seemed out of sorts and not her normal self; they were terrified she was going to have a fall or get ill from overdoing things, which would be bad for her and disastrous for the baby. If Alex could phone her, without fail, every day, that would be a huge help.

'Lately she hasn't been picking up my calls,' said Lauren. 'You may have better luck. If you sense there's a problem, let me know straight away.'

Dan cut in: 'Laurie thinks your mum's avoiding her, but I've told her she's imagining it.'

Alex looked unconvinced. 'I wouldn't be too sure, she's still beating herself up about what she was like as a mother to us. I think that's why she's not sleeping.'

'You're wrong,' Lauren countered. 'Disrupted sleep is completely normal at this stage, all the books say so.'

'Come on, she told you about something that was worrying her, which she'd never revealed to anyone, and you threw it back in her face and told her what a crap mother she'd been. Think about it.'

'That's *not* what happened,' said Lauren hotly. 'She was deliberately undermining me, flaunting her fertility.' She was close to tears. 'In any case, I apologised, but now she's punishing me – maybe because there was some truth in what I said.'

'Can we stop this and focus on practicalities?' Dan said. 'I've plotted everyone's availability and created a rota. From tomorrow, Sheila, Laurie or I will visit every day and deliver anything Ruth needs. That way we can keep a close eye on her. I'll slot your phone calls into the spreadsheet, Alex.'

The following evening Lauren and Dan turned up on Ruth's doorstep, unannounced, carrying two large Sainsbury's carrier bags. They marched into the kitchen and unpacked the shopping, then moved back and forth, wiping worktops, stacking the dishwasher and sweeping the floor. Dan explained his rota and pinned a copy on the noticeboard. Ruth watched in dismay from the sofa; she felt like a hostage in her own home. When she attempted to fetch a glass of water, Lauren restrained her: she mustn't lift a finger, that's why they'd brought chilled soup and bread for supper.

'I'm not sure I can manage any.'

Lauren ignored her. She said Ruth needed some decent food for a change: it looked as though she'd been snacking on biscuits, toast and jam for days, which was bad for the baby's blood sugar. They were going to sit at the table and have a proper meal.

Ruth felt an explosion of anger in her chest. 'No,' she said, 'I'm not a child to be bossed around. It's too uncomfortable, sitting over there. *This* is where I eat,' she patted the coffee table, 'so I can keep my legs up.' She added loudly, 'The two of you haven't a clue what I'm going through.'

Lauren bit her lip and busied herself with the soup. Dan pulled up two chairs opposite the sofa, then started to clear books and papers from the table, but Ruth told him to leave them: there was plenty of room for three bowls and a bit of bread.

Spoons clinked against china in a thickening silence, then Dan said, 'Delicious, Laurie, courgette and Parmesan, you said?'

'Yes.'

'It's all organic, Ruth. We got it from the farmers' market, specially for you.'

'Thank you,' she said, forcing down a spoonful.

'And now there's fresh fruit and some yogurt.'

Ruth said she'd be sick if she ate any more, but accepted the offer of a herbal tea, to placate them.

Dan cut up a peach and handed half to Lauren, then he turned to Ruth. 'As I said, one of us will be here every day from now on, to help you with stuff.'

'What stuff?'

'Bringing you food and shopping; sorting out the garden.'

Ruth followed his gaze: the lawn was a foot high and everything in the borders was brown and desiccated. 'Adam used to do all the watering and I haven't had the energy,' she said defensively.

'We'll come over this weekend, mow the grass, get the sprinkler going and stick some plants in. Then you'll be able to lie here and look out at some flowers and greenery, which will cheer you up, won't it?'

He looked to Lauren for confirmation but she wasn't listening. She'd picked up a pile of papers from the table and was flicking through them. She stared at Ruth. 'Are you thinking of moving to Cornwall?'

'It's just a vague idea.'

'And you'd live there on your own?'

'Yes, but it probably won't happen. I picked those up in Penzance, I was just—'

'Why have you written "very close to Ofsted 'excellent' school" on this one, and "two nurseries within walking distance" here? And "lovely, but would need three beds minimum"?' Lauren handed the sheets to Dan.

'It's nothing.' Ruth was very tired.

Lauren was reading out another note: '"Move into Erin's Mommune as a stop-gap, then rent or buy?"'

'What's a Mommune?' asked Dan.

'It's a place where single mothers live together and bring up their children. Have I got that right, Mum?' Lauren turned to Ruth, her eyes like slits.

Ruth closed her eyes.

'Look, Dan, there are *tons* of houses here and she's researched the school and nursery catchment areas for all of them and written notes—' Lauren broke off, then started reading aloud: *'I know you better than anyone, your cells are in my brain. You know my voice, my heartbeat, my breathing – I am your home, so cruel to abandon you.'* She looked towards Ruth. 'You want to keep him, don't you?'

If she didn't answer maybe the questions would stop.

'Ruth?' said Dan.

Ruth opened her eyes. 'That's private. I was being—'

'Being *what*?' Lauren was shouting now and her face was scarlet.

'Imaginary.'

Lauren leant down until her face was almost touching her mother's. 'Are you taking him to Cornwall? Is that the plan?'

Ruth felt very hot and confused, and her breasts were leaking again; she folded her arms over the dark circles on her tunic and sighed heavily. 'It's not what I want, it's about him. Who can look after him best. He's the one who matters, not the rest of us. And we've bonded, him and me. It's what happens.'

Lauren turned to Dan. 'Are you hearing this?' She started to sob.

'Laurie, let's not jump to conclusions, shall we?' Dan gently prised the sheaf of paper out of her hands, then laid the pages out on the table and photographed them one by one on his phone.

As an afterthought he took a photo of his mother-in-law; her eyes were closed again.

He went over and squatted next to her. 'Ruth, I think you're very tired and a bit confused. For the last nine months you've always said that you're our incubator, that you're carrying the baby until he's ready to be born and you'll hand him over to us straight away. That's what we've agreed, isn't it?'

She couldn't bear how complicated everything was: Lauren, Dan, the baby; they all wanted different things from her.

'Can you promise me you're going to stick to that agreement?'

Her head was throbbing and she couldn't work out what was best. She said, 'Please leave.'

But they took no notice. Maybe she hadn't said it out loud?

'Ruth, can we just talk sensibly and get things straight?'

She was surprised by the noise that erupted from her throat, *'Get out of my house or I'll call the police.'* Her scream filled the room. They were staring. She was breathless with exertion. Her heart was hammering and the baby seemed to be moving inside her lungs. 'Go,' she gasped. *'Now.'*

Dan got up and took Lauren's hand. The two of them were standing over her. 'We're leaving,' he said. 'But this baby belongs to us and we'll do whatever's necessary to protect him. There's no *way* you're keeping him, Ruth.'

Adam was eating a Sainsbury's ready meal while working his way through a pile of defence papers. When he opened the door and saw their faces, he feared the worst.

'Your mother?' He looked at Lauren. 'What's happened?'

'How did you know?' She burst into tears.

It was some time before Dan managed to reassure Adam that both Ruth and the baby were physically fine. But they'd hit a problem, he said, and needed advice, urgently.

Adam led them inside. They sat at the table and Dan told him what had happened. They were scared that Ruth would leave London and they wouldn't know where the baby was or if it was safe and well. He'd taken the photos as evidence, in case she absconded. There was an antenatal appointment scheduled for first thing the following morning, but as things stood they were worried that she wouldn't turn up. She'd screamed at them like a mad woman. She seemed to be thinking of joining a women's commune with someone called Erin; for all they knew, she might have left Hammersmith already. Lauren started to cry again.

Adam thought for a while, then he said, 'We may end up having to go to a Family Court to get an injunction, but for now let's try to deal with this informally. I'll contact Ruth straight away. My hunch is that she will go to the check-up tomorrow, but if she doesn't turn up and you can't reach her by phone, then call me and I'll drop everything to sort things out.'

He turned to Lauren and hugged her to him. 'I'm so sorry you're having to go through this, it's not fair.' She buried her head against his chest. 'Listen to me.' He put his hands on her shoulders and waited until she looked up at him. 'This baby is yours and I *promise* you will have it. I'll do whatever is necessary.'

'Thank you, Dad,' she said, between sobs.

'I'm sorry,' he repeated. 'This shouldn't have happened.'

'It's not your fault,' said Dan. 'For whatever reason, Ruth has gone back on her word. It's unforgiveable of her.'

Adam stood up. 'Who knows what's going on, Dan?' He ushered them towards the door. 'I wouldn't presume to judge.'

Ruth had fallen deeply asleep in the kitchen, now she was woken by a bleeping noise. The sound of an email arriving. She opened her eyes and peered at the clock: ten minutes past midnight. She leant towards the coffee table, struggled with the zip of her bag and extracted her phone, then lay back on the sofa and opened her inbox. All she could see were the first three lines:

Adam Furnival
LUNCH?
Ruth

Her heart leapt: he'd come round! The four words slid and swam. Her fingers kneaded the thin edges of her phone as she stared at the screen, holding on to this moment in which he yearned to see her, in which he loved her again. If he came back to her, everything would be all right.

She opened the email:

Ruth,
Under English law I am the father of the baby you are carrying and thus have an ethical and legal interest in your intentions towards 'our' child after it is born.
May we meet to discuss? I can come to Hammersmith if that is easier for you.
I should prefer to settle this matter informally and amicably, so please could you email me some times that are convenient for you?
Adam Furnival
Erasmus Chambers
6 Stick Walk,
Middle Temple

The legal formality of the email sent a chill through her. Best ignore it, she told herself. She pressed delete.

29

Lauren and Dan sat either side of Ruth in the waiting room of the antenatal clinic. She felt like a pregnant convict with her guards. No one spoke. Lauren's face was red and puffy. When her name was called Ruth walked straight to the examination room without looking back and pulled the door closed behind her.

'Your daughter not with you today?' asked the midwife, just as Lauren and Dan entered the room.

There was a tense silence as she tested Ruth's urine sample.

'Excellent, no trace of protein.' She looked up at them and her voice was gratingly jolly: 'That's what we like to see, isn't it?'

Eventually Dan said, 'Yes. Great.'

The midwife measured the length of Ruth's bump with a tape and cross-checked it against a graph on the wall. 'You're thirty-five weeks and six days pregnant and your measurement is spot on.'

Her hands probed Ruth's abdomen, feeling for the contours of the baby, then she pressed a sonic aid against it and showed them the readout: 138 beats per minute, perfectly normal.

She looked at Ruth. 'He seems very happy in there, but how are *you* feeling?' Her face was plump and creased with sympathy.

'Tired,' said Ruth. 'Hardly sleeping.'

'So hard in this weather, isn't it? All my ladies are complaining. Not got much longer to go, though.' She turned to Lauren and Dan. 'You must be *so* proud of Mum?'

'Yes,' they said flatly.

'Just make sure you give her as much cosseting as you can over the next couple of weeks before her C-section.' She reached for the blood pressure cuff and turned back to Ruth. 'Let me quickly check your BP, then you can go away and put your feet up, my love.' Ruth wanted to ask this kindly middle-aged woman to take her home and look after her – protect her from everyone and everything.

The midwife was watching the figures on the face of the machine; she frowned. 'Mmm, it's quite a bit higher today. Let's have another go.'

She took it a second time, but the numbers were the same. 'It could be the heat . . . ' Her voice was less jolly now. She looked down at Ruth. 'Apart from the tiredness, how have you been feeling?'

'Not great. But I've been very stressed recently.' She looked over at Lauren and Dan. 'Haven't I?' she said pointedly.

'We don't want any of that, do we?' said the midwife, following Ruth's gaze. 'Won't do your little chap any good at all.' There was a hint of reproof in her voice.

As the midwife gently unwound the cuff from Ruth's arm Lauren said, 'Does blood pressure that high harm the baby?' Her face was tense with anxiety.

'It's OK, Laurie, it's OK.' Dan put his arm round her. He turned to the midwife. 'Could this be dangerous?'

'Your mum's other indicators are all fine and he's moving around well.' She looked at Ruth as if weighing the options. 'I don't *think* we need to admit you at this point, but I'd like you to come back early next week for another check. In the meantime, take things very quietly and phone us *immediately* if you're worried about anything.'

*

When they reached the hospital foyer, Dan said, 'Ruth, can we go to the café for a coffee?'

'Herbal tea, I think you mean,' said Ruth. 'That was one of your many specifications, Dan, when you commissioned my uterus.'

'Please Mum, we need to talk,' pleaded Lauren.

'You heard what the midwife said: I need to rest. I'm exhausted.'

'We'll give you a lift home.'

'I'll get a minicab. I can't cope with any more stress.'

As she turned away a wave of resentment hit her. 'And if you intend to goad your father into sending me any more threatening emails, can I please have some warning? For the baby's sake, if nothing else.'

She trudged down the corridor away from them.

In the taxi she switched on her phone. Four missed calls from Lauren, three from Dan, one from Adam, two from Alex, two from Sheila. Why wouldn't they leave her alone? They were making her *ill*. She switched it off again.

Lauren and Dan called Adam on speakerphone from the car to update him. When he told them he'd so far had no response to his email, Lauren said she wanted to start legal proceedings against Ruth straight away.

Adam counselled patience. 'I've left a voicemail asking her to call me. She may be sleeping, or mulling things over.'

Dan said, 'She's behaving very oddly. She refused to engage with us at the clinic and she was very hostile. I'm wondering whether she's got some kind of pre-natal psychosis.' He hesitated. 'Do you think she needs to be sectioned?'

'Er, no Dan,' said Adam drily, 'on the basis of what you've told me so far I doubt she'd meet any of the clinical or legal criteria.'

'Even though she poses a risk to our baby's safety and our peace of mind?' said Dan. He'd spent a sleepless night online, reading news reports about surrogates who'd kept babies.

'OK, here's what we'll do,' Adam's voice was decisive. 'There's no point in going nuclear at this stage, let's give it another twenty-four hours and if she hasn't got back to you or me by tomorrow afternoon I'll go over to Hammersmith and we'll take it from there.'

Ruth had slept for most of the afternoon and early evening. Now it was getting dark and she was in the kitchen, eating toast and marmalade. As she filled the kettle to make some tea she caught sight of her fingers. They were swollen and rather shiny, like the succulent plants that grew on the cliffs at Porthcurno. She stretched out both hands under one of the spotlights: they looked redder than usual, with tense cream blotches at the joints. Her wedding ring was tight, too tight. She tried to pull it off, but it wouldn't budge. She poured a drop of olive oil onto the finger and massaged it in. Still no good.

On *News at Ten* a man was talking about a demonstration at Heathrow, how flights were being disrupted, but Ruth couldn't concentrate: the ring was hurting now. She wrestled it backwards and forwards and finally managed to rock it over the joint. The skin was hot and almost raw. The effort exhausted her and she lay back on the sofa. Now victims of a terrorist attack were talking about what they'd been through and their little girl who'd lost a leg was learning to walk with a frame. She'd never taken the ring off before. She looked at her naked finger and felt apprehensive, as if something bad might happen to her without it. Nonsense, she told herself, it was obsolete now: nothing but a scrap of metal. Her phone made a rattling sound: Alex again. Ruth ignored it, she didn't feel like talking and she needed to pee urgently. It was a huge effort to drag herself to the loo. In the hall mirror her face was flushed and strangely puffy.

She fell asleep and was woken by the unfamiliar sound of the landline. It rang for a long time, then went to voicemail. A disembodied voice filled the kitchen and she turned the TV down to listen.

'Ruth, this is Sheila, can you pick up? . . . I know you're there, Ruth. Talk to me. *Please.* Say something – anything – so I know you're all right.

'OK, the reason I'm leaving this message is that Adam's been calling me. Lauren and Dan think you're going to kidnap their baby. I've told him that you'd *never* do that, not under *any* circumstances, because you're a compassionate and ethical person, Ruth. That's true, isn't it?

'I'd come round right now, but I'm still up in Leeds. Adam wants to talk to you, urgently.

'You can call me at any hour of the day or night. Just pick up the phone. I'll be waiting for you.

'I love you and I'm concerned about you. We all are.

'I'll be back tomorrow evening and I'll come straight over.

'I'm going to hang up now. Unless you want to say something, Ruth?

'*Ruth?*

'OK, night, night.'

Then silence.

30

A stifling day, close and humid, the temperature already twenty-six degrees at ten in the morning. It felt as though the air was being squeezed tight and would soon explode with a crack of thunder and a torrent of relieving rain. Ruth had brought a blanket into the garden to escape the heat of the house and now she was lying on the grass, with cushions under her head and back. She stretched, sighed and inspected her feet again. The ankles had completely disappeared into the puffy wedges at the bottom of her legs and the skin was satiny and splodged with purple: she'd grown hooves overnight. Her fingers were fat pink sausages, unbiddable; when she tried to bend them they curled inwards then stopped. This morning the face in the bathroom mirror had been *really* swollen, little black eyes peeping out of puffy sockets that merged into rigid cheeks. Not her face. There was something disconnected and alarming about this body, she felt like Alice, after she'd eaten the cake that made her bigger. She wondered vaguely whether she should phone the hospital, but couldn't face it.

A plane growled overhead. She looked up and watched the heavy grey body until it disappeared behind the roof of the house. Suddenly the yellow bricks blackened and the house was falling towards her; a pain in the front of her head, sharp and sickening. She sat up and the building righted itself, but the garden was screaming a warning: sour, electric green splattered with purple and blinding white, it vibrated with menace. Something very bad was happening.

The baby was pushing her lungs up into her throat, making it hard to breathe. She felt screams congealed like lead weights in her chest – she wanted to howl, but the neighbours would hear. People would come running and ask her what was the matter, and she wouldn't have a satisfactory answer.

Ruth put both hands on her tummy and felt a dolphin lurch: he was there, alive, that was something. She ran a hand over her face and looked down at her fat palm, it was running wet; sweat was pouring from her. The idea that the house might be a safer place formed slowly. She heaved herself forward and tried to stand, but her head screamed in protest: safer to keep close to the ground where the pain was just about manageable. She got down on all fours and crawled over the grass, then up the steps, onto the terrace and into the kitchen, where everything she looked at was obscured by flickering silver chrysanthemums. Ruth shook her head to dislodge them, but more came, showering her field of vision. All the windows were black, as if an assiduous child had crayoned them in.

Her breath was coming too fast. It made the sound of a dog panting alongside her. She tried to slow it down. In – *hold* – Out. In – *hold* – Out. But the feeling of dread overcame her again and she lost the rhythm. Her heart was thundering. A thought sliced through the chaos of her body, clean and sharp as a knife: *Hospital is the best place to die.*

The phone was on the kitchen table and she had to swim through air thick as molasses to get there. She reached up and touched it; it fell off its cradle and onto the floor. A taxi would be faster than an ambulance. She tried to dial the minicab number, but her fingers wouldn't work and she sobbed with frustration. Finally she managed to stab nine three times, then the speaker button.

The voice that filled the room asked her to choose an emergency service.

'Ambulance.'

'Connecting you.'

'London Ambulance Service, can you tell me your name and location?'

Ruth gave the details and a woman's voice repeated them back.

'Can I call you Ruth?'

'Yes.'

'What's the problem, Ruth.'

'I'm thirty-six weeks pregnant and something's wrong. I can't see properly, there are flickering things everywhere.' Ruth let out a sob of terror. 'I think I'm dying.'

'Is there someone with you, Ruth?'

'No.'

'You sound breathless, is that right?'

'Hard to breathe.'

'Is your heart beating faster than usual?'

'Very.'

'Are you having any contractions? Is the baby starting to come, Ruth?'

'No.'

'Can you feel it moving at all?'

'Yes.'

'How old are you Ruth?'

'Fifty-four.'

'Can you repeat your age for me, love?'

'Fifty-four.'

'As in, number *five* and then number *four*?'

'Yes.'

'And you think you're thirty-six weeks pregnant?'

'Yes.'

A pause.

'Have you fallen or had any head injuries today or in the recent past, Ruth?'

'No.'

'Do you have any other medical or psychiatric conditions that you take medication for, or see doctors or nurses regularly about?'

'No.'

'OK. An ambulance is on its way. It should be there in less than ten minutes. I'm going to stay on the line until they get to you. Now is there any chance you could get to your front door and open it for me, so the paramedics don't have to break it down?'

'I'll try.'

'OK, I want you to take the phone with you as you go to the door and I'll keep talking to you. Take your time.'

Ruth crawled down the hall, pushing the phone in front of her. Seagulls were flying across her path, and bumblebees. Such a long way. Suffocating, this heat on the clifftops. She couldn't reach the latch, it was too high, and her fingers wouldn't connect.

She lunged and caught it, yanked it back, then collapsed next to the phone.

'Door's open.'

'Well done Ruth, that's fantastic. Can you wedge it open somehow? The ambulance is nearly there.'

Ruth stretched out an arm as a doorstop then rested her head on it.

'Is there anyone you'd like me to call? Husband, partner, other family? Or a friend?'

She sobbed. 'No one.'

A flickering blue noise and boots on the garden path. Yellow men lifted her up and took her on a stretcher to the ambulance. Cold inside, as they pulled off her clothes, put jelly on her chest

343

and attached electrodes. Cuff on her arm, tightening. Fingers prodding her legs.

She closed her eyes. The paramedic was talking on the phone.

'It's not psychiatric, we found her antenatal notes in the house. Dead on thirty-six weeks and aged fifty-four. Looks like she's having it for someone else . . .

'No, there's no sign of labour or rupture of membranes. Blood pressure's a hundred and ninety-five over a hundred and fifteen. Bilateral pitting oedema. Vomiting . . .

'Yes, confusion but no fitting . . . OK, be there in ten minutes.'

Her head was in a vice of pain: if she moved or opened her eyes she would die from the light entering and exploding.

Too ill and tired to sort it out. Someone was moaning, 'The baby, help the baby.'

'It's all right, Ruth, we're taking you to the labour ward. The doctors know you there, and they'll do what's best for your baby. Not long to wait now.'

Clunk of doors. Exhaust fumes, hot air, street noise. Lifted up and down, onto something hard. Rattling wheels. Whoosh of floppy hospital doors: cooler air and corridor echo. Trolley stopping, skitter of curtains. Murmur of people.

She opened her eyes the smallest fraction and squinted through a mesh of lashes. Faces with auras. *The company of saints?* One looming in. Finger plucking eyelid. Sharp lights into bald eyes, swoop of killer pain. Bowl under chin, acid in her throat and mouth, sick smell. A woman talking, 'Slow dilation response.' Loud now, against her ear, 'Ruth, I'm Debbie Morgan, one of the obstetric specialist registrars. You've come into hospital because you're quite unwell. Can you tell me how long your hands and legs have been swollen?'

'Bad yesterday, took my ring off.'

'Have you got any pain?'

'Terrible headache; can't see. I'm frightened.'

'I know, my love, all your symptoms are being caused by your very high blood pressure; we need to bring it down.'

'Can't bear it.'

'Is it hurting anywhere else?'

Ruth touched her right ribcage. 'Here.' She was whimpering.

'We need those bloods, plus liver and kidney chemistry. Now.'

'Am I dying?'

'Not if we can help it.' Her hand on Ruth's, squeezing, but the voice more hopeful than reassuring. 'We want to stabilise you and monitor the baby to make sure he's OK. We'll give you painkillers and something to stop you feeling so sick. We found your daughter's details in your notes, so she knows you've been admitted.'

Trolley wheels, quieter place. Where they put the dead people? Arms heaving her onto a bed; blood pressure cuff biting her arm and pumping more pain inside her head; a voice, 'Two hundred over a hundred and eighteen.'

Hands fumbling between her legs, sorting between flaps of flesh and pushing a catheter inside her; urethra rearing against the hard plastic, furious and sore.

'Protein in urine.'

'Has someone called the paediatricians?'

'I'm inserting a cannula, Ruth, so we can take blood for testing and start giving you drugs to make you feel better ... sharp prick coming.' Needle slashing back of hand; jumble of jolts, cold tubes against skin. 'And another prick in your arm ... there.' Hurtling down a tunnel towards obliteration. Cold jelly on tummy, stick probing: ultrasound. Memento mori.

Fingers in her mouth, fumbling, big dry thing under tongue. Retch it away. 'Try to keep still for me Ruth, this tablet will bring down your blood pressure. Take some deep breaths.'

So tired and heavy. Everything. Couldn't keep watch, couldn't keep eyes open. Floating ...

*

345

A long time in limbo, then everything whirling and crashing. Blur of blue body overhead, swaying. 'My baby's dead?'

'At the moment he's OK, but . . . ' The voice tailed off.

Save baby. Save baby. Save . . .

' . . . decent flow in umbilical artery, considering . . . '

' . . . brisk reflexes and ankle clonus . . . '

' . . . magnesium sulphate is indicated in a case like this . . . '

' . . . platelets and coagulation are normal, she'd be OK for a spinal.'

A man's voice, loud and decisive: 'OK, call theatre and let them know we're on our way, if we hang around much longer she could start fitting. The next of kin are on their way, you said?'

She closed her eyes to stop the patterns, but the yellows and crimsons were inside her eyes, and the foetus with the smashed skull, staring. She'd smashed him, now he was smashing her. A life unled. But if him, no Lauren, no Alex. Too hard to put together. Everything broken, disconnected. It could have her, *but it mustn't kill the baby.*

'Ruth, this is Tom Fenton, your consultant, we've met in the antenatal clinic. We're going to prepare you for an emergency C-section because you have pre-eclampsia. Your blood pressure is very high and it isn't responding to treatment. We're going to have to deliver the baby and placenta to make you better. Do you understand?'

There are risks, Mrs Furnival, you need to understand the risks of contemplating childbirth at your age . . . Eclampsia. Stroke. Haemorrhage. Then death, of course. Maternal death.

Ruth opened her eyes. Giant snowflakes were falling, blotting out the people, so many people. But the consultant's voice was loud. 'Ruth? Are you happy to give your consent to the Caesarean?'

What was the right answer this time?

So easy to get it wrong.

346

Mustn't forge his signature.

'Ruth, we need to move fast. If you're in agreement, say yes.'

'Yes.'

'We'll let your family know, OK?'

'Yes.'

The face disappeared and she was wheeled along corridors and in and out of lifts. The sticky thud of feet on lino beside her, then a space full of light and the low thrum of machines. Heaven or hell?

A woman's voice: 'Ruth, you're in the operating theatre and I'm going to give you a spinal anaesthetic, so you'll be awake but won't feel anything during the surgery. We're going to roll you onto your side.' A needle sliding through skin, then pressure and a jolt in her spine; now she was on her back, someone's hand on her leg. 'The drugs will start working in about eight minutes.'

The lower half of her body was full of warm treacle, it surged through her pelvis, down her legs to her toes. Then all feeling below her waist disappeared. The pain in her head was there still, but bearable. She opened her eyes: a wall of green cloth reared up above her chest; she couldn't see what was happening. An anaesthetist on her right, next to a wall of machines; a midwife on the other side, holding her hand, watching her face. Above the green wall, masks, eyes and blue hats moved like puppets, the consultant in the middle, higher than the rest. He was talking quietly; metal clattered, monitors bleeped. Then a tugging in the numbness.

Suddenly footsteps and talking, loud, staccato and urgent. The midwife let go of Ruth's hand. The consultant was looking at the anaesthetist. 'She's bleeding heavily. I need to get this baby out now.'

Then different voices:

'How many units of blood do we have here?'

'Two.'

'Major obstetric haemorrhage. We need a shock pack. NOW.'

A figure moving to the door. Sliding. Falling. Scrambling upright, the gown, dark and wet, clinging to its body. Her blood.

'Go. Just *GO.*'

Post-partum haemorrhage is a medical emergency where you can bleed to death very fast.

'Ruth, look at me. Just focus on me.' The midwife took her hand and moved to hide the carnage.

The consultant was saying HOLD and PRESS and RELEASE. Ruth felt something give at her centre as they tried to prise the baby out of her.

Out of harm's way. Doctors have done this before. Where did that one go? She can't help any of it now, she's floating away. Not hers, this one. *Must tell the others.*

'Give them a message,' she said. 'My family.'

The midwife's ear was next to Ruth's mouth. She pulled out a piece of paper, balanced it on her palm and started writing.

Then a creature, close by, shrieking with pain.

The foetus?

The baby?

Something against her face, warm and damp. 'Here he is, Ruth. Alive and in good condition. Well *done*, you *did* it, you've been so brave.'

People with boxes, hooking little bags onto a rail. Receding.

A long way below her, now, all of them.

Getting colder.

'Need any more?'

'Another pack. She's losing it as fast as we put it in.'

The phrase we were taught at medical school was 'a sense of impending doom'.

'Blood pressure falling.'

Sloshing. Smell of meat. Killing field.

Die now. Tit for tat. Bye bye, baby. Bye bye.

'Ruth, I've got the placenta out but you're still bleeding heavily and we've tried everything. I need to give you a general anaesthetic and perform a hysterectomy. You'll lose your uterus, but there's no alternative. I need your consent.'

All the blood gone. Motherblood. Lifeblood. Nothing left.

'Ruth, this could save your life, I need you to say yes.'

A mask over her face. Bleeping and buzzing.

Too cold now. Too late . . .

Darkness.

31

Adam was the first to arrive at the hospital. He'd been in court, midway through his summing-up, when a clerk passed him a note; the judge called an early adjournment and wished him well. Dan had driven from his office and couldn't find a parking space, so he'd parked the car on a double yellow line. They waited tensely in reception until Lauren arrived, then a nurse took them up in a lift to a small room near the operating theatres. Ruth was being monitored, she said; one of the doctors would come and talk to them as soon as possible. Would they like tea or coffee while they waited?

Lauren said, 'There's no time for that, please take us to her, straight away, we're supposed to be with her, it's in the notes.' She was breathing fast and her voice was strangled. 'I got here as soon as I could.' The nurse looked at her, confused.

Dan interposed himself and said, loudly, almost shouting, 'We are Daniel and Lauren Ryan, the baby's real parents. Ruth Furnival is our surrogate. We're entitled to be present.'

Adam's face was chalk white and he was hugging himself. 'Why was she admitted?' he asked. 'What's going on exactly?'

The nurse said, 'I'm sorry, but I'm agency cover. All I know is I was called down from the gynae ward, because there's an emergency in obstetrics, and told to fetch you and bring you here. I don't really know my way around, but if you like I'll try and find out what's going on.' Adam nodded and she hurried away.

They sat down on uncomfortable plastic chairs around a small, low table. A fan whirred in one corner and a broken Venetian blind clattered uneasily against the window from time to time. The initial call had come mid-morning, while Lauren was putting the finishing touches to a mural in the nursery: Ruth had been admitted to hospital in a serious condition; they were trying to stabilise her before delivering the baby; immediate family members should get there as soon as possible. She'd called Dan, messaged Adam, then ordered an Uber. On the way she'd phoned Alex and told her to get on a plane. Her hands and hair were still covered in green paint. She cried in bursts, then sniffed loudly every so often to stop herself and pulled at the red band on her wrist.

Dan, full of pent-up anger and frustration, was worrying aloud about fines and clamping. 'Why aren't there designated bays for emergencies, or ways of overriding parking restrictions when it's this urgent? Being towed away is the last thing we need. They need to fix the system.'

Eventually Adam said tensely, 'In the great scheme of things, Dan ...'

'Sorry. I'm in a state.'

'So are we all.'

Lauren said, 'Why hasn't the nurse come back? Why aren't they telling us anything? I can't *bear* this.' She turned to Adam. 'Did Mum reply to your email?'

'No,' said Adam. 'But it's hardly surprising. She's clearly been seriously ill for some time.'

Dan said, 'Then why didn't they admit her yesterday, when they *knew* her blood pressure was high? It's beyond irresponsible,

351

letting this happen. Yet again . . . ' He didn't finish the sentence. 'If our baby comes to any harm because of Ruth's illness, we're going to sue this hospital for negligence.'

Lauren said, 'Dad, could Mum have made legal arrangements to keep the baby between receiving your email and first thing this morning?'

Adam looked at her in disbelief. 'What kind of question is that?'

'It's the question I'm asking you.' Lauren's face was blotched and belligerent.

'It is *theoretically* possible that your mother went straight to a solicitor after the clinic appointment yesterday and began the process of opposing any future application by you for a parental order.' He sighed. 'But it's highly unlikely, given the state she's in now. And to be frank I really don't think this is the time—'

Lauren shook her head. 'No, Dad, I'm sorry, but you've just said it's a possibility and we *know* we can't trust her. I want you to help us take out an injunction now. Do you know a solicitor we can call?'

Before Adam could reply there was a knock on the door and a junior doctor, very young and looking shell-shocked, came into the room. The three of them stood up and encircled him. Ruth was being prepared for a C-section, he said, but unfortunately it wasn't appropriate for anyone else to be present.

Dan protested, 'We were given cast-iron guarantees by the consultant that both of us would be there for the birth. We are the baby's biological parents. It says so in all the hospital paperwork.'

The doctor waited until he'd finished, then said flatly that everyone was aware of that plan, but it had been overtaken by events. 'Mrs Furnival has fulminant pre-eclampsia and has developed complications that could be life-threatening. There are already a lot of people in theatre and you'd just be in the way.'

'Will the baby be all right?' Lauren gripped the doctor's arm so hard that he winced.

'We're doing our best.' He turned to Adam. 'I'm sorry.'

Adam reached for the back of a chair to support himself. 'Are you saying ... ' But he couldn't risk the words.

The doctor said, 'I have to go, they need me in there.'

They sat down again, Dan with his arm around Lauren, both of them rigid with anxiety; Adam opposite, his head in his hands.

The door was slightly open and a man strode past carrying a padded freezer bag.

'Blood,' said Lauren.

Adam sat up. 'What for?'

'It could be for the baby, but it's most likely to be Mum. Haemorrhaging.'

Adam's phone buzzed. It was Alex, calling from the airport, wanting to know the latest. He put her on speaker and they leant forward as he brought her up to speed. 'They've been bringing blood, lots of blood. Lauren thinks it's for your mother.'

'Don't let her die,' said Alex. 'She's *not allowed to die*. Tell her I love her and I always have. She's been a great mother. Remember to tell her that.'

After she'd rung off, Lauren looked at Dan and Adam. 'What have we done?' she said.

They sat slumped in silence, struggling to control their terror, longing for and dreading the next knock on the door.

When it came their heads snapped up and their breath stopped, as if they'd been punched. They stared, hearts pounding, unable at first to make sense of the shape in the doorway. A woman holding a bundle of pale blue cloth.

'Ruth, where's Ruth?' said Adam.

Lauren gave an involuntary cry and held out her arms.

'Here's the little fellow you've been waiting for all this time.' The midwife laid the baby in Lauren's lap, 'Safe and sound. There you go, Mummy.'

Lauren was laughing and weeping, Dan moved closer to her and they gazed at the face of their son. He was the colour of a radish and had a shock of black hair. His eyes were closed but his mouth was working away, searching for something. Lauren bent her little finger, the way she'd seen so many mothers do over the years. She offered it to him and he began to suck furiously. Then he paused, opened his eyes and they locked on to hers.

She grinned at Dan, tears streaming down her cheeks. 'Our baby. Can you believe it?'

Dan touched one of the tiny hands and the fingers splayed in response. He started to cry, great racking male sobs. 'Hello, my son.'

Adam couldn't stop rocking. It was the only way he could hold himself together.

The midwife was flicking through her notebook. 'The paediatricians have checked him over. His Apgar score was nine out of ten, despite everything.'

Adam couldn't restrain himself any longer, 'But my *wife*?'

The midwife's face contracted. 'She's still in there. I was with her until he was born.' She reached into her pocket and fished out a piece of paper, folded small. 'She gave me a message for you.'

Lauren and Dan got up and came to stand next to Adam.

'My handwriting's not great, would you like me to read it?' Adam nodded. 'It was hard to hear her, but I think I got everything.'

The baby snuffled and started to cry – a dry, insistent bleat – Lauren rocked him backwards and forwards and he stopped.

'"This baby belongs to Lauren and Dan. I want them to take him straight away. I want him to have a good life. I love my daughters. I love my husband Adam. I'm sorry about everything."' As she read the final words the midwife's voice faltered. She folded the paper and handed it to Adam.

He pressed it against his chest. 'Will she be ...?' He couldn't go on.

'She's very poorly and they're still working on her. Mr Fenton says he'll come and see you as soon as they've finished in theatre.' There were tears in the midwife's eyes.

Lauren was rocking her baby and crying for her mother. Adam leant forward, elbows on his knees, braced. She was going to die. All on her own. And it would be his fault. He'd let it happen.

Lauren, Dan and the baby went up to the postnatal ward where a room had been prepared for the three of them. Adam sat alone for what seemed like hours. Eventually the consultant came. He said that after they'd delivered the baby the bleeding got much worse and the only way to stop it was to remove Ruth's uterus. She was too ill to give her consent, but he'd had to go ahead, otherwise she'd have died.

'*Thank God.*' Adam's whole body was trembling. 'So she's out of danger?'

The consultant's expression was pained. 'I'm afraid not, Mr Furnival. She's still critically ill and we've just sent her up to Intensive Care. She's lost so much blood that her body has started to shut down.' He looked intently at Adam, his face creased in sympathy. 'It's not looking good. I'm sorry.'

32

Before she opened her eyes, Ruth heard the bleeping. Necklaces of sound were draped all around her, every one of them a different rhythm and pitch. Feet squished and clattered back and forth on the floor. Someone was coughing, a crescendo of sound that ended with a series of wheezing groans, then started up again. There was pressure on her nose, as if she had a bad cold, but tighter; she attempted to move her head, in order to escape it, but couldn't, then tried to touch it, but her hands wouldn't move: something was holding them down. She lifted one eyelid a fraction and white acid filled her head. Something was blocking her throat, making her retch. An alarm sounded and her eyes came open. She shut them tightly, but pink and green had got inside them. The noise continued and feet were coming. She gave a phlegmy sigh.

'Ruth,' the voice was very close, 'you're in Intensive Care.'

She looked and looked until the shadow above her resolved itself into a face. She tried to say Adam, but no sound came.

Doctors were shining lights in her eyes and staring at the machines. They were pulling out tubes from her throat and nose. They were smiling. Now she was disappearing again.

*

356

Ruth was awake now and could move more freely, but the pain was terrible: it was as if someone had beaten her up. They said it was because they were trying to wean her off the morphine, but she didn't understand. Sometimes torturers came, but no one could hear her screaming. They said she was having flashbacks. Adam was still there. He said that he and Alex had been doing shifts by her bed for the past ten days. She didn't know why. Alex was sleeping, he said, but she'd be back soon. Lauren was at home and would come when Ruth was stronger.

After a while a memory erupted: *there was a baby*. Her hands went down to find him. But the flesh under the hospital gown was collapsed and soft: she was empty as a ransacked tomb. There was a long knobbly ridge above her pubic bone; as she explored it with her fingers pain sliced through her pelvis. The men with knives were back. She remembered someone holding her hand and a small face nuzzling hers.

Adam took her through it, slowly. She'd had a Caesarean and the baby was fine. He'd been handed to Lauren and Dan straight away and the three of them were at home in Brockley. All was well and Lauren was breastfeeding. They'd named him after Ruth. It had been Lauren's idea.

He pulled a fragment of newspaper from his pocket and held it in front of her. She couldn't make out the words, so he read it to her.

RYAN On 11th July, to Lauren (née
Furnival) and Daniel, a much-wanted
son, Jago Patrick.
With love and deepest gratitude to
Ruth Furnival.

'Jago?' said Ruth huskily, because the tubes had bruised her throat and vocal cords. 'My name?'

'Yes.' He was smiling at her.

'Dan agreed?'

'He was so thrilled, he'd have agreed to anything. They're so grateful for what you've done for them, and so thankful you pulled through.' His voice gave way. 'We all are.'

When Ruth was stronger they moved her to a general ward and Adam sat by her bed for most of every day; at first she took it for granted, then she wondered why he wasn't at work.

'I handed over my case the day after Jago was born. The judge agreed the circumstances were exceptional.'

'Why?'

'They told me you were dying.'

Ruth looked at him. 'And you minded?'

'I minded.'

Adam explained how ill she'd been, sedated and on a ventilator. It was a miracle she'd survived. Twice they'd been warned she wouldn't make it through the night.

A few days later, he told her that the surgeon had removed her womb, to save her life.

She said nothing for a long time, then, 'So we're both neutered now.'

Alex came often. She'd taken a sabbatical from work and was spending three months in England, to get to know her nephew and spend time with the rest of the family.

'I guess everything that's happened has made me appreciate what I've got,' she said, brushing the corner of her eye. 'The doctors say that being on a ventilator has a lot in common with torture, both physically and mentally,' she told Ruth. 'It takes a long time to recover and when they let you out of here you'll need a carer at home, at least for a while. I thought I might add the role to my CV.'

*

Lauren visited, with the baby. It was awkward, as Ruth had known it would be. Jago was fast asleep, cocooned in his car seat, his face obscured by a blanket. Lauren kissed Ruth and offered to wake him, but Ruth said no, leave him in peace, she wouldn't be able to hold him: her tummy was still too sore.

'That's a shame.' But Lauren sounded relieved. 'Is the pain bad?'

'It's worse since I came off the morphine, but getting a bit less every day.'

'I bought you some fruit, but you seem to have plenty already.' Lauren put a basket of grapes on the table and sat down on a chair by the bed. 'I'm sorry you've had such a terrible time.'

Ruth said, 'I'm the one who needs to apologise, for putting you and Dan through so much. I went mad just before he was born. I had fantasies about bringing him up myself. I think they were a way of coping with what I was going through. The loneliness, and the dread of losing him, and not being sure who I was any more. But I would never have done it.' Lauren nodded, but her face was impassive. 'That night when you came over I was tired and confused. I realise now that I was probably already ill. I completely lost sight of your feelings. Please forgive me.'

Lauren smiled distantly and said, 'Mum, it's all in the past and completely forgotten. We're both beyond grateful for all the sacrifices you made to give us Jago.' It sounded strangely formal: a little speech that she'd practised in advance. The old Lauren, reserved and judgemental, keeping her real feelings tucked away.

Ruth leant sideways to look at her grandson. The blanket had fallen away from his face and he was moving his head from side to side as if searching for something; he had the scrawny, vulnerable look of all premature babies and he seemed to be peering at her. She was moved, but he seemed very far away. She couldn't connect him with the creature she'd sung to and confided in – her close companion for all those lonely months.

She turned back to Lauren and said flatly, 'Be honest: are you ever going to feel the same way about me, after what happened?'

Lauren stared at her lap for a moment, then back at Ruth. 'For the forty-eight hours before Jago was born I hated you – more than I've ever hated anyone in my whole life. I would have killed you with my bare hands to stop you stealing him.

'Then we got to the hospital and they brought him to us and read out your message and your life was in danger. And suddenly you stopped being this big, powerful figure who was going to take my baby.' Lauren stopped to blink away tears. 'I was terrified. All I wanted was for you to stay alive.' She reached out and stroked Ruth's hand. It was the hand of an old woman: the skin dry and wrinkled, livid with the bruises and puncture marks left by scores of needles and cannulas. 'I love you, Mum. I wish I could hug you and make you believe me.'

'I believe you,' said Ruth. 'And thank you for calling him Jago.' She smiled. 'It's weird, for years my surname was an embarrassment, but now it feels as if I'm starting to reclaim it.'

She looked over at the baby; he was restless and starting to grizzle. Lauren picked him up, then sat him upright in her lap. Ruth wondered what it would be like to touch him. She held out her hand and Lauren moved Jago towards it. Ruth put her forefinger against his cheek and began to stroke it very gently.

Ruth and Lauren were both breathing fast, aware of the hammering of each other's hearts. They understood the necessity and danger of this moment. Jago turned his face until his mouth found Ruth's finger, then he sucked on her like a famished creature. His black eyes were open and he was looking at her with fierce concentration. *As if he recognised her.* She was engulfed by a physical longing for the child.

Finally she found words that would do. 'Do you know, I can't believe he was *ever* inside me? He seems so entirely separate now. Totally *your* baby. What is it they say about being a grandparent? Lovely to have them, but even better to be able to hand them back.'

Then, with deliberate cruelty, she wrenched her finger from Jago's mouth. He looked at her with astonishment, then rage, and started to scream. Ruth felt sick; it was all she could do not to snatch him from her daughter's arms.

Lauren laughed with the particular complacency of a lactating mother as she lifted her T-shirt and put Jago to her breast. He whimpered briefly, then began to feed, gasping with greedy pleasure every few seconds. Lauren looked across at Ruth. 'Thank you for saying that, Mum. You've no idea how much it means to me.'

Ruth managed a smile, but her whole body was trembling.

Lauren said that Dan was waiting in the day room. He hadn't wanted to intrude, but could he pop in for a second and say hello before they drove home? She messaged him and he bounded in, kissed Ruth and said she'd given him the most precious thing imaginable: their lives were transformed and he'd never thought he could be so happy. They would never, ever, be able to thank her enough. He loved her. This Dan was euphoric and expansive, laughing with delight as he gazed at his son.

She watched them as they walked the length of the ward and out into the world, carrying Jago between them: she felt pride and desolation.

Adam's visits were the highlight of Ruth's day, something she looked forward to during the broken nights, ward rounds and physiotherapy sessions. In view of his hatred of hospitals, his constancy was heroic, she told him. He laughed: it had been like an intensive course of aversion therapy, he admitted, but now he felt surprisingly at home in the wards and corridors. Once Ruth was able to manage short walks, they spent most of their time together outside, in a small courtyard garden; surrounded on three sides by tall buildings, it offered a refuge from the heat of the sun.

One afternoon Adam said, 'Out of interest, why did you tell Lauren about my vasectomy?'

'I'm sorry, I shouldn't have, but I was so upset when I found out you were having an affair with Emily.'

Adam didn't respond.

'You were, weren't you?'

He smiled and shook his head.

Ruth stared at him. 'But you did have sex with her?'

'No.'

Ruth was confused. 'But Sheila said . . .'

Adam stretched his arms above his head and stared at the sky. 'Things might have been heading in that direction. But after Lauren turned up and accused me of adultery, I decided abstinence was the order of the day.'

'Wise move.' Ruth smiled, rueful.

Adam was looking at her with curiosity. She wondered whether to tell him about Sam. She hesitated, not wanting to hurt him, or incriminate herself. But they seemed past all that now: familiar, comfortable and kind to one another, nothing more. So almost as a penance – and because honesty was easier now – Ruth described her short-lived dalliance, told as a comedy of manners rather than a humiliation. Adam laughed, but betrayed no sign of jealousy. She felt relief, tinged with disappointment.

Because there was nothing to lose, she said, 'I told Lauren about the abortion, too. I didn't mention you, just that I'd had one. I was in a bad state at the time and having terrible dreams. They frightened me.' She stopped, unsure whether to go on. Adam placed his arms across his chest, but he was listening. 'Nightmares really. A bashed-up foetus kept looking at me. And after that I couldn't stop thinking about it. Then somehow it got all mixed up with Lauren's baby. I wanted to make up for everything – for not being around when the girls were small, for not being a good mother to them. I wanted to raise one child *properly*. That was why ...'

'I know,' said Adam, gently. 'I found some papers in the kitchen. It looked as though you were keeping a sort of diary?'

Ruth nodded.

'I read them, when you were so ill and I thought you weren't going to pull through. I hope you don't mind.' He paused, took out a handkerchief and blew his nose hard. 'It made me understand.'

Ruth was dry-eyed, she felt empty of tears now. She asked him if he remembered going to hear Elgar's Cello Concerto in New College Chapel the night before the abortion. Of course, he said, he'd driven home that afternoon to fetch his mother's car and there was a bad traffic jam on the way back to Oxford, he'd almost missed the beginning. His friend Richard had been the soloist. She told him that whenever she heard the music now, it took her straight back to that evening; sitting, cold, scared and utterly out of her depth, in the medieval chapel, the sad, heavy yearning of the second movement expressing something that she was undergoing, but too numb to feel. It seemed now like a sort of elegy – for their youth, for the child that would never be, and for all the wounds they'd inflicted on one another.

Next time he visited, Adam had downloaded the concerto onto his phone, and they sat in the garden with an earphone each and listened to all four movements, their arms wrapped round one another. Afterwards they spoke for hours about things they'd thought and felt, but never said.

Ruth told him she'd sometimes wondered whether it would have helped if there had been some sort of ritual, a means of acknowledging that something had been lost.

'Do you regret it, now?'

'At the time I didn't feel anything but horror and hatred for the thing inside me. I was fighting for my survival. That's why I couldn't discuss it with you beforehand. I was too scared of losing my nerve. Then, after the dreams, I forced myself to imagine everything, and I was sad.' She sighed. 'But do I regret it? No. It was the right decision and I'm grateful beyond words that I had the choice.' She gave him a steady look. 'I know you think I didn't take your feelings into account, but I couldn't afford to.'

There was a silence between them, then Adam said, 'I think I needed you to acknowledge that it was complicated and difficult and damaging, as well as being necessary to you. Then I'd have understood. But I felt shut out. As it was, we went through it together, but separately.'

'Together but separate.' She shook her head. 'You could be describing our marriage.'

Adam was fumbling in his trouser pocket. 'That reminds me.' She couldn't see what he was holding. 'I've been carrying this around with me for three weeks. I found it down the back of the sofa in the kitchen.'

He opened his hand: her wedding ring.

She stared at the thin gold band, remembering her panic as she'd wrenched it off her finger, the sweltering heat, the sense of looming catastrophe. 'I took it off the night before Jago was born. Every bit of me was starting to swell up and the ring was cutting off the blood supply. It got stuck and I had to use oil. It felt weird, without it, but then I thought what's the point—'

She broke off because of the way Adam was looking at her.

He picked up the ring and held it towards her.

'Marry me, Ruth?'

33

They celebrated her fifty-fifth birthday at lunchtime, to accommodate Adam's dinner for newly appointed judges and Jago's exacting bedtime routine. Ruth sat at the kitchen table in a high-backed chair padded with cushions, gazing at a mass of presents. She'd asked them not to bother – there was nothing she wanted or needed – but they'd taken no notice. Adam and Alex sat either side of her, attentive and solicitous to a fault; Lauren and Dan were opposite, with Jago perched like a trophy on the table in front of them. It was the first time they'd been together as a family for several weeks.

Dan clinked his wine glass against her tumbler of water. 'To Ruth, who made our family possible—'

'Please, no speeches.'

But Adam was sliding his arm around her shoulder and clearing his throat. 'Today was your deadline for giving birth, and you delivered, with ten weeks to spare.' He looked over at Jago, then back at Ruth. 'I'm so proud of what you did. And the way you saw it through. And everything ...'

The others looked away, as if they'd trespassed on something private. Alex leant across the table to break the silence. 'We're *all* very proud of your granny, aren't we, Jago?' She rubbed his tummy. 'Yes, we *are.*' He grinned and gurgled, avid for more.

Lauren reached forward abruptly and pulled him out of reach. 'He'll be hungry,' she said, unbuttoning her shirt and pushing Jago's face against her breast. He sucked half-heartedly, then spluttered, arched his back and began to cry. Ruth felt a surge of heat and sweat; she looked away. Defeated, Lauren shifted the baby onto her shoulder, where he quietened. 'He's better without an audience,' she said, her face reddening.

'I think it's maybe a bit soon, Laurie.' Dan checked his phone. 'His last feed was only two hours and twenty-five minutes ago.'

Alex said, 'Why don't you give him to Mum for a bit, then the two of us can get lunch on the table?'

Lauren turned to Dan; his nod was almost imperceptible, but Ruth caught it.

'It's OK,' she said. 'You keep him.' But Lauren was already sliding Jago across the table.

Ruth took him in her arms. He was solid now, more at ease in the world. She pulled off one of the yellow socks that Alex had knitted and tickled his bare foot with her little finger; he stared up at her, eyes crinkling with pleasure. She started to sing softly, as she had when he was inside her, and he fell into a beaming, dribbling trance. Ruth could sense Lauren moving around behind her back, watchful and poised to intervene. The rest of them were ranged around her, like figures frozen in a masque, their smiles taut as grimaces. This was how it would be from now on, she thought to herself.

She kissed the top of Jago's head, then held him out to Dan. 'He wants his daddy,' she lied.

The room came back to life: Alex and Lauren laughed as a skein of pasta overflowed its serving dish; they put sliced tomatoes, basil leaves and a slug of olive oil on top, then stood back to admire their handiwork; Dan held Jago aloft while Adam took photos and agreed that his grandson's head control was truly remarkable. Ruth watched them all: she felt detached and uncertain of her place. It had been a year of tumult and confusion: a hurricane had passed through their lives. The debris had been cleared away and the external fabric repaired, but they were still trying to re-establish themselves.

Lauren clearly felt that she'd fought for possession of Jago and won. He was in *her* gift now and she took palpable pleasure in dispensing him in very small spoonfuls – even Alex's share was rationed. Ruth sensed that her own illness and frailty had enabled something in Lauren, giving her the space to move centre stage. They understood each other better now, but Ruth knew that the primordial bond she had with her grandson – the price of his existence – would always rankle with Lauren: it was something to be forgotten or denied.

Adam was on edge. During the weeks of hospital visits he'd talked longingly of the moment when Ruth would be well enough to return home and they could live as a couple again after all the months of estrangement. But she craved silence and solitude. She spent most of her time reading, writing, or walking alone by the river. He kept telling her that he loved her, but that he wasn't sure where he stood: whether they had a future. And she couldn't give him an answer; the question was too big, too complicated.

In truth, Ruth was still recovering from the onslaught of Jago's birth and the trauma of Intensive Care. There were no words for the hellish intensity of the experience, so she couldn't explain it to anyone. Every so often a hallucination swept her back to a blood-soaked birthing room. She was shackled to a table and people in masks and gowns slashed at her and forced plastic down her throat while she retched and thrashed. Afterwards it took hours to recover her equanimity. Her physical strength was improving, but she hadn't yet come to terms with her brutal

367

return to the menopause. The night sweats, hot flushes, memory lapses and mood swings would continue for a year, the doctors had warned her, maybe longer.

She'd avoided mirrors the whole time she was in hospital, and when she came home she had to screw up her courage before confronting her body for the first time. She looked older than fifty-five, which is to say that she looked older than most affluent women of her age in London contrived to appear. Greyish-brown hair surrounded a thin, worn face, and there was the shadow of a moustache on her upper lip; her breasts and tummy were like empty containers made of a smart material that had under-performed; her skin was thin, and marbled in places with a network of broken blood vessels. A thick, wide scar traversed her lower abdomen, marking the place where first Jago, then her uterus, had been removed. Her legs were scrawny from lack of exercise and her pubic hair was mostly white now, as if the travails of the past months had shocked it into senescence.

A few months ago, she would have gazed at this careworn body through borrowed eyes and throbbed with disgust and self-loathing. She would have tidied herself up and papered over the cracks, spending time and money she couldn't afford on ever more frequent maintenance. The option was still there. Go back to Lorenzo, get botoxed and filled, pump herself up again with HRT, *pretend she was fertile*. But what would be the point? Her year of re-fertilisation and rejuvenation had been a means to an end: the creation of Jago. But she'd learnt in the process that you couldn't go back. It was the road to self-annihilation, a surrogate life, driven and derided by vanity.

Now, facing up to herself, she felt disquiet, but also a deep recognition. It was creased and battle-scarred, this body, but uniquely *hers*. To disguise it would be to deny who she was, what she'd been through and all she'd achieved. She needed to scrape away the expectations of others, and all the accommodations that had shaped and stunted her, in order to find out who she really was. Now. While there was still time.

She thought often of Ruth Jago, the girl who climbed trees with fearless abandon, ran like the wind and commanded the waves on Marazion Beach. Her primary self, untrammelled by menstruation, gestation and birth. Before fertility threw its big red cloak over her. Before all those other selves – student, wife, worker, mother – took over. As she struggled to find her bearings in this new land, parched of oestrogen, where she might live for the next forty years, she needed to reclaim that child – curious, truthful, androgynous and free – who had delighted in being by herself and for herself. She was still there, somewhere, crouching on the tideline, searching in the seaweed for cowrie shells, mermaid's purses and agate pebbles. Waiting to be found.

Acknowledgements

Warmest thanks to everyone who has helped me during the research, writing and editing of this book.

On the research front I'm very grateful to: the surrogates and intended parents who told me their stories; the women who shared their experiences of fertility and infertility; Dr Valentine Akande, Dr Stuart Lavery, Dr Jane MacDougall and Dr Sarah Martindale, who lent their medical expertise and advice; and Rachel Bright, who explained life at the criminal bar. Particular thanks to fertility specialists Dr Sarah Martins da Silva and Dr Julija Gorodeckaja; midwife (medical and editorial!) Sadie Holland; and solicitor Tim Langton. All of them read the manuscript in detail, made comments and answered my endless questions with patience and good humour. Any errors of fact or interpretation that remain are mine, not theirs.

At Bath Spa University I was taught by three formidable and generous writers: Maggie Gee, who read the early chapters, shared her craft and gave me the confidence to keep going; Fay Weldon, who was both astutely critical and encouraging; and Tessa Hadley, who offered inspiration and support throughout the time I was writing and whose penetrating reading of the completed manuscript was invaluable. My fellow students

Richard Crowe, Peter Kingston, Beth Mann and Rachel Shorer read fragments and helped to shape my ideas.

Kate O'Sullivan gave me a place to write and much other practical assistance. Guy Baily, Caroline van den Brul, James and Victoria Fraser, Alison and Roger Ward, and Clive and Anna Wolman all provided shelter and a desk while I was between homes or in quarantine. My son Toby and daughter-in-law Rachel sent dispatches from the frontline of pregnancy and parenthood as they welcomed first Jess, then Daniel. My son Matthew solved innumerable technical problems and created a website for me. Kathy Barnby, Jasmine Daines Pilgrem and Fiona Maddocks were pillars of support who also read the manuscript and gave valuable feedback.

Huge thanks to my editors, Clare Smith and Sarah Savitt, for their wisdom and insight, and for guiding me through the final drafts with such acuity and kindness. Thanks also to Celeste Ward-Best, Hayley Camis, Nico Taylor, Alison Tulett, Rachel Cross and the ever-patient Nithya Rae, together with everyone else in the wider Virago and Little, Brown teams, who between them brought this book to fruition; and to Susanna Peden at Susanna Lea Associates.

Four final debts of gratitude. My daughter Imogen badgered me to start writing, prodded me to keep going and was an incisive early reader. Cathy Wells-Cole has been the best accomplice any writer could wish for, unstinting with her time and critical intelligence. My wonderful agent Kerry Glencorse believed in *Surrogate* from the outset, nurtured it, then found it the perfect home. Last and most heartfelt thanks are due to my husband Peter: I'm more grateful than I can say for his sustenance, encouragement and advice – everything, really.